P9-DTN-055

Volume 37

ELLERY QUEEN'S WINGS OF MYSTERY

Edited by
ELLERY QUEEN

The Dial Press

DAVIS PUBLICATIONS, INC.
380 LEXINGTON AVENUE, NEW YORK, N.Y. 10017

FIRST PRINTING

Library of Congress Catalog Card Number: 59-13341
Printed in the U.S.A.

COPYRIGHT NOTICES AND ACKNOWLEDGMENTS

Grateful acknowledgment is hereby made for permission to reprint the following:

Fourth of July Picnic by Rex Stout; from AND FOUR TO GO by Rex Stout; copyright c 1957 by Rex Stout; reprinted by permission of The Viking Press, Inc. and Pola Stout.
The Fall of a Coin by Ruth Rendell; c 1975 by Ruth Rendell; reprinted by permission of Georges Borchardt, Inc.
B As in Bribe by Lawrence Treat; c 1975 by Lawrence Treat; reprinted by permission of Robert P. Mills, Ltd.
The Breaking Point by Miriam Sharman; c 1974 by Miriam Sharman; reprinted by permission of the author.
The Scrabble Clue by Francis M. Nevins, Jr.; c 1974 by Francis M. Nevins, Jr.; reprinted by permission of the author.
The Big Bunco by William Bankier; c 1974 by William Bankier; reprinted by permission of Curtis Brown, Ltd.
Miss Phipps on the Telephone by Phyllis Bentley; c 1973 by Phyllis Bentley; reprinted by permission of Harold Matson Company, Inc.
Walking Hubert Down by John Pierce; c 1974 by John Pierce; reprinted by permission of the author.
Gideon and the Innocent Shoplifter by J. J. Marric; c 1975 by the Estate of John Creasey; reprinted by permission of Harold Ober Associates, Inc.
The Lost Heir by Lillian de la Torre; c 1974 by Lillian de la Torre; reprinted by permission of Harold Ober Associates, Inc.
Undue Influence by E. X. Ferrars; c Elizabeth Ferrars 1974; reprinted by permission of Harold Ober Associates, Inc.
Miss Ferguson Versus JM by Gerald Tomlinson; c 1975 by Gerald Tomlinson; reprinted by permission of the author.
The Most Tattooed Man in the World by Janet Green; copyright 1960 by Janet Green; reprinted by permission of Curtis Brown, Ltd.
The Intricate Pattern by Donald Olson; c 1974 by Donald Olson; reprinted by permission of Blanche C. Gregory, Inc.
The Scene of the Crime by Ellen Arthur; c 1973 by Ellen Arthur; reprinted by permission of the author.
A Matter of Disturbing Incidents by Michael Innes; c 1974 by J. I. M. Stewart; reprinted by permission of Curtis Brown, Ltd.
Kirinyaga by Joe Gores; c 1975 by Joe Gores; reprinted by permission of the author.
Mr. Strang and the Cat Lady by William Brittain; c 1975 by William Brittain; reprinted by permission of the author.
Return of the Hero by Michael Gilbert; c 1974 by Michael Gilbert; reprinted by permission of John Cushman Associates, Inc.
Captain Leopold and the Ghost-Killer by Edward D. Hoch; c 1974 by Edward D. Hoch; reprinted by permission of the author.
The Adventure of Abraham Lincoln's Clue by Ellery Queen; copyright c 1965, 1968 by Ellery Queen; reprinted by permission of the author.

CONTENTS

1 SHORT NOVEL

20 NOVELETS AND SHORT STORIES

(CONTINUED ON NEXT PAGE)

CONTENTS ***(CONTINUED FROM PAGE 5)***

EDITOR'S NOTE

Dear Reader:

Mystery stories have wings.

When you read mystery stories, you fly. As the plots unfold, at each unexpected turn, at each new twist of events, you soar, spin, dip, loop. You have no fear of flying when your airplane is a story of detection or crime or mystery. And when you touch down, all mysteries solved, you sigh with satisfaction.

Mystery stories have other wings too.

Visualize each mystery story as the stage of a theater, with the proscenium arch above, the orchestra seats in front, the dressing rooms in the back, the wings on both sides. From these wings you have the vantage position. You can see the action onstage as each character "struts and frets his hour upon" the scene of the crime while "all our yesterdays have lighted" murderers and victims "the way to dusty death."

But none of the 21 stories in this collection is "a walking shadow"; none is "a tale told by an idiot, full of sound and fury, signifying nothing." No, indeed: the short novel and the 20 novelets and short stories are all full-bodied tales told by some of the greatest mystery writers of the past and present, and while you will find some sound and fury (as you should in mysteries), the 21 tales in this volume signify action, suspense, excitement, drama, characterization, style—sheer reading pleasure.

So—rev up with J. J. Marric and Commander George Gideon. Contact! Taxi with Michael Gilbert and Inspector Patrick Petrella. Take flight with Lawrence Treat and E. X. Ferrars. Ride the skies with Ruth Rendell and Lillian de la Torre. Soar with Rex Stout and Nero Wolfe. Perform aerobatics with Edward D. Hoch and Captain Leopold. Maneuver with Michael Innes and Sir John Appleby. Fly through the air with Phyllis Bentley and Miss Marian Phipps.

Economy flights, with no frills? Not on your first-class ticket! Luxury flights only—with thrills!

Happy landings with

ELLERY QUEEN

Rex Stout

Fourth of July Picnic

The United Restaurant Workers of America—10,000 strong—celebrated the Fourth of July by holding a picnic at Culp's Meadows on Long Island. It seemed to be a typical Independence Day celebration, complete with speeches—although "the eagle didn't scream as much or as loud" as Archie Goodwin had expected. But this Fourth of July observance, for all its ceremonies and festivities, had one added feature—something not on the calendar of events . . .

One of Rex Stout's liveliest Nero Wolfe short novels—a detective delight to read, and, as Archie makes clear just before the climactic scene, a challenge to your wits. Indeed, this short novel, complete in this volume, might have been titled "The Locked Tent" . . .

Detective: NERO WOLFE

Flora Korby swiveled her head, with no hat hiding any of her dark brown hair, to face me with her dark brown eyes. She spoke:

"I guess I should have brought my car and led the way."

"I'm doing fine," I assured her. "I could shut one eye too."

"Please don't," she begged. "I'm stupefied as it is. May I have your autograph—I mean when we stop?"

Since she was highly presentable I didn't mind her assuming that I was driving with one hand because my right arm wanted to stretch across her shoulders, though she was wrong. I had left the cradle long ago. But there was no point in explaining to her that Nero Wolfe, who was in the back seat, had a deep distrust of moving vehicles and hated to ride in one unless I drove it, and therefore I was glad to have an excuse to drive with one hand because that would make it more thrilling for him.

Anyway, she might have guessed it. The only outside interest that Wolfe permits to interfere with his personal routine of comfort, not to mention luxury, is Rusterman's restaurant. Its founder, Marko Vukcic, was Wolfe's oldest and closest friend; and when Vukcic died, leaving the restaurant to members of the staff and making Wolfe executor of his estate, he also left a letter asking Wolfe to see to it that the restaurant's standards and reputation were maintained; and Wolfe had done so, making unannounced visits there once or twice a week, and sometimes even oftener, without ever grumbling—well, hardly ever. But he sure did grumble when Felix, the maître d'hôtel, asked him to make a speech at the Independence Day picnic of the United Restaurant Workers of America. Hereafter I'll make it URWA.

He not only grumbled, he refused. But Felix kept after him, and Wolfe finally gave in when Felix came to the office one day with reinforcements: Paul Rago, the sauce chef at the Churchill; James Korby, the president of URWA; H. L. Griffin, a food and wine importer who supplied hard-to-get items not only for Rusterman's but also for Wolfe's own table; and Philip Holt, URWA's director of organization. They also were to be on the program at the picnic, and their main appeal was that they simply had to have the man who was responsible for keeping Rusterman's the best restaurant in New York after the death of Marko Vukcic.

Since Wolfe is only as vain as three peacocks, and since he had loved Marko if he ever loved anyone, that got him. There had been another inducement: Philip Holt had agreed to lay off of Fritz, Wolfe's chef and housekeeper. For three years Fritz had been visiting the kitchen at Rusterman's off and on as a consultant, and Holt had been pestering him, insisting that he had to join URWA. You can guess how Wolfe liked that.

Since I do everything that has to be done in connection with Wolfe's business and his rare social activities, except that he thinks he does all the thinking, and we won't go into that now, it would be up to me to get him to the scene of the picnic, Culp's Meadows on Long Island, on the Fourth of July. Around the end of June, James Korby phoned and introduced his daughter Flora. She told me that the directions to Culp's Meadows were very complicated, and I said that all directions on Long Island were very complicated, and she said she had better drive us out in her car.

I liked her voice, that is true, but also I have a lot of foresight, and it occurred to me immediately that it would be a new and exciting experience for my employer to watch me drive with one hand; so I told her that, while it must be Wolfe's car and I must drive, I would deeply appreciate it if she would come along and tell me the way.

That was how it happened, and that was why, when we finally rolled through the gate at Culp's Meadows, after some thirty miles of Long Island parkways and another ten of grade intersections and trick turns, Wolfe's lips were pressed so tight he didn't have any. He had spoken only once, around the fourth or fifth mile, when I had swept around a slowpoke.

"Archie. You know quite well."

"Yes, sir." Of course I kept my eyes straight ahead. "But it's an impulse, having my arm like this, and I'm afraid to take it away because if I fight an impulse it makes me nervous, and driving when you're nervous is bad."

A glance in the mirror showed me his lips tightening, and they stayed tight.

Passing through the gate at Culp's Meadows, and winding around as directed by Flora Korby, I used both hands. It was a quarter to three, so we were on time, since the speeches were scheduled for three o'clock.

Flora was sure a space would have been saved for us back of the tent, and after threading through a few acres of parked cars I found she was right, and rolled to a stop with the radiator only a couple of yards from the canvas. She hopped out and opened the rear door on her side, and I did likewise on mine.

Wolfe's eyes went right to her, and then left to me. He was torn. He didn't want to favor a woman, even a young and pretty one, but he absolutely had to show me what he thought of one-handed driving. His eyes went right again, the whole seventh of a ton of him moved, and he climbed out on her side.

The tent, on a wooden platform raised three feet above the ground, not much bigger than Wolfe's office, was crowded with people, and I wormed through to the front entrance and on out, where the platform extended into the open air. There was plenty of air, with a breeze dancing in from the direction of the ocean, and plenty of sunshine. A fine day for the Fourth of July.

The platform extension was crammed with chairs, most of them empty. I can't report on the condition of the meadow's grass because my view was obstructed by ten thousand restaurant workers and their guests, maybe more. A couple of thousand of them were in a solid mass facing the platform, presumably those who wanted to be up front for the speeches, and the rest were sprayed around all over, clear across to a fringe of trees and a row of sheds.

Flora's voice came from behind my shoulder. "They're coming out, so if there's a chair you like, grab it. Except the six up front; they're for the speakers."

Naturally I started to tell her I wanted the one next to hers, but didn't get it out because people came jostling out of the tent onto the extension. Thinking I had better warn Wolfe that the chair he was about to occupy for an hour or so was about half as wide as his fanny, to give him time to fight his impulses, I worked past to the edge of the entrance, and when the exodus had thinned out I entered the tent.

Five men were standing grouped beside a cot which was touching the canvas of the far side, and a man was lying on the cot. To my left Nero Wolfe was bending over to peer at the contents of a metal box there on a table with its lid open.

I stepped over for a look and saw a collection of bone-handled knives, eight of them, with blades varying in length from six inches up to twelve. They weren't shiny, but they looked sharp, worn narrow by a lot of use for a lot of years. I asked Wolfe whose throat he was going to cut.

"They are Dubois," he said. "Real old Dubois. The best. They belong to Mr. Korby. He brought them to use in a carving contest, and he won, as he should. I would gladly steal them." He turned. "Why don't they let that man alone?"

I turned too, and through a gap in the group saw that the man on the cot was Philip Holt, URWA's director of organization. "What's the matter with him?" I asked.

"Something he ate. They think snails. Probably the wrong kind of snails. A doctor gave him something to help his bowels handle them. Why don't they leave him alone?"

"I'll go ask," I said, and moved.

As I approached the cot James Korby was speaking. "I say he should be taken to a hospital, in spite of what that doctor said. Look at his color!"

Korby, short, pudgy, and bald, looked more like a restaurant customer than a restaurant worker, which may have been one reason he was president of URWA.

"I agree," Dick Vetter said emphatically. I had never seen Dick Vetter in person, but I had seen him often enough on his TV show—in fact, a little too often. If I quit dialing his channel he wouldn't miss me, since twenty million Americans, mostly female, were convinced that he was the youngest and handsomest MC on the waves. Flora Korby had told me he would be there, and why. His father had been a bus boy in a Broadway restaurant for thirty years, and still was because he wouldn't quit.

Paul Rago did not agree, and said so. "It would be a pity," he declared. He made it "peety," his accent having tapered off enough not to make it "peetee." With his broad shoulders and six feet, his slick black hair going gray, and his mustache with pointed tips that was still all black, he looked more like an ambassador from below the border than a sauce chef. He was going on:

"He is the most important man in the union—except, of course, the president—and he should make an appearance on the platform. Perhaps he can before we are through."

"I hope you will pardon me." That was H. L. Griffin, the food and wine importer. He was a skinny little runt, with a long narrow chin and something wrong with one eye, but he spoke with the authority of a man whose firm occupied a whole floor in one of the midtown hives. "I may have no right to an opinion, since I am not a member of your great organization, but you have done me the honor of inviting me to take part in your celebration of our country's independence, and I do know of Phil Holt's high standing and wide popularity among your members. I would merely say that I feel that Mr. Rago is right, that they will be disappointed not to see him on the platform. I hope I am not being presumptuous."

From outside the tent, from the loudspeakers at the corners of the platform, a booming voice had been calling to the picnickers scattered over the meadow to close in and prepare to listen. As the group by the cot went on arguing, a state trooper in uniform, who had been standing politely aside, came over and joined them and took a look at Philip Holt, but offered no advice.

Wolfe also approached for a look. Myself, I would have said that the place for him was a good bed with an attractive nurse smoothing his brow. I saw him shiver all over at least three times. He decided it himself, finally, by muttering at them to let him alone and turning on his side to face the canvas.

Flora Korby had come in, and she put a blanket over him, and I noticed that Dick Vetter made a point of helping her. The breeze was sweeping through and one of them said he shouldn't be in a draft, and Wolfe told me to lower the flap of the rear entrance, and I did so. The flap didn't want to stay down, so I tied the plastic-tape fastening to hold it, in a single bowknot.

Then they all marched out through the front entrance to the platform, including the state trooper, and I brought up the rear. As Korby passed the table he stopped to lower the lid on the box of knives, real old Dubois.

The speeches lasted an hour and eight minutes, and the ten thousand URWA members and guests took them standing like ladies and gentlemen. You are probably hoping I will report them word for word, but I didn't take them down and I didn't listen hard enough to engrave them on my memory. At that, the eagle didn't scream as much or as loud as I had expected. From my seat in the back row I could see most of the audience, and it was quite a sight.

The first speaker was a stranger, evidently the one who had been calling on them to gather around while we were in the tent, and after a few fitting remarks he introduced James Korby. While Korby was orating, Paul Rago left his seat, passed down the aisle in the center, and entered the tent. Since he had plugged for an appearance by Philip Holt I thought his purpose might be to drag him out alive or dead, but it wasn't. In a minute he was back again, and just in time, for he had just sat down when Korby finished and Rago was introduced.

The faces out front had all been serious for Korby, but Rago's accent through the loudspeakers had most of them grinning by the time he warmed up. When Korby left his chair and started down the aisle I suspected him of walking out on Rago because Rago had walked out on him, but maybe not, since his visit in the tent was even shorter than Rago's had been. He came back out and returned to his chair, and listened attentively to the accent.

Next came H. L. Griffin, the importer, and the chairman had to lower the mike for him. His voice took the loudspeakers better than any of the others, and in fact he was darned good. It was only fair, I thought, to have the runt of the bunch take the cake, and I was all for the cheers from the throng that kept him on his feet a full minute after he finished. He really woke them up, and they were still yelling when he turned and went down the aisle to the tent, and it took the chairman a while to calm them down.

Then, just as he started to introduce Dick Vetter, the TV star suddenly bounced up and started down the aisle with a determined look on his face, and it was easy to guess why. He thought Griffin was going to take advantage of the enthusiasm he had aroused by hauling Philip Holt out to the platform, and he was going to stop him. But he didn't have to.

He was still two steps short of the tent entrance when Griffin emerged alone. Vetter moved aside to let him pass and then disappeared into the tent. As Griffin proceeded to his chair in the front row there were some scattered cheers from the crowd, and the chairman had to quiet them again before he could go on. Then he introduced Dick Vetter, who came out of the tent and along to the mike, which had to be raised again, at just the right moment.

As Vetter started to speak, Nero Wolfe arose and headed for the tent, and I raised my brows. Surely, I thought, he's not going to involve himself in the Holt problem; and then, seeing the look on his face, I caught on.

The edges of the wooden chair seat had been cutting into his fanny for nearly an hour and he was in a tantrum, and he wanted to cool off a little before he was called to the mike. I grinned at him sympathetically as he passed and then gave my ear to Vetter. His soapy voice (I say soapy) came through the loudspeakers in a flow of lather, and after a couple of minutes of it I was thinking that it was only fair for Griffin, the runt, to sound like a man, and for Vetter, the handsome young idol of millions, to sound like whipped cream, when my attention was called. Wolfe was at the tent entrance, crooking a finger at me.

As I got up and approached he backed into the tent, and I followed. He crossed to the rear entrance, lifted the flap, maneuvered his bulk through the hole, and held the flap for me. When I had made it he descended the five steps to the ground, walked to the car, grabbed the handle of the rear door, and pulled. Nothing doing. He turned to me. "Unlock it."

I stood. "Do you want something?"

"Unlock it and get in and get the thing started. We're going."

"We are like hell. You've got a speech to make."

He glared at me. He knows my tones of voice as well as I know his. "Archie," he said, "I am not being eccentric. There is a sound and cogent reason and I'll explain on the way. Unlock this door."

I shook my head. "Not till I hear the reason. I admit it's your car." I took the keys from my pocket and offered them. "Here. I resign."

"Very well." He was grim. "That man on the cot is dead. I lifted the blanket to adjust it. One of those knives is in his back, clear to the handle. He is dead. If we are still here when the discovery is made you know what will happen. We will be here all day, all night, a week, indefinitely. That is intolerable. We can answer questions at home as well as here. Confound it, unlock the door!"

"How dead is he?"

"I have told you he is dead."

"Okay. You ought to know better. You do know better. We're stuck. They wouldn't ask us questions at home, they'd haul us back out here. They'd be waiting for us on the stoop and you wouldn't get inside the house."

I returned the keys to my pocket. "Running out when you're next on the program, that would be nice. The only question is do we report it now or do you make your speech and let someone else find it, and you can answer that."

He had stopped glaring. He took in a long deep breath, and when it was out again he said, "I'll make my speech."

"Fine. It would be a shame to waste it. A question. Just now when you lifted the flap to come out I didn't see you untie the tape fastening. Was it already untied?"

"Yes."

"That makes it nice." I turned and went to the steps, mounted, raised the flap for him, and followed him into the tent. He crossed to the front and on out, and I stepped to the cot.

Philip Holt lay facing the wall, with the blanket up to his neck, and I pulled it down far enough to see the handle of the knife, an inch to the right of the point of the shoulder blade. The knife blade was all buried.

I lowered the blanket some more to get at a hand, pinched a fingertip hard for ten seconds, released it, and saw it stay white. I picked some fluff from the blanket and dangled it against his nostrils for half a minute. No movement.

I put the blanket back as I had found it, went to the metal box on the table, lifted the lid, and saw that the shortest knife, the one with the six-inch blade, wasn't there.

As I went to the rear entrance and raised the flap, Dick Vetter's lather or whipped cream, whichever you prefer, came to an end through the loudspeakers, and as I descended the five steps the meadowful of picnickers was cheering.

Our sedan was the third car on the right from the foot of the steps. The second car to the left of the steps was a 1955 Plymouth, and I was pleased to see that it still had an occupant, having previously noticed her—a woman with careless gray hair topping a wide face and a square chin, in the front seat but not behind the wheel.

I circled around to her side and spoke through the open window. "I beg your pardon. May I introduce myself?"

"You don't have to, young man. Your name's Archie Goodwin, and you work for Nero Wolfe, the detective." She had tired gray eyes. "You were just out here with him."

"Right. I hope you won't mind if I ask you something. How long have you been sitting here?"

"Long enough. But it's all right, I can hear the speeches. Nero Wolfe is just starting to speak now."

"Have you been here since the speeches started?"

"Yes, I have. I ate too much of the picnic stuff and I didn't feel like standing up in that crowd, so I came to sit in the car."

"Then you've been here all the time since the speeches began?"

"That's what I said. Why do you want to know?"

"I'm just checking on something. If you don't mind. Has anyone gone into the tent or come out of it while you've been here?"

Her tired eyes woke up a little. "Ha," she said, "so something's missing. I'm not surprised. What's missing?"

"Nothing, as far as I know. I'm just checking a certain fact. Of course you saw Mr. Wolfe and me come out and go back in. Anyone else, either going or coming?"

"You're not fooling me, young man. Something's missing, and you're a detective."

I grinned at her. "All right, have it your way. But I do want to know, if you don't object."

"I don't object. As I told you, I've been right here ever since the speeches started, I got here before that. And nobody has gone into the tent, nobody but you and Nero Wolfe, and I haven't either. I've been right here. If you want to know about me, my name is Anna Banau, Mrs. Alexander Banau, and my husband is a captain at Zoller's—"

A scream came from inside the tent, an all-out scream from a good pair of lungs. I moved, to the steps, up, and past the flap into the tent.

Flora Korby was standing near the cot with her back to it, her hand covering her mouth. I was disappointed in her. Granting that a woman has a right to scream when she finds a corpse, she might have kept it down until Wolfe had finished his speech.

It was a little after four o'clock when Flora Korby screamed. It was 4:34 when a glance outside through a crack past the flap of the tent's rear entrance, the third such glance I had managed to make, showed me that the Plymouth containing Mrs. Alexander Banau was gone.

It was 4:39 when the medical examiner arrived with his bag and found that Philip Holt was still dead. It was 4:48 when the scientists came, with cameras and fingerprint kits and other items of equipment, and Wolfe and I and the others were herded out to the extension, under guard.

It was 5:16 when I counted a total of seventeen cops, state and county, in uniform and out, on the job. It was 5:30 when Wolfe muttered at me bitterly that it would certainly be all night. It was 5:52 when a chief of detectives named Baxter got so personal with me that I decided, finally and definitely, not to play.

It was 6:21 when we all left Culp's Meadows for an official destination. There were four in our car: one in uniform with Wolfe in the back seat, and one in his own clothes with me in front. Again I had someone beside me to tell me the way, but I didn't put my arm across his shoulders.

There had been some conversing with us separately, but most of it had been a panel discussion, open air, out on the platform extension, so I knew pretty well how things stood. Nobody was accusing anybody. Three of them—Korby, Rago, and Griffin—gave approximately the same reason for their visits to the tent during the speechmaking: that they were concerned about Philip Holt and wanted to see if he was all right. The fourth, Dick Vetter, gave the reason I had guessed, that he thought Griffin might bring Holt out to the platform, and he intended to stop him.

Vetter, by the way, was the only one who raised a fuss about being detained. He said that it hadn't been easy to get away from his duties that afternoon, and he had a studio rehearsal scheduled for six o'clock, and he absolutely had to be there. At 6:21, when we all left for the official destination, he was fit to be tied.

None of them claimed to know for sure that Holt had been alive at the time he visited the tent; they all had supposed he had fallen asleep. All except Vetter said they had gone to the cot and looked at him, at his face, and had suspected nothing wrong.

None of them had spoken to him. To the question, "Who do you think did it and why?" they all gave the same answer: someone must have entered the tent by the rear entrance, stabbed him, and departed. The fact that the URWA director of organization had got his stomach into trouble and had been attended by a doctor in the tent had been no secret, anything but.

I have been leaving Flora out, since I knew and you know she was clear, but the cops didn't. I overheard one of them tell another one it was probably her, because stabbing a sick man was more like something a woman would do than a man.

Of course the theory that someone had entered by the back door made the fastening of the tent flap an important item. I said I had tied the tape before we left the tent, and they all agreed that they had seen me do so except Dick Vetter, who said he hadn't noticed because he had been helping to arrange the blanket over Holt; and Wolfe and I both testified that the tape was hanging loose when we had entered the tent while Vetter was speaking.

Under this theory the point wasn't who had untied it, since the murderer could have easily reached through the crack from the outside and jerked the knot loose; the question was when. On that none of them was any help. All four said they hadn't noticed whether the tape was tied or not when they went inside the tent.

That was how it stood, as far as I knew, when we left Culp's Meadows. The official destination turned out to be a building I had been in before a time or two, not as a murder suspect—a county courthouse back of a smooth green lawn with a couple of big trees. First we were collected in a room on the ground floor, and, after a long wait, were escorted up one flight and through a door that was inscribed DISTRICT ATTORNEY.

At least 91.2 per cent of the district attorneys in the State of New York think they would make fine tenants of the governor's mansion at Albany, and that should be kept in mind in considering the conduct of D.A. James R. Delaney. To him at least four of that bunch, and possibly all five, were upright, important citizens in positions to influence segments of the electorate. His attitude as he attacked the problem implied that he was merely chairing a meeting of a community council called to deal with a grave and difficult emergency—except, I noticed, when he was looking at or speaking to Wolfe or me. Then his smile quit working, his tone sharpened, and his eyes had a different look.

With a stenographer at a side table taking it down, he spent an hour going over it with us, or rather with them, with scattered contributions from Chief of Detectives Baxter and others who had been at the scene, and then spoke his mind.

"It seems," he said, "to be the consensus that some person unknown entered the tent from the rear, stabbed him and departed. There is the question, how could such a person have known the knife would be there at hand? But he need not have known. He might have decided to murder only when he saw the knives, or he might have had some other weapon with him, and, seeing the knives, thought one of them would better serve his purpose and used it instead. Either is plausible. It must be admitted that the whole theory is plausible, and none of the facts now known are in contradiction to it. You agree, Chief?"

"Right," Baxter conceded. "Up to now. As long as the known facts are facts."

Delaney nodded. "Certainly. They have to be checked." His eyes took in the audience. "You gentlemen, and you, Miss Korby, you understand that you are to remain in this jurisdiction, the State of New York, until further notice, and you are to be available. With that understood, it seems unnecessary at present to put you under bond as material witnesses. We have your addresses and know where to find you."

He focused on Wolfe, and his tone changed. "With you, Wolfe, the situation is somewhat different. You're a licensed private detective, and so is Goodwin, and the record of your high-handed performances does not inspire confidence in your—uh—candor. There may be some complicated and subtle reasons why the New York City authorities have stood for your tricks, but out here in the suburbs we're more simple-minded. We don't like tricks."

He lowered his chin, which made his eyes slant up under his heavy brows. "Let's see if I've got your story straight. You say that as Vetter started to speak you felt in your pocket for a paper on which you had made notes for your speech, found it wasn't there, thought you had left it in your car, went to get it, and when, after you had entered the tent, it occurred to you that the car was locked and Goodwin had the keys, you summoned him and you and he went out to the car.

"Then Goodwin remembered that the paper had been left on your desk at your office, and you and he returned to the tent, and you went out to the platform and resumed your seat. Another item: when you went to the rear entrance to leave the tent to go out to the car, the tape fastening of the flap was hanging loose, not tied. Is that your story?"

Wolfe cleared his throat. "Mr. Delaney. I suppose it is pointless to challenge your remark about my candor or to ask you to phrase your question less offensively." His shoulders went up an eighth of an inch, and down. "Yes, that's my story."

"I merely asked you the question."

"I answered it."

"So you did." The D.A.'s eyes came to me. "And of course, Goodwin, your story is the same. If it needed arranging, there was ample time for that during the hubbub that followed Miss Korby's scream. But with you there's more to it. You say that after you and Wolfe re-entered the tent, and he continued through the front entrance to the platform, it occurred to you that there was a possibility that he had taken the paper from his desk and put it in his pocket, and had consulted it during the ride, and had left it in the car, and you went out back again to look, and you were out there when Miss Korby screamed. Is that correct?"

As I had long since decided not to play, when Baxter had got too personal, I merely said, "Check."

Delaney returned to Wolfe. "If you object to my being offensive, Wolfe, I'll put it this way: I find some of this hard to believe. Anyone as glib as you are needing notes for a little speech like that? And you thinking you had left the paper in the car, and Goodwin remembering it had been left at home on your desk and then thinking it might be in the car after all?

"Also there are certain facts. You and Goodwin were the last people inside the tent before Miss Korby entered and found the body. You admit it. The others all state that they don't know whether the tape was tied or not when they visited the tent; you and Goodwin can't very well say that, since you went out that way, so you say you found it untied."

He cocked his head. "You admit you had had words with Philip Holt during the past year. You admit he had become obnoxious to you—your word, obnoxious—by his insistence that your personal chef must join his union. The record of your past performances justifies me in saying that a man who renders himself obnoxious to you had better watch his step. I'll say this, if it weren't for the probability that some unknown person entered from the rear, and I concede that it's quite possible, you and Goodwin would be held in custody until a judge could be found to issue a warrant for your arrest as material witnesses. As it is, I'll make it easier for you."

He looked at his wristwatch. "It's five minutes to eight. I'll send a man with you to a restaurant down the street, and we'll expect you back here at nine thirty. I want to cover all the details with you, thoroughly." His eyes moved. "The rest of you may go for the present, but you are to be available."

Wolfe stood up. "Mr. Goodwin and I are going home," he announced. "We will not be back this evening."

Delaney's eyes narrowed. "If that's the way you feel about it, you'll stay. You can send out for sandwiches."

"Are we under arrest?"

The D.A. opened his mouth, closed it, and opened it again. "No."

"Then we're going." Wolfe was assured but not belligerent. "I understand your annoyance, sir, at this interference with your holiday, and I'm aware that you don't like me—or what you know, or think you know, of my record. But I will not surrender my convenience to your humor. You can detain me only if you charge me, and with what?

"Mr. Goodwin and I have supplied all the information we have. Your intimation that I am capable of murdering a man, or of inciting Mr. Goodwin to murder him, because he has made a nuisance of himself, is puerile. You concede that the murderer could have been anyone in that throng of thousands. You have no basis whatever for any supposition that Mr. Goodwin and I are concealing any knowledge that would help you. Should such a basis appear, you know where to find us. Come, Archie."

He turned and headed for the door, and I followed. I can't report the reaction because Delaney at his desk was behind me, and it would have been bad tactics to look back over my shoulder. All I knew was that Baxter took two steps and stopped, and none of the other cops moved.

We made the hall, and the entrance, and down the path to the sidewalk, without a shot being fired; and half a block to where the car was parked. Wolfe told me to find a phone booth and call Fritz to tell him when we would arrive for dinner, and I steered for the center of town.

As I had holiday traffic to cope with, it was half-past nine by the time we got home and washed and seated at the dinner table. A moving car is no place to give Wolfe bad news, or good news either for that matter, and there was no point in spoiling his dinner; so I waited until after we had finished with the poached and truffled broilers and broccoli and stuffed potatoes with herbs, and salad and cheese, and Fritz had brought coffee to us in the office, to open the bag.

Wolfe was reaching for the remote-control television gadget, to turn it on so as to have the pleasure of turning it off again, when I said, "Hold a minute. I have a report to make. I don't blame you for feeling self-satisfied; you got us away very neatly, but there's a catch. It wasn't somebody that came in the back way. It was one of them."

"Indeed." He was placid, after-dinner placid, in the comfortable big made-to-order chair back of his desk. "What is this, flummery?"

"No, sir. Nor am I trying to show that I'm smarter than you are for once. It's just that I know more. When you left the tent to go to the car, your mind was on a quick getaway, so you may not have noticed that a woman was sitting there in a car to the left, but I did. When we returned to the tent and you went on out front, I had an idea and went out back again and had a talk with her. I'll give it to you verbatim, since it's important."

I did so. That was simple, compared with the three-way and four-way conversations I have been called on to report word for word. When I finished he was scowling at me, as black as the coffee in his cup.

"Confound it," he growled.

"Yes, sir. I was going to tell you, there when we were settling the details of why we went out to the car, the paper with your notes; but as you know we were interrupted, and after that there was no opportunity that I liked, and anyway I had seen that Mrs. Banau and the car were gone, and that baboon named Baxter had hurt my feelings, and I had decided not to play.

"Of course the main thing was you, your wanting to go home. If they had known it was one of us six, or seven counting Flora, we would all have been held as material witnesses, and you couldn't have got bail on the Fourth of July, and God help you, I can manage in a cell, but you're too big. Also if I got you home you might feel like discussing a raise in pay. Do you?"

"Shut up." He closed his eyes, and after a moment opened them again. "We're in a pickle. They may find that woman any moment, or she may disclose herself. What about her? You have given me her words, but what about her?"

"She's good. They'll believe her. I did. You would. From where she sat the steps and tent entrance were in her minimum field of vision, no obstructions, less than ten yards away."

"If she kept her eyes open."

"She thinks she did, and that will do for the cops when they find her. Anyhow, I think she did too. When she said nobody had gone into the tent but you and me she meant it."

"There's the possibility that she herself, or someone she knew and would protect— No, that's absurd, since she stayed there in the car for some time after the body was found. We're in a fix."

"Yes, sir." Meeting his eyes, I saw no sign of the gratitude I might reasonably have expected, so I went on. "I would like to suggest, in considering the situation, don't bother about me. I can't be charged with withholding evidence because I didn't report my talk with her. I can just say I didn't believe her and saw no point in making it tougher for us by dragging it in. The fact that someone might have come in the back way didn't eliminate us.

"Of course I'll have to account for my questioning her, but that's easy. I can say I discovered that he was dead after you went back out to the platform to make your speech, and, having noticed her there in the car, I went out to question her before reporting the discovery, and was interrupted by the scream in the tent. So don't mind me. Anything you say. I can phone Delaney in the morning, or you can, and spill it, or we can just sit tight and wait for the fireworks."

"Pfui," he said.

"Amen," I said.

He took in air, audibly, and let it out. "That woman may be communicating with them at this moment, or they may be finding her. I don't complain of your performance; indeed, I commend it. If you had reported that conversation we would both be spending tonight in jail." He made a face. "Bah. As it is, at least we can try something. What time is it?"

I looked at my wristwatch. He would have had to turn his head almost to a right angle to glance at the wall clock, which was too much to expect. "Eight after eleven."

"Could you get them here tonight?"

"I doubt it. All five of them?"

"Yes."

"Possibly by sunup. Bring them to your bedroom?"

He rubbed his nose with a fingertip. "Very well. But you can call them now, as many as you can get. Make it eleven in the morning. Tell them I have a disclosure to make and must consult with them."

"That should interest them," I granted, and reached for the phone.

By the time Wolfe came down from the plant rooms to greet the guests, at two minutes past eleven the next morning, there hadn't been a peep out of the Long Island law. Which didn't mean there couldn't be one at three minutes past eleven. According to the morning paper, District Attorney Delaney and Chief of Detectives Baxter had both conceded that anyone could have entered the tent from the back and therefore it was wide-open. If Anna Banau read newspapers, and she probably did, she might at any moment be going to the phone to make a call.

I had made several, both the night before and that morning, getting the guests lined up; and one special one. There was an address and phone number for an Alexander Banau in the Manhattan book, but I decided not to dial it. I also decided not to ring Zoller's restaurant on Fifty-second Street. I hadn't eaten at Zoller's more than a couple of times, but I knew a man who had been patronizing it for years, and I called him.

Yes, he said, there was a captain at Zoller's named Alex, and yes, his last name was Banau. He liked Alex and hoped that my asking about him didn't mean that he was headed for some kind of trouble. I said no trouble was contemplated, I just might want to check a little detail, and thanked him. Then I sat and looked at the slip on which I had scribbled the Banau home phone number, with my finger itching to dial it, but to say what? No.

I mention that around ten thirty I got the Marley .38 from the drawer, saw that it was loaded, and put it in my side pocket, not to prepare you for bloodshed, but just to show that I was sold on Mrs. Banau. With a murderer for a guest, and an extremely nervy one, there was no telling.

H. L. Griffin, the importer, and Paul Rago, the sauce chef, came alone and separately, but Korby and Flora had Dick Vetter with them. I had intended to let Flora have the red leather chair, but when I showed them to the office, Rago, the six-footer with the mustache and the accent, had copped it, and she took one of the yellow chairs in a row facing Wolfe's desk, with her father on her right and Vetter on her left. Griffin, the runt who had made the best speech, was at the end of the row nearest my desk.

When Wolfe came down from the plant rooms, entered, greeted them, and headed for his desk, Vetter spoke up before he was seated.

"I hope this won't last long, Mr. Wolfe. I asked Mr. Goodwin if it couldn't be earlier, and he said it couldn't. Miss Korby and I must have an early lunch because I have a script conference at one thirty."

I raised a brow. I had been honored. I had driven a car with my arm across the shoulders of a girl whom Dick Vetter himself thought worthy of a lunch.

Wolfe, adjusted in his chair, said mildly, "I won't prolong it beyond necessity, sir. Are you and Miss Korby friends?"

"What's that got to do with it?"

"Possibly nothing. But now nothing about any of you is beyond the bounds of my curiosity. It is a distressing thing to have to say, in view of the occasion of our meeting yesterday, the anniversary of the birth of this land of freedom, but I must. One of you is a miscreant. One of you people killed Philip Holt."

The idea is to watch them and see who faints or jumps up and runs. But nobody did. They all stared.

"One of us?" Griffin demanded.

Wolfe nodded. "I thought it best to begin with that bald statement, instead of leading up to it. I thought—"

Korby cut in. "This is funny. This is a joke. After what you said yesterday to that district attorney. It's a *bad* joke."

"It's no joke, Mr. Korby. I wish it were. I thought yesterday I was on solid ground, but I wasn't. I now know that there is a witness, a credible and confident witness, to testify that no one entered the tent from the rear between the time that the speeches began and the discovery of the body. I also know that neither Mr. Goodwin nor I killed him, so it was one of you. So I think we should discuss it."

"You say a witness?" Rago made it "weetnuss."

"Who is he?" Korby wanted to know. "Where is he?"

"It's a woman, and she is available. Mr. Goodwin, who has spoken with her, is completely satisfied of her competence and bona fides, and he is hard to satisfy. It is highly unlikely that she can be impeached. That's all I—"

"I don't get it," Vetter blurted. "If they've got a witness like that why haven't they come for us?"

"Because they haven't got her. They know nothing about her.

But they may find her at any moment, or she may go to them. If so you will soon be discussing the matter not with me but with officers of the law—and so will I. Unless you do discuss it with me, and unless the discussion is productive, I shall of course be constrained to tell Mr. Delaney about her. I wouldn't like that and neither would you. After hearing her story his manner with you, and with me, would be quite different from yesterday. I want to ask you some questions."

"Who is she?" Korby demanded. "Where is she?"

Wolfe shook his head. "I'm not going to identify her or place her for you. I note your expressions—especially yours, Mr. Korby, and yours, Mr. Griffin. You are skeptical. But what conceivable reason could there be for my getting you here to point this weapon at you except the coercion of events? Why would I invent or contrive such a dilemma? I, like you, would vastly prefer to have it as it was, that the murderer came from without, but that's no good now. I concede that you may suspect me too, and Mr. Goodwin, and you may question us as I may question you. But one of us killed Philip Holt, and getting answers to questions is clearly in the interest of all the rest of us."

They exchanged glances. But they were not the kind of glances they would have exchanged five minutes earlier. They were glances of doubt, suspicion and surmise, and they weren't friendly.

"I don't see," Griffin objected, "what good questions will do. We were all there together and we all know what happened. We all know what everybody said."

Wolfe nodded. "But we were all supporting the theory that excluded us. Now we're not. We can't. One of us has something in his background which, if known, would account for his determination to kill that man. I suggest beginning with autobiographical sketches from each of us, and here is mine.

"I was born in Montenegro and spent my early boyhood there. At the age of sixteen I decided to move around, and in fourteen years I became acquainted with most of Europe, a little of Africa, and much of Asia, in a variety of roles and activities. Coming to this country in nineteen-thirty, not penniless, I bought this house and entered into practice as a private detective.

"I am a naturalized American citizen. I first heard of Philip Holt about two years ago when Fritz Brenner, who works for me, came to me with a complaint about him. My only reason for wishing him harm, but not the extremity of death, was removed, as you know, when he agreed to stop annoying Mr. Brenner about joining your union if I would make a speech at your blasted picnic. Mr. Goodwin?"

I turned my face to the audience. "Born in Ohio. Public high school, pretty good at geometry and football, graduated with honor but no honors. Went to college two weeks, decided it was childish, came to New York and got a job guarding a pier, shot and killed two men and was fired, was recommended to Nero Wolfe for a chore he wanted done, did it, was offered a full-time job by Mr. Wolfe, took it, still have it. Personally, was more entertained than bothered by Holt's trying to get union dues out of Fritz Brenner. Otherwise no connection with him or about him."

"You may," Wolfe told them, "question us later if you wish. Miss Korby?"

"Well—" Flora said. She glanced at her father, and, when he nodded, she aimed at Wolfe and went on. "My autobiography doesn't amount to much. I was born in New York and have always lived here. I'm twenty years old. I didn't kill Phil Holt and had no reason to kill him." She turned her palms up. "What else?"

"If I may suggest," H. L. Griffin offered, "if there's a witness as Wolfe says, if there *is* such a witness, they'll dig everything up. For instance, about you and Phil."

She gave him an eye. "What about us, Mr. Griffin?"

"I don't know. I've only heard talk, that's all, and they'll dig up the talk."

"To hell with the talk," Dick Vetter blurted, the whipped cream sounding sour.

Flora looked at Wolfe. "I can't help talk," she said. "It certainly is no secret that Phil Holt was—well, he liked women. And it's no secret that I'm a woman, and I guess it's not a secret that I didn't like Phil. For me he was what you called him, a nuisance. When he wanted something."

Wolfe grunted. "And he wanted you?"

"He thought he did. That's all there was to it. He was a pest, that's all there is to say about it."

"You said you had no reason to kill him."

"Good heavens, I didn't! A girl doesn't kill a man just because he won't believe her when she says no!"

"No to what? A marriage proposal?"

Her father cut in. "Look here," he told Wolfe, "you're barking up the wrong tree. Everybody knows how Phil Holt was about women. He never asked one to marry him and probably he never would. My daughter is old enough and smart enough to take care of herself, and she does, but not by sticking a knife in a man's back." He turned to Griffin. "Much obliged, Harry."

The importer wasn't fazed. "It was bound to come out, Jim, and I thought it ought to be mentioned now."

Wolfe was regarding Korby. "Naturally it raises the question how far a father might go to relieve his daughter of a pest."

Korby snorted. "If you're asking it, the answer is no. My daughter can take care of herself. If you want a reason why I might have killed Phil Holt you'll have to do better than that."

"Then I'll try, Mr. Korby. You are the president of your union, and Mr. Holt was an important figure in it, and at the moment the affairs of unions, especially their financial affairs, are front-page news. Have you any reason to fear an investigation, or had Mr. Holt?"

"No. They can investigate as much as they damn please."

"Have you been summoned?"

"No."

"Had Mr. Holt been summoned?"

"No."

"Have any officials of your union been summoned?"

"No." Korby's pudgy face and bald top were pinking up a little. "You're barking up the wrong tree again."

"But at least another tree. You realize, sir, that if Mr. Delaney starts after us in earnest, the affairs of the United Restaurant Workers of America will be one of his major concerns. For the murder of Philip Holt we all had opportunity, and the means were there at hand; what he will seek is the motive. If there was a vulnerable spot in the operation of your union, financial or otherwise, I suggest that it would be wise for you to disclose it now for discussion."

"There wasn't anything." Korby was pinker. "There's nothing wrong with my union except rumors. That's all it is, rumors, and where's a union that hasn't got rumors with all the stink they've raised? We're not vulnerable to anything or anybody."

"What kind of rumors?"

"Any kind you want to name. I'm a crook. All the officers are crooks. We've raided the benefit fund. We've sold out to the big operators. We steal lead pencils and paper clips."

"Can you be more specific? What was the most embarrassing rumor?"

Korby was suddenly not listening. He took a folded handkerchief from his pocket, opened it up, wiped his face and his baldness, refolded the handkerchief at the creases, and returned it to his pocket. Then his eyes went back to Wolfe.

"If you want something specific," he said, "it's not a rumor. It's a strictly internal union matter, but it's sure to leak now and it might as well leak here first. There have been some charges made, and they're being looked into, about kickbacks from dealers to union officers and members. Phil Holt had something to do with some of the charges, though that wasn't in his department. He got hot about it."

"Were you the target of any of the charges?"

"I was not. I have the complete trust of my associates and my staff."

"You said 'dealers.' Does that include importers?"

"Sure, importers are dealers."

"Was Mr. Griffin's name mentioned in any of the charges?"

"I'm not giving any names, not without authority from my board. Those things are confidential."

"Much obliged, Jim," H. L. Griffin said, sounding the opposite of obliged. "Even exchange?"

"Excuse me." It was Dick Vetter, on his feet. "It's nearly twelve o'clock and Miss Korby and I have to go. We've got to get some lunch and I can't be late for that conference. Anyway, I think it's a lot of hooey. Come on, Flora."

She hesitated a moment, then left her chair, and he moved. But when Wolfe snapped out his name he turned. "Well?"

Wolfe swiveled his chair. "My apologies. I should have remembered that you are pressed for time. If you can give us, say, five minutes?"

The TV star smiled indulgently. "For my autobiography? You can look it up. It's in print—*TV Guide* a couple of months ago, or *Clock* magazine, I don't remember the date. I say this is hooey. If one of us is a murderer, okay, I wish you luck, but this isn't getting you anywhere. Couldn't I just tell you something I felt like?"

"You could indeed, Mr. Vetter. But if inquiry reveals that you have lied or have omitted something plainly relevant that will be of interest. The magazine articles you mentioned—do they tell of your interest in Miss Korby?"

"Nuts." Many of his twenty million admirers wouldn't have liked either his tone or his diction.

Wolfe shook his head. "If you insist, Mr. Vetter, you may of course be disdainful about it with me, but not with the police once they get interested in you. I asked you before if you and Miss Korby are friends, and you asked what that had to do with it, and I said possibly nothing. I now say possibly something, since Philip Holt was hounding her—how savagely I don't know yet. Are you and Miss Korby friends?"

"Certainly we're friends. I'm taking her to lunch."

"Are you devoted to her?"

His smile wasn't quite so indulgent, but it was still a smile. "Now that's a delicate question," he said. "I'll tell you how it is. I'm a public figure and I have to watch my tongue. If I said yes, I'm devoted to Miss Korby, it would be in all the columns tomorrow and I'd get ten thousand telegrams and a million letters. If I said no, I'm not devoted to Miss Korby, that wouldn't be polite with her here at my elbow. So I'll just skip it. Come on, Flora."

"One more question. I understand that your father works in a New York restaurant. Do you know whether he is involved in any of the charges Mr. Korby spoke of?"

"Oh, for God's sake. Talk about hooey." He turned and headed for the door, taking Flora with him. I got up and went to the hall and on to the front door, opened it for them, closed it after them, put the chain-bolt on, and returned to the office. Wolfe was speaking.

". . . and I assure you, Mr. Rago, my interest runs with yours—with all of you except one. You don't want the police crawling over you and neither do I."

The sauce chef had straightened up in the red leather chair, and the points of his mustache seemed to have straightened up too. "Treeks," he said.

"No, sir," Wolfe said. "I have no objection to tricks, if they work, but this is merely a forthright discussion of a lamentable situation. No trick. Do you object to telling us what dealings you had with Philip Holt?"

"I am deesappointed," Rago declared. "Of course I knew you made a living with detective work, everybody knows that, but to me your glory is your great contributions to cuisine—your *sauce printemps*, your oyster pie, your *artichauts drigants*, and others. I know what Pierre Mondor said of you. So it is a deesappointment when I am in your company that the only talk is of the ugliness of murder."

"I don't like it any better than you do, Mr. Rago. I am pleased to know that Pierre Mondor spoke well of me. Now about Philip Holt?"

"If you insist, certainly. But what can I say? Nothing."

"Didn't you know him?"

Rago spread his hands and raised his shoulders and brows. "I had met him. As one meets people. Did I know him? Whom does one know? Do I know you?"

"But you never saw me until two weeks ago. Surely you must have seen something of Mr. Holt. He was an important official of your union, in which you were active."

"I have not been active in the union."

"You were a speaker at its picnic yesterday."

Rago nodded and smiled. "Yes, that is so. But that was because of my activity in the kitchen, not in the union. It may be said, even by me, that in sauces I am supreme. It was for that distinction that it was thought desirable to have me." His head turned. "So, Mr. Korby?"

The president of URWA nodded yes. "That's right," he told Wolfe. "We thought the finest cooking should be represented, and we picked Rago for it. So far as I know, he has never come to a union meeting. We wish he would, and more like him."

"I am a man of the kitchen," Rago declared. "I am an artist. The business I leave to others."

Wolfe was on Korby. "Did Mr. Rago's name appear in any of the charges you spoke of?"

"No. I said I wouldn't give names, but I can say no. No, it didn't."

"You didn't say no when I asked about Mr. Griffin." Wolfe turned to the importer. "Do you wish to comment on that, sir?"

I still hadn't decided exactly what was wrong with Griffin's left eye. There was no sign of an injury, and it seemed to function okay, but it appeared to be a little off center. From an angle, the slant I had from my desk, it looked normal.

He lifted his long narrow chin. "What do you expect?"

"My expectations are of no consequence. I merely invite comment."

"On that, I have none. I know nothing about any charges. What I want, I want to see that witness."

Wolfe shook his head. "As I said, I will not produce the witness—for the present. Are you still skeptical?"

"I'm always skeptical." Griffin's voice would have suited a man twice his size. "I want to see that witness and hear what she has to say. I admit I can see no reason why you would invent her—if there is one it's too deep for me, since it puts you in the same boat with us—but I'm not going to believe her until I see her. Maybe I will then, and maybe I won't."

"I think you will. Meanwhile, what about your relations with Philip Holt? How long and how well did you know him?"

"Oh, to hell with this jabber!" Griffin bounced up, not having far to bounce. "If there was anything in my relations with him that made me kill him, would I be telling you?" He flattened his palms on Wolfe's desk. "Are you going to produce that witness? No?" He wheeled. "I've had enough of this! You, Jim? Rago?"

That ended the party. Wolfe could have held Korby and Rago for more jabber, but apparently he didn't think it worth the effort. They asked some questions, what was Wolfe going to do now, and what was the witness going to do, and why couldn't they see her, and why did Wolfe believe her, and was he going to see her and question her, and of course nobody got anything out of that. The atmosphere wasn't very cordial when they left. After letting them out I returned to the office and stood in front of Wolfe's desk. He was leaning back with his arms folded.

"Lunch in twenty minutes," I said cheerfully.

"Not in peace," he growled.

"No, sir. Any instructions?"

"Pfui. It would take an army, and I haven't got one. To go into all of them, to trace all their connections and dealings with the man one of them murdered . . ."

He unfolded his arms and put his fists on the desk. "I can't even limit it by assuming that it was an act of urgency, resulting from something that had been said or done that day or in the immediate past. The need or desire to kill him might have dated from a week ago, or a month, or even a year, and it was satisfied yesterday in that tent only because circumstances offered the opportunity.

"No matter which one it was—Rago, who visited the tent first, or Korby or Griffin or Vetter, who visited it after him in that order—no matter which, the opportunity was tempting. The man was there, recumbent and disabled, and the weapon was there. He had a plausible excuse for entering the tent. To spread the cloud of suspicion to the multitude, all he had to do was untie the tape that held the flap. Even if the body were discovered soon after he left the tent, even seconds after, there would be no question he couldn't answer."

He grunted. "No. Confound it, no. The motive may be buried not only in a complexity of associations but also in history. It might take months. I will have to contrive something."

"Yeah. Any time."

"There may be none. That's the devil of it. Get Saul and Fred and Orrie and have them on call. I have no idea for what, but no matter, get them. And let me alone."

I went to my desk and pulled the phone over.

There have been only five occasions in my memory when Wolfe has cut short his afternoon session with the orchids in the plant rooms, from four o'clock to six, and that was the fifth.

If there had been any developments inside his skull I hadn't been informed. There had been none outside, unless you count my calling Saul and Fred and Orrie, our three best bets when we needed outside help, and telling them to stand by.

Back at his desk after lunch, Wolfe fiddled around with papers on his desk, counted the week's collection of bottle caps in his drawer, rang for Fritz to bring beer and then didn't drink it, and picked up his current book, *The Fall* by Albert Camus, three or four times, and put it down again. In between he brushed specks of dust from his desk with his little finger.

When I turned on the radio for the four o'clock newscast he waited until it was finished to leave for his elevator trip up to the roof.

Later, nearly an hour later, I caught myself brushing a speck of dust off my desk with my little finger, and said something I needn't repeat here, and went to the kitchen for a glass of milk.

When the doorbell rang at a quarter past five I jumped up and shot for the hall, realized that was unmanly, and controlled my legs to a normal gait. Through the one-way glass panel of the front door I saw, out on the stoop, a tall lanky guy, narrow from top to bottom, in a brown suit that needed pressing and a brown straw hat.

I took a breath, which I needed apparently, and went and opened the door the two inches allowed by the chain-bolt. His appearance was all against it, but there was no telling what kind of specimen District Attorney Delaney or Chief of Detectives Baxter might have on his staff.

I spoke through the crack. "Yes, sir?"

"I would like to see Mr. Nero Wolfe. My name is Banau, Alexander Banau."

"Yes, sir." I took the bolt off and swung the door open, and he crossed the sill. "Your hat, sir?" He gave it to me and I put it on the shelf. "This way, sir." I waited until I had him in the office and in the red leather chair to say, "Mr. Wolfe is engaged at the moment. I'll tell him you're here."

I went to the hall and on to the kitchen, shutting doors on the way, buzzed the plant rooms on the house phone, and in three seconds, instead of the usual fifteen or twenty, had a growl in my ear. "Yes?"

"Company. Captain Alexander Banau."

Silence, then: "Let him in."

"He's already in. Have you any suggestions how I keep him occupied until six o'clock?"

"No." A longer silence. "I'll be down."

As I said that was the fifth time in all the years I have been with him. I went back to the office and asked the guest if he would like something to drink, and he said no, and in two minutes there was the sound of Wolfe's elevator descending and stopping, the door opening and shutting, and his tread. He entered, circled around the red leather chair, and offered a hand.

"Mr. Banau? I'm Nero Wolfe. How do you do, sir?"

He was certainly spreading it on. He doesn't like to shake hands, and rarely does. When he was adjusted in his chair he gave Banau a look so sociable it was damn close to fawning, for him.

"Well, sir?"

"I fear," Banau said, "that I may have to make myself disagreeable. I don't like to be disagreeable. Is that gentleman"—he nodded at me—"Mr. Archie Goodwin?"

"He is, yes, sir."

"Then it will be doubly disagreeable, but it can't be helped. It concerns the tragic event at Culp's Meadows yesterday. According to the newspaper accounts, the police are proceeding on the probability that the murderer entered the tent from the rear, and left that way after he had performed the deed. Just an hour ago I telephoned to Long Island to ask if they still regard that as probable, and was told that they do."

He stopped to clear his throat. I would have liked to get my fingers around it to help. He resumed.

"It is also reported that you and Mr. Goodwin were among those interviewed, and that compels me to conclude, reluctantly, that Mr. Goodwin has failed to tell you of a conversation he had with my wife as she sat in our car outside the tent. I should explain that I was in the crowd in front, and when your speech was interrupted by the scream, and confusion resulted, I made my way around to the car, with some difficulty, and got in and drove away. I do not like tumult.

"My wife did not tell me of her conversation with Mr. Goodwin until after we got home. She regards it as unwise to talk while I am driving. What she told me was that Mr. Goodwin approached the car and spoke to her through the open window. He asked her if anyone—"

"If you please." Wolfe wiggled a finger. "Your assumption that he hasn't reported the conversation to me is incorrect. He has."

"What! He has?"

"Yes, sir. If you will—"

"Then you know that my wife is certain that no one entered the tent from the rear while the speeches were being made? No one but you and Mr. Goodwin? Absolutely certain? You know she told him that?"

"I know what she told him, yes. But if you will—"

"And you haven't told the police?"

"No, not yet. I would like—"

"Then she has no choice." Banau was on his feet. "It is even more disagreeable than I feared. She must communicate with them at once. This is terrible, a man of your standing, and the others too. It is terrible, but it must be done. In a country of law the law must be served."

He turned and headed for the door.

I left my chair. Stopping him and wrapping him up would have been no problem, but I was myself stopped by the expression on Wolfe's face. He looked relieved; he even looked pleased. I stared at him, and was still staring when the sound came of the front door closing.

I stepped to the hall, saw that Banau was gone and hadn't forgotten his hat, and returned and stood at Wolfe's desk.

"Goody," I said. "Cream? Give me some."

He took in air, all the way, and let it out. "This is more like it," he declared. "I've had all the humiliation I can stand. Jumping out of my skin every time the phone rang. Did you notice how quickly I answered your ring upstairs? Afraid, by heaven, afraid to go into the tropical room to look over the Renanthera imschootiana! Now we know where we are."

"Yeah. Also where we soon will be. If it had been me I would have kept him at least long enough to tell him—"

"Shut up."

I did so. There are certain times when it is understood that I am not to badger, and the most important time is when he leans back in his chair and shuts his eyes and his lips start to work. He pushes them out, pulls them in, out and in, out and in.

That means his brain has crashed the sound barrier. I have seen him, dealing with a tough one, go on with that lip action for up to an hour. I sat down at my desk, thinking I might as well be near the phone.

That time he didn't take an hour, not having one. More like eight minutes. He opened his eyes, straightened up, and spoke.

"Archie. Did he tell you where his wife was?"

"No. He told me nothing. He was saving it for you. She could have been in the drug store at the corner, sitting in the phone booth."

He grunted. "Then we must clear out of here. I am going to find out which of them killed that man before we are all hauled in. The motive and the evidence will have to come later; the thing now is to identify him as a bone to toss to Mr. Delaney. Where is Saul?"

"At home, waiting to hear. Fred and Orrie—"

"We need only Saul. Call him. Tell him we are coming there at once. Where would Mr. Vetter have his conference?"

"I suppose at the MXO studio."

"Get him. And if Miss Korby is there, her also. And the others. You must get them all before they hear from Mr. Delaney. They are all to be at Saul's place without delay. At the earliest possible moment. Tell them they are to meet and question the witness, and it is desperately urgent. If they balk I'll speak to them and—"

I had the phone, dialing.

After they were all there and Wolfe started in, it took him less than fifteen minutes to learn which one was it. I might have managed it in fifteen days, with luck. If you like games you might lean back now, close your eyes, and start pushing your lips out and in, and see how long it takes you to decide how you would do it. Fair enough, since you know everything that Wolfe and I knew.

But get it straight; don't try to name him or come up with evidence that would nail him; the idea is, how do you use what you now know to put the finger on him? That was what Wolfe did, and I wouldn't expect more of you than of him.

Saul Panzer, below average in size but miles above it in savvy, lived alone on the top floor—living room, bedroom, kitchenette, and bath—of a remodeled house on Thirty-eighth Street between Lexington and Third. The living room was big, lighted with two floor lamps and two table lamps, even at seven o'clock of a July evening, because the blinds were drawn. One wall had windows, another was solid with books, and the other two had pictures and shelves that were cluttered with everything from chunks of minerals to walrus tusks. In the far corner was a grand piano.

Wolfe sent his eyes around and said, "This shouldn't take long."

He was in the biggest chair Saul had, by a floor lamp, almost big enough for him. I was on a stool to his left and front, and Saul was off to his right, on the piano bench. The chairs of the five customers were in an arc facing him. Of course it would have been sensible and desirable to arrange the seating so that the murderer was next to either Saul or me, but that wasn't practical since we had no idea which one it was, and neither did Wolfe.

"Where's the witness?" Griffin demanded. "Goodwin said she'd be here."

Wolfe nodded. "I know, Mr. Goodwin is sometimes careless with his pronouns. The witness is present." He aimed a thumb at the piano bench. "There. Mr. Saul Panzer, who is not only credible and confident but—"

"You said it was a woman!"

"There is another witness who is a woman; doubtless there will be others when one of you goes on trial. The urgency Mr. Goodwin spoke of relates to what Mr. Panzer will tell you. Before he does so, some explanation is required."

"Let him talk first," Dick Vetter said, "and then explain. We've heard from you already."

"I'll make it brief." Wolfe was unruffled. "It concerns the tape fastening on the flap of the rear entrance of the tent. As you know, Mr. Goodwin tied it before we left to go to the platform, and when he and I entered the tent later and left by the rear entrance it had been untied. By whom? Not by someone entering from the outside, since there is a witness to testify that no one had—"

James Korby cut in. "That's the witness we want to see. Goodwin said she'd be here."

"You'll see her, Mr. Korby, in good time. Please bear with me. Therefore the tape had been untied by someone who had entered from the front—by one of you four men. Why? The presumption is overwhelming that it was untied by the murderer, to create and support the probability that Philip Holt had been stabbed by someone who entered from the rear. It is more than a presumption; it approaches certainty. So it seemed to me that it was highly desirable, if possible, to learn who had untied the tape; and I enlisted the services of Mr. Panzer." His head turned. "Saul, if you please?"

Saul had his hand on a black leather case beside him on the bench. "Do you want it all, Mr. Wolfe? How I got it?"

"Not at the moment, I think. Later, if they want to know. What you have is more important than how you got it."

"Yes, sir." He opened the lid of the case and took something from it. "I'd rather not explain how I got it because it might make trouble for somebody."

I horned in. "What do you mean 'might'? You know damn well it would make trouble for somebody."

"Okay, Archie, okay." His eyes went to the audience. "What I've got is these photographs of fingerprints that were lifted from the tape on the flap of the rear entrance of the tent. There are some blurry ones, but there are four good ones. Two of the good ones are Mr. Goodwin's, and that leaves two unidentified." He turned to the case and took things out. He cocked his head to the audience. "The idea is, I take your prints and—"

"Not so fast, Saul." Wolfe's eyes went right, and left again. "You see how it is, and you understand why Mr. Goodwin said it was urgent. Surely those of you who did *not* untie the tape will not object to having your prints compared with the photographs. If anyone does object he cannot complain if an inference is made. Of course there is the possibility that none of your prints will match the two unidentified ones in the photographs, and in that case the results will be negative and not conclusive. Mr. Panzer has the equipment to take your prints, and he is an expert. Will you let him?"

Glances were exchanged.

"What the hell," Vetter said. "Mine are on file anyway. Sure."

"Mine also," Griffin said. "I have no objection."

Paul Rago abruptly exploded. "Treeks again!"

All eyes went to him. Wolfe spoke. "No, Mr. Rago, no tricks. Mr. Panzer would prefer not to explain how he got the photographs, but he will if you insist. I assure you—"

"I don't mean treeks how he gets them." The sauce chef uncrossed his legs. "I mean what you said, it was the murderer who untied the tape. That is not necessary. I can say that was a lie! When I entered the tent and looked at him it seemed to me he did not breathe good, there was not enough air, and I went and untied the tape so the air could come through. So if you take my print and if it is like the photograph, what will that prove? Nothing at all. Nuh-theeng! So I say it is treeks again, and in this great land of freedom—"

I wasn't trying to panic him. I wasn't even going to touch him. And I had the Marley .38 in my pocket, and Saul had one too, so if he had tried to start something he would have got stopped quick. But using a gun, especially in a crowd, is always bad management unless you have to, and he was twelve feet away from me, and I got up and moved merely because I wanted to be closer.

Saul had the same notion at the same instant, and the sight of us two heading for him, with all that he knew that we didn't know yet, was too much for him. He was out of his chair and plunging toward the door as I took my second step.

Then, of course, we had to touch him. I reached him first, not because I'm faster than Saul but because he was farther off. And the damn fool put up a fight, although I had him wrapped. He kicked Saul where it hurt, and knocked a lamp over, and bumped my nose with his skull. When he sank his teeth in my arm I thought, That will do for you, mister, and jerked the Marley from my pocket and slapped him above the ear, and he went down.

Turning, I saw that Dick Vetter had also wrapped his arms around someone, and she was neither kicking nor biting. In moments of stress people usually show what is really on their minds, even important public figures like TV stars. There wasn't a word about it in the columns next day.

I have often wondered how Paul Rago felt when, at his trial a couple of months later, no evidence whatever was introduced about fingerprints. He knew then, of course, that it had been a treek and nothing but, that no prints had been lifted from the tape by Saul or anyone else, and that if he had kept his mouth shut and played along he might have been playing yet.

I once asked Wolfe what he would have done if that had happened.

He said, "It didn't happen."

I said, "What if it had?"

He said, "Pfui. The contingency was too remote to consider. It was as good as certain that the murderer had untied the tape. Confronted with the strong probability that it was about to be disclosed that his print was on the tape, he had to say something. He had to explain how it got there, and it was vastly preferable to do so voluntarily instead of waiting until evidence compelled it."

I hung on. "Okay, it was a good trick, but I still say what if?"

"And I still say it is pointless to consider remote contingencies. What if your mother had abandoned you in a tiger's cage at the age of three months? What would you have done?"

I told him I'd think it over and let him know.

As for motive, you can have three guesses if you want them, but you'll never get warm if you dig them out of what I have reported. In all the jabber in Wolfe's office that day, there wasn't one word that had the slightest bearing on why Philip Holt died, which goes to show why detectives get ulcers.

No, I'm wrong; it was mentioned that Philip Holt liked women, and certainly that had a bearing. One of the women he had liked was Paul Rago's wife, an attractive blue-eyed number about half as old as her husband, and he was still liking her, and, unlike Flora Korby, she had liked him and proved it.

Paul Rago hadn't liked that.

"Q"

Ruth Rendell

The Fall of a Coin

The story of a marriage on the rocks, with Ruth Rendell the acute observer of all the telling details, the acute listener to all the mean, petty, accusing, recriminating thrusts and counter-thrusts in the duel of the sexes . . .

The manager of the hotel took them up two flights of stairs to their room. There was no elevator. There was no central heating either and, though April, it was very cold.

"A bit small, isn't it?" said Nina Armadale.

"It's a double room and I'm afraid it's all we have left."

"I suppose I'll have to be thankful it hasn't got a double bed," said Nina.

Her husband winced at that, which pleased her. She went over to the window and looked down into a narrow alley bounded by brick walls. The cathedral clock struck five. Nina imagined what that would be like chiming every hour throughout the night, and maybe every quarter as well, and was glad she had brought her sleeping pills.

The manager was still making excuses for the lack of accommodations. "You see, there's this big wedding in the cathedral tomorrow. Sir William Tarrant's daughter. There'll be five hundred guests and most of them are putting up in the town."

"We're going to it," said James Armadale. "That's why we're here."

"Then you'll appreciate the problem. Now the bathroom's just down the passage—turn right and it's the third door on the left. Dinner at seven thirty and breakfast from eight till nine. Oh, and I'd better show Mrs. Armadale how to work the gas fire."

"Don't bother," said Nina, enraged. "I can work a gas fire." She was struggling with the wardrobe door which at first wouldn't open, and when opened refused to close.

The manager watched her, apparently decided it was hopeless to assist, and said to James, "I really meant about working the gas *meter*. There's a coin-in-the-slot meter—it takes fivepence pieces—and we really find it the best way for guests to manage."

James squatted on the floor beside her and studied the gray metal box. It was an old-fashioned gas meter with brass fittings of the kind he hadn't seen since he had been a student living in a furnished room. A gauge with a red-arrow marker indicated the amount of gas paid for, and at present it showed empty. So if you turned the dial on the gas fire to ON, no gas would come from the meter unless you had previously fed it with one or more fivepence pieces.

But what was the purpose of that brass handle? There were differences between this contraption and the one he'd had in his college days. Maybe, while his had been for the old toxic coal gas, this had been converted for the supply of natural gas. He looked at the manager and asked her.

"No, we're still waiting for natural gas in this part of the country and when it comes the old meters will have to go."

"Then what's the handle for?"

"You turn it to the left like this, insert your coin in the slot, and then turn it to the right. Have you got fivepence on you?"

James hadn't. Nina had stopped listening, he was glad to see. Perhaps when the inevitable quarrel started, as it would as soon as the manager had gone, it would turn on the awfulness of going to this wedding for which he could hardly be blamed, instead of the squalid arrangements in the hotel for which he could.

"Never mind," the manager was saying. "You can't go wrong, it's very simple. When you've put your fivepence in, you just turn the handle to the right as far as it will go and you hear the coin fall. Then you can switch on the fire and light the gas. Is that clear?"

James said it was quite clear, thanks very much, and immediately the manager had left the room, Nina, who wasted no time, said, "Can you tell me one good reason why we couldn't have come here tomorrow?"

"I could tell you several," said James, getting up from the floor, turning his back on that antediluvian gadget and the gas fire which looked as if it hadn't given out a therm of heat for about thirty years. "The principal one is that I didn't fancy driving a hundred and fifty miles in a morning coat and tophat."

"Didn't fancy driving with your usual Saturday morning hangover, you mean."

"Let's not start a row, Nina. Let's have a bit of peace for just one evening. Sir William is my company chairman. I have to take it as an honor that we were asked to this wedding, and if we have an uncomfortable evening and night because of it, that can't be helped. It's part of my job."

"Just how pompous can you get?" said Nina with what in a less attractive woman would have been called a snarl. "I wonder what Sir William-Bloody-Tarrant would say if he could see his sales director after he's got a bottle of whiskey inside him."

"He doesn't see me," said James, lighting a cigarette, and adding because she hadn't yet broken his spirit, "That's your privilege."

"Privilege!" Nina, who had been furiously unpacking her case and throwing clothes onto one of the beds, now stopped doing this because it sapped some of the energy she needed for quarreling. She sat down on the bed and snapped, "Give me a cigarette. You've no manners, have you? Do you know how uncouth you are? This place'll suit you fine, it's just up to your mark—gas meters and a loo about five hundred yards away. That won't bother you as long as there's a bar. I'll be able to have the *privilege* of sharing my bedroom with a disgusting soak."

She drew breath like a swimmer and plunged on. "Do you realize we haven't slept in the same room for two years? Didn't think of that, did you, when you left booking until the last minute? Or maybe—yes, that was it, my God!—maybe you did think of it. Oh, I know you so well, James Armadale. You thought being in here with me, undressing with me, would work a miracle. I'd come round. I'd—what's the expression?—*resume marital relations*. You got them to give us this—this cell—on purpose. You bloody well fixed it!"

"No," said James. He said it quietly and rather feebly because he had experienced such a strong inner recoil that he could hardly speak at all.

"You liar! D'you think I've forgotten the fuss you made when I got you to sleep in the spare room? D'you think I've forgotten about that woman, that Frances? I'll never forget and I'll never forgive you. So don't think I'm going to let bygones be bygones when you try pawing me about after the bar closes."

"I won't do that," said James, reflecting that in a quarter of an hour the bar would be opening. "I shall never again try what you so charmingly describe as pawing you about."

"No, because you know you wouldn't get anywhere. You know you'd get a slap on the face you wouldn't forget in a hurry."

"Nina," he said, "let's stop this. It's hypothetical, it won't happen. If we are going to go on living together—and I suppose we are, though God knows why—can't we try to live in peace?"

She flushed and said in a thick sullen voice, "You should have thought of that before you were unfaithful to me with that woman."

"That," he said, "was three years ago—*three years*. I don't want to provoke you and we've been into this enough times, but you know very well why I was unfaithful to you. I'm only thirty-five, I'm still young. I couldn't stand being permitted *marital relations*—pawing you about, if you like that better—about six times a year. Do I have to go over it all again?"

"Not on my account. It won't make any difference to me what excuses you make." The smoke in the tiny room made her cough and, opening the window, she inhaled the damp cold air. "You asked me," she said, turning round, "why we have to go on living together. I'll tell you why. Because you married me. I've got a right to you and I'll never divorce you. You've got me till death do us part. Till death, James. Right?"

He didn't answer. An icy blast had come into the room when she had opened the window, and he felt in his pocket. "If you're going to stay in here till dinner," he said, "you'll want the gas fire on. Have you got any fivepence pieces? I haven't, unless I can get some change."

"Oh, you'll get some all right. In the bar. And just for your information, I haven't brought any money with me. That's *your* privilege."

When he had left her alone, she sat in the cold room for some minutes, staring at the brick wall. Till death do us part, she had told him, and she meant it. She would never leave him and he must never be allowed to leave her, but she hoped he would die.

It wasn't her fault she was frigid. She had always supposed he understood. She had supposed her good looks and her capacity as housewife and hostess compensated for a revulsion she couldn't help. And it wasn't just against him, but against all men, any man. He had seemed to accept it.

In her sexless way she had loved him. And then, when he had seemed happier and more at ease than at any time in their marriage, when he had ceased to make those painful demands and had become so sweet to her, so generous with gifts, he had suddenly and without shame confessed it.

She wouldn't mind, he had told her; he knew that. She wouldn't resent his finding elsewhere what she so evidently disliked giving him. While he provided for her and spent nearly all his leisure with her and respected her as his wife, she should be relieved, disliking sex as she did, that he had found someone else.

He had said it was the pent-up energy caused by her repressions that made her fly at him, beat at him with her hands, scream at him words he didn't know she knew. To her dying day she would remember his astonishment. He had genuinely thought she wouldn't mind. And it had taken weeks of nagging and screaming and threats to make him agree to give Frances up.

She had driven him out of her bedroom and settled into the bitter unremitting vendetta she would keep up till death parted them. Even now, he didn't understand how agonizingly he had hurt her. But there were no more women and he had begun to drink.

He was drinking now, she thought, and by nine o'clock he would be stretched out, dead-drunk, on that bed separated by only a few inches from her own.

The room was too cold to sit in any longer. She tried the gas fire, turning the switch to ON; but the match she held to it refused to ignite it, and presently she made her way downstairs and into the little lounge where there was a coal fire and people were watching television.

They met again at dinner.

James Armadale had drunk half a pint of whiskey, and now, to go with the brown Windsor soup and hotted-up roast lamb, he ordered a bottle of burgundy.

"Just as a matter of idle curiosity," said Nina, "why do you drink so much?"

"To drown my sorrows," said James. "The classic reason. Happens to be true in my case. Would you like some wine?"

"I'd better have a glass, hadn't I, otherwise you'll drink the whole bottle."

The dining room was full and most of the other diners were middle-aged or elderly. Many of them, James supposed, would be wedding guests like themselves. He could see that their own arrival had been noted and that at the surrounding tables their appearance was being favorably commented upon. It afforded him a thin wry amusement to think that they would be judged a handsome, well-suited, and happy couple.

"Nina," he said, "we can't go on like this. It's not fair on either of us. We're destroying ourselves and each other. We have to talk about what we're going to do."

"Pick your moments, don't you? I'm not going to talk about it in a public place."

She had spoken in a low subdued voice, quite different from her hectoring tone in their bedroom, and she shot quick nervous glances at the neighboring tables.

"It's because this is a public place that I think we stand a better chance of talking about it reasonably. When we're alone you get hysterical and then neither of us can be rational. If we talk about it now, I think I know you well enough to say you won't scream at me."

"I could walk out though, couldn't I? Besides, you're drunk."

"I am not drunk. Frankly, I probably shall be in an hour's time and that's another reason why we ought to talk here and now. Look, Nina, you don't love me—you've said so often enough—and whatever crazy ideas you have about my having designs on you, I don't love you either. We've been into the reasons for that so many times that I don't need to go into them now, but can't we come to some sort of amicable arrangement to split up?"

"So that you can have all the women you want? So that you can bring that bitch Frances into my house?"

"No," he said, "you can have the house. The court would probably award you one-third of my income, but I'll give you more if you want. I'd give you half." He had nearly added, "to be rid of you," but he bit off the words as being too provocative. His speech was already thickening and slurring.

It was disconcerting—though this was what he had expected—to hear how inhibition made her voice soft and kept her face controlled. The words she used were the same, though. He had heard them a thousand times before. "If you leave me, I'll follow you. I'll go to your office and tell them all about it. I'll sit on your doorstep. I won't be abandoned. I'd rather die. I won't be a divorced woman just because you've got tired of me."

"If you go on like this," he said thickly, "you'll find yourself a widow. Will you like that?"

Had they been alone, she would have screamed the affirmative at him. Because they weren't, she gave him a thin, sharp, and concentrated smile, a smile which an observer might have taken for amusement at some married couple's private joke.

"Yes," she said, "I'd like to be a widow, *your* widow. Drink yourself to death, why don't you? That's what you have to do if you want to be rid of me."

The waitress came to their table. James ordered a double brandy and "coffee for my wife." He knew he would never be rid of her. He wasn't the sort of man who could stand public disruption of his life, scenes at work, the involvement of friends and employers. It must be, he knew, an amicable split or none at all.

And since she would never see reason, never understand or forgive or forget, he must soldier on. With the help of this, he thought, as the brandy spread its dim cloudy euphoria through his brain.

He drained his glass quickly, muttered an "excuse me" to her for the benefit of listeners, and left the dining room.

Nina returned to the television lounge. There was a play on and its theme was a marital situation that almost paralleled her own. The old ladies with their knitting and the old men with their after-dinner cigars watched it apathetically.

She thought she might take the car and go somewhere for a drive. It didn't much matter where—anywhere would do that was far enough from this hotel and James and that cathedral clock whose chimes split the hours into fifteen-minute segments with long brazen peals. There must be someplace in this town where one could get a decent cup of coffee, some cinema maybe where they weren't showing a film about marriage or what people, she thought shudderingly, called sexual relationships.

She went upstairs to get the car keys and some money.

James was fast asleep. He had taken off his tie and his shoes, but otherwise he was fully dressed, lying on his back and snoring. Stupid of him not to get under the covers. He'd freeze. Maybe he'd die of exposure. Well, she wasn't going to cover him up, but she'd close the window so it wouldn't be too cold when she came in.

The car keys were in his jacket pocket, mixed up with a lot of loose change. The feel of his warm body through the material made her shiver. His breath smelled of spirits and he was sweating in spite of the cold. Among the change were two fivepence pieces. She'd take one of those and feed that gas meter.

It would be horrible dressing for that wedding in here at zero temperature. Why not feed it now so that the room would be ready for the morning, ready to turn the gas fire on and give her some heat when she came in at midnight, come to that?

The room was faintly illuminated by the yellow light from the street lamp in the alley. She crouched down in front of the gas fire and noticed she hadn't turned the dial to OFF after her match had failed to ignite the jets. It wouldn't do to feed that meter now with the dial turned to ON, and have fivepence worth of old-fashioned toxic gas flood the room. Not with the window tight shut and not a crack round that heavy old door. Slowly she put her hand out to turn the dial to OFF.

Her fingers touched it. Her hand remained still, poised. She heard her heart begin to thud softly in the silence as the idea in all its brilliant awfulness took hold of her. Wouldn't do? Was she mad? It wouldn't do to feed that meter now with the gas fire dial turned to ON? What would do as well, as efficiently, as finally? She withdrew her hand and clasped it in the other to steady it.

Rising to her feet, she contemplated her sleeping husband. The sweat was standing on his pale forehead. He snored as rhythmically, as stertorously, as her own heart was beating. A widow, she thought, alone and free in her own unshared house. Not divorced, despised, disowned, laughed at by judges and solicitors for her crippling frigidity, not mocked by that Frances and her successors, but a widow all the world would pity and respect.

Comfortably off too, if not rich, with an income from James's life assurance and very likely a pension from Sir William Tarrant.

James wouldn't wake up till midnight. No, that was wrong. He wouldn't *have* wakened up till midnight. What she meant was he wouldn't wake up at all.

The dial on the gas fire was still on. She took the fivepence coin and tiptoed over to the meter. Nothing would wake him, but still she tiptoed. The window was tight shut with nothing beyond it but that alley, that glistening lamp, and the wall of the cathedral.

She studied the meter, kneeling down. It was the first time in her sheltered, cosseted, snug life that she had ever actually seen a coin-in-the-slot gas meter. But if morons like hotel servants and the sort of people who would stay in a place like this could work it, she could.

There was the slot where the coin went in, there the gauge whose red arrow showed empty. All you had to do, presumably, was slip in the coin, fiddle about with that handle, and then, if the gas fire dial was left on, toxic coal gas—the kind of gas that had killed thousands in the past, careless old people, suicides, accident-prone fools—would rapidly begin to seep out of the unlighted jets.

James wouldn't smell it. Drink had paralyzed him into an unconsciousness as deep as that which her own sleeping tablets brought to her.

Nina was certain it wouldn't matter that she hadn't paid close attention to the manager's instructions. What had she said? Turn the handle to the left, insert the coin, then turn it to the right.

She hesitated for a moment, just long enough for brief fractured memories to cross her mind—James when they were first married, James patient and self-denying on their honeymoon, James promising that her coldness wouldn't matter, that with time and love . . . James confessing with a defiant smirk, throwing Frances' name at her, James going on a three-day bender because she couldn't pretend the wound he'd given her was just a surface hurt, James drunk night after night . . .

She didn't hesitate any longer.

She got her coat, put the car keys in her handbag. Then she knelt again, between the gas fire and the meter. First she checked that the dial, which was small and almost at ground level, was set at ON. She took hold of the brass handle on the meter and turned it to the left. The coin slot was now fully exposed and open. She pressed in the fivepence piece and flicked the handle to the right. There was no need to wait for the warning smell, oniony, acrid, of the escaping gas. Without looking back, she walked swiftly from the room, closing the door behind her.

The cathedral clock chimed the last quarter before nine.

When the bar closed at eleven thirty, a crowd of people coming upstairs and chattering in loud voices would have awakened even the deepest sleeper. They woke James. He didn't move for some time but lay there with his eyes open till he heard the clock chime midnight. When the last stroke died away he reached out and turned on the bedside lamp.

The light was like a knife going into his head, and he groaned. But he felt like this most nights at midnight and there was no use making a fuss. Who would hear or care if he did? Nina was evidently still downstairs in that lounge. It was too much to hope she might stay there all night out of fear of being alone with him.

No, she'd be up now that television was over, and she'd start berating him for his drunkenness and his infidelity—not that there had been any since Frances—and they would lie there bickering and smarting until gray light mingled with that yellow light, and the cathedral clock told them it was dawn.

And yet she had been so sweet once, so pathetic and desperate in her sad failure. It had never occurred to him to blame her, though his body had suffered. And his own solution, honestly confessed, might have worked so well for all three of them if she had only been rational.

He wondered vaguely, for the thousandth time, why he had been such a fool to confess when, with a little deception, he might be happier now than at any time in his marriage. But he was in no fit state to think. Where had that woman said the bathroom was? Turn right down the passage and the third door on the left. He lay there till the clock struck the quarter before he felt he couldn't wait any longer and he'd have to find it.

The cold air in the passage—Lord, it was more like January than April—steadied him a little but made his head bang and throb. He must be crazy to go on like this. What the hell was he doing, turning himself into an alcoholic at thirty-five? Because there were no two ways about it, he was an alcoholic all right. And if he stayed with Nina he'd be a dead alcoholic by forty.

But how can you leave a woman who won't leave you? Give up his job, run away, go to the ends of the earth . . . It wasn't unusual for him to have wild thoughts like this at midnight, but when the morning came he knew he would just soldier on.

He stayed in the bathroom for about ten minutes. Coming back along the passage, he heard footsteps on the stairs, and knowing he must look horrible and smell horribly of liquor, he retreated behind the open door of what proved to be a broom closet. But it was only his wife.

She approached their room door slowly as if she were bracing herself to face something—himself, probably, he thought. Had she really that much loathing of him that she had to draw in her breath and clench her hands before confronting him? She was very pale. She looked ill and frightened, and when she had opened the door and gone inside he heard her give a kind of shrill gasp that was almost a shriek.

He followed her into the room, and when she turned and saw him he thought she was going to faint. She had been pale before, but now she turned paper-white. Once, when he had still loved her and had hoped he might teach her to love him, he would have been concerned. But now he didn't care, and all he said was, "Been watching something nasty on the TV?"

She didn't answer him. She sat down on her bed and put her head into her hands. James undressed and got into bed. Presently Nina got up and began taking her clothes off slowly and mechanically. His head and body had begun to twitch as they did when he was recovering from the effects of a drinking bout. It left him wide-awake. He wouldn't sleep again for hours.

He watched her curiously but dispassionately, for he had long ago ceased to derive the slightest pleasure or excitement from seeing her undress. What intrigued him now was that, though she was evidently in some sort of shock, her hands shaking, she still couldn't discard those modest subterfuges of hers, her way of turning her back when she stepped out of her dress, of pulling her nightgown over her head before she took off her underclothes.

She put on her dressing gown and went to the bathroom. When she came back her face was greasy where she had cleaned off the makeup and she was shivering.

"You'd better take a sleeping tablet," he said.

"I've already taken one in the bathroom. I wanted a bath but there wasn't any hot water." Getting into bed, she exclaimed in her normal fierce way, "Nothing works in this damned place!"

"Put out the light and go to sleep. Anyone would think you have to spend the rest of your life here instead of just one night."

She made no reply. They never said good night to each other. When she had put out her light, the room wasn't really dark because a street lamp was still lit in the alley outside. He had seldom felt less like sleep, and now he was aware of a sensation he hadn't expected because he hadn't thought about it. He didn't want to share a bedroom with her.

That cold modesty, which had once been enticing, now repelled him. He raised himself on one elbow and peered at her. She lay in the defensive attitude of a woman who fears assault, flat on her stomach, her arms folded under her head. Although the sleeping pill had begun to take effect, her body seemed stiff, prepared to galvanize into violence at a touch.

She smelled cold. A sour saltiness emanated from her as if there were sea water in her veins instead of blood. He thought of real women with warm blood, women who awoke from sleep when their husband's faces were near theirs, who never recoiled but smiled and put out their arms. She would keep him from them forever until drink or time made him as frozen as she was.

Suddenly he knew he couldn't stay in that room. He might do something dreadful—beat her up perhaps or even kill her. And much as he wanted to be rid of her, spend no more time with her, no more money on her, the notion of killing her was as absurd as it was grotesque. It was unthinkable. But he couldn't stay here.

He got up and put on his dressing gown. He'd go to that lounge where she'd watched television, take a blanket and spend the rest of the night there. She wouldn't wake till eight or nine and by then he'd be back, ready to dress for the wedding.

Funny, really, their going to a wedding, to watch someone else getting into the same boat. But it wouldn't be the same boat, for if the office gossip was more than that, Sir William's daughter had already opened her warm arms to many men.

The cathedral clock struck one. By morning the room would be icy and they'd need that gas fire. Why not put a fivepence piece in the meter now so the fire would work as soon as he wanted it?

The fire itself lay in shadow, but the meter was clearly illuminated by the street lamp. James knelt, trying to remember the instructions of the manager. Better try it out first before he put his coin in, his only fivepence coin. Strange, that. He could have sworn he'd had two when he first went to bed.

What had the manager said? Turn the handle to the left, insert the coin, then turn the handle to the right. No, turn it to the right as far as it will go until *you hear the coin fall*. Keeping hold of his coin—he didn't want to waste it if what Nina said was true and nothing worked in this place—he turned the handle to the left, then to the right as far as it would go.

Inside the meter a coin fell with a small dull clang. The red-arrow marker on the gauge, which had stood at empty, moved along to register payment. Good. He was glad he hadn't wasted his money. The previous guest must have put a coin in and failed to turn the handle until the coin fell. So Nina had been wrong about things not working. Still, it wasn't unusual for her to get the wrong idea, not unusual at all.

Gas would come through as soon the dial was switched to ON. James checked that the window was shut to keep out as much of the cold as possible, gave a last look at the sleeping, heavily sedated woman, and left the room, closing the door behind him.

Lawrence Treat

B As in Bribe

In which Mitch Taylor, Homicide Squad, gets tangled in a professional football caper, and maybe he should have stood in bed. You see, Mitch's wife Amy had this cousin of hers, this Hamilton (Ham) Burney, who was an all-league defensive guard, and Ham had big ideas. And a big idea in the gambling racket can lead to big trouble . . . Another brash, breezy police procedural that, so far as it goes, tells it like it is . . .

Detectives: MITCH TAYLOR and the HOMICIDE SQUAD

What with the way the world was going these days, Mitch Taylor figured he was doing all right. Here he was pulling down his regular weekly bunch of green stuff, he was getting along with the rest of the gang on the homicide squad, and he had his health and a couple of pretty good kids.

But most of all, even after ten years of marriage, Amy was still something special. Not just the way she looked, which was okay in any language, but the kind of dame she was and the way she backed him up, and irregardless, too. About the only trouble with her was this cousin of hers, and nobody could call him *her* fault.

The thing was, while Amy wasn't exactly interested in football, every once in a while Mitch happened to leave the paper open at the sports section and she couldn't help seeing it. There was maybe a picture or else a news item on Ham Burney, all-league defensive guard.

"He's my cousin," she said the first time she noticed his name. "We practically grew up together."

"No kidding!" Mitch said. "How come you never mentioned it before?"

"There was no particular reason to. And besides, I was only seven when his family moved away."

"How old was he?"

"Nine," she said. "He's handsome, isn't he?"

She kind of sighed, and Mitch figured there was something more to this, so he said, "Seen him lately?"

"Oh, no. Not since he was nine. But he did something wonderful for me. I don't think I ever told you, did I?"

"Did what?"

"Told you about the time he rescued me? Some boys got hold of me and wanted to do things. They were much older than Ham, and although he was big for his age it was a brave thing for him to do, to take them all on. He could have been killed. I'll never forget it. I'll never be able to do enough for him." She sighed again and said, "I wonder what he's like now."

Mitch, who knew his statistics, answered that one. "Six-four, and weighs two-seventy."

"His name's Hamilton," Amy said, "although people always called him Ham."

And maybe he was, Mitch told himself. Still, why bother thinking about him? Except once in a while when they were all talking football in the squad room and somebody happened to mention Burney, Mitch would say, kind of casual-like, "Oh, him? That's Amy's cousin."

It would have been okay, too, if that was as near as Ham came into Mitch's life, but a lot of things can happen. While Mitch couldn't say that the breaks were always against him, on the other hand he could have used a little more luck, and used it nicely, too.

It was one of those days you could forget ever happened. Mitch had to hang around court most of the morning, and then the case got held over on account some lawyer maybe had a cousin who knew the judge's wife and had gone and whispered something in the judge's ear, maybe about a tip on the stock market or else a pinochle game tonight.

Anyhow, around noon the judge decided to let Mitch and the rest of the witnesses go home, so Mitch had himself a submarine over at the Greek's before hoofing it back to headquarters. By then there was no squad car available, and it started to rain and Mitch had to scout around knocking on doors down on James Street to see if he could dig up a witness to that assault business last night.

Most of the doors got slammed in his face and he got called a pig a few times. Then when he walked out of Number 347 East, some dame spit down from an upstairs window, and the trouble was, her aim was good. While the rain washed most of it off, it didn't help things, either.

What with all that rain, the buses were jammed, and the one Mitch got on, he didn't know the driver and he had nobody to talk to. So he was glad to get off at his corner, and finally he got to feeling better. Like always, Amy heard him stick his key in the door of the apartment and she met him coming in and gave him the news.

"Ham called today," she said. "He's coming to visit us for a few days."

"Here?" Mitch said.

"Yes, of course."

"He pulls down fifty or a hundred grand a year and he wants to stay here?"

"I asked him to," Amy said.

"Tell him he'd be better off at the Hilton. He maybe thinks we got a mansion waiting for him."

"I told him we had a small place and I suggested a hotel, but he said he had reasons and would rather come here if we had room for him."

"Only we don't," Mitch said, feeling he'd had a narrow escape.

"But it's all arranged," Amy said. "Joey's going to sleep downstairs with the O'Connors, and Mamie's going to stay with her friend Beth. We'll use their room, and Ham can take ours."

"Why not the other way round?" Mitch said, trying to rescue something out of the argument.

"A big man like that," Amy said. "He needs a double bed. And what if we're uncomfortable for a few nights? It's the least we can do for him."

"I guess so," Mitch said. On account if Amy wanted it that way, it was okay with him. Still—

Ham flew in on an early afternoon plane, and that evening Mitch found him making himself at home in the living room. Amy was beaming and she'd cooked one of those stews of hers, the kind you could sniff when you came up the landing and everybody in the building wished they'd get invited.

The kids weren't saying much, they were just staring goggle-eyed at one of the biggest guys they'd ever seen. He was talking football, but even Mamie hardly looked at Mitch when he came in. Joey was up on Cloud Nine, but the worst of it was, this Ham guy took a shine to Mitch right off.

"Amy's been talking about you," he said, holding out a paw the size of a Frisbee. "Did she tell you about the time I beat up five kids that were trying to drag her into a back lot?"

"Yeah," Mitch said, wondering why the guy had come here instead of to a hotel. "Must have been quite a battle."

"They were older than me," Ham said, "and I just happened down the street when—"

Mitch sort of half-listened, and then managed to break away and head for the bedroom. There he unholstered his gun and stuck it up on the top shelf of the closet, where he always put it so it would be out of reach of the kids. When he turned around, Amy was standing there.

"I know it's going to be hard for you," she whispered, "but I owe him so much, I can never do enough for him. You'll be nice to him, won't you?"

"Sure," Mitch said. "Why wouldn't I?"

She kissed him and said in a low voice, "I knew you would."

Mitch wondered what all the fuss was about. Granted he'd rather see Ham play than hear him talk, but the guy was here, and what could you do about it? So Mitch settled down and listened, and every once in a while he kind of muttered something, while he hoped Ham would tire himself out and go to bed early.

Naturally, though, it didn't work out that way, because right after dinner, when Amy was in the kitchen, Ham took Mitch aside. Ham spoke confidentially, like he was tipping Mitch off to a secret play. "Mitch," he said, "let's go down the street and have ourselves a drink."

Mitch did his best to get out of it. "Thanks," he said, "but I got to hit the sack early. Maybe some other time."

Only Ham wouldn't let him go. "Something I want to tell you," he said. "Something in your line."

That was different, so they went down to the corner bar. After everybody'd said hello to Ham and wanted his autograph, him and Mitch sat down by themselves and Ham got down to business. He leaned over the table and spoke like he was still tipping Mitch off to a new play.

"Mitch," he said, "ever hear of Bluebird Yancy?"

"Blue?" Mitch said, wondering what Ham had to do with a crooked gambler that half a dozen police departments wanted to nail and couldn't. "Him? What about him?"

"Or Nate Brigham and Jerry Nick?"

"Who you trying to kid?" Mitch said.

Ham looked pleased, like he'd just blocked a field-goal kick that would have tied it all up. "Well," he said, "I can see what it is to live on your salary. If you were on the vice squad, for instance, the dough would be pouring in, but for a homicide man it must be kinda tough."

"I get along," Mitch said. "What's on your mind, Ham?"

"I got an appointment to meet Bluebird and a couple of his boys," Ham said. "That's why I'm here, and not registered at any hotel—so I can get together with them in private and talk things over."

"Are you nuts?" Mitch said. "Lay off or you'll end up in the clink. Unless they put a knife in your big belly first."

Ham thought that was funny. "I can take care of myself," he smirked.

"Not with them," Mitch said. "Stay away from them or you'll get hurt. I'm not kiddin'."

"I got a scheme," Ham said. "First off, I'll see them this once, and then never again. After the arrangement is made, I call from a pay phone and all I tell them is what the team feels like, who's injured that nobody knows about. Things like that. Nothing crooked, nothing I can go to jail for, but they pay for that kind of inside dope, and particularly for a team like ours that figures to win the title. And while I make plenty, I don't mind telling you that I'm in hock up to my neck. So—are you with me?"

Mitch didn't answer right off. While it was poison to sit down at a table with Ham and a gambler like Blue, and while this was straight bribery, still—he was Amy's cousin. And she wanted to do something for him, didn't she?

Maybe there wasn't much of the gray stuff inside that skull of Ham's, but Amy'd take it hard if he got in real trouble. And he was heading straight for it, because a guy like Blue would pick him clean and then throw out the soup bones. And besides, if Mitch played it cagey, maybe he'd get something on Blue and those pals of his.

It took Mitch a while to think things out. Because, while he wasn't going to get trapped into anything, there was no reason why he couldn't say okay, then talk it over with the lieutenant in the morning. If the lieutenant vetoed it, all Mitch had to do was tell Ham he'd changed his mind. And if the lieutenant told Mitch to go ahead, then Mitch was covered.

Ham kept waiting for Mitch's answer, and while Mitch didn't usually put on an act, this time he kind of poured it on. He frowned, licked his lips, took another gulp of beer, and finally gave his answer.

"Okay," he said. "Why not?"

He checked with Lieutenant Decker the next morning. First off, Decker was against it. "A character like Blue will spot you a mile away," he said. "And even if he doesn't, it's not our bailiwick. Our jurisdiction is crimes against the person, so where do we come in?"

"If Blue scares off when he sees me," Mitch said, hoping it would work out that way and keep Ham on the up and up, "then what do we lose? But if he goes through with it and thinks I'm there for my shake, then maybe I can get enough evidence on him to turn over to the rackets squad. Maybe, for instance, you could tape me."

"It's the other way round," Decker said. "*They'll* be taping *you*. And maybe that tape will be worth getting hold of. It might even be a piece of evidence we're entitled to, on the theory that it's an invasion of privacy and therefore a crime against the person." The lieutenant leaned back in his chair, let the swivel squeak, and said kind of slow, "Maybe. Just maybe. But brother! Somebody's sure being devious."

There was nothing devious about Ham, though. He ate up practically everything on the table, and Joey and Mamie looked kind of bewildered that there was nothing left for seconds. And when Ham took a shower he stayed in the bathroom a half hour or so and left the place a mess. He busted a chair on account he was too heavy for it, and he broke Joey's bat in half just to show how strong he was.

Mitch kind of wondered how long Amy could take it. She still had this "thing" going for Ham. No matter what he did, she couldn't hold anything against him, but it was pretty tough on the rest of the family. Mitch was starting to figure out a few ways of getting Ham to leave when Ham said he'd heard from Blue. The meeting was all set and would Mitch come along? And that was how come he and Ham came to take a cab to some bar over in the river area, where Yancy and his troops were waiting.

They shook hands all around, and they all got introduced. Nate Brigham, Jerry Nick, Mitch Taylor. It could have been a business conference, and in a way it pretty much was.

Mitch had got a description of the Bluebird, but even so, it was hard to believe that this little dumpy guy with the bald head and the sad eyes was one of the top gamblers in the country, who'd been mixed up in a dozen kinds of dirty business but never got nailed down. Except that when he spoke up and you heard that voice of his, rich and deep enough to drown out everybody else, you knew he was something more than the little squirt he looked like.

Right off it seemed that Blue hadn't tumbled to who Mitch was, and Mitch was a little surprised that Blue didn't handle himself better. Because the way he blocked off the side of the booth where he wanted to sit, it was pretty obvious what he was after. He wanted a view of Brigham over at the bar, so he could signal or get signals. Jerry Nick sat on the inside, next to Blue, with Ham opposite Nick and next to Mitch.

When they were all sorted out, Blue said, taking over in that voice of his, "I guess we have some things to decide, but first I'd like to make myself clear. I don't go in for any crooked stuff. Ham, I don't want you to miss a tackle or do anything except play your best game. And if you have anything else in mind, then we all may as well go home right now."

For Mitch that was the tipoff. The conversation was being taped, and Blue wanted to sound like he was clean, while he roped Ham in and got Ham to suggest a bribe. Mitch had expected something along those lines, but he'd figured Blue to be a much smoother operator. Although with Ham, you didn't have to be smooth. Ham worked on heavyweight principles; anything under a ton or so didn't count.

It was pretty easy to read Blue, too. What he was after was, he was setting up a frame, because if the football commissioner ever heard this tape, Ham would be through in professional football. So Blue could then blackmail him, and Ham would have to do whatever Blue told him to. Mess up a play. Leave a hole for a back to come through. Set up a penalty. Knock out an opposing back. Anything at all. And Ham could spell the difference between winning and losing, because he wasn't an all-league defensive guard for nothing.

Meanwhile Blue went ahead and made like the host offering drinks all around. Ham took a Scotch and soda, and Mitch settled for a beer.

"Just bring me a can," he said, on account he was taking no

chances with getting a mickey slipped in his drink. "That's the way I like it. Glass, it spoils the taste."

"A connoisseur," Blue said. "A real connoisseur."

After that they horsed around a little, talking about the league and who had a chance of knocking off Ham's club. Stuff like that. Blue got into personalities and found out a few things, but nothing important. At first Mitch wasn't sure what the guy was after, but when the drinks came and the waiter put a whole bottle in front of Ham, Mitch caught onto that little trick.

The idea was simple—to get Ham drunk, just in case he was smart enough when sober to tumble to how he was getting suckered. Anyhow, Ham laid himself wide open and asked pointblank how much they'd pay him for you-know-what. Which maybe Ham thought was a way of putting it real cagey.

After a while Mitch couldn't help getting a pretty good idea of what the tape was going to sound like after it got listened to, edited, cut, spliced, and put together again. Around then, say by the time Ham was on his third or fourth drink and Blue was leading him along like he was getting rehearsed for a TV commercial, Mitch got to thinking things out.

Maybe it was Blue's voice, maybe the way he kept looking over at the bar where this Nate Brigham was, or maybe it was one of those hunches that you can't ever pin down, only you know they're right—anyhow, after a while Mitch knew that this guy wasn't Bluebird Yancy at all. He was just a stand-in.

Yancy's reasons for not coming weren't hard to figure out. If the tape showed Ham discussing a bribe with Yancy, then Yancy could be in trouble, too. But this way his voice wouldn't even be on the tape. and he could probably prove he'd been a few hundred miles away on the night the tape had been made.

Maybe Mitch should have walked out of here and gone home. Maybe he should have let Ham drown in his own soup. And certainly Mitch should have gone over to a phone, or tried to, and called headquarters and told them where he was and asked for help. Except that Ham was Amy's cousin and she wanted to do something for him, and she'd expect Mitch to take care of Ham. So Mitch had to do things on his own and in his own way, even if he was riding for a fall.

He kind of fidgeted around, like he was sitting on a splinter or something, until he had himself smack in the line of sight between Blue and Brigham, over at the bar. That way Blue couldn't get his signal across, and Mitch was safe for long enough to take his wallet out of his pocket, stick the thing down on the table with his identification in full view, and start talking.

"Let's level on this," he said. "I'm Taylor, Homicide, and what I came for was to get the goods on Bluebird Yancy. That's why I'm here and that's what Ham brought me here for. He's working with the police, and this bribery pitch—it's nothing but an act. Only it looks like you were too smart to fall for it, so let's have the tape and call it quits. Because you're not Yancy, and I know it."

You could tell that guy, whatever his name was, hadn't expected anything like this, and the idea of a cop scared him. So Mitch was all set to tell Ham to pick up Jerry Nick and spread him out on the table while Mitch located the tape. And it would have worked out that way, Ham and Mitch could have been there in the center of the room and on their way out before Brigham got wise. Except nothing got through into that big head of Ham's in less than five or ten minutes.

He looked blank and said to Mitch, "What are you trying to pull? I ought to throw you up against the wall and watch you bounce back, because you're queering the whole deal." And at the same time he grabbed Mitch and shook him with that big paw of his.

Still, Mitch made a stab at getting things back on the right track. "Amy told you, didn't she?" he said, figuring the magic of her name would stop Ham. Which it did, except it was too late. Because when Ham had grabbed the little guy, it gave Brigham a clear view of the booth and of Blue's S.O.S. signal. The result was, Brigham walked over, took his gun out, and stuck it against Mitch's spine.

It was a pretty smooth maneuver, too, because his body screened what was happening inside the booth, so nobody could see that gun of his, and he held his voice low. "Keep your hands where they are," he said to Mitch. "I want your gun, so sit tight."

There was nothing much Mitch could do except wish Amy'd never had a cousin or that he'd never showed up or that he'd had enough sense to go along with Mitch right off the bat. Anyhow, Mitch let Nate take his gun. Then Mitch turned around and saw that nobody in the bar had noticed what was going on in the booth. And even if they had, nobody was going to come over and help him out.

You take a setup like this, with a couple of professional hoods ready to gun you down if they have to, and you don't mess around. You stall, and you hope for some kind of a break.

"Where's Yancy?" Mitch said, real innocent and speaking to Nate. "What happened to Bluebird Yancy?"

"Sitting right in front of you," Brigham said.

"Him?" Mitch said. "Who you kidding? He's no more Yancy than I'm the King of Siam."

"That's right," Blue said, real quick. "They paid me to play a part. I don't want trouble. I—"

Then a bunch of things happened all at once, including Nate Brigham getting sore and losing his head. Sort of snarling at Blue and telling him to shut up, Brigham swung his gun, with the barrel as a whip, and hit Blue in the jaw. Blue let out a howl, on account not just because he was hurt, but he was an actor and what good is an actor with a busted jaw?

At this moment Ham sort of came to, his mind began working pretty much the way it worked when a play was coming at him. Or maybe his mind wasn't working, but the result was about the same, because Ham went into action.

The table in front of Mitch seemed to lift up and hit the wall of the booth and knock it over, along with everybody else. Only the booth kept on going and hit the wall of the room and stove part of it in. There must have been some electrical wiring in there that shorted, because suddenly the lights went out. Some dame back there at the bar started screaming, and somebody heaved a bottle for no reason except when things get rough in a bar somebody always heaves a bottle.

For a second or two Mitch was kind of left alone. Blue and Jerry Nick and Brigham were all off balance, what with Ham's charge. So Mitch hooked the nearest leg, which turned out to be Brigham's. Brigham went down, and Mitch socked him, got a knee in Brigham's face, and grabbed at his hand. It had a gun in it, so Mitch banged down the wrist and kept banging until the hand let go of the gun.

You don't exactly think when you're in a spot like that, but in the back of his mind Mitch had a couple of things he wanted to get hold of. First off, there was his own gun, and second, he wanted that tape.

The gun business was easy, on account he now had the drop on Brigham, and he located the tape with that pocket flashlight he always carried with him. He switched the light on and spotted the dispatch case that must have had the tape recorder in it. Everybody else seemed busy untangling themselves, and what with there being no regular light, nobody even saw Mitch pick up the case. Once he had it, it was easy to get Ham to dust out of the joint along with him.

They found a cab about a block away and got inside and Mitch told the driver to go to the airport. Then Mitch went to work on Ham.

"You jackass!" he said. "You know what you got yourself into? They framed you. Every time you opened your big mouth and said you wanted dough and that you'd help them out any way you could, it got taped. They could blackmail you for the rest of your life. And the tape's right here, in this case. So when you hole up somewheres, and it better be a long ways from here, you can turn it on and listen to yourself. Then you can think about what would have happened if somebody went to the football commissioner and told them about this tape."

"I could explain it," Ham said, but Mitch didn't bother waiting for any half-baked excuses.

"Consorting with known gamblers," Mitch said. "And with Yancy's hoods. Beginning to see the picture?"

"I guess so," Ham said weakly.

"So what you're going to do when we get to the airport," Mitch said, "is take the first plane out. Anywheres. Just get out of town and out of the state. In the morning you can fly any place you want to, except here. If you're lucky, nobody's going to know about tonight. Because if it ever comes out, you're through, finished, kaput. Understand?"

Ham did. And he paid the cab fare out to the airport, and prepaid it back to Mitch's apartment, where Amy was waiting up.

"Where's Ham?" she said. "Isn't he with you?"

"He had some business somewheres else," Mitch said, "and he had to beat it."

"Why? Where?"

"I don't know where," Mitch said, "but he got in a kind of a jam and had to take off."

"Wouldn't you help him?"

"Oh, sure. I did all I could."

"I'm glad of that. Because, while he was a nuisance, he's still my cousin and he's still wonderful, isn't he?"

"Well," Mitch said cautiously, "he's something all right."

So everything was fine with Amy, but he ran into a little trouble with the lieutenant next morning, when Decker called him into that cubbyhole of an office of his.

"How did that business with Ham Burney work out?"

"Well," Mitch said, "he was supposed to meet Bluebird Yancy. Remember?"

"Did he?"

"No. Yancy never showed."

"It wouldn't have anything to do with an actor named Travis Stanley, would it? He's in the hospital with a broken jaw and he says somebody hit him, only he won't say who."

"Anybody get arrested?" Mitch asked.

"Some dame did, for throwing a bottle and starting a ruckus. Burney was there all right, but the precinct is handling the case and they haven't called us in. In case they do I ought to know what the score is."

"This Burney," Mitch said, playing it close to the chest, "they wanted to get some bribery evidence on him."

"Did they?"

Mitch shook his head. "No. It didn't work out."

"Anything else?"

"It's kind of a family matter," Mitch said, "so if nobody's going to prefer charges and if nobody got hurt except this actor guy, then that's the whole ball game. It's all over."

The lieutenant didn't like it. He was the commanding officer here. He had a right to know what his men were doing, and their duty was to report to him, and in full. So Mitch tried to smooth things over a little.

"You were right about the tape," he said.

The lieutenant didn't say anything, and after a while Mitch got up, kind of looked around, then walked out.

He was in the doghouse all right, but what of it? Because you take a guy like Ham, raking in the big dough and being famous and all that, and what did he have? Not much. And while Mitch didn't exactly have everything in the world and wasn't making big dough, he was doing all right. In fact, if you wanted to sit down and think about it, it looked like he was in pretty good shape, what with Amy and the kids and a good job and a regular paycheck.

Miriam Sharman

The Breaking Point

Mark Venner had a nightmare, the same nightmare, night after night. And he had good reason to have it. But now he was near the breaking point – a danger to himself, to his wife Ann, and to the company for which he worked. And Ann too was near the end of her rope.

The dramatic story of the aftermath of a crime . . .

The dashboard clock, livid in the darkness, registered 9:55. The shrill whistle of the oncoming train rose to a shrieking crescendo. His car crashed against it, splintering into a thousand fragments.

Mark Venner struggled out of his tormented sleep, soaked in perspiration, shivering with shock. In the twin bed his wife was already awake.

"I'm sorry, Ann," he mumbled. "I've disturbed you again."

"It doesn't matter," she replied gently. He put on his dressing gown. "I'll come down with you," she added quickly.

His reply came mechanically. "Don't get up. I'll be all right."

She shook her head, smiled, wrapped her housecoat round her small slight body, and followed him downstairs. In a few minutes they were seated on the comfortable sofa in front of the electric fire, sipping hot milk.

He leaned back wearily. "I never want to sleep again. It's always the same nightmare. . .every night now." He shut his eyes as if to blot it out. "It's always the. . .accident." He turned to look into his wife's face. "Always the. . .accident."

Harsh racking sobs shook him. Ann leaned forward and rested her hand in his. He clutched it. "Mark, dear," she said gently. "You mustn't give way. It's over now, it happened eighteen months ago, why can't you forget it? Let me help you."

His haggard eyes rested on her, weighing her, finding her wanting. "You talk as if it was all my doing!"

"No, no." For the moment she had forgotten how touchy he had become. "I mean, we'll help each other."

"But I was there, on the spot! *You* don't have to live with that shrieking train, that speeding car, John's blood!" He turned away from her. "If only I could get some sleep, dreamless sleep. . .no nightmares. . ."

There was a long silence. Ann cast around her mind for something to say that would not trigger off another surge of self-pity. It was better to remain silent than say the wrong thing. Mark took a small bottle from his dressing-gown pocket and emptied a tablet from it onto the table. Then he lit a cigarette and inhaled it deeply. He took a sip of his milk and swallowed the tablet.

"Take two tonight," she said. She glanced at her watch. "It's only quarter to three—five hours to go before you need get up." Her voice trailed away as he suddenly faced her, his mouth hard, his eyes suspicious. "It's quite safe," she added hurriedly. "I've done it myself in the past, after an operation."

He relaxed a little, shrugged, then swallowed a second tablet. "Won't do any good," he muttered. "Takes more than that to put me to sleep."

She moved closer to him, slipped her arm through his, and he sighed resignedly. They leaned back, shoulders touching, the physical contact seeming to soothe.

Mark's voice was firmer. "You're quite right, of course. What's done can't be undone. I might just as well enjoy all this—" He indicated the smart modern house with an all-embracing gesture. "And you," he added, slipping an arm round her, "as I did, at first."

"You will again. This phase you are going through will pass. Then everything will be all right."

"Yes, yes, everything will be all right. It's a phase, I'll get over it, don't you worry."

He felt her trembling as she turned toward him. His embrace was rough and passionate and she responded, as always, with equal passion. His fears and doubts dissolved in sheer physical sensation. This magic, Ann thought, with a small part of her mind, must be retained. It was her only hope of nursing Mark through these critical days.

The directors' meeting was coming to an end. Mark's pad was covered with his doodling. He had been unaware, or uncaring, of the disapproving frowns of the directors at his badly shaven face, his neglected hair, his messy chain-smoking.

"We come to the last item on the agenda," Sir Henry said. "The libel action."

Mark felt four pairs of eyes boring into him, hostile eyes, impatient eyes. He made an effort to pull himself together, but he couldn't keep the truculence out of his voice.

"I'm sorry, gentlemen. I take full responsibility. . .most unfortunate."

"As head of our legal department, Mark, you surely have some suggestion as to how we might cope with this unfortunate matter?" Sir Henry asked, with surprising restraint.

"Yes, yes, of course." Mark spoke quickly. "Settle it, admit liability with a good grace. I'll beat 'em down, get them to take a couple of thousand in settlement."

Arbuthnot, the Managing Director, exploded. "Really, Venner, is that all you have to say! You're supposed to vet every word we put into print! Pretty free and easy with the company's profits, aren't you? Seems an odd mistake for a lawyer to make, to fail to notice what everybody says is an obvious libel."

"I admit I made a mistake," Mark interrupted, his voice raised. He gripped the edge of the table, trying to control his trembling. What did it matter, he thought, what did anything matter? Night after night, no sleep, recurring nightmares, and Ann's panacea no longer effective. No word of forgiveness from these hard-faced colleagues either, he told himself, as he looked round the table.

"Can't a man make a mistake without everybody sitting in judgment on him as if he were a murderer—" He broke off abruptly and, in the indignant silence, stared unseeingly.

Sir Henry took matters in hand, politely but firmly. "Venner has a point, gentlemen. Men are only human after all and mistakes are made. I declare the meeting now closed."

He signaled to the others to go. Mark remained seated. Sir Henry sat down close to him. "I've known you too long, Mark, to take offense at your behavior. I've known you as a conscientious and loyal member of the staff of this company for years and we were grateful when you stepped into John Croft's shoes."

"Leave him out of this, Sir Henry, leave John out of this, please."

Sir Henry dropped his conciliatory manner. His voice became sharp. "That accident upset you more than you admitted at the time. And you've not spared yourself in your work here. But now, a big mistake. You've been overdoing it, you must take a rest."

Mark struggled to his feet. He felt as if he was suffocating under Sir Henry's tolerance. "The way you have been for the past months," the Chairman continued, now at his most syrupy, "you're no use to yourself, nor, actually, to the firm."

There it was, Mark told himself, the veiled threat, the thing he had been expecting, the end of everything. "I feel done in," he muttered.

"That's what I'm saying," Sir Henry said briskly. "You need a rest. Take a month's leave, right away. I'll take the responsibility with the other directors." He patted Mark affectionately on the back. "And don't worry about that libel. I'll get young Lawrence to deal with it."

"Lawrence?" Mark sounded as alarmed as he felt. "But he's an outside lawyer, not one of ours!"

Sir Henry did not meet Mark's eyes as he shrugged his answer. "What of it? Let him handle this one case for us. There'll be plenty of work for you to do when you come back. Provided you're fit, of course." He was at the door. "Remember me to that charming wife of yours. Lucky man!"

Mark stared at the door for seconds after Sir Henry had closed it behind him. The words "lucky man" kept going round in his mind. He walked across the room, threw open the long windows, stepped forward onto the balcony, and looked down to the distant street with its toy cars and miniature people.

He felt dizzy and shut his eyes. He recalled the many times he had parachuted from airplanes during the war, yet here he was, turning dizzy just looking down from a high building. There was little of his manhood left to him, he thought, welcoming the all too familiar wave of self-pity. Ann could no longer do anything for him. Whiskey was the only thing that could blunt his over-active imagination.

Ann telephoned three pubs before she located Mark.

"Yes, Mrs. Venner," the barmaid said. "He's here, been here since six o'clock."

Ann swallowed her pride. "Is he—has he had a lot to drink?"

The barmaid was matter-of-fact. "He's had too many double whiskies, but he's not drunk. He's just sitting here, by himself, just sitting. Do you want me to call him to the phone?"

"No, no, thank you," Ann said hurriedly. "I—it's just that he's had no food." She hung up abruptly.

She was deeply worried and, unusual for her, uncertain how to handle the deteriorating situation. She must do something to stop the rot, to restore Mark to the man he had been—assured, virile, alight with charm. She phoned Sir Henry.

"Ann? How are you, my dear?" She was relieved at the friendliness in his voice. "Nice to hear from you," he added.

"I was wondering when you were coming to dinner, Sir Henry. You haven't been for a very long time."

"Hadn't we better leave it till you and Mark come back from holiday?"

Ann kept the surprise out of her voice. "Is the holiday so urgent, then?" she asked warily.

Sir Henry sounded wary, too. "Is Mark there? Or are you alone?"

"He's not here at the moment. He had to go out."

"Well, I can speak freely. Obviously he hasn't told you what happened today." She listened with dismay to Sir Henry's account of the scene in the boardroom. "I say he's in need of a good long rest," he ended.

"I'm glad you're on my side, Sir Henry," she said. "I've been trying to persuade him to have a break for ages now, but you know how he is—can't possibly leave the office at the moment, too much to do." A little light laugh accompanied the last words.

"That accident's preying on his mind," Sir Henry went on. "And he needs to have all his wits about him for his work, you know."

"I'm sure he'll take a holiday when he realizes it's your wish, Sir Henry. Leave it to me," she added firmly.

"I'm sure I can, my dear. We all know your determination and single-mindedness—and that's a compliment."

"Thank you, Sir Henry, you're good for my morale. Goodbye."

She would need all her single-mindedness, Ann thought as she hung up, now that she could no longer depend on Mark's physical need of her. It would come back, of course, it must come back, she told herself fiercely. She loved him, she wanted nobody else, she must win him back.

She crossed to the fireplace and looked at herself in the mirror above it, seeking reassurance. The bloom on the pale clear skin owed nothing to make-up. The deep blue eyes looked back at her steadily. The soft dusky hair framed her face in contemporary fashion. She didn't look her 32 years.

The clock on the mantelpiece caught her eye. It was 9:40. There was nothing she could do but wait. She had barely settled herself in an armchair in front of the television set, determined to sit it out, when the telephone rang.

"Mark! For heaven's sake, where are you?"

His voice had the underlying whine with which she had become so familiar of late. "It's usual to leave a note," he said. "But I can't leave a note, so I'm phoning instead. I can't take any more, my beauty. You see, no more. . .it'll be just another accident. . .that damn level-crossing."

"Please, Mark, don't drive the car. Wait for me! I'll come for you. Mark, please!" She knew her last words had not reached him. He had hung up.

She took stock for a few moments, fighting down her panic. Her mind worked clearly enough when action was needed. The phone call had been an appeal for help even if Mark had been unaware of it himself. She could take the short cut from the house and reach the level-crossing before him.

She put on a coat, tied a scarf round her head, and started to walk briskly. Soon she found herself running.

Mark drove away from The Blue Anchor, increasing his speed as he reached the quiet country road he used so much. His thoughts were a jumble of images and words and he was mumbling to himself. He had drunk a lot of whiskey, but it had brought no relief this time. He'd practically lost his job and if whiskey let him down, where could he turn for forgetfulness? To Ann? Ann. . .the cause of his troubles.

The night was clear, the sky starlit. He heard the train's whistle in the near distance and glanced at the car clock. 9:55. On time, as usual. He pressed his foot down on the accelerator and sped forward. His timing was perfect, he thought; and so it should be, he had rehearsed it often enough. There it was—the open crossing. If he kept up this speed it would soon be over.

The noise in his ears was deafening now. His sweating hand slithered on the steering wheel. He felt his resolution weakening, he pictured the impact—of metal and flesh—his flesh. He took his foot off the accelerator, the car's speed dropped to 40, to 30, to 20. He was within a few yards of the train when he slammed on his brakes.

The sudden jerk flung him forward but did him no damage. His staring eyes followed the train's disappearing tail. Shaking and spent, he sat for several seconds slumped over the wheel.

He looked up and saw Ann's white-coated figure running across the rails toward him. She was at the car in a moment, her eyes frantic. At the sight of Mark, who turned his head slowly to look at her, she sighed with relief. She slipped into the passenger seat beside him, careful not to touch him.

"Lost my nerve. Hadn't the guts to do to myself what I did to John." His voice was bitter. "Rotten coward, that's what I've become."

Ann picked her way carefully through the brittle moment.

"Mark, let's go home. I'll drive."

He licked his lips and rubbed his dirty, sweaty hands together. "I've got to get out of this thing." He fumbled with his door handle. "I'm suffocating. I'll walk."

"I'll come with you."

He looked at her, wanting to reject her, but he could not. He shrugged and got out of the car. Ann slipped into the driver's seat and steered the car onto the verge.

"I'll empty the petrol tank," she said.

"You think of everything." At the sneering words Ann whirled around, taken aback. She braced herself for worse to come. He would take it out on her because he had just failed himself. "Like you did with John," he said harshly. "The clocks, the door handles of the car—your brains and my brawn!"

She kept all emotion out of her voice. "If you don't go away for a complete change, you'll collapse, for good and all."

"And that would never do, would it? I might give the game away altogether and then where would you be?"

"You'll lose your job if you go on like this."

"Now there's a thought! Got John out of the way so as to step into his job, but John's still in the way!"

"Mark, what about us?" She made the direct appeal deliberately. "We wanted each other, that was why. The job was a secondary consideration. Wasn't it, Mark?"

He gestured miserably, his resentment melting as he let memories flood back. "It all seemed worth it at the time. So much to gain. And I was a man then, not the wreck I am today." Anger mounted. "And you're to blame for that, for everything, everything!"

He leaned against a fender and buried his head in his hands. Ann hesitated, then came round the car and stood beside him.

"Look, Mark, we're in a mess and we've got to get out of it and we can only do that by our own efforts. You have to rest or there's no saying what will happen."

"You mean I'm a danger to you," he snapped. "I might make a clean breast of it and then you'd be in trouble."

Ann wondered at her own patience. She had never shown it toward John. "It's as much a danger to you as it is to me," she said quietly. "If you say too much, what will happen to you?"

"You don't give a damn what they do to me!"

"I care more than anything in the world. I have no life apart from you, Mark. I love you."

He turned to look at her. "I'd like to believe that," he sighed. "But John, he keeps getting in the way, he's everywhere, and I can't get rid of him."

She placed her hand on his arm and there was a moment of tenderness as they sat together. "As long as we keep close to each other," she said, "no rows, no recriminations, we'll see it through."

He nodded wearily. His dark haggard eyes and gaunt face looked at peace. He stood up and gently pulled her to her feet. She leaned toward him and as their bodies touched, he accepted her kiss, warm enough on her part but utterly without feeling on his. She swallowed her disappointment. They started the short walk home, side by side, but with a twelve-inch gap between them.

The police were on the telephone early the following morning.

"Yes. Mrs. Venner speaking. Oh, thank you. We were just going to do something about it. Yes, ran out of petrol. Thank you, I'll be right over."

Mark was on his third cup of black coffee and chain-smoking. He watched Ann as she crossed to the writing desk. "I'll need the insurance certificate," she murmured.

"You're in a hurry to get off."

"Well, it wouldn't do if I didn't seem anxious to get the car back," she pointed out reasonably.

"I'm not letting you go to the police on your own."

She looked at him in amazement. "If I wanted to go to the police station, Mark, I wouldn't need to wait for this kind of opportunity." But she had little hope that logic would influence him.

"I'm not letting you out of my sight, see?"

"Well, come with me."

"Exactly what I intend to do."

He went out of the sitting room. Ann found what she needed in the desk, also several brochures of holiday resorts abroad. She flicked them over, sensed rather than heard Mark stealing up close behind her.

"Let's make it Venice," she said, without turning round. "We could be ready in a couple of days. Would you prefer to fly?"

She turned round and met his eyes. For a second there was an answering flicker of interest in his. Then he turned away.

"Oh, do what you want. I can't be bothered."

Ann drove them to the police station in her Mini. As she started up the short drive to the entrance, she suddenly realized that Mark was hanging back.

"I can't go in there," he mumbled. "All those policemen, asking questions. . .the way they did before."

There was no use starting an argument here, she thought. "I won't be long. Will you wait here?"

"I'll wait."

Inside the police station all was informal and friendly. "Ah, Mrs. Venner," the sergeant said. "We've got Mr. Venner's car in the garage. Now, if I could just have the insurance certificate and the driving license—"

Ann switched on her best smile as she handed over the documents. "I'm sorry to give you all this bother, Sergeant. We thought we'd just push the car out of the way and call for it this morning with a can of petrol. Had no idea it would cause you all this extra work."

"That's all right, Mrs. Venner." He pushed the book toward her and indicated the place for her to sign. "We had a phone message about it early this morning. We had to investigate. Thank you." He restored the book to its position on the desk. "Be a good thing when they bring that level-crossing up to date, with modern signals and warnings and everything."

"Oh, they're starting on that, at last?" Her voice sounded strained.

"Day after tomorrow. Trains are being diverted round Kidstock while the work is being done. Pity they didn't get on with it sooner."

He broke off in embarrassment, as Ann showed signs of agitation. "Oh, sorry, Mrs. Venner. I forgot myself for the moment. . .bringing back such unhappy memories to you."

"Yes, Sergeant, horrible coincidence, wasn't it?"

Ann swung round at the sound of Mark's voice. "Leaving our car there, of all places," he muttered.

The sergeant looked at him, puzzled. Ann felt panic rising up in her. "We'll get the car now," she said.

Mark made no move. He looked round slowly. "So this is what a police station looks like. Not so terrible, almost inviting."

"This is just our shop window, sir. As long as you don't have to go past those doors—" The sergeant laughed rather feebly as he pointed in the direction of the doors leading to the cells.

Mark stared straight at Ann. Her outward control was near the breaking point. "I don't think I'd mind it so much," he said quietly. "It would be an end, one could just give up. . ." His voice trailed away and the sergeant could barely have heard the last words.

"Heavens!" Ann, glancing at the clock on the wall, broke into the role of the flurried, busy young woman. "It's nearly eleven o'clock and we've such a lot to do!"

She crossed quickly to Mark, slipped her arm through his, and steered him through the door.

"The garage is round the back, Mrs. Venner," the sergeant called. . .

Two exhausting days later Ann had completed the arrangements for their trip to Venice. Mark had made no objection to going but neither had he helped her. He had spent most of his time just sitting and smoking and brooding.

"We're all ready now," she said. "The packing's finished. I'm tired, Mark. Let's go out to dinner tonight, there's no food in the house."

"I'm not hungry. I don't want to go out and face people."

"All right, we'll have an early night and be fresh for the journey tomorrow." She sat down near him. He looked at her, but his eyes were empty. "We'll be away from all this," she went on, "in a few hours and you'll get well. And it will be like old times, the two of us."

He drew back. "The two of us!" he shouted. "You fool, can't you see it will never be just us two! John won't stay behind, he'll always be with us, no matter where I run to!"

Ann's iron self-control, rigidly maintained for weeks past, suddenly snapped, stretched beyond endurance. "I don't need any reminders!" Her voice was like a whip. "You've made sure of that, with your whining and scenes and suspicions. You've made our life a hell because you haven't the guts to see the job through. So you blame me all the time. I've had to carry the burden alone. Where would you be today if it weren't for me!"

"Back in my old life—a million times better off than I am now."

"Then why don't you clear out?" She was trembling with frustration and anger. "You hate me, there's nothing left for us. Why don't you clear out and leave me in peace?"

He was taken aback at this outburst, so different from her reactions in the past.

"I daresay that's what you'd like," he sneered. "But it's not so easy. We can't get away from each other."

"No? Well, I can get away from you. I'm leaving tomorrow morning as planned." She suddenly gave in to her despair. A flood of bitter sobs shook her. "I've stood as much as I can."

He heard her run upstairs and slam the bedroom door. He tried to sort himself out. If he let her go, he'd be rid of her. Perhaps, without her, he'd be able to come to terms with his guilt. But he didn't want her to leave him—it could be dangerous for him. She might decide to go to the police and then how would he know?

He felt confused. He went slowly upstairs and listened at the bedroom door, expecting to hear her crying. He opened the door quietly and went in. She was seated on the edge of the bed, not yet undressed, deep in thought, with set, tired face. As she looked at him, quiet now and subdued, with something of the former Mark Venner looking out of his eyes, her heart turned over. "Mark, darling, forgive me. I'm sorry for what I said just now."

"It was quite true. How were you to know I had a conscience?" He sat down beside her. "Pity I didn't have the nerve to do myself in the other night, not even when I was full of whiskey. That would have solved all my problems, and yours."

The outburst had done her good, she thought; her mind was clear, her patience restored, her longing for him intense. She smiled faintly. "I don't have any problems of my own, I only have your problems. You're eaten up with guilt. I'm not. I've wondered why I'm not, but it's not so easy to explain. I suppose it's too much a matter of emotions and temperament and I can live with it, Mark. John was a bore; he was in the way of our wonderful life together. It was a clever scheme and it worked."

"Clever because you thought of it," he said harshly.

"But it worked because of you—your iron nerve and timing.

And it's over and done with and nothing can undo it, so why not bury it, Mark?"

"You feel nothing?" he said slowly. "Nothing?"

She shook her head. "Not even when you began talking about it—the crash—and how it felt. Then my only concern was for you." She held his eyes. "I've only got feelings and thoughts for you, my darling."

"You're the strong one," he said. "I'm the weakling. Look at me."

She shook her head. "I need you, Mark, more than you need me. I'll never leave you, whatever I say."

"You feel nothing, nothing at all for John?" he asked again, wonderingly. "You have no doubts, no remorse, not just a little, now and then?"

"No." The word was emphatic. It was how she felt. She put out her hand to his cheek.

He struck it aside. "Then how can you know how I feel? How can you help me? You're not flesh and blood." He stood up, shaking. "You're right—you're not leaving *me*—I'm leaving *you*!"

He ran downstairs and picked up his suitcase. He had no idea where he would go but he felt, suddenly, that he must drive away, anywhere, and never come back. He felt more alive and alert than he had done for months.

He drove carefully at first, then increased his speed. He felt almost intoxicated, although he had only had a couple of whiskies. He felt fine, in fact. He would go on for another six or seven miles and then turn off, along the road to the level-crossing. He could take that, the way he felt tonight, and then he would be free.

He'd drive along the deserted stretch of road to the crossing, drive straight over it, without hesitation or fear. Tonight he would lay his ghosts—once and for all. He turned into the long straight road that no longer held any terrors for him. In a few minutes the level-crossing would come into sight.

In the far distance behind him a car's headlights streamed into his mirror. He glanced quickly behind, suddenly suspicious. It could be Ann, it was a small car. He slowed down just enough to try to identify it. It looked like Ann's car. So—she was following him. Well, he'd show her. She hadn't a hope of keeping up with his Jaguar.

He glanced at the dashboard clock. 9:55. And suddenly an icy streak cut through him. No, he wouldn't think about it. The level-crossing was coming into view but still far enough away for him to pull himself together.

Ann's car was creeping up on him. He'd beat the lot of them, John included. He increased his speed, touching 80 now. 80. That was what he was doing on the night—that night—

The exhilaration was evaporating, yielding to confusion. He drove by instinct, the shrieking sounds so familiar to him in his nightmare blurring his senses. Without turning his head, he slowly reached out with his left hand toward the passenger seat beside him. He felt a man's leg.

Relief flooded over him. As if in a spell, he turned his eyes toward his companion. He fully expected to see John and he was not startled when he met the other man's eyes. He heard him grunt and sink down drowsily into his seat.

He heard the shrill whistle of the oncoming train, its clattering wheels, its relentless din. The car was speeding directly into it.

"John, John!" he yelled. "Jump, for God's sake!"

A few seconds later came the crash and a few seconds after that Ann's car pulled up. She ran from it like someone demented and found Mark's shattered body in the debris. He was alive, barely conscious. Very gently she lifted his head onto her lap. He stirred.

"Thank heaven," she said. "You're all right."

He spoke with difficulty, but he made it; he had something important to say. "John—I saved him. . .this time. . ."

"Mark, Mark!" Ann was frantically willing him to cling to life. "Hang on, try to hang on for a bit. There was no train, they're going round the other way. You hit the lamps and things."

It took a few seconds for this to sink in. During that last moment before death, his eyes and mind seemed to clear. His words came distinctly. "But I made it right with John—to hell with *you*."

People and police arrived some minutes later. She was still sitting there, hunched over him, desolate, defeated. John's murder had left her unscathed. But Mark had died hating her, and her life was over.

"Q"

Francis M. Nevins, Jr.

The Scrabble Clue

Introducing Fred Buford, retired cop and former instructor at the Police Academy, in, paradoxically, his last case. . .We all like detective stories that end with a whiplash of revelation. Here's one that ends with a double whiplash. . .

When Fred Buford swung the coupe into his home street he found a police car blocking the entrance to the parking area. Two more official cars stood in the paved crescent in front of the apartment building, their red roof globes whirling in the five o'clock twilight.

Fred made a K-turn and pulled into a vacant space on the street, hefted the armful of sporting periodicals he had checked out of the library, and entered the high-rise. The brown-uniformed doorman sat in an alcove off the foyer, being questioned by two hard-eyed men in shapeless gray suits. Fred punched the elevator button for 22.

Even out in the hall, as he fumbled the key into the front door, he could smell the aroma of Bunny's meatloaf. Finest cook an old man ever had, he reflected, and the finest daughter too, turning the biggest bedroom in the apartment over to him, buying him that earphone attachment so he could listen to the radio late into the night without disturbing her.

He shambled into the large airy apartment and Bunny Buford, tall and slender in green blouse and slacks, came into the front room from the kitchen to greet him. Fred lowered his bulk onto the sofa and unlaced his shoes with a sigh, replacing them with soft-soled slippers. When he was comfortable he looked up at his daughter and asked in his cracked rumble, "What's all the excitement downstairs?"

"There's been a murder in the building, Daddy." Bunny's calm tone was the product of 28 years lived in the shadow of violent crime. She took off her glasses and wiped the steam of cooking from their lenses with the edge of her apron. "The Umber woman down in 16-C, the blonde who liked purple miniskirts. Someone cut her up with a carving knife. A Detective-Sergeant Duffy came by two hours ago looking for you and I told him I expected you back about this time."

Where else can a widower ex-cop past the mandatory retirement age spend his days but at the library, Fred wondered. He cupped his chins in a liver-spotted hand and shook his fringe of sparse white hair in disapproval. "Duffy, huh? There was a Duffy in my course on Techniques of Crime Detection at the Academy year before last. Flaming idiot if you ask me. If he's in charge five will get you ten the case goes into the Unsolved basket."

"He looked upset when I saw him." The girl's brown eyes brightened and her button nose twitched in sudden excitement so that for a moment she almost looked like a real rabbit. "Daddy, you don't think he wants you to help with the case?"

Fred tried to suppress his own soaring hope of relief from the stagnation of eleven months' retirement. "Who the hell would he ask for help if not me?" he demanded. "If he doesn't come back here with hat in hand he's a bigger fool than—"

At which point the door chime sounded and the veteran Police Academy instructor jumped to his feet in expectation.

"Great meatloaf, Miss Buford, best I've had since my mother passed away," mumbled tall gawky Sergeant Duffy around his final mouthful of meat and baked potato.

"She's a great cook," Fred agreed heartily, "and a fine freelance commercial artist too, I'll have you know. You should have her show you the sketches in her workroom sometime when you're not on a case. You won't believe this, Duffy, but when she was born I was very disappointed I didn't have a son. Now I wouldn't trade her for all the sons in the world." He threw a fatherly arm around Bunny's shoulders and she smiled up at him proudly.

The young sergeant neatly laid his knife and fork on the edge of his plate. "Gosh, sir, I'm so glad I noticed that F. BUFORD on the apartment-house directory downstairs and figured it must be you. And I'm even gladder," he went on, inadvertently cutting off something Fred had begun to say, "that you don't mind helping out on this one, Captain, ah, I guess it's Mr. Buford now, isn't it?"

"Let's take our coffee over to the couch while my daughter is clearing the table," Fred suggested, "and you can tell me the details."

"Well, Cap, ah, sir," the rookie sergeant began, "as you know, the victim's name was Trudy Umber. She used to be married to Will Umber of Craven and Umber, the ad agency downtown, but they separated two years ago and she moved in here and has been living off a separation allowance. Off that and a little sideline she had. The old badger game. She'd let herself be picked up by a well-to-do older man—a married man, of course—and jump into the sack with him a few times while her accomplice made like Cecil B. DeMille with a camera hidden in the bedroom closet of her apartment. Then a few weeks later she'd put the bite on the guy—money in return for the negatives.

"The only unusual thing about the way she played it is that she'd put the bite on the guys herself; most of the time, as you know, it's the male accomplice, the cameraman, who makes the approach to the sucker. She had six guys paying off regularly until today, when it seems one of them got fed up."

"If you know so much about her activities," Fred rumbled, "why didn't you go after her while she was still alive?" He swallowed black coffee from a tall thick mug.

"Oh, we just found all this out today, sir, from her diary and the victims. We found a, well, a sex diary hidden inside a stereo speaker on a wall mount. Names all her marks, gives them report cards, tells how much she collected from each—the whole works, except there's no mention of who her partner is, but we'll get him soon enough."

Fred crossed his slippered feet and folded his hands on his bulging abdomen. "The dubious pleasure of wading through the tramp's diary is all yours," he grunted. "Who found her body?"

"Today's the day the window washers come around to do the outside of the building. One of the crew happened to look in from the outside of 16-C and saw her lying in a pool of blood and wooden chips in the dining room and gave the alarm. She was stabbed seven times with a long-bladed knife which the killer took away with him. Very messy. Medical examiner gives the time of death as between twelve thirty and two o'clock."

"Wooden chips?" Fred's gruff tone suggested annoyance.

"Yessir. She must have been a brainy sort of tramp. Instead of watching soap operas or game shows on TV during the day she played Scrabble with herself. You know, the game where you make words out of little wood blocks with letters of the alphabet printed on one side?"

"I've played the game, Sergeant," Fred remarked drily.

"Well, sir, she had the board set up on the dining-room table and was in the middle of a game with herself when the killer rang the bell. Apparently he brought his own knife—none seems to be missing from her apartment. Anyway, he stabbed her seven times, wiped the knife on a bathroom towel, and took the knife away with him.

"But she wasn't quite dead yet. Mass of blood that she was, she dragged herself over to the table and pulled down the Scrabble box with all the letters in it and rooted around among those scattered little letters on the floor and palmed two of them before she died. When we found her, her other hand was clawed among the letters like she was looking for more of them."

"What two letters did she pick up?"

"An R and an F," Duffy said. "No way of telling which letter was meant to come first, of course."

"It's still a damned good clue," his old instructor pointed out, "if you know how to use it."

"Sir, I learned from you." Duffy's voice rang with pride. "The woman's diary gives the full names of all six men she was blackmailing. And it happens that two of them have initials that match."

"Who are they?"

"One of them is Roger Farris, a vice-president at the United Electronics main office. Tall, good-looking, fiftyish, standard executive-type complete with a society wife and two kids in college that hate his guts and a big fancy house out in Spruceknoll. In other words, one hell of a lot of respectability to preserve and a strong motive for killing the tramp who threatened his respectability. The other one is Franklin Roosevelt Quist. You've heard of him, I guess. The big civil rights lawyer?"

"I've heard," Fred replied laconically. "Had a run-in with him the year before I retired over something one of his clients had decided in his infinite wisdom was a case of police brutality. Of course, as you pointed out, Duffy, there's no way of telling which of the two letters was meant to be read first."

"There's a bigger problem than that, sir," Duffy said. "The boys have already talked to both suspects and both of them claim to have alibis. Between twelve thirty and two o'clock this afternoon Roger Farris says he was sitting at the head table at the Sheraton Central campaign luncheon for Senator Huggins, and our friend the defender of the oppressed was downtown in Superior Court arguing a civil rights case."

"Political lunches are organized chaos," Fred reminded the younger man. "Courts take recesses. If you can't crack one of those two alibis, you'd better find another line of work."

"Oh, we're working on them, sir," Duffy assured his former instructor hastily. "But of course we have no positive proof that the killer is one of those two. Maybe the girl's partner was named Roy Fox or Frank Rush or something and maybe he killed her in a dispute over sharing the payoff money. Maybe a homicidal maniac did it. Anyway, just as a matter of routine we've been checking out every person in this building whose initials are RF or FR or whose first or last name begins with one of those combinations." The young sergeant lowered his eyes for a moment in embarrassment. "Uhh—were you in the library all day today, sir?" he asked Fred Buford.

In the sudden silence they could hear the friendly clink of dishes from the kitchen.

Fred glared at the hapless rookie. "Don't you think you should read me your damn Miranda warning before you ask a question like that, *Sergeant?*" Then he spread his cracked lips in a feeble attempt at a grin. "I went for a bite to eat at Leo's Luncheonette around the corner from the library sometime after noon. I always eat there when I spend the day browsing in the Reading Room. Leo's is jammed at lunchtime, I don't remember my waitress and didn't see anyone there I knew." He held out his wrists as if for the handcuffs.

Duffy raised his hands almost in horror. "Oh, no, sir, that was just a routine question. I was just being thorough like you taught us at the Academy. You were the last FR in the building that I hadn't covered, but, my gosh, you're no more a suspect than—well, than I am!"

"Glad to hear it, Duffy. You're showing good cop sense." The thought crossed Fred's mind that the sergeant had not been quite as thorough as he stated he had been, but residual resentment of the rookie's line of questioning led him to give Duffy no more than the subtlest hint. "Actually, I never talked to the Umber woman more than to say hello in the elevator. I only knew her name because an old man with no job gets curious about his neighbors, but I doubt she even knew my name or my daughter's."

"Uhhh—but you will come down to headquarters tomorrow and help me work on those alibis?" Duffy requested awkwardly.

"Oh, hell, sure I'll help. Nothing better to do." Fred carefully kept all his joy at being asked out of his voice.

"Gee, thanks a million, sir, I sure appreciate it!" Duffy rose fumblingly from his armchair. "Would ten o'clock be too early for you?"

Fred frowned as he hoisted his thick-bellied bulk to his feet. "Old folks don't need much sleep. I'll see you at eight."

"Yessir."

"Just one thought before you go," he said at the door. "Husband and wife are separated, husband has to lay out cash to live up to their separation agreement. If husband finds out wife is also getting goodies from lovers, he might be tempted to cut off his payments the fast way, with a knife. And he might be even more tempted to stick a couple of Scrabble letters in her hand so as to make things hot for a couple of her lovers, assuming of course that he first took a peek into her diary like you did and found out who they were, or learned some other way. If I were you I'd look into what Mr. Will Umber was doing early this afternoon."

"Yes, sir! I'll do that. And thanks again for all your help. And for dinner. See you tomorrow, sir!" They shook hands in the corridor by the elevator and Fred shuffled back into the apartment and into the kitchen where Bunny was finishing the dishes.

"I heard most of what you two were saying," his daughter said, handing him the meat platter to dry. "You haven't had that light of excitement in your eyes since the day you retired."

Fred picked up a dishtowel and wiped the water from the dinnerware with vigorous strokes. "Yes, indeed," he crowed, "when the kids get stuck they got to call in the old man. And with a lump like that Duffy in charge you can be damn sure it won't be solved without me! Why, throughout this entire day and evening he's believed that F. BUFORD on the board downstairs meant me, and never even wondered how an old man on a cop's retirement pension could afford the rent on a big apartment like this. I threw him enough hints, too, like when I mentioned that a long time ago I'd wanted a son. Just like I said before he came—a flaming idiot."

Bunny almost dropped a plate laughing. "Oh, Daddy! Were you seriously going to suggest *me* as a suspect?"

Fred chuckled back at his daughter, enjoying the joke hugely.

"Well, as a point of routine he should have covered it. After all, look at the case a really good cop could build against you. When can't a woman working the badger game do the usual thing and have her male accomplice make the approach to the marks? When the accomplice is a female, too. What's the most convenient way for the accomplice to operate the hidden camera in the other girl's apartment? Live in the same building herself and use the fire stairs. When someone's dying and using her last breath to spell out her murderer's name, is she going to reach for the killer's initials or try to spell out the name? Spell out the name, of course. It's an open-and-shut case—a dispute between the partners over the payoff money like Duffy suggested."

"Oh, Daddy, you're beautiful." Bunny blew a playful kiss at her father in appreciation of the jest. "But I think you've been hitting too many whodunits down in that Reading Room. For the sake of my reputation you'd better switch to some nice safe biographies! Seriously, Daddy, who do you think did it?"

"My money's on Franklin Roosevelt Quist." The old policeman savored every syllable of the civil-rights lawyer's name. "That last point I made about the Umber woman going for the name instead of the initials makes a lot of sense, you see. And even if she was going for the initials, if she was trying to name Roger Farris she wouldn't have been clawing out for more letters at the moment she died, the way Duffy said she was, because she already had Farris' initials. In the game of Scrabble, daughter, there is only one Q—and she couldn't find it. That's what she was hunting around for, desperately trying to add it to the F and R in her hand before the curtain came down. We'll crack his alibi tomorrow."

"Be careful drying that meat knife," cautioned Frederika Buford, known to her father as Bunny. "It's very sharp."

"Q"

William Bankier

The Big Bunco

When you are scriptwriters for a TV sit-com series and you're bogged down on page 10 of episode number 52 and the deadline was yesterday, you might feel pretty desperate. Desperate enough to do something really wild. Well, that's how writer Joe Huck and idea-man Stan Percival felt when Stan dreamed up that impossible dream. Imagine one of the oldest con games in the history of bunco, but all dressed up in ultra-mod clothes—and don't forget what P. T. Barnum said . . .

I have a crazy partner. Which is not so bad most of the time because our job is writing scripts for a television situation-comedy series called "Rooms Without Doors" and when you're sweating to come up with a funny premise for episode number 46 and the deadline is yesterday afternoon, a little crazy can be a good thing.

"Stan, we are dead," I will say from my place at the typewriter, little strands of spiderweb stretching from my cramped fingers to the dusty keys. "That rumbling sound you hear above us is clods of earth hitting the lid of our coffin."

And then Stan Percival will heave up his 260 pounds from the folding canvas deck chair, which is the only other piece of furniture in our cubbyhole office, and he will say, "No, Joe. No. We are not dead. We are on the verge of a great idea. All I have to do is say it."

He is looming over me, six feet four inches, his hands working the air like clay, and I know he doesn't have an idea, not in his conscious mind anyway. But there is a look on his face like a man who has a chicken bone in his throat and is trying to work it back up and spit it out. Stan's eyes are bulging, his lips are pursing, and there are beads of sweat on his big round face.

"And this is the idea," he says. "Cousin Mary is locked in a church overnight." It is insane; there is no reason for a church to be mentioned, but I keep listening. "She doesn't know how to get out but she has a bottle of brandy with her because she'd been to the liquor store to get supplies for their anniversary party. Back home Uncle Walt misinterprets a phone call because he's lost his hearing aid, so he thinks she's been kidnaped. The police are called in which gets Larry uptight because he's expecting a delivery of forged lottery tickets. And at the end Mary will be up in the bell tower playing 'I'll Be with You in Apple Blossom Time' with her feet, which tips Larry off because this is *their song*."

The whole thing is sheer madness, but I start laughing and I start typing and pretty soon we have a script. Which is why I say a little crazy can be a good thing. Sometimes but not always. Because the time Stan got it into his head that we should sell somebody the Jacques Cartier Bridge was something else. And that is the time I propose to tell you about.

It all began one morning in August when Stan arrived late. We had quit work at nine o'clock the night before, solidly blocked and frustrated at page ten of a difficult, no an impossible, script. I had always feared this day.

When Stan came into the office he didn't go to his deck chair. Instead he went to the window which was open a few inches and flung it up all the way so that the glass rattled. Then he thrust the top of his body through the aperture and screamed across Ste. Catherine Street, "Freedom now!"

There must have been some response from the street because he hung out there for a few minutes and I heard one end of an abusive conversation before he drew himself back in and said to me, "Bore, bore, bore! I can't do this any more, Joe Huck. I am dying of boredom." Then he prostrated himself, not in the chair but on the floor.

"Ready when you are, Stanley," I said.

But he went on, "I couldn't sleep last night. I lay awake asking myself where's the excitement? Where's the adventure? Man was not created to lurch round and round on a treadmill. You know who has it all figured out? That former playwright what's-his-name. who wrote *African Genitals*. Robert Aardvark."

"Robert Ardrey. *African Genesis*."

"That's the guy. He has a new book in which he theorizes that man's Number One need is not security, it's excitement. Freedom from boredom. I think he's right."

"Okay. How do we work that into episode number 52?"

Stan Percival reared up on one elbow, his large head appearing over the edge of my desk like the Kraken's. "Damn it, that's the point. I am not going to write episode number 52. I am off the treadmill as of now. I seek a new adventure."

"Fine. And what will you do for money?"

Our weekly situation comedy on CBC Television was an imitation of similar American series and we never kidded ourselves. Its existence was predicated on a political demand for Canadian content on the taxpayers' network. But the pay was good and there were no other jobs like it for writers in Montreal.

"Money," said Stan, "will have to be one of the essential ingredients of our new adventure."

"You've got me in it, too?"

"Of course. You're just as bored as I am. You're just too security-bound to show it."

It was clear he needed humoring. "Okay, partner, tell me about *our* adventure."

Stan sat up on his blue-denimed haunches. "It has to be some sort of crime."

"Crime?"

"Right. That's where the adventure is. I figured it all out last night. I'm convinced half the people involved in criminal acts do it because the straight-and-narrow bores them stiff."

"But we can't kill anybody. I doubt we could even rob a bank. No experience."

"Pay attention, oh, Lucky Huck. There is crime and there is crime. The category I have in mind is the kind that involves no violence. It demands ingenuity on the part of the criminal, and usually a degree of crookedness in the victim who wants something for nothing. I speak, noble Huck, of the big con, the big bunco."

I shook my head. "These things are not easy."

"Of course not. That's precisely the challenge. But aren't we in the con game already? Don't we spend our days making up preposterous stories that involve the manipulation of a lot of characters to achieve a desired end?" He was on his knees now, sprawled halfway across the desk. "All we have to do is apply our skills to inventing a con. Some sort of plot that feeds on human greed and ends up milking some sucker who deserves it because he goes along."

I sensed the momentum in Stan's persuasion. but it was too late to get off the track. "And I suppose you have something in mind."

"It hit me in the wee hours," he said. "We are going to sell the Jacques Cartier Bridge."

I raised my eyes to the window and saw in the distance the massive steel structure vaulting the St. Lawrence River to the South Shore. "Stanley," I said, "this is another fine mess you're getting us into."

"It's an idea. We've had crazier ones. Now all we have to do is work out the details."

I must admit it was an interesting exercise. I went along because there was no way Stan Percival would get back to the script until he had played out his game. By late afternoon we had hacked out a scenario which, given a bit of luck, might just work.

It involved our actor-friend Yves Paquette doing his uncanny impersonation of the Mayor of Montreal and it included an important role for Stan's girl friend, Portia Fleming. If all went well, the plan ended with a payoff to us of $50,000.

When I raised my eyebrows at that, Stan said, "I won't kid you, I need the money. My alimony payments are killing me." He stood up, displaying his denims and faded T-shirt. "You think I enjoy dressing like a middle-aged hippie?"

My $200 sports jacket hung majestically on the back of the chair. "I've tried to tell you—" I began.

"I know. I waste money. But I'm trying to change." He went to the door. "Come on, I'll buy us both dinner."

That evening we prowled hotel lobbies looking for a setting. We were lucky. We had covered the Mount Royal and the Laurentian. Then, in the Queen Elizabeth, we saw listed on the bulletin board: CANADIAN CONSTRUCTION INDUSTRY CONVENTION.

"These are the guys we want," Stan said.

"But it's today, Thursday, Friday, and Saturday. That's too sudden."

"Nonsense. 'Mission Impossible' converts a warehouse into the Freedonian Museum overnight. The faster we have to work, the better. Verve, Brother Huck, panache, élan."

I drifted past a table where ticketed conventioneers were registering and I picked up a membership roster. Then Stan and I went into the bar, ordered a beer, and perused the list for a potential bridge buyer. We were halfway through when I spotted a familiar name and a jolt of adrenalin made my hand tremble.

"Lewicki," I said. "E. J. Lewicki from Baytown, Ontario."

Stan's grinning face was clenched like a fist. "It's working, isn't it? The pieces are falling into place."

"Back home in Baytown everybody's heard of E. J. Lewicki. Made his fortune building airfields for the Commonwealth Training Plan during the war. Always in the papers. A hint of scandal one year about kickbacks."

"Our man," Stan said. "Our pigeon."

"Keeps getting hassled by the Provincials for driving fast under the influence. Usually has a pretty chick beside him."

"Oh, my goodness." Stan was cracking his huge knuckles like walnuts. "We couldn't have written a better character ourselves. You say he likes pretty girls? I'll go and get Portia. You pick up Yves Paquette and we'll meet back at the office in half an hour."

We did. Yves and I had possession of the two chairs when Stan arrived with Portia and a paper bag containing six quarts of beer and a roll of paper cups. Drinking beer out of a paper cup is an abomination, but it is just one of the things I hate and yet keep doing when working with Stan Percival. Another is embarking on a venture like selling the Jacques Cartier Bridge to a rich unscrupulous Ontario construction magnate. But I knew there would be no getting my partner back to episode number 52 until he got this quirk out of his system. If it were done, it were best done quickly.

I offered Portia my chair, but she preferred to recline on the desk, which caused Stan's huge face to assume a thoughtful expression. I was afraid he might cancel the meeting and order me and Yves out of the office, but the caper held too firm a grip on his mind.

A word about Portia. She is 23 years old and features miles of cascading blonde hair at one end and miles of devastating leg at the other. Her torso is generous too, and stretched out as she was now on one elbow with one knee up, a backless sandal dangling from the other foot and her blouse losing the battle to stay closed three buttons to two, you had to admit nothing more was required of Portia Fleming. Which was just as well because she is a terrible actress.

"Stanley," she said now, "how is my part coming in the series? Are you writing me more lines?"

This was Stan's current trap. Only by using extreme persuasion had he wangled her a bit part in "Rooms Without Doors." The director, a good judge of talent, abhorred any script in which she appeared and was urging Stan to write her out. Meanwhile, from Portia's side the pressure was maintained for a fatter part. And when Portia applied pressure, it was warm and fragrant and sweet. Stan was caught in the vise of life; someday soon he would have to find a way to escape its squeeze.

"This is not a script conference," Stan said. "We are here on a more important matter." And he proceeded to outline our plan. At this point you may be wondering why these two newcomers did not reject the scheme which was, of course, strictly illegal. You must remember Stan was talking to actors. As long as he is playing a part, an actor will do anything from undressing in a department-store window to selling a shoddy product on TV. An actor must act.

"Portia, you will make contact with E. J. Lewicki—Joe will point him out to you. Remember, you are playing the part of a confidential secretary to Mayor Martel of Montreal. All you have to do is drop a hint about the plans to build a new University on Ste. Helen's Island. Just let him know that it will be a big project. A lot of steel will be used."

Yves Paquette said, "I guess you want me to play the part of the Mayor." He put on a tiny twisted smile and let his eyes slip into the famous glazed, maniacal stare and we had to laugh. Even without makeup he was almost His Worship.

"Remember," I said to Yves, "Lewicki will have seen the real Mayor addressing the dinner a few hours earlier, so you'll have to be good."

Yves opened his private door just enough to let me catch a glimpse of the giant ego lurking inside. "I am good," he said.

We confirmed our times, rehearsed our lines, finished the beer, then went home to bed—I to mine, Yves to his, and Stan, presumably, to Portia's.

Next afternoon I telephoned the hotel and reserved a room in the name of Finn, a clever alias since my name is Huck. I checked in at 5:00, telephoned Stan, and he showed up an hour later carrying the inevitable paper bag. This time it contained a bottle of rye. Stan phoned for ice. Then he called Yves and gave him the room number.

At eight o'clock we met Portia in the doorway of the main salon where the Construction Conventioneers had just finished dinner. The real Mayor was beginning his speech. Portia had trouble spotting us because we were both wearing glasses we didn't need and Stan had pasted on a false mustache. I tipped the headwaiter and he let us lurk along the wall until I spotted E. J. Lewicki and pointed him out to Portia.

It was years since I had seen the affable millionaire cruising the streets of Baytown, but he had not changed much. His hair was whiter, but it still covered his head like Good King Wenceslas's snow—deep and crisp and even. And the symbolic unlighted cigar still projected from between his teeth untouched by his fastidious lips which were drawn away from the tobacco in a rigid grin.

We left Portia Fleming thus loaded and pointed in the right direction and went back to the room to wait for Yves. Professional to the core, he showed up on the stroke of 9:00, hatted and cloaked to conceal his uncannily Mayorish appearance. At 9:30 we left him and went down to the bar where, according to plan, Portia was supposed to be drinking with Lewicki. And she was, seated at a table in the far corner, their heads so close that she could have bitten the other end of his cigar.

Portia greeted us with surprise as we passed by. "Carl, Peter," she called, using our assumed names, "did you hear the boss's speech?"

"Hello, Jenn. No. We just got here. His Worship wants to see us upstairs to ask how we're making out on the project."

Portia, as Jenny, introduced us in our roles as executive assistants to the Mayor of Montreal. We sat down, accepted a drink, and soon had our plot rolling along in high gear. Lewicki, unscrupulous and avaricious, was everything a con man could ask.

"You guys," he soon said, "must be right in there where the action is."

"Oh, we hear a thing or two."

"The young lady mentioned something about building a new University down on the island. I'd sure like to get in on that."

"Well, sir," Stan said, "there's no reason why you shouldn't. You've certainly made a good friend in Jenny."

"I wonder," I said, "if Mr. Lewicki might not be the man for the Mayor's special project?"

I had let the cat out of the bag and Stan almost overplayed his horror. I sensed that we were flirting with a Laurel and Hardy interpretation. But Lewicki seemed interested. Thank goodness for booze and bar lighting.

"Peter, the Mayor's project is not for public consumption."

"You can talk freely at this table, boys. E. J. Lewicki can keep a secret."

Stan apologized, changed the subject, and for the time it took to finish our drinks and order another round he made empty conversation. But I could tell where Lewicki's thoughts were. Finally he said, "Your Mayor is famous for his big ideas. I guess this new one is a beauty."

My partner appeared to reconsider. He glanced at me. I nodded. "Very well," he said. "Part of our assignment is to find an entrepreneur who is big enough and fast enough to help put this deal over."

Lewicki said, "I just got up and ran twice around the room and you didn't even miss me."

"The deal is this. Now that the subway is running under the river to the South Shore, and the new Champlain Bridge is operating, the Mayor plans to close the old Jacques Cartier Bridge and dismantle it. The city will accept an offer of five million dollars for the steel in the bridge."

"But if I do that, I end up with a lot of steel on my hands and nowhere to go with it."

"That's where the new University fits in. The proposed site is Ste. Helen's Island, right beneath the bridge. You won't have to go anywhere with the steel. You will sell it to the city for use in the new construction. In effect, you will be a broker, buying the bridge and selling it back almost on the same day. At a nice profit. And the company that dismantles the bridge will be working on a very nice municipal contract, too."

E. J. Lewicki turned his glittering eyes first on me, then on Stan. The cold cigar pierced our hearts, one after the other. "That's a handsome project. I expect the bidding will be fierce."

"Mayor Martel doesn't work that way," Stan said. "He is, as you may have heard, somewhat of an autocrat. He works fast and he has the power to initiate projects as he sees fit. No, this contract will go to the company the Mayor chooses."

"And you boys are expected to make a recommendation."

"We are."

The elderly millionaire turned to Portia. "What do you say, Jenny?"

She put her hand on his. "I know the Mayor would like you."

"Done," Lewicki said. "Tell His Worship I'm interested."

"We can do better. We can take you to him right now."

So there we all were twenty minutes later in my room on the fifteenth floor, raising our glasses of rye and tap water while the Mayor of Montreal, played to the hilt by Yves Paquette, proposed a toast.

"*Félicitations á Monsieur Lewicki,*" he said, "and success to all of us. May this project be brought to a very speedy and profitable conclusion."

We drank and Yves drew Stan into a corner for a few words. Then Yves put down his glass, shook hands with everyone, took his coat and hat, and made his departure.

The room seemed empty after Yves's large performance. Stan said to Lewicki, "The Mayor just reminded me of a detail I neglected to mention. There are certain requirements he has to fulfill in order to expedite these projects as quickly as he does. It is normal, in these cases, for the successful contractor to pay a deposit—"

"What you're saying is there's a payoff."

"That's a harsh word. I would never use it to describe—"

He was interrupted again, this time by Lewicki's hearty laughter. "Don't be embarrassed, my boy. I've been in this game a long time. I was wondering when you were going to ask for it. How much do you want?"

"Fifty thousand dollars."

"Cash, I suppose?"

"Yes, sir. Used bills, small denominations."

When Lewicki and Portia left ten minutes later, Stan and I fell on the floor. Literally. "He went for it!" Stan said. "We have sold that man the Jacques Cartier Bridge!"

"I can't believe it!"

"Believe it, my son. Tomorrow morning, right after the banks open, Mr. Lewicki will be here with the money."

And it was so. We slept fitfully, woke at eight, shaved and dressed and had a large room-service breakfast. At 10:30 Lewicki and Portia arrived together with a satchel which, when opened, revealed the sum of $50,000, all in used, low-denomination banknotes.

"Jenny," Stan said, still playing everything according to our beautiful script, "you'd better deliver this cash to the Mayor's office and tell His Worship that the deal has been completed, consummated."

She took the satchel and left. . .

"Meanwhile," Stan said, "Peter and I will work fast drawing up the necessary papers to get this project underway. You'll be hearing from us very soon."

Lewicki was standing at the window looking downriver at his newest possession. "Fine," he said. "And now I wonder if you boys have any of that good Canadian whiskey left."

I am not a morning drinker, but for $50,000 I figured I could go along. We sipped and chatted while my impatience grew. The show was over. I wished to be gone.

Finally Lewicki set down his empty glass. Then he patted his pockets. "Oh, boys," he said, "I have just given the young lady all the cash I have. I'm checking out now and I have a lot of people to tip. How much money can you spare me?"

Stan said, "How much do you need?"

Lewicki pondered and mumbled. "Bellhops, maid, garage, waiters—they've all been real good to me. Can you let me have a couple of hundred?"

Stan and I pooled our funds. We just made $200 with cab fare left over. Back in the office, waiting for Portia to show up, I said, "Imagine that old bird hitting us up like that."

Stan said, "Relax, he said he'd mail it back. Besides, we pay out $200, we get back $50,000 less expenses. If you don't speculate, you can't accumulate."

By now we were hungry. By two o'clock we were tired and surly. By 3:30 we were suspicious. At 4:00, when Portia's telegram was delivered, we were angry and sick. I gave my last quarter to the boy while Stan took a long yellow sheet from the envelope. He read it aloud.

HI BOYS. I ALWAYS WANTED TO BE ABLE TO AFFORD TO SEND A LONG WIRE. NOW I'M RICH SO HERE GOES. STAN, I ALWAYS THOUGHT MY FAILURE IN TV WAS NOT BECAUSE I'M A BAD ACTRESS BUT BECAUSE YOU ARE A BAD WRITER. THIS PROVES IT. THE MOTIVATION YOU PROVIDED ME IN THIS CON GAME WAS VERY FLIMSY. WHY SHOULD I CHEAT THAT SWEET MR. LEWICKI JUST SO YOU AND YOUR DUMB PARTNER CAN MAKE A KILLING? ANYWAY E.J. TELLS ME YOUR PLAN WOULDN'T HAVE FOOLED ANYBODY. THE STEEL FROM A BRIDGE WOULD NEVER BE USED IN CONSTRUCTING UNIVERSITY BUILDINGS. JUST ANOTHER EXAMPLE OF YOUR CARELESS PLOTTING. YOU DO IT ALL THE TIME. GOOD ENOUGH FOR YOUR TACKY TELEVISION PLAYS BUT NOT FOR REAL LIFE. SO I AM HERE NOW IN BAYTOWN WITH SOMEBODY

WHO REALLY KNOWS HOW TO BE NICE TO ME. TELL JOE I LIKE HIS HOMETOWN. HE SHOULD NEVER HAVE LEFT. LOVE. PORTIA.

After Stan had torn up the telegram and kicked the deck chair to pieces, nobody said anything for a while. Then I went over and tried to cheer him up.

"Well, at least you're rid of Portia Fleming. She was a problem in the series and now she's gone forever."

I said it, but I took no comfort from it, and I don't think Stan did either. We wanted her gone because she was supposed to be dumb. But the way things worked out, it looks like the smart cookies flew away to Baytown and left the dumb guys in Montreal, out $200 plus expenses.

Phyllis Bentley

Miss Phipps on the Telephone

Everything is grist to the writer's mill—and to the detective's. Even a midnight phone call that is apparently a wrong number can arouse Miss Phipps's creative impulses . . .

Detective: MISS MARIAN PHIPPS

The telephone rang. Miss Phipps, dragged up from the cosy depths of her first sleep, mumbled, rolled over, and took up the phone from the table beside her bed. The time, she noted from the illuminated electric clock, was three minutes past midnight.

"Tettenham three four one eight," Miss Phipps said crossly.

"*Tettenham* three four one eight?" queried a voice.

"Yes," said Miss Phipps, noting that the voice was young, girlish, not very well educated, with a definitely northern intonation. She corrected herself and gave the new exchange, formerly known as Tettenham.

"Are you Miss Phipps?"

"Yes."

"Miss Marian Phipps?"

"Yes."

In anguish Miss Phipps ran rapidly over in her mind all her friends and relations and their present whereabouts. There was her niece with her family, there was Inspector Tarrant with his family. Which of them had had an accident? Which were near enough to London to warrant the police calling her rather than a relative? Which? Why? Where?

"Have you a brother called Randall Harvey?" continued the voice.

"No!" said Miss Phipps explosively, remembering her well-loved brother who had perished in the Normandy landing.

"No?" said the voice incredulously. "Are you sure?"

"Absolutely sure."

"Or a half brother?"

"No!"

"Perhaps your housekeeper has a brother of that name?"

"I have no housekeeper."

"Oh. Well." There was a pause in which the voice could be heard calling briskly, "Mr. Harvey! Mr. Harvey!" Then there was a pause in which nothing could be heard. Finally the voice resumed. "There's been some mistake," it said on a note of disappointment. "Good night. Sorry to have troubled you."

"Well, good night," said Miss Phipps, taken aback.

She replaced the telephone with an angry clash, and, rolling over, buried her head in the pillow and tried to fall asleep again.

But she could not. It was not so much a matter of sleep interrupted as of wounded pride. Miss Phipps was a novelist and a writer of detective stories. She often began a story by imagining some mysterious situation, then thinking up circumstances which would explain it. But try as she would, she could not explain that telephone call.

It was a local call, since the girl had not begun with the 01 which nowadays preceded all London calls from a distance. The girl was northern, probably Yorkshire, so that she may have been somebody connected with Miss Phipps's niece, who lived in that county. But she seemed to think some Mr. Harvey had known Miss Phipps and claimed to be her brother.

Miss Phipps, as a woman living alone with her name in the telephone directory, was not unfamiliar with calls from young men who wanted to "Come round and have a good time," promising to be her friend if she would let them. All such callers she terrified out of their wits by assuming a booming schoolmistressy Oxford-English voice, addressing them as "young man," reminding them of their mothers, and threatening to inform the police. But young men of that sort, in that kind of situation, did not employ a young girl to do their telephoning for them. Moreover—and this puzzled Miss Phipps—the girl had sounded genuinely disappointed. She seemed really sorry that Miss Phipps had no brother named Randall. Or was she sorry for some other reason?

A mistaken identity, that's all it was, Miss Phipps told herself. Randall Harvey wanted another Miss Marian Phipps, of course. He was a visitor from Yorkshire who had a friend in London who had a sister named Marian Phipps who lived in Tettenham. Miss Phipps sat up crossly, put on the light, and took up the telephone directory. There was no other Marian Phipps in the Tettenham section. In fact, there were no other Phippses there at all.

Miss Phipps gave a loud angry snort. From under the pillow she drew the notebook and pencil she put there every night. She found her reading glasses and put them on. Sighing, she took up her pencil and wrote down carefully the exact time of the call and every word of the conversation.

At ten o'clock the next morning, as Miss Phipps was sitting at her desk struggling with a plot which declined to grow, a ring sounded at the door of her flat. Exclaiming irritably at the interruption, she bounced to the door and flung it open.

A young man stood there. He was in his twenties, Miss Phipps judged, personable, even handsome, dark, with hair and sideburns longish, but not too long to be acceptable to Miss Phipps's old-fashioned taste. His eyes were brown and sparkling, his suit, shirt, tie, and shoes almost up to advertisement standards. Miss Phipps looked at him with interest but coldly, suspecting a salesman.

"Good morning," he said.

Miss Phipps remained markedly silent.

"I came to apologize for that stupid telephone call last night," he went on.

Miss Phipps, unable to resist an expression of genuine human feeling, thawed.

"What was it all *about?*" she asked.

"Well—" began the young man.

His pause and perplexed eyebrows skillfully suggested that the tale was too long to be told from a threshold.

"Well, come in," said Miss Phipps, still rather cross. "Sit down and tell me all. But I warn you," she added grimly, "the story had better be good."

The young man, seating himself, cleared his throat.

He's going to lie to me, reflected the experienced Miss Phipps.

"We wanted to find out if you were in. So my sister—"

"Now listen to me," said Miss Phipps kindly. "The young lady was probably not your sister, and there was no need to invent Mr. Randall Harvey in order to find out whether or not I was in."

"Well, my wife then."

"That's better. Is she really your wife, eh?"

"Yes!" shouted the young man. "What do you take me for?"

"Keep cool. Why did you invent Mr. Randall Harvey?"

"I didn't invent him," said the young man. "We landed in France together on D-Day!"

"Now, come, young man!" Miss Phipps said with some anger. "You're far too young for that. On D-Day you would be how old? Let's say, three?"

"My father and Mr. Harvey—" began the young man.

"Your father! Well, at least your chronology is improving."

"As a matter of fact—"

"That phrase usually precedes a lie, my dear boy."

"You're too clever for me, and *that's* a fact," admitted the young man, starting to rise.

"Why not tell me the truth?" suggested Miss Phipps mildly. "I am curious to know why you invented a Mr. Randall Harvey."

"I didn't invent him. He's all too real. He cheated me out of a sum of money, then said his sister would pay."

"But my name is not Harvey."

"He said you were a best-selling novelist who wrote under a pseudonym."

"Ha!"

"I saw paperbacks by you on the station bookstall."

"And so?"

"He had a northern accent and I saw a picture of a mill chimney on one of your book jackets, so it seemed a good guess you were from the north."

"Better and better."

"I have heard," faltered the young man, suddenly turning scarlet, "that you could write a check for ten thousand pounds and never feel it."

"Oh, my dear boy," said Miss Phipps sadly. "Very few people can write a check for ten thousand pounds and not feel it. Those who can are usually not aging novelists. How were you proposing to make me write this check?"

"Oh, I didn't have any such grand aspirations. I just hoped—for a little help."

"Now at last you're talking some sense."

"You sounded kind on the telephone," said the lad hopefully.

"How much do you want, and why?"

"My wife and I are actors in a touring group," began the young man. "And you see—"

"Don't tell me the manager went bankrupt and there was no salary for you?"

"Why shouldn't I tell you that?" said the young man on a note of pique.

"Because it's not *with it,* my dear boy—it's out of date. That sort of thing doesn't happen nowadays. You have a trade union, Equity, you know; you can appeal to them for help."

"Unfortunately it isn't an Equity matter. This fellow Harvey is—was—a friend of mine. He's been stealing money from people's coat pockets; somebody suspected and threatened to bring a court action if he didn't pay it all back. Of course, if he once got hauled up by the police his career would be done for—and he's quite a good actor, you know. That's the pity of it. Yes, really a very promising actor. So I lent him the money on his assurance he'd pay me back, but he didn't, and now we haven't the money to pay our hotel bill."

"Where is this hotel?"

"In Yorkshire."

"What are you doing in London, then?"

"We came last night after the show." (After the show, mused Miss Phipps, reflecting sadly on the distance from Yorkshire, the probable curtain time of the show, and the hour of the telephone call.) "To see if we could touch my wife's father. He's not a bad old boy, and the sum isn't very large. But he's away—"

"On holiday?"

"In New York on business."

"Do you know," said Miss Phipps with some solemnity, "I'm rather surprised that when you found out I was alone—for that was really the object of the Harvey ploy, wasn't it?"

"Well, y-yes."

"I thought so. I'm rather surprised," repeated Miss Phipps, "that you didn't try a spot of burglary."

"Oh, I wanted to," confessed the young man with a paradoxical air of virtue, "but Celeste was afraid you might get hurt. She's having a baby, you know."

"I'm glad Celeste has so much sense. And so you thought you'd come round this morning and try a sob story on a silly old spinster-novelist living alone."

"I don't understand you, Miss Phipps," said the young man haughtily, springing to his feet.

"By the way, what is your name?"

"Mark."

"Mark what?"

"You can't expect me to tell you that," said the young man.

"No. I don't expect so. Ah, there you are, Harrison," said Miss Phipps cheerfully, as the door opened and a large solid man in a doorman's uniform filled the gap. She now remembered with gratitude Inspector Tarrant's insistence on the installation of an emergency summoning bell from her flat to the front entrance.

"You rang, Madam?"

"Yes. Just see Mr. Mark out, will you? *Off* the premises, please."

"Is he annoying you? Shall I ring for the police, Miss Phipps?"

"No. I don't wish to prefer charges," said Miss Phipps.

With some care Mark suppressed a sigh of relief.

"You, Mark, are a confidence trickster," Miss Phipps told him. "I don't recall what the modern phrase is—con man, is it?—but I'm sure you understand what I mean. I don't believe a single word of anything you've told me. Would a five-pound note be any use to you?"

"No!" Mark burst out in a fury.

"I thought not. Your suit is too expensive. To conclude, if there is a choice for me between tricking and being tricked, I prefer to be tricked. I prefer being the lamb to the tiger."

"You can keep it. It's a silly choice."

"Not in the long run, young man. Next time things won't go so well for you. I seriously suggest that you turn to honest work."

"What sort of honest work is open to me, do you think?" cried Mark with bitter resentment.

"Why not try writing for the magazines?" suggested Miss Phipps, handing him a copy of *Ellery Queen's Mystery Magazine*. "You have a genuine gift for story-telling. But my dear Mark, you must get your details right. Verisimilitude matters, you know—"

"Thanks for the advice," said the young man sarcastically.

"And I also suggest that you get married."

Mark snorted and withdrew, clutching, Miss Phipps noted with satisfaction, the magazine.

"Q"

John Pierce

Walking Hubert Down

Much has been written about the quality of plot in fiction. Not too much has been written about the quantity of plot in fiction. How much plot should there be in a short-short of 1500 to 2500 words? How much in a short story of 5000 to 7000 words? In a novelet of 10,000 to 15,000 words? In a short novel of 35,000 words? In a novel of 50,000 words or more? Opinions will differ, of course—some readers (and critics) prefer style to substance; others like their stories fully packed.

Here is the story of the fully packed variety. And yet note how the author, the gifted John Pierce, meshing substance and style, cunningly controls his plot material, artfully releases its details until the whole truth is slowly, inexorably revealed . . .

Four of them studied Spanish in a small town in Mexico. They had dark airless rooms in the Hotel Espléndido and took classes in the mornings at the *Alianza*. Evenings they could be seen on a stone bench near the bandstand in the Plaza. There they blinked and scratched themselves and waited for the Main Event. She appeared with no regularity in any of several fine cars. She was Pamela Sykes-Coddington, the tungsten heiress, sometime film starlet and international beauty queen.

Multiple marriages had but ripened her. She wore the surname of her latest husband, a departed Englishman of means. To him they attributed her rather droll, rather touchingly pretentious British accent. Or she could have, perhaps as easily, absorbed it in drama school (she was briefly visible in a pair of Japanese late-show monster films).

She lived in the hills above the Pacific not far from Acapulco, but it was in Ecija, the village where they (on veterans' benefits) attended classes, that she was most often seen. And they—Farrow, Dewey, Sprague, and the repellent Griggs—watched intently as that lissome figure with string shopping bag made its silken rounds of the knick-knack and liquor stores. They studied her nubile locomotion and devised orgiastic dreams.

All were surprised when Masden Farrow married her. Farrow, too, was surprised. He met her in a used-book shop one morning and took her to coffee with his last 163 pesos. She Mercedes-Benzed him through the hills to her blinding white establishment above the cove where rode her white yacht. They lunched on her terrace, swam in her natural-rock pool, drank her liquor, suppered among her fireflies and drank anew, and were wedded in a simple secret four A.M. ceremony—this in less than a day.

We are in the late summer of the middle sixties. You may have read of it: misplaced love and conjugal perfidy; blood on a white carpet and the inexcusable behavior of Edward Griggs. The cleric who joined them, an unshaved retired Idahoan dredged up by her from the American colony in the pre-dawn, took generous payment and was chauffeured back down the hill.

They trudged up the marble stairs to her seaside bedroom with a fresh pail of champagne to toast the morn. Their slurred repartee calved silly laughter. They slept and woke to new champagne. On the bedside table were airplane tickets to Nassau for late tonight or the following morning—whenever, she now interjected, they had disposed of her father.

"Repeat?" said Farrow. He was fastening the belt of a yellow silk robe, the property, he assumed, of Cecil Sykes-Coddington. "Dispose of father, you said?"

"Yes, he's flying in from Schenectady this evening, dolling. I'm sure I explained."

"Did you?" Very little was clear to him.

She said, "Then listen carefully now. This is most important. For the brief while that dad is here tonight I must ask that you pose as Hubert W. Poundstone."

"Say again? Didn't get you."

She repeated the instructions.

"Who is Hubert W. Poundstone?"

"Oh, Masden," she lamented. "I *told* you all this last night."

"Told me what?"

"I told you painstakingly. I said, I thought about three weeks ago I was going to marry Hubert."

"And didn't?"

"Now, how could I have? I married you."

"Ah, yes," he said. "Go ahead."

"Everything was arranged. We were driving off to get married. We stopped off at a restaurant in Chilpancingo so I could telephone father to give him some good news for a change. Father's been awfully *miffed* at me. So I laid it on like fertilizer—how happy I was, how this was forever, how fine and steady Hubert was. 'Hubert's put it all together,' I said. And dad was happy. And when I went back to the car—*my* car, my *Bentley*—Hubert had picked up some waitress and driven off."

"Why, the skunk."

"To put it lightly. I had to hire a taxi back. *Couldn't* call home again. Couldn't *do* that to father. Result, he thinks we—Hubert and I—*are* married. He sent us that damned yacht as a wedding gift. He's flying in tonight. So tonight you're Hubert."

Cloudily Farrow recalled lingering over a portrait on the bureau before they slept. The portrait was no longer visible. "I thought that was your latest ex, Sykes-Coddington, in the picture."

"What picture? What *are* you talking about?"

"Portrait on the bureau."

"No, no, that was Hubert. I threw it away. Threw *him* away. That's all over. He's gone to Hong Kong."

"Who has?"

"*Pound*stone."

"Where is Sykes-Coddington?"

"My God, how do I know? Merrie England, I suppose."

"Do continue."

"I said it's father's periodic audit of my life, Masden. He'll look things over, satisfy himself I've at last got a decent marriage, and make provision for our needs for the year ahead."

Dawn pinked the balustrade outside the walk-in windows and touched the white hull of the yacht below. "We have needs?"

"Of course we do, dumbbell. I live off the proceeds of capital I can't touch till I'm thirty."

"And you've exhausted said yearly proceeds by July?"

"Every ruble. Don't look so obtuse. It's nothing; it's a tedious ritual dance we perform semiannually. It gives dad the most vulgar sense of power and of being loved. Nudging people around is what he understands. He wants this time to evaluate my husband; there've been some that didn't work."

Farrow's mind fought its traces. Only now, sobering, did the incongruity of this—his marriage to a nymph millionairess—present itself as a phenomenon to be analyzed.

"And I'm to be Hubert Poundstone."

"Well, if dad finds out you're not he'll be back at that Acapulco airport before I can mix him a loaded drink."

"Describe Poundstone."

"Tall, rotund, conceited, overbearing. It has nothing to do with anything. I said father's never laid eyes on Hubert, never will."

"If I must," Farrow said tepidly.

"Oh, but you definitely must. Let's face it, dolling, as Masden Farrow of the G. I. Bill at age thirty you're hardly the social or financial catch of the summer season. Go to sleep. Get yourself some cash from one of those bureau drawers when you wake up. Look through the garage for a car you like and drive down to a good store in Ecija for some decent clothes."

"What sort would Hubert wear?"

"Please don't start making things difficult, dolling. I'm getting the most awful headache. Get anything that isn't army surplus and torn tennis shoes. And do *not* rush to tell your local schoolmates about this. If the wire services get it and father reads it before getting here—well, he just won't get here."

No father, no money? Farrow pondered it and slept until noon. He rose and showered. Petty cash in large bills stuck out from the bureau drawers. He dressed and left Pamela prettily *non compos* in her bare flesh and large black eyeshades. On the terrace he received breakfast from a portly smiling servant named Pilar.

He went to the garage and selected a Tsetse-Fly GTX-400C 3.8 bearing British plates and slipped down the winding asphalt to Ecija. At a clothing shop well removed from his hotel and student haunts he picked out a small but respectable beginner's wardrobe. He gave them his own clothes to present to charity and, in maroon slacks, white sandals, aloha shirt, black glasses, and yachting cap, debouched into the bright sunlight with armfuls of wares.

He was not halfway to the Tsetse-Fly when he smelled it—the sour dreadful odor of Edward Griggs's socks. Griggs was waiting in the passenger seat for him, his wise smirk too exultant to be controlled.

Farrow threw the boxes into the jump seat. "Griggs."

Griggs showed his yellow teeth in a grin. "We were wondering if you'd forgotten your old pals."

He was shorter than Farrow, but fat and heavier. His complexion was coarse and pinkish. Horrid local toilet waters failed to compensate for his disinclination to bathe. He used a cloying, grease-based tonic on his unwashed blond hair.

"Pals?" Farrow asked.

"Share and share alike; you know our motto."

"Do I? No, I didn't know we had a 'motto.' Certainly never heard it from you." He had the keys in the ignition but Griggs made no move to disembark.

"Back to the big snow-white hacienda?" Griggs asked.

"Beat it, Griggs. Find your own girl."

Griggs chuckled. "Girl or wife?" he purred. "I know you got married to her."

Farrow felt an arctic chill. "Who said that?"

"Well, now, you didn't show up at class yesterday or at the hotel last night and I got sort of worried. I know a little friend of a housemaid who's an in-law of a gardener at Pamela's. An old technique of mine—con one of these local girls into thinking you might take them to the States, you can get anything." This last he gave gamy significance with his vulpine grin.

Farrow looked tiredly at him. All Griggs's character assessments ended on some variation of "get." "That Kepelhoff is a good guy; he'll do anything in the world for you," Griggs would say.

An armada of swirling flies announced the grand arrival of the ice-cream vendor. A wobbly wheeled burro cart supporting a gross, dirty, shaveless man hove to. When small children came running he blew his nose, wiped grimy hands on his stained trousers, and began to issue cones.

Farrow shuddered. The scene evoked the squalor of that rancid bedbug hotel from which he had by sheer miracle escaped. Everything about it, like Griggs, induced a leaden vertigo.

"Well," he said, "nice seeing you, but right now I've got to go."

"I thought you might invite me up."

"No. We just got married at dawn."

"Maybe I'd like a nice lunch too," Griggs whined. "Meet someone from the upper classes for a change. Have a few drinks and bat some ideas around."

"That sounds stimulating, but not today. I've got to go."

Griggs shook his head dolorously. "I surely would like to meet her."

"*No*, Griggs, you can't. Some other time. Right now I'm hurrying back to try," he lied, "to get her on a plane to Mexico City for the day. She has things to do there."

"On her wedding day?" He smiled.

"Do I have to throw you out of here?"

Smiling, Griggs dug a limp Fatima cigarette from his spotted plaid jacket. "I was worried about Saenz, the *hotelero*. Knowing you'd moved out, he might start handing out your stuff willy-nilly, so I put it all in my room for safekeeping."

"Find anything you needed?"

"Something fell out."

"I'll bet it did," Farrow began, but then disintegrated. Something uninvited had taken lodgment in his skull; it was his spine up there, coiled compactly as an eel.

He knew what Griggs, prowling in Farrow's luggage, had found. Among his papers was a Las Vegas wedding certificate dated six or seven years ago. In those days he had the means to drink too much. Her name was, regrettably, Mary Smith. She was a shill in a gambling club where he'd won $30. Somehow he married her. Two days later he lost her in a Los Angeles bus terminal. Never saw her or heard from her or of her again. Did not know where she came from. Could never find her for divorce purposes. Maybe she was dead. "That's been over," he said.

"Over how? She never divorced you or you her. Nobody ever had the dough to hire people to find the other one, or so you said one night."

"I said that?"

"That night you got the insurance refund and we did all that drinking."

Farrow sighed. "So all right, Griggs, what's your angle?"

"There's no angle."

"Come on, you're too dumb to be subtle. We all know you. What are you planning, to take that piece of paper up to Pamela? She'll laugh in your face."

"I doubt if the Mexican cops would. Bigamy in a Catholic country?"

"It has nothing to do with Mexico," Farrow argued inanely. "The guy was a U.S. nondenominational minister."

"Operating in Mexico."

"Okay. You, wedding certificate, cops. Is that it?"

"No, what I said was, if any of the rest of us had fallen into something good *we'd* have shared."

"The day anyone authorizes you to include yourself in their 'we'—all right, so you take it to the cops and then sit there in triumph while you count up the nothing that's left to share, is that it?" Farrow drummed the wheel in the sour smell and watched the ice-cream vendor pull away. How (abed this morning) he had rejoiced at being clear of it—lumpy bedding and perspiration and dirty toilets and Griggs. Years of nothing, then deliverance—and now Griggs again. One thing only would be worse: consignment for half a lifetime to the mud floor of a village jail.

He had roughly 3000 pesos—or $240—left from the clothing appropriation. With wife Pamela he would be on that Nassau flight tonight or tomorrow morning—beyond Griggs, beyond local jurisdiction. He gave Griggs 2000 pesos. "This is on condition you try to keep your mouth shut for a couple of days," he said. "Her father is coming down. You spread this news around and I'll guarantee you there'll be instant disinheritance problems—for her, for me, for you."

"*De acuerdo,*" quoted Griggs from their textbook.

"I'm serious about this. I'm telling you. Blow your mouth off about this and there's nothing. Zero."

"*Convenido.*" Done.

"Split some of that money with Sprague and Dewey. They haven't got a dime between them. And now I've got to go."

"No need to be huffy," Griggs said from the sidewalk. "All we expect is a modest share."

"I'll ask Dewey later how much of it you shared with them." His tires threw gravel getting away. He lacked the composure for that perilous, climbing road. The rage at the thought of Griggs in his luggage dimmed his eyesight. He drove a few blocks to a small prim bar. Inside it was quiet, cool, and mahogany. Keeping the barman awake was a lone gringo philosopher drinking dacquiris. Farrow ordered a cognac. He could not chase the stench of Griggs's socks from his sinuses. They had poisoned the air through the Hotel Espléndido.

Disconsolately he tapped his glass for a second cognac. He had everything or he had nothing, contingent on his playing ball with Edward Griggs. He should never have come down to Ecija in a $20,000 car. He should have sent for his luggage.

Three cognacs diluted his anger and he previsioned Nassau. Idly he contemplated the mirror behind the serried bottles. In that mirror the Englishman two stools from him read his considerable mail. He was small and wiry with a military mustache and receding brownish hair. He finished with his correspondence and swept it aside. He took up the local newspaper and looked it over. In the mirror he caught Farrow's vacant eyes.

"Bit of a glaze on the sea this morning," he said cheerily. "Care for a look at the paper? What's bloody Osgood doing in the bloody Grand Prix?"

Farrow had quit reading newspapers.

"Bit depressing, eh? Fishwick," he said, extending his hand. "Farrow? Yes. Knew a chap named Farrow once. Can't think where. No, erase. Friend of mine knew him. Any relatives in Algiers?"

Farrow thought not.

"Just as well. The Farrow my friend knew was a bit dotty. Claimed 'Farrow' derived from Pharaoh. Studied Egyptian land records. Instigated legal claims. Then, too, there was a Farrer, from Dorking where I once lived. Dead at the turn of the century, long before my time. Offspring? Let me think . . ."

Farrow nodded and smiled at the monologue that followed, though he did not hear the words. Griggs weighed upon him; he needed drink, not conversation. When next Fishwick departed for the door marked *Caballeros*, Farrow glanced at the mail beside him. There were ten or twelve envelopes—all addressed to Cecil Sykes-Coddington, Esq., c/o *Correspondencia General*, Acapulco, Gro., Mexico. Definitely not the man in the portrait on Pamela's bureau, but her ex-husband he was.

Farrow came off the bar in all directions. The Tsetse-Fly with British plates was visible from the window. Sykes-Coddington's car? He tipped the bartender and quickly made his exit.

He regained the automobile. *It* was his error. Better to have come to town by oxcart, or on foot. Who in town didn't know the car? It spelled Pamela.

"*Hola, Farrow!*" A woman ran toward him in her high heels. "*Ay, Farrow, me debes dos mil pesos!*"

Owe you 2000 nothing, he muttered, and shot forward with a howl of burning rubber. Clever tart. Posing as a nice girl and handing him a bill. Her name was Lucrecia. He left her shouting and waving angry arms. "*Dorty peeg!*"

They had late lunch on the terrace. They spoke perfunctory, mid-afternoon words and heard somewhere the snip of a gardener's shears. Farrow's sorties into levity did not fool her. "Badders, dolling?" she asked.

"If not bad a little spicy."
She exposed her pink tongue at the guacamole. "Tell mama."
"I sat next to a guy in a bar a while ago. He was reading his mail. The addressee on the envelopes was Cecil Sykes-Coddington."
The pink tongue froze. "*Describe* him."
This was done.
"Well, *blast* the man," she exploded. Her wine overturned on the tablecloth and Farrow's trousers. Smoldering, she watched the maid Pilar in a chiding mop-up. "Bloody, bloody," she said. "I should have known."
"Yes."
"His showing up. He keeps showing up. Showing up, showing up. When I divorced him I hadn't much cash to give him, that's why."
"I thought he was a big businessman."
"He was, till we married. My husbands all quit their jobs and take a bottle to bed." She pushed her food away in favor of the cigarette which she smoked in incisive, angry breaths. "Let's figure this dreadful nonsense out. Cecil knows I'd planned a meeting with father about this time of year. He damn well knows I never married Hubert. He'll undoubtedly be royally smashed by evening. Drunk he's impossible. No, we can't have him bumbling up here."
"Would he bumble up?"
"When he's drinking?" She gestured fatigue. "He wasn't sticky about the break-up, but he'd thrown away his source of income. I told him I'd help him along later if we could just prevent a lot of newspaper mishmash reaching father."
"Something strange is going on. He's using the name 'Fishwick.' That's how he introduced himself."
She regarded him sharply. "Don't tell me you sat there and had a *conversation* with him?"
"To answer, yes and no."
"But of course he'd have to be Fishwick. Or Turner or Goines or something equally dull. He's a jump ahead of about fifty bill collectors."
"And your problem is his showing up loaded and spoiling our domestic charade for your dad."
"My problem, *your* problem. Or even worse. He's just too unpredictable. Foul temper, bitter about money, there's just no telling."

She stood abruptly. "I've got to go find him, that's all. You didn't notice the rest of the address on those envelopes?"

"*Correspondencia General,* Acapulco. General Delivery."

"Good old Cecil. Better waiting in a general delivery line like some shipping clerk than giving people the name of an un-chic hotel. Tell me how to find this bar where you saw him."

Chicanery on a large scale, Farrow deduced, was like stomping out a grassfire in a shifting wind. There was Griggs, there was Sykes-Coddington, and there was Lucrecia, and he and Pamela hadn't been married twelve hours. With relief he watched Pamela scoot away. While she dealt with Sykes-Coddington he could run down and defer Lucrecia, the public lady. She did business from an ornate room in the Hotel De Oro, a nomenclature she celebrated with a largess of golden teeth.

It was isolated; it was deluxe; it hung grimly to a cliff above the sea. Better run down to the hotel. Better anything than have her burst in here at supper time squawling for her fee. It was a human error, a linguistic misunderstanding. The kind of thing one's (male) company might chuckle over while one showed one's vacation film slides in Duluth. Briefly Farrow had, a year ago, accompanied Lucrecia to her pleasure chamber where a vigorous night was enjoyed. Only toward dawn did it register that the basis of their amour was commercial. While Lucrecia slept he had gone out a window, fallen down a mountainside, and crawled torn and battered to a highway.

He rummaged in the money drawer. Enough was here for everybody. He sought, in the garage, a less conspicuous conveyance. He settled on a smaller machine—a Reno-Simpson 4-4-2 Demi-Hydro (Modified)—and sped briskly down the road.

He hummed a jaunty tune. Could one, he debated, under the carefree statutes of the Bahamas, locate and divorce (by long distance) someone named Mary Smith (no middle initial, no address) without it infringing on the sanctity of one's present marriage? Something like removing one's long underwear while wearing a frogman's suit, he thought. But this was an age of impossibles. Just tonight he would substitute entertainingly for a man he had never seen. Downhill he hurtled toward complication number four.

The voice was satin-suave but imperious, the words were spaced and given emphasis like breechblocks on an assembly line. *"You maid take sheets off bed in my room,"* declaimed Hubert W. Poundstone to the dapper desk clerk in the lobby of the De Oro. "I not want sheets changed. Sheets mine," pointing to himself. "U.S. sheets. *Estados Unidos* sheets, *sabe,* Pedro?"

"Yes, certainly," said the clerk, but had then to pick up the buzzing telephone. His name was not Pedro. Abiding the interruption, Poundstone, a tall porpoise-shaped man with smooth pink cheeks, let his hooded eyes drift lazily and arrogantly over the lobby and its potted plants and human baggage. He saw nothing worth the oiled turn of his head. He wore an ascot and a blue blazer with brass buttons and smelled of high-priced cologne.

Farrow, who had quickly recognized him from the bureau portrait, drew closer and leafed through travel brochures. Poundstone's was a familiar attack. He toured countries like a farm tractor through a garden. Americano, spoken slowly and loudly enough, should be understandable anywhere in the universe. Or to people of any intelligence.

"I bring own sheets when I make travel," he persisted. "Sheets mine personally. You maid put my *Estados Unidos* sheets in you laundry. I want back."

"Yes, I understand perfectly, Mr. Poundstone. Our most sincere apologies. I'll give instructions for—"

"Bonos," Poundstone acknowledged, and glided to an open elevator. Farrow stepped in behind him. He stepped out after Poundstone on the second floor. He dawdled to inspect a so-so wall painting while Poundstone strode away to unlock a door on a balcony overlooking the patio swimming pool and the Pacific. Farrow waited for the door to close and went to look at the number. Number 16.

He followed the balcony back and around its U to Number 28 where Lucrecia did business. Her window faced, across the patio, the closed door which Poundstone, back from Hong Kong—did what and why?

His conversation with Lucrecia, a not uncomely dark-eyed lady, was in Spanish. Reproduction in that tongue would be ostentatious. Bygones were bygones, she smiled glitteringly, counting the money. Would Farrow, perhaps (she was not *occupado* now), did he. . . ?

Not today, Farrow said politely. But for another category of service he was ready to settle on her an additional 2000 pesos.

She was puzzled. Then quickly she beamed and nodded agreement. Boots and whips?

No, no, Farrow explained. If she could, between now and mid-evening, defer all engagements and keep a sharp eye on the comings and goings of the señor in Room 16 across the patio, noting, for example, what visitors came and went. . . ?

In a warm bath in a blue sunken tub he prepared for Pamela's father. He dried himself and searched for the yellow silk robe, but could not find it. He was humming as he poured a glass of wine. The telephone rang. It was Pamela.

"Dolling, where *have* you been? Didn't Pilar tell you I've been calling?"

"Didn't see Pilar." He dilated his nostrils to an unpleasant odor. "She seems to be downstairs cooking something unorthodox. I've been out for a drive."

"But you know one of us has to be there when father calls. Hasn't he?"

"Not if Pilar didn't tell you."

"Double-damn. *Bad* father. Well, then listen. I've almost got Cecil cornered, the drunken sod. He's been bar-hopping down the coast. He left the place I'm in not five minutes ago."

"Where is that?"

"*Miles* from you. Toward Acapulco. And he's said to be acting very badly, so I'll have to catch him and bribe him with half the moon. I wouldn't doubt father might be en route in a rent-a-car, and I'll try to be there in a jiffy, but meanwhile you be on hand, and don't forget you're Poundstone."

"From where? Where did he grow up and go to school?"

"Just make something up, it doesn't matter."

"*De acuerdo,*" answered Farrow from the text.

He was enjoying his wine; then he wasn't. He vaulted from his lounge chair. The affront to his nostrils was not Pilar's cooking. No, he knew the sour odor. He hurried down the hall and opened doors—a bedroom, a linen closet, a study-library, then a bedroom on whose bed rested Griggs's battered suitcase. Clothes were strewn about. On the floor, moist and crusted, like objects fallen off an Art League collage, were two discarded socks.

Heavily he sat down. He rose. He continued the length of the hall and stared down at the swimming pool. The yellow robe lay over the back of a lawn chair. Beside it, on another, flabby and maggot-white, reclined Griggs with a drink in his hand. The robe meant he had been foraging about in their bedroom. And where else? Had he pocketed the Nassau air tickets? Farrow had not seen them on the bedside table.

He retraced his steps, closing the doors he had thrown open. In the study the red telephone on the desk made him think of Lucrecia. He stepped inside, closed the door, and, in the swivel chair, massaged his face while he pondered Griggs, the telephone, and the desk's scattered papers. He picked up the telephone, then put it down. He looked for a telephone book. There was unopened mail addressed to Sykes-Coddington, postmarked days and weeks ago but never forwarded. Complex legal letters choked a basket; reports of fund dividends, charity solicitations. He pulled open one drawer, then a second. He skimmed a typewritten letter and frowned. He read it through from the start. He read others, then opened other drawers.

He swiveled the leather desk chair and stared at the Pacific. He looked in the phone book and called Lucrecia who, as it happened, had some news. He thanked her, replaced the phone, and looked in the book for a second number. This was an alcoholic retiree who drank in the Ecija barrooms and inhabited the American colony. Farrow asked him if he knew a minister named Ricketts.

By the pool he had a highball and talked to Griggs.

"Oh, yes, by way of curiosity, the money I gave you this morning, did you share-and-share-alike with Dewey and Sprague according to our motto?"

"Didn't even have any for myself," Griggs confessed. "You know that little dark arcade near where the cathedral is? Four guys jumped me and took everything I had."

"Jumped you in broad daylight outside the church?" Farrow whistled softly.

"Gone before I could get up off the ground."

"Knocked you down, did they?"

Griggs stretched his arms and arched his head back. "Anyway, I didn't even have the rent money, so I figured I could stay up here until I get organized."

"Did you bring my stuff too?"

"No, I was going to but it wouldn't fit in the cab."

"Little tiny cab, eh? Taxicab twelve miles up here? I thought they cleaned you out."

"They did," Griggs said, "but I was buddies with this particular cab driver. I'd done him a favor and he drove me up free."

"What kind of favor did you do the taxi driver, Griggs?"

"It's been a long time. I don't remember exactly."

"Good man. That's the true kind of Christianity. You don't keep score. Maybe you saved him from drowning in the Pacific or took care of his hospital bills or told his family you'd take them all to the States."

Griggs turned his head in a grin. "Be as smart as you want to, old buddy," he cautioned. "Just so you remember where we stand."

"Oh, I remember, all right."

"I don't even know Pamela—yet—but I've as much claim to what's here as you have. At least I'm eligible."

"Eligible? Why, you're the John Gilbert of the western tropics. I just wish, since you don't know her, you'd quite calling her by her first name. Somehow it degrades her. And the only reason I'm grilling you, I was worried about my luggage and that wedding certificate lying around."

"It's safe, old sport. It's with a friend of mine somewhere, all enveloped and stamped and addressed to the right people in case anything should happen to me."

Farrow glanced at his watch. "Just don't let it disarrange your judgment, piggy. One dumb remark at that supper table to-night with her father sitting there and he'll—from what I hear of him—boot you off that cliff ahead of me."

"A little suspense never hurt anybody," Griggs grinned. "You know what I've just about decided? Using one of these fancy cars of hers, I could live up here and have breakfast in the morning before spinning down for classes at the *Alianza*."

"Sounds terrific, Griggs, but the house belongs to her father and he'll be coming in very soon. He's meticulous about some things. Right now I'd suggest you get up there and take a bath and shave. You smell bad. Brush your teeth. And find some clothes that don't smell."

"Was thinking of doing that." Griggs stood and put on the yel-low robe.

"You'll find your luggage in the big room down the hall. You'd thrown it in the room her father uses."

"I thought that big room was Pamela's."

"It was before she married me. We're in a bigger one at this end of the hall. To narrow your souvenir hunting, I locked the door."

He watched Griggs's departure. He finished his drink. Dusk was coming. He took a slow stroll on the grounds, passing the six-car garage and lingering along the balustrade above the waves pounding and sucking at the rocks. Beyond the yacht the orange rim of the sun disappeared. Time for dressing in the bedroom with Pamela preparatory to a splendid dinner. Time, nearly, for daddy and the Hubert Poundstone act.

In the upstairs bedroom—their bedroom—he saw the lights go on. Griggs, in the yellow bathrobe, prowled about. A bit of looting, perhaps; anything he might have overlooked before he knew the room was Farrow's.

Farrow took a bench facing the ocean. It grew dark. What a pretty little dream. Ricketts was no minister; he was a disbarred lawyer from Chicago who had fled south from his creditors and did odd jobs along this coast. Some odd job.

Pamela? Ah, yes, Pamela. Well, Pamela, not a quarter hour after his own departure from the De Oro (and a half hour before she telephoned him), had rapped on the door of Room 16 and departed *allegro con hot sauce* with the real Hubert W. Poundstone and his U.S. sheets and luggage.

Farrow threw a handful of gravel over the low wall at the sea. He thought he heard something, but did not. Then he saw the dim sweeping halos of two headlights making the road turns, coming up. He watched them grow brighter and now flicker in the vegetation. The engine came moaning and the car appeared and circled to stop at the wide front door. The headlights went off and the driver dismounted and went inside. Hard to make out that figure, but he knew who it wasn't. For eleven years, according to the correspondence upstairs, Pamela's father had been confined to a New York sanitarium. Farrow lifted his eyes to the lighted upstairs window.

Here is how that went. A figure in yellow was in the room. A second figure, dressed darkly, came into the light. There were three pistol shots. There was no one in yellow.

Farrow left the bench and crossed damp grass and caliche to the front screen door. He punched the chime and pushed open the screen as Sykes-Coddington walked leisurely down the stairs. "Did I hear shots?" Farrow asked.

"Yes, three," Sykes-Coddington said cheerily. He strained in the darkness to see his questioner. "Ah, Farrow. Good fellow. Just in time for a drink." He led the way into an adjoining room with a bar. "Know a chap named Griggs by any chance? Afraid I just killed him by mistake. Thought he was someone named Poundstone before I checked his I.D. Soda? No loss, I wouldn't guess—Griggs. Bloody sneak. Ruined my favorite silk bathrobe. Stealing money out of the bureau drawers—money scattered everywhere. Where on earth does Pam get these people?"

He handed Farrow a drink as the phone rang.

"Ah, yes, Pamela," he said into the phone. "Cecil here . . . At the airport, are you? . . . I *know* you are, dear, I hear the bloody planes . . . Won't tell me where you're going? Well, I'll find out and be along . . . Me? Nothing much. Just sitting here enjoying a drink with a very pleasant young chap named Farrow.

"Hello? Hello, Pamela . . . " He listened hard at the phone, looked at it, shook it in his hand, smiled, and put it down. "Not very complimentary. I mentioned your name and she hung up."

"I'm supposed to be dead, that's why. She recruited me to stand in for Poundstone to impress her father."

"Her *father?* Man's an invalid, bedridden. Couldn't walk three feet. Why on earth should she want *you* dead? What have you done to poor Pamela?"

"I think the idea was to get you jailed for murdering me, wasn't it?"

"Yes, she keeps trying to do that kind of thing. Hare-brained, muddling female. Do my best to keep her off balance. Led her London detectives to believe I'd fly in at eight tonight. Gave them the slip and came early, as Fishwick. Thought sure I'd surprise them. Too bad. She's gone again. Well. Another time."

"You won't give her a divorce? Is that it?"

"Not for Poundstone. Bloody fortune-hunting swine. Never have laid eyes on the man, that's the problem. No photographs extant except one she's said to carry around. I don't mind. Gives added zest. You see, Pam, on film location in the Orient, had a mad fling with him and, back home, passed him off as her half brother adrift in the East needing something to do. I put him, by mail, in our Hong Kong office. Not only embezzled me blind but cheated my best customers. Gave my whole name and operation such a black eye it's cost me a couple of million. I'm not poor. I'm interested in what oafish clog-dance she led you."

Farrow told him everything. The "cleric" Ricketts, Griggs, Lucrecia, and Poundstone were included. The Englishman laughed outrageously, slapping his leg, spilling part of his drink. "Had a go at her, did you? Don't look sheepish. Everyone does. And so you found out about Ricketts, and how your marriage was bogus, and her father wasn't coming, and she'd bolted with Poundstone, and so you offered up Griggs as a substitute Poundstone."

He laughed again. He poured fresh drinks. "Shouldn't laugh, should I? Grubby business for you. Apologize. Yes, I see their scheme now. Through her gumshoes she ascertains I'm due in, hunting for Poundstone. She picks you up and rigs the fake marriage, grooms you as Hubert's surrogate. I arrive, you mistake me for her father, say, 'Good evening, I'm Poundstone,' and I blast you through the middle and go to jail forever. Whereupon Hubert moves in up here. Too complex for Pam to have thought up. I suspect Poundstone hatched it from the shadows."

"Except Griggs got me mad enough to go into that bar where I happened to meet you. I told her about talking to you, so she could hardly go on presuming you'd mistake me for Poundstone. She eloped with the airplane tickets but must have stopped somewhere en route to collect him. I beat her to the De Oro and discovered him."

"But she still nourished the possibility I just might show up in the gloom and shoot the first chap I saw," the other said. "That I did. Fatuous Poundstone. Doesn't he realize I could have him in prison for embezzlement even if I were in jail?"

"Why haven't you?"

"I'm a sporting man," Sykes-Coddington said. "So what's for you now, Farrow? Back to bedbug, book, and candle?"

Farrow gestured limply. "What else?"

"No, I think you ought to be better compensated for your troubles. But for our accidental meeting it could be you on that floor upstairs instead of your sneak thief, Griggs. Let me think. I've never seen Poundstone. You have. Might have a job for you if you're interested. And I'd pay well."

Where the Buunjak feeds its crocodiles to the Niastomiz; where the giant nasturtiums and orange trumpet flowers strive among the lilishwa bushes beneath the creeper-choked branches of the cedar and wattle and gibbet tree; where night excites the lion's roar and cry of hyrax and hyena, the bark of African cricket and scream of parrot, the chatter of the colobus monkey, shrill of spurfowl, croak of frog, and ting-tang of the bell bird—where these sights, sounds, rot odors, and cloudbursts interlace, Farrow, in the bar of the New Day Hotel, had a drink. The drink was pink gin.

Rain pounded the iron roof and gurgled on the sodden ground outside. He listened and his right eyebrow twitched. He sought to make sense of the past year's disorder: there were planes and ships and dugouts on the Amazon; mosquito netting and customs sheds and snowmobiles across Greenland; skin rashes, quinine pills, berserk elephants, Land Rovers bogged down in malarious swamps, and six thousand games of gin rummy. What had he started out to do?

The door opened and Sykes-Coddington bent in from the downpour. He shook out his drenched mackintosh and stamped his gumboots on the bare wood floor. He had been off at a telephone somewhere. "*Uwee? Uwee!* Ever hear that? Kikuyu war cry." He joined Farrow and signaled the native barman.

"Onto something," he said. "Couple passed through Kimogu on the run. Man fits Poundstone's description. Pamela they were certain of. For the last fourteen months, twice a night, her first film has been the only one available to their cinema. Whole town's seen it eight-hundred-and-fifty-odd times. *Lizard Man Meets the Purple Fungus*. Love it. Love Pamela. Swarmed around her, cooked up some *posho* and caterpillar; drums and dances. She chartered an aircraft near there. Connecting flight north out of Ubendi. Ever seen Sweden?"

Farrow's eye twitched. He never had.

"That's where they're headed. We'll catch up with them in Stockholm."

"We never seem to get any closer," Farrow said.

"Thought you knew by now, old boy," the Englishman said. "Don't think I really want to catch them until they're ready for it. Killed that one blighter—Griggs. One's enough. No, I've decided to just walk them down."

"Walk them down?"

Cecil Sykes-Coddington lifted his gin. "Always amazes me how little Americans know about their own country. Never heard of how they used to catch the wild mustang? Nuisance animals, really, not good for much. Led good horses astray. Not very intelligent. Stuck to their own small preserve of twenty or thirty square miles, wouldn't leave it. So relays of horsemen simply followed them in circles at a steady, unending walk, walking twenty-four hours a day, giving the poor beasts no rest until they pulled up from sheer exhaustion. Then it was easy."

"Walking Hubert down," Farrow said. "Are we getting a relay?"

"Don't need any. We have trains and planes and telephones and ample money. Imagine Pam and Poundstone dashing through airports, creeping down alleys, hiding in doorways, slipping incognito into backstreet hotels like your Espléndido, and never getting a decent night's sleep without snapping awake a dozen times a night to what they think is my footstep in the hall. Drive them wacky."

"So," proposed Farrow. "We walk them down, we exhaust them. They're sick, underweight, dirty, half deranged, and by then they hate each other's guts. What then?"

"Ah, what then?" Cecil Sykes-Coddington smiled.

J. J. Marric (John Creasey)

Gideon and the Innocent Shoplifter

About Commander George Gideon, Chief of the C.I.D. (the Criminal Investigation Department at New Scotland Yard)... There are times when Gideon is deeply troubled about his job, times when he stops being a policeman and lets his emotions get the better of his reason. (Who would want it any other way?)...

Detective: COMMANDER GEORGE GIDEON

It was bad enough when the Metropolitan Police had to deal with criminals born and bred in the British Isles, and there were plenty of them. It was worse when a foreigner—an "alien" in the official terminology—was the suspect. It was worse still, in the opinion of George Gideon, the Commander of the Criminal Investigation Department at New Scotland Yard, when this foreigner was a young American.

Gideon seldom gave personal attention to petty larceny, unless there was something very special about it, and shoplifting normally became his worry only when it reached major proportions. But an American teenager under suspicion of shoplifting was a different matter.

And so Gideon sent for the boy, now in custody at Cannon Row, the police station across the narrow road from Scotland Yard. At first sight Gideon was troubled. This was little more than a boy, small, fragile-looking, pale. Standing opposite Gideon, and completely dwarfed by him, Morris K. Barnes from Chicago looked like a Lilliputian confronting Gulliver.

Nevertheless, appearances could be deceptive, Gideon reminded himself. This might well be a hard, tough, professional criminal; in Chicago, as in nearly every large city in the world, they trained criminals young. He must not be swayed by the youth and apparent innocence of the lad now facing him.

"Your name is Morris K. Barnes?"

"Yes, sir."

"You came from Chicago to London by air last month?"

"That's right."

"You have a work permit for this country, and you said that you had a job at Hooper's, a department store, but this is not true."

"No, sir, it isn't true."

"Why did you lie?"

"I believed I could find a job when I came to England—but to get this job I had to have a permit, and to obtain the permit I had to have a job."

"Have you tried to find work since you've been in England?"

"Yes, sir."

"What kind of work?"

"Every kind, sir, from soda jerk to bellboy, but no one is interested in someone who only wants to stay for a few weeks."

"Can you give me any proof that you've applied for these jobs?"

"Yes, sir, I can show you letters received from employers who decided not to hire me."

"Why did you want to come to this country in the first place?"

"My grandparents came from London, and I always wanted to spend a summer in England. I'm still in high school, but I saved the money for my passage from a newspaper route."

"Have you ever been accused of any crime before?"

"No, sir, I have not."

"How much money did you have when you were arrested and charged with stealing goods from the chemist's shop?"

For the first time Morris K. Barnes looked puzzled.

"What's that, sir?"

"The chemist's shop. What you call a drug store."

The pale face cleared. "I had what you call a sixpence and some coppers," young Barnes said respectfully.

"Where were you planning to sleep tonight?"

"In one of your parks, I guess."

"Have you slept out before?"

"Yes, sir, most nights since I've been in England. After my first week here I realized that all the money I'd brought with me was going on hotel bills. And I couldn't earn any more because I couldn't get a job."

"How much money did you bring with you?"

"Twenty-five dollars."

"Often been hungry?" demanded Gideon, almost angrily; but his heart was growing heavier within him, and the severity of his manner became harder to maintain.

"Yes, sir, I've been very hungry plenty of times."

"You had nowhere to sleep, you had no money, you were hungry, you had lied about your work permit and doubted if you could get a job. Is that the picture?"

"Yes, sir, that's right," the youth admitted slowly.

"So you went into the chem—the drug store and stole some cosmetics, hoping to sell them and get some food, at least."

The young American did not reply immediately. He drew himself up to his full height, and pride was like a cloak about him. He looked Gideon straight in the eyes, and said, "No, sir, I did not steal."

"You went into this drug store. You took certain articles from the counter. The manager asked you for payment and you admitted that you could not pay. So the manager sent for a policeman."

"That is true, sir."

"Why did you take the goods from the counter?"

The pale cheeks were touched with pink, but the steady gaze did not falter.

"I had an idea, sir. Oh, I know it sounds crazy now, but then—well, I was so desperate I just didn't stop to work it all out. I thought that if the manager would let me try to sell some of the goods in the street—there were lots of people outside, but none of them came into the shop—I might earn a commission. I didn't know you had to have a permit—*another* permit"—the boy's lips curved in a wry smile—"to do this. Oh, yes, sir, I see now that the whole thing was impossible—even if I'd *had* the permit, how was he to know I wouldn't just walk off with the stuff and not come back? But *I* knew I'd come back, and somehow—well, I just thought *he* would know it, too.

"I *was* taking the stuff to the manager, sir, I really was. I thought if I actually had the things in my hand he couldn't refuse to let me try, especially as he had no customers. I told him this, sir, but he wouldn't believe me. He thought I was stealing them."

"I'm not sure I blame him," said Gideon dryly. "What did he say to you?"

"He said I was a bloody lying Yank, sir."

"And what did you do then?"

"I hit him, sir."

"I understand you have a powerful punch," Gideon remarked.

"I box featherweight, sir. I'm the high school champion. I'm sorry I hit the man. I really am."

"He is not proceeding with a charge of assault, only with a charge of shoplifting," Gideon said. "Did you tell anyone else about your idea?"

"No, sir. It came to me suddenly. There was a bar next door to the drug store and I thought if I could only make enough commission for one meal, maybe my luck would change."

Gideon contemplated the boy for what seemed a long time. The young American moistened his lips and Gideon thought he was fighting back tears.

"Do you like London?" Gideon asked abruptly.

The boy's expression changed.

"Yes, sir. I—yes, *sir!* I think London's a wonderful city. Every day I visit someplace I haven't seen before." His eyes were bright with enthusiasm. "I've been to all the places I've read about, like the Tower of London and the National Gallery and the Monument and the markets and—oh, almost everywhere, sir. I certainly like London. In one way I was glad I couldn't get work, because I had plenty of time to visit these places."

"Which did you like most?" asked Gideon.

The youth did not answer at first, but his eyes clouded; a question intended to lighten the mood had in fact brought tension. Gideon, by now more than half convinced of the boy's honesty, concentrated on this change of expression.

Slowly and deliberately Barnes answered.

"I guess it was the day I spent at the Old Bailey. I had heard a lot about British justice, and I certainly saw it in action."

His answer could be cleverly calculated; or it could be genuine. Was there any way in which Gideon could make absolutely sure whether or not Barnes spoke the truth? After a long pause he put a very different question, wondering as he did so at his concern to establish the boy's innocence; it was almost as if he were dealing with the future of his own son.

"If you stood trial by jury, and the evidence given was exactly what you've told me, what verdict would you expect?"

The answer came almost at once.

"Guilty, I guess."

"So you know your story doesn't sound convincing?"

Another pause, and the boy answered, "I know that very few people will believe me, sir." He stopped abruptly, as if checking himself from going on, and Gideon waited. Now the expressive face showed a certain diffidence. "May I ask you a question, sir?"

"Yes."

"Do *you* believe me?" demanded Morris K. Barnes.

I should have expected it, thought Gideon, deeply troubled. I've stopped being a policeman, I've let my emotions get the better of my reason. He did not answer, still cudgeling his brain for a way to make absolutely sure of the boy's honesty. But he could see none. He could, however, see the disappointment which began to affect the other, and could imagine the despair which had begun to creep over him. Still silent, Gideon faced the fact that, demanding the truth from this boy, he himself had now to give an answer which must be true.

At last he spoke. "Before I tell you what I think you must understand this. My opinion doesn't affect the law. The law is served by evidence, not by opinions. Is that clear?"

"Yes, sir."

"Very well. I do believe you."

After the first shock of surprise, happiness shone from the dark eyes, but Gideon was still troubled. He might believe that the boy's story was true. But would a magistrate believe it?

"Thank you," said Morris K. Barnes.

"You still have to satisfy the magistrate," Gideon reminded him. "And I can't prove, and you can't prove, what was really in your mind when you took those things from the counter." He frowned. This was a charge brought by the company concerned; there was no way in which the police would now drop it, no way in which they could try to persuade the company to drop it. Yet much of what the lad had said *could* be proved, if he, Gideon, was prepared to take a little extra trouble.

Gideon's sense of responsibility toward this boy suddenly seemed very great indeed.

He stood up, walked slowly round the heavy desk, and placed a hand on the boy's shoulder. "I want you to plead not guilty when you are charged, and I shall arrange for someone to ask you some of the questions I have asked you today. I'll have your answers checked, so they had better be the same ones you've given me. Then you'll have to hope for the best from British justice."

"The answers are true, sir," Morris K. Barnes said, "so they will be the same."

That evening Gideon was totally unable to dismiss the boy from his mind, and the next morning found him sitting in court listening intently to questions and answers. Each reply given by the young American was the identical one he had given Gideon the previous day; each emotion throbbing in his voice, passing over his face, was the same emotion he had shown before.

And the impression he made on the court was the same impression he had made on Gideon.

The solicitor for the complainants conferred in whispers with the gray-haired shop manager. The elderly magistrate frowned, as Gideon had frowned, obviously of two minds.

"Is anything known about the accused?" the magistrate asked sharply.

A police officer stood up.

"We have made certain inquiries, sir, and the accused's statements on all matters which can be proved have been verified up to the moment when he stepped inside the shop. That is all, sir."

There was a short pause Then the solicitor for the complainants stood up, looked about him, stared at the pale-faced American boy in the dock, and said, "With your permission, your worship, my clients would like to withdraw the charge. They feel there is sufficient doubt, in view of all that has been said, as to whether the accused *did* intend to steal. Moreover, they would be glad to take Mr. Barnes into their employ while he remains in London, your worship."

It was one of the few occasions on which Gideon had seen that particular magistrate smile.

"A very sensible decision," the magistrate said. "I hope you enjoy the rest of your stay with us, young man."

But the young man did not seem to hear him; he was looking at Gideon.

"Q"

Lillian de la Torre

The Lost Heir

(as told by James Boswell, London & Kent, 1772-1773)

If you are meeting Dr. Sam: Johnson, the great Eighteenth Century criminologist, for the first time, we envy you a rare reading experience. In his MORTAL CONSEQUENCES, *Julian Symons wrote: "The detective stories about Johnson and Boswell . . . are perhaps the most successful pastiches in detective fiction . . . Miss de la Torre caught most happily the tone and weight of Johnson's conversation . . ."*

In this newest investigation of "crime and chicane" the plot does not derive from any famous Eighteenth Century case—neither the Annesley (1743) nor the Douglas (1769). "If coming events cast their shadows before," the author tells us, "this story may suggest, here and there, the mystery of the Tichborne claimant a century later . . . you may even discern a plausible explanation of the inexplicable features of that puzzling case. In certain fictitious elements, of course, including the outcome, it has nothing to do with Tichborne" . . .

Detective: DR. SAM: JOHNSON

"I implore you, Dr. Johnson, help a grieving mother to find her lost son!"

Thus impulsively spoke Paulette, Lady Claybourne, as she crossed the threshold at Johnson's Court. We saw a delicate small personage, past youth indeed, but slim and erect in the most elegant of costly widow's weeds. Her face was a clear oval, cream tinged with pink, and her large dark eyes looked upon us imploringly under smooth translucent lids. In Dr. Johnson's plain old-fashioned sitting room, she looked like a white butterfly momentarily hovering over the gnarled bole of an oak tree.

Dr. Sam: Johnson, *detector* of crime and chicane, and friend to the distrest, bowed over the small white hand. Then in his sixty-third year, tall and burly, aukward and uncouth, he yet valued himself upon his complaisance to the ladies. His large but shapely fingers engulfed the dainty digits of our guest as he led her to an armed chair, the while replying:

"'Twere duty, no less. But first, ma'am (seating her), you must tell me how you came to lose the child. Pray attend, Mr. Boswell, I shall value your opinion. Ma'am, I present Mr. Boswell, advocate, of Edinburgh in Scotland, my young friend and favourite companion."

Smiling with pleasure to hear myself thus described, I bowed low. The lady inclined slightly, and began her story:

"My son, Sir Richard Claybourne, is no child. He is in his twenty-seventh year, if—if he is in life. His father, Sir Hubert Claybourne, of Claybourne Hall in Kent, left me inconsolable ten years ago, and our only son, Richard, then sixteen, acceded to the title and estate.

"Well, sir, 'tis a common story. Tho' we had been close before, once he came into his estate, I could not controul him. Claybourne Hall saw him but seldom, for he preferred raking in London, running from the gaming tables to—to places more infamous yet.

"Then, as he approached his majority," the soft voice went on, "Richard fell deeply in love, and proposed to marry. 'Twas against my wishes, for tho' the young lady's fortune was ample, she was brought up in a household where I, alas, have no friends. But being neighbours, Cynthia Wentworth drew Richard home to Kent, and at Claybourne, on a day in spring, they were wedded and bedded.

"Alas the day! That very night, Richard burst into my chamber, where I lay alone waking and fretting. He was dishevelled and wild, and, Damn the bitch, says he (pardon me, gentlemen), she has broken my heart, I shall leave England this night. I'll go for a soldier, and never return while she lives. Nothing I said could disswade him. Take care of Claybourne estate, cried he to me, and was gone."

The low voice faltered, and went on:

"With the help of Mr. Matthew Rollis, my trusted solicitor, I kept up the estate. Cynthia Wentworth, mute and grim, went back to her foster folk at Rendle. No word came from Richard; but enquiring of returning soldiers, once or twice I heard a rumor of him in the New World, at New-York, at Jamaica. Since then, nothing. Six years have now passed. I can bear it no longer. I must find my boy."

Dr. Johnson looked grave.

"'Tis long for a voluntary absence. Who is the next heir? Who had an interest to prevent Sir Richard's return?"

"Good lack, Dr. Johnson, you do not think—?"

"I do not think. I ask meerly."

"You alarm me, sir. The next heir is Jeremy Claybourne, a lad now rising twenty. He springs from the Claybournes of Rendle, a family I have long lived at enmity with. His father, my husband's late brother Hector—well, I say nothing of him; he was kind to me while he lived. But his wife was a venomous vixen, and never spared to vilify me. In that house Cynthia was brought up and her mind poisoned against me. On them I blame the whole affair.

"Indeed it is pressure from that quarter that drives me to action. The lawyers will have Richard declared dead, and his cousin Jeremy put in possession. On that day they will turn me out into the world without a friend. He must come home and protect me."

"Then we must find him. You say your son departed on his wedding night. How did he depart?"

"I know not how, sir, but Claybourne estate is on the coast; I have thought he went by sea, perhaps in some smuggler's vessel."

"A course full of peril," commented my friend, who considered that being in a ship was like being in gaol, with the likelihood of being drowned. "Alas, madam, what assures you that he is still in life?"

"A mother's heart! I *know* that, somewhere, he is alive!"

"Then we must appeal to him to shew himself, wherever he may be. Bozzy, your tablets. By your leave, ma'am, we'll address him thus in all the papers (dictating):

> "SIR RICHARD CLAYBOURNE went from his Friends in the year '66, & left his Mother bereft & his Affairs in disorder. Whosoever makes known his whereabouts shall be amply rewarded, & he himself is implored to return to the Bosom of his grieving Mother.
>
> Claybourne Hall in Kent
> April ye 10th, 1772"

"There, madam, let this simple screed be disseminated, especially in the seaports of the New World, where he was last heard of; and my life upon it, if he be alive, Sir Richard will give over his sulks and return to his duties."

"I pray it may be so," murmured my Lady.

Dr. Johnson looked after the crested coach as it left the court, and shook his head.

"Let us all pray, for her sake, it may be so."

Time passed. I returned to Edinburgh, and quite forgot the problem of the missing Sir Richard Claybourne and his whereabouts; until once more, in the spring of 1773, I visited London.

I was sitting comfortably with my learned friend in his house in Johnson's Court, when a billet was handed in. Dr. Johnson put up his well-shaped brows as he read it, and passed it to me.

> "By the grace of Heaven, Sir Richard Claybourne is found! Come at once to the Cross Keys.
>
> P. Claybourne
>
> at the Cross Keys,
> Wednesday, 10 of ye clock"

"I suppose we must go," said Dr. Johnson.

Wild horses would not have kept me away. We found Lady Claybourne in the wainscotted room abovestairs at the Cross Keys, sitting by the fire in a state of agitation. By her side, in silent concern, stood a grave, smooth-faced person in a decent grey coat. He proved to be Mr. Rollis, the manager of the Claybourne estate.

My Lady started up at our advent.

"O bless you, Dr. Johnson, your screed has brought my Richard home to me!"

"Is he here?"

"Not yet. He is but now come into port, and gives me the rendezvous here."

"That is so," murmured Mr. Rollis in a low caressing voice, seating her gently.

"Then, my Lady, how are you sure it is he?" asked Dr. Johnson gravely.

"Old Bogie says so."

"And who is old Bogie?"

"My son's bodyservant from his childhood. To this trusted retainer I gave the task of disseminating your screed in the New World. You understand, Dr. Johnson, I am of French extraction, and come from the island of Hispaniola, where I still possess estates. There Bogie was born and bred, and there, his task done, he was instructed to await developments."

"And there he found Richard?"

"Sir, strolling in the gardens at Port au Prince, by chance he comes face to face with Richard. What, 'tis Bogie! cries Richard. Master Dickie! cries Bogie, and they embrace. In letters sent before, they describe this affecting scene."

"Indeed, my lady, so they do," asseverated Rollis.

What more these letters imported was not revealed, for just then there was a knock at the door, and two men appeared on the threshold. One of them, a little old Negro with such a face as might have been carven on a walnut shell, was but a shadow behind the shoulder of the other. On this one all eyes fixed.

We saw a tall young man, dark tanned and very thin. His swarthy face, tho' gaunt and worn, yet strikingly resembled my Lady's about the eyes, which were brilliant and dark, with smooth deep lids under arching brows. He smiled her very smile, his delicately cut mouth, so like hers, flashing white teeth. His own dark hair was gathered back with a thong. His right sleeve hung empty.

The length of a heartbeat the room was poised in silence. Then my Lady rose slowly to her feet.

"'Tis Richard," she whispered.

"Aye, 'tis Richard," murmured Rollis.

"'Tis Richard: but O Heaven, how changed!"

In an instant the tall young man went to her, and she gathered him to her bosom. Let us draw the veil over a mother's transports.

After these sacred moments, Richard made known to us his story.

"I went from England," he said, "resolved never to return. But I soon tired of the soldier's restless life, and I resolved to seek some idyllic shade, far from the haunts of man, and there forget the past. From Jamaica I made my way to Hispaniola. With forged letters and a false name I obtained employment from our own factor on our own plantation. There all went on to a wish, marred only when in the late earthquake I was pinned by a fallen linten, which paralyzed my right arm (touching the empty sleeve). Alas, Mother, I have brought you back the half of a man."

"Not so!" cried my Lady stoutly. "The arm is there. (So it was, close-clipped to his side within his fustian coat.) We'll have the best surgeons to it, and it shall mend!"

"Meanwhile," he smiled, "you shall see how my left hand

serves."

To proof, he took her white fingers in his brown ones, and kissed them the while my Lady melted in smiles.

"Tho' 'twas my intent never to return," he went on, "your eloquent appeal, making its way to me, moved my heart towards England."

"The thanks be yours, Dr. Johnson," uttered my Lady.

"Aye, our thanks to you," seconded Rollis.

"And so I came down to Port au Prince, with intent to take ship, and there at the dock I met with dear Bogie—"

The black man bowed, and wiped a tear with the heel of a dusky pink palm.

"—and here I am!"

"There will be rejoicing at Claybourne," smiled my Lady. "You must be present, Dr. Johnson, Mr. Boswell."

Assenting, we parted with a promise to visit the Hall for the coming festivities of the Claybourne Dole on St. George's Day.

'Twas April, with spring in the air. We proceeded forthwith into Kent, tho' not to Claybourne Hall. Dr. Johnson had a mind first to visit friends at Kentish Old Priory, hard by.

Our welcome at the Priory, and our diversions thereat, form no part of this tale, except insofar as diversion was afforded at every social gathering by speculation upon the romantic recrudescence of Sir Richard Claybourne. Those who had caught a glimpse of him importantly expatiated on his resemblance to his lady mother. Some even saw in him a look of his late father, Sir Hubert. Others again thought he resembled nobody, and suspected my Lady had been bamboozled by an impostor. She was just asking to be bamboozled, added certain cynics; while the sentimental joyed to share the bliss of a mother's heart.

As to myself, being a lawyer I took it upon me to expatiate in all companies on the great principle of filiation, by which the romantick Douglas Cause had been newly won; that, in brief, if a mother declared *This is my son*, it is so.

Heedless, the young ladies would twitter the while over the folk at Rendle. How were they taking it? How would Cynthia receive the return of her long-lost bridegroom? What would Jeremy say, now that his cousin had returned to cut him out?

As the group around the tea table was enjoyably speculating thus, one afternoon, a servant announced:

"Lady Claybourne. Mr. Claybourne."

At the names silence fell, and every head turned. Into the silence stepped a blonde girl in sea-green tissue, snug at her slender waist, and draping softly over a swaying hoop. Her sunny hair was lightly piled up à la Pompadour. There was pride in her carriage, and reserve in her level blue gaze and faint smile.

Attending her, nay, hovering over her, came a broad-shouldered youth in mulberry, whose carelessly ribbanded tawny hair, square jaw, and challenging hazel eye delineated a very John Bull in the making.

Thus I encountered at last Cynthia, Lady Claybourne, whom Richard had loved and left, and Jeremy Claybourne, his cousin and heir.

Constraint fell on the tea table. After a few observes on the weather (very fair for April), the company dispersed. The Claybournes lingered, having come of purpose to bespeak Dr. Johnson's advice in the matter of the claimant at Claybourne Hall.

"They say you have met this person," said Cynthia. "I have not. Tell me, is he Richard indeed?"

"Of course he is not!" uttered Jeremy angrily.

"The great principle of filiation—" I began.

"As you say, Mr. Boswell: the mother avers it is her son. Moreover," added Dr. Johnson, "the man of business says it is Richard; and the old-time servant asserts it is Richard."

"My Lady's too tender heart is set on the fellow," growled Jeremy, "and everybody knows Rollis and Bogie will never gainsay her. She has them under her spell with her coaxing ways: as she has everybody. Only my mother saw thro' her. Cupidity, adultery, bastardy—in such terms my mother spoke of her."

"Enough, Jeremy," said Cynthia quickly, "your mother ever spoke more than she knew about her sister Claybourne."

"Never defend Lady Claybourne," muttered Jeremy, "for she is no friend to you."

"Yet Richard loved me," said the girl. "Can he be Richard, and never come near me?"

"Yet, my dear—if he left you in anger?" murmured Dr. Johnson.

"That is between me and Richard," said Cynthia stiffly.

"Then there's no more to be said."

"Oh, but there is," countered Cynthia quickly. "I'll not see

Jeremy dispossessed by a pretender. Pray, Dr. Johnson, will you not scrutinize this fellow, and detect whether he be Richard indeed, or an impostor?"

"Why, if he be an impostor, 'tis my hand in the business has raised him up," observed Dr. Johnson. "I'll scan him narrowly, you may be sure. But why do you not confront him yourself?"

"The door is closed against me."

"We'll confront him at the Dole," said Jeremy grimly.

"What is this Claybourne Dole we hear so much about?" I enquired curiously.

"Sir," replied Cynthia, " 'tis a whimsy from the Dark Ages, of a death-bed vow to relieve the poor forever, and a death-bed curse, that if 'tis neglected, the Claybourne line shall fail. For six years past Jeremy, as the heir, has upheld the custom; and all Claybournes, even I, must play their part on St. George's Day."

"Which is this day week," remarked Dr. Johnson. "Well, well, I'll note Sir Richard's proceedings in the meantime."

Next day, according to our invitation at the Cross Keys, we became guests at Claybourne Hall. We found the Hall to be a stately Palladian mansion, with classical pilasters and myriad sashwindows taking the light. Here the dowager Lady Claybourne reigned in splendour, and now that her Richard was beside her, all was love and abundance.

Richard indeed moved as one waking out of a dream, from the formal garden to the bluffs above the sea, from the great hall to the portrait gallery. As he stared at the likenesses of his ancestors in the latter, we were enabled to stare at him, as a youth on canvas, as a man in the flesh. As my Lady had said, how changed!

The youthful face in the portrait was smooth and high-coloured. The face of flesh was now thin and sallow. But in both countenances, the fresh and the worn, the look of my Lady was apparent in the large thin-lidded eyes and the curve of lip. In the portrait, young Richard rested his left hand on the hilt of his sword, and held in his right the bridle of his favourite horse.

"Gallant Soldier, remember, Mother?" murmured Richard. "He bade fair to be the fastest horse in the county."

"He is so still. You shall ride him yet, my son, when the arm mends."

Following her glance, I perceived that the useless arm had been coaxed into its sleeve, and saw in the hand the ball of crimson wool whereby, with continual kneading and plying, the atrophied muscles were to be, by little and little, restored to use. The slack fingers with an effort tightened about the crimson wool and loosed it again, tightened and loosed.

"I'll ride Gallant Soldier yet," vowed Sir Richard.

Meanwhile, the swift steed was Richard's delight and wherever he went, out of doors in the fresh April weather, horse and groom were sure to be near him.

The out of doors was Richard's element. The old gamekeeper rejoiced to have him back, and marvelled at his undiminished skill, tho' with the left hand, at angling and fencing and shooting with the pistol; tho' the sporting gun was no longer within his power.

Indoors, other times, the restored Sir Richard would be busied with Mr. Rollis, turning over old deeds or signing new ones, as to the manor born. Mr. Rollis exclaimed in wonder, that the new signature, tho' left-handed, so closely resembled the old.

In certain respects, methought, the long sojourn in the wilds shewed its effects. The skin was leather-tanned by the furnace of the West Indies. The voice was harsh, and so far from smacking of his upbringing in Kent, the manner of speech had a twang that spoke of the years in Hispaniola.

At table, also, the heir's manners, to my way of thinking, left something to be desired. But what can a man do who must feed himself with one hand? Old Bogie hovered ever at his shoulder, ready to cut his meat; while at his knee, rolling adoring eyes, sat Richard's old dog, a cross fat rug of a thing named Gypsy. I noticed she got more than her share of titbits.

Only once during that week was the name of Cynthia mentioned, when Dr. Johnson took opportunity to say:

"Sir, will you not see your wife?"

Richard shook his head.

"Not yet. Do not ask it. Let me mend first."

"Cynthia's suspense must be painful," observed Dr. Johnson.

Wherever Richard was, my Lady was sure to be close at hand. Now she came between to say coldly:

"Cynthia has Jeremy to console her. Let her alone."

Richard turned away in silence.

St. George's Day, April 23, 1773, dawned fair. Claybourne Hall hummed and was redolent with final preparations. At the farther edge of the south meadow they were roasting whole oxen, and putting up long tables on trestles to set forth the viands to come. At the near end a platform under a red and white striped canopy offered shelter against sun or shower, whatever April weather might ensue.

At the Hall as morning advanced, Lady Claybourne bustled about; but Richard did not appear. Soon he would face his first meeting with the world. How would he be received?

At mid-morning, we all attended Sir Richard's levee in the old-fashioned way. A rainbow of splendid garments had been kept furbished for him from his raking days. For this great occasion, he chose a suit of cream brocaded and laced with gold, in which he looked like a bridegroom. A modish new wig with high powdered fore-top well became his flashing dark eyes and haggard face. In this he shewed his only trace of foppery, the outmoded hats and wigs of past days having been condemned *en masse*, and new ones bespoke from London.

My Lady, too, was adorned most like a bride, for she had given over her mourning weeds upon Richard's return, and now wore silver tissue edged with bullion lace. As to me, I had donned my bloom-coloured coat, while Dr. Johnson was satisfied to be decent in chestnut broadcloth.

On the stroke of noon we issued forth to greet the quality and commonalty already gathering to honour the day. Richard vibrated like a wire; my Lady, glowing with joy, never left his side. Thus, strolling in the meadow, we exchanged bows with the neighbouring squires, and nodded condescendingly to the assembling tenantry. Sometimes Richard uttered a name; sometimes he only made a leg, bowed and smiled. His eyes shewed the strain he was under.

As we strolled, suddenly my Lady took in a sibilant breath, and gripped her son's fingers. Two persons stood in our way. Richard uttered one word: "Cynthia!"

Her hand on Jeremy's, the girl stood and eyed the speaker, utterly still. At last she spoke:

"Who are you?"

"I am Sir Richard Claybourne, your humble servant, and your husband that was."

She searched him deep, the sallow face, the dark eyes, the useless arm.

"Make me believe it," she said. "Answer me but three questions."

"Not now," snapped Lady Claybourne. "The Dole begins."

"I think you must, Sir Richard," said Dr. Johnson gently.

"Very well, sir. But think well, Cynthia, you may not like the answers."

"If true, I shall like them very well. One: when we began our loves (the clear skin rosied), what was my name for you?"

"Dickon," said the claimant instantly.

"No, 'Rich,' you are wrong. Now say: where was our secret post office?"

"In a hollow tree."

"That is true. Which one?"

"Ah, that I have forgotten."

"Never mind. Why did you leave me as you did?"

"You know why."

"I know why. Do you?"

"I beg you, Cynthia, spare me saying it."

"I do not fear to hear it."

Eyes downcast, Richard uttered low: "You force me to say it. Because I found you to be used goods."

Jeremy doubled his fists and aimed a blow, which Richard swiftly fended with his own.

"Stand back, Jeremy," said Cynthia coolly: "he knows he lies."

Jeremy, muttering, dropped his arms, and the claimant followed suit, as the dowager cried:

"Of course the little trollop must deny it. Enough of this farce!"

"Answer me but this, if you be Richard," pursued Cynthia steadily, "what did you say in your farewell note?"

"An unworthy trick, Cynthia, I left you no farewell note."

"Shall I shew it you?"

"I forbid it!" cried the dowager angrily. " 'Tis clear Cynthia will tell any lie, pass any forgery, to do away with you and get the estate for Jeremy. Come, begin the Dole!"

She swept Richard away. At her gesture, he mounted the platform and spoke:

"My people—my dear friends, companions of my youth! Richard is returned, and we shall have better days at Claybourne Hall. I am too moved to say more."

A silence. Would they reject him? Then the cheer burst forth: *Huzza!* It was Mr. Rollis who gave the triple "Hip hip!"

Bowing, the master of Claybourne reached his hand to his lady mother, and descended to the level. Old Bogie with a basket of loaves and Mr. Rollis with a purse of crown pieces fell in on either side. Jeremy and Cynthia, stiff-backed, followed; and we, Sir Richard's guests, brought up the rear.

Drawn up before the dais, shepherded by friends and relations in gala array, stood two dozen hand-picked and hand-scrubbed antients of days. Clean smocks cloathed the toothless gaffers, and snowy aprons adorned the silver-haired gammers. The Dole began: to each, a gracious word from Sir Richard, a crown piece from Rollis's purse, and a fat brown loaf from Bogie's basket.

The entourage had gone part way down the line, when a boy with a billet pushed through the crowd and handed the folded paper to Sir Richard. The latter snapped it open, read, and scowled. Then he shrugged, threw down the crumpled paper (which in the interest of neatness I retrieved and pocketed for future destruction) and stepped forward to the next curtseying old crone.

There was still bread in the basket and silver in the purse when again a newcomer pushed his way importantly through the crowd. I recognized the burly fellow with his staff and his writ. 'Twas the parish constable, come as I supposed to bear his part in the drama of the Claybourne Dole. At sight of him, Richard stopped stock-still. Then he bowed abruptly, and strode swiftly away. We saw him reach the edge of the meadow, where as usual the favourite steed, Gallant Soldier, saddled and bridled, stood with his groom. The Dole party stood and gaped as Richard leaped to the saddle, slapped the reins two-handed, and tore off at a gallop.

As we stood staring, the dowager rounded on Cynthia.

"You wicked, wicked girl!" she cried. "Now what have you done! You have driven Richard from home a second time!"

"Be that as it may," said Dr. Johnson, "continue the Dole, Sir Jeremy, lest the Curse fall upon you."

Under his commanding eyes, the Dole party re-formed about Jeremy. I noticed that the constable, stately with writ and staff, belatedly brought up the rear; and so the Dole was completed.

Cheering, the tenantry broke ranks and attacked the tables; but there was no feasting for us. Marshalled by Dr. Johnson, we found ourselves indoors in the withdrawing room, sitting about on the stiff brocaded chairs as the late sunlight slanted in along the polished floor. We seemed to sit most like a select committee, myself and Cynthia and Jeremy, Lady Claybourne and Rollis and Bogie, with Dr. Johnson as it were in the chair, and the constable like a sergeant-at-arms, solidly established just outside the door.

"Where is Sir Richard?" demanded Mr. Rollis.

"Vanisht," replied Dr. Johnson with a broad smile. "We have put the genie back in the bottle."

"How do you know he is vanisht?"

"Because 'twas I conjured him away."

"Alas for my Lady!" cried generous-hearted Cynthia, "to lose her son a second time."

With a heart-broken gesture, Lady Claybourne put her kerchief to her eyes.

"Save your sympathy, she has not lost him," said Dr. Johnson calmly.

"Unravel this mystery, sir," exclaimed Cynthia.

"I have not all the strands in my fingers, but the master string I have pulled, and the unravelling begins. You have heard the cynical saying, if you should send word to every member of Parliament, *Fly, all is discovered*, the floor would be half empty next day."

In a trice I had out of my pocket the note the claimant had thrown down. *Fly, all is discovered,* it read.

"But he did not fly," I objected.

"Not then," conceded my friend. "But upon the heels of the warning came the constable with his staff and a great writ in his hand—instructed by me, I confess—and that did the business. The false Richard is off, and I venture to suppose he'll not return."

"How could you be so sure he was not the true Richard?" I asked curiously.

"Sir, the affair of Susanna and the elders was my first hint. As the lying elders could not say with one voice under which tree she sinned, so there was no agreement on the scene of that romantick meeting with old Bogie, whether the gardens or the docks. Was there such a meeting? It occurred to me to doubt it. Yet the positive voices of all three, mother, man of business, and old servant, overbore me for the nonce."

"Not to mention," said I, "the devotion of the dog Gypsy at Claybourne."

"Cupboard love," smiled Johnson. "Had you fed her, she would have drooled in *your* lap. No, the dog did not move me. For at Claybourne, I was again observing matter for doubt. There was, for instance, the affair of the wigs and hats. The false Richard wore his predecessor's garments very well. But the headgear would not fit; he was obliged to obtain a new supply.

"Moreover," my friend continued, "the real Sir Richard was right-handed. The sword in his portrait was scabbarded to the left, as it must be for a right-handed man to draw. But I soon perceived this fellow was always left-handed. He wrote, he shot, he fished left-handed with the perfect ease of a lifetime. Therefore must his right arm seem to be stricken. Then if he had learned from someone to write like Sir Richard, yet perforce not perfectly, the shift of hand explains all. Thus too, the arm must seem to mend. Who would willingly go one-armed forever?"

"And it mended miraculously," added Jeremy drily, "when I struck at him and he struck back two-fisted."

"So I saw," remarked Dr. Johnson, "tho' 'twas over in the blink of an eye. Yet it shook him, and Cynthia's tests still worse, making him all the more ready to believe *All is discovered,* and fly at once, by that mount he had always ready."

"Then where is the real Sir Richard?" I put the question that was hanging in the air.

"Ah, there's the question," said Dr. Johnson. "Let us ask Cynthia. Forgive me, my dear, do not answer unless you will; but had you really a note of farewell?"

"I will answer," said Cynthia in a low voice, "for Jeremy has the right to know. There was a note of farewell left for me in our hollow tree." Reaching into her bodice, she brought it forth. "Here it is."

With compressed lips, Lady Claybourne turned away. Three heads bent over the yellowing scrap. The message we read was brief and bitter:

> "Now you know me, I am unworthy to touch you. But be comforted, you shall be rid of your incubus when the tide goes out. Farewell, for you'll never see me more.
>
> Rich"

"I made sure he had thrown himself into the sea," whispered Cynthia.

"Dear heart," cried Jeremy, "on his wedding night, why would he so?"

"Because," said Cynthia, low, "he came to me with the French disease, and left me rather than infect me. He was half mad with remorse and drink taken, and I feared what he might do. 'Twas pure relief when I heard his mother had seen him and set him on his way."

"But had she?" asked Johnson gravely. "—Sit down, Lady Claybourne. You need not answer. I will answer for you. You never saw Richard that night. He was drowned. But you were determined still to rule Claybourne estate, and you had the wit and the will to invent a story to keep you there tho' Richard was gone. How long, think you, Cynthia, could she have remained, had you displayed this everlasting farewell?"

"I was but fourteen, and I wanted so to believe," murmured Cynthia. "But now—I know not."

"Perhaps," said Dr. Johnson, turning a stern face on the old Negro, "perhaps Bogie knows."

The dark eyes darted left and right. No sign came from my Lady, but Jeremy spoke with gruff gentleness:

"Speak up, Bogie. Tell us the truth; it shall not be held against you."

"I know," whispered the black painfully. "When Sir Richard was gone, none knew whither, I was set to search, and so 'twas I found at the cliff top his wedding coat folded, and a note held down by a stone."

"What said the note? Or can you not read?"

"I can read. It began: Honoured Mother, When you read this I shall be dead—"

Cynthia hid her face in her hands.

"I read no more," went on Bogie, "but took coat and note to my Lady in her chamber. She read it dry-eyed, and mused long. At last, Bogie, says she, I learn by this billet that your young master has left England, and we are to keep all things in readiness for his return. Was I to gainsay her?"

Lady Claybourne sat like a figure carved in ice.

"Yet Sir Richard would never return," went on Dr. Johnson, "and Jeremy's guardians became more and more pressing. I suggest that as Jeremy approached his majority, a scheam was conceived to hold the estate, a scheam in which you three—you, my Lady, and Rollis and Bogie—had your parts to play."

"And you too, Dr. Johnson," smiled Rollis, unabashed.

"And I too," said the philosopher wryly. "My part was to be the dupe, and lend my authority to the comedy of 'The Return of the Long Lost Heir.' 'Twas all too pat. He will be found, predicts my Lady like a sybil, and found he is, on her own ground, in Hispaniola. How? Because she arranged it—through a trusted messenger, her old slave from Hispaniola, our friend Mr. Bogie."

The old man almost smiled as he inclined his head.

"But who was he, then, whom Bogie found in Hispaniola," I demanded, "so miraculously suited to the part?"

"I know not," replied Dr. Johnson; "but I can guess. I think we shall find that there was someone in Hispaniola whom my Lady sent there out of the way long ago; someone whom she would gladly establish for life at Claybourne Hall; someone who so closely resembled her that he could win wide acceptance as the lost heir. To speak plainly: her son."

"Her *son?*"

"Her bastard son, Sir Jeremy, whose existence your mother railed at in years past. Is that not so, Lady Claybourne?"

My Lady disdained to answer.

"Is that not so, Mr. Rollis?"

"That is so, Dr. Johnson." Mr. Rollis smiled thinly. "The lad was troublesome, and 'twas I who secretly shipped him off for her to the Hispaniola plantation. Thither my Lady sent Bogie, to instruct him and bring him back. Bogie is not as simple as he seems. Come, my Lady, say this is so, for our best course now is to compound the matter with Sir Jeremy."

"Compound, will you?" said Jeremy darkly. "I'll look to the strong-box first."

"As to the strong-box," said Rollis calmly, "you may set your mind at rest, for I have kept the keys. Tho' in indifferent matters I was ruled by my Lady—"

"D'you call it an indifferent matter, raising me up a false husband!" cried Cynthia indignantly.

"As to that," returned the solicitor coolly, "I never expected my Lady's mad scheam to prevail; and as to the estate, I have kept it faithfully for whoever comes after."

"What impudence!" cried Jeremy. "Dr. Johnson, say, shall we not give these conspirators into custody, and send after the fleeing impostor?"

Lady Claybourne spoke for the first time:

"He'll hang for it. Would you hang your brother, Jeremy?"

"My *brother?*"

"Your father's son."

"Of the blood on both sides!" exclaimed Dr. Johnson. "Small wonder he passed for the heir!"

"And small wonder my mother railed," added Jeremy.

"Sir Jeremy will not desire a scandal at Claybourne," said my

Lady with perfect calm. "He will prefer that I should take my dower right and withdraw to Hispaniola. My son Paul—whom, as you say, I have not lost—shall join me. Now I will bid you good night. Come, Rollis. Come, Bogie."

" 'Tis for the best. Let it be so, Sir Jeremy," said my wise friend.

My Lady, head held high, sailed out at the door, and Rollis and Bogie followed.

"Be it so," assented Jeremy gravely, and the constable let them pass. "Now," he went on, his face softening, "there is but one more word to say. Cynthia (taking her hand)—Lady Claybourne, will you wed with me, and be Lady Claybourne still?"

"Yes, Jeremy," said Cynthia.

E. X. Ferrars

Undue Influence

Mrs. Margery Gosse was 82, a widow, self-reliant, and independent-minded. But people in their eighties, especially when they live alone, are prone to accidents. Mrs. Gosse tripped, fell, and fractured a femur in her leg. Luckily she still had one blood relative, a niece, who insisted on taking care of Mrs. Gosse after she left the hospital. Luckily? Taking care? A story of "loneliness and fear and hopelessness"...

"Why, Evelyn!" Mrs. Gosse exclaimed. "What a lovely surprise! I never dared to expect you."

"And how very, very naughty of you not to have let us know what happened straight away," Evelyn Hassall said, stooping to kiss the old wrinkled forehead, sallow against the snowy white of the pillows. "To leave it to that daily of yours to tell us—which it took her a fortnight to think of doing. We only had her letter this morning."

"Ah, Mrs. Jimson, so well-meaning, but she shouldn't have bothered you." Mrs. Gosse smiled up at her niece as she stood by the bedside, holding a bunch of jonquils and some magazines. "But it's sweet of you to have come, dear. I know what a busy life you lead."

"Well, really! The hospital people should have phoned me at once."

Mrs. Gosse was touched by the concern in Evelyn's voice. Yet the truth was that the old woman was a little surprised by it. It was two years since Evelyn had been over to see her, and Evelyn and Oliver lived only 50 miles away, a distance which, if they had happened to feel, say, like dropping in for lunch some Sunday, was nothing nowadays. So Mrs. Gosse had slipped into the habit of believing that her niece and her husband did not really want to be bothered too much about her.

That occasion, two years ago, when Evelyn, as now, had come over bearing gifts, had been Mrs. Gosse's eightieth birthday party.

A lovely party. Her stepdaughter Judith, with her two little girls, had been there, and of course Mrs. Gosse's darling husband Andrew had still been alive then. He'd had his coronary about six months later, although he had been a year younger than his wife and no one had ever dreamed he would die before her. Evelyn and Oliver had not been able to come to the funeral because they had been away on a Caribbean cruise, but they had sent a beautiful wreath.

The strong scent of the jonquils that Evelyn now laid on the bedside locker, saying that she supposed a nurse would bring a vase for them if she rang, made Mrs. Gosse suddenly remember that wreath. And that made her think of death. Naturally she had been thinking of death a good deal since her accident, and sometimes it had been with a dreamy sort of fascination. But more often it had been with a quietly stubborn resistance. She did not want to die yet.

Evelyn sat down on the chair by the bed and undid the collar of her fur coat. She was a pretty woman in a pallid, fluffy-haired way, not much over 40 though she looked rather more, because behind the pink and white softness of her face there was a certain hardness of bone, a tightness of the muscles.

"Now tell me what happened," she said. "Mrs. Jimson isn't the most literate of letter writers."

"Well, dear, really nothing much happened," Mrs. Gosse replied. "I fell, that was all. I was on the way to the kitchen to get my breakfast, and you know those three steps in the passage—I just tripped there and fell. And I don't really remember much about it, because apparently I fainted—and d'you know, I've never, I mean never, fainted in my life before. Then when I came to I was here. So I hardly know anything about it.

"But I've been told Mrs. Jimson came in at her usual time and found me and got Dr. Bryant at once, and he called for an ambulance and sent me here. And it turns out that what I've got is a fractured femur and I'm going to be stuck here for quite a time. But really I'm very lucky, because I understand a good many people of my age would simply have got pneumonia and died. And they're so kind to me here—nuns, you know, mostly Irish—I've never been called 'darlin'' so often in my life before!"

"Well, it just shows I've always been right, doesn't it?" Evelyn said. "You shouldn't be living alone. I hope Oliver and I can persuade you to be more reasonable about that now."

Actually Mrs. Gosse could not remember when Evelyn had protested at her living alone. Judith, Andrew's daughter, had tried hard after Andrew's death to persuade her stepmother to live with her and her husband, Ronald. But Ronald, who was in the oil business, had just been posted to Venezuela, and Mrs. Gosse had not been able to see herself, past 80, pulling up all her roots and going to live in such a strange and distant place. Besides, loving as Judith and Ronald had always been to her and dearly as she loved their children, Mrs. Gosse had always had a dread of becoming a burden to others, particularly to those for whom she cared the most.

"Anyway, when they let you out, of course you'll come to us," Evelyn went on. "No, don't argue about it. You couldn't possibly go home alone. You must come and stay with us as long as you need to."

"That's very kind of you, dear," Mrs. Gosse said. "It's a very tempting suggestion. I suppose I'll find it rather difficult to manage on my own for a time. I'll think it over."

But really there was nothing to think over. It was obvious that even when Mrs. Gosse could move about on her two aluminum crutches and go to the bathroom by herself, she could not possibly have looked after herself in her own apartment, with only Mrs. Jimson coming in to help her in the mornings. It was inevitable that she should accept Evelyn's invitation. So when at last Mrs. Gosse left the hospital it was in an ambulance that was to carry her to the Hassalls' home.

Mrs. Gosse was rather dismayed by the ambulance. She had imagined she was well enough to make the journey by car. But Evelyn reminded her that her spare bedroom was on the second floor and that as Mrs. Gosse would not be able to manage the stairs, she would have to be carried upstairs on a stretcher. Regretfully Mrs. Gosse thought of her own apartment in which she would quite soon have been able to hobble out into the garden to look at the crocuses coming out under the beech trees and to sit on the bench there in any early spring sunshine that might brighten an occasional day, and to pick big yellow bunches of forsythia for the vases in the sitting room.

In the Hassalls' house she would be cooped up in one room until she could go up and down the stairs, and who knew how many weeks that would be? However, it was a very attractive room with pale gray walls and a dark red carpet and pearly white closets and some nice photographs of Greece on the walls and a beautiful little bathroom opening out of it.

Oliver carried Mrs. Gosse's luggage up for her. He was a short round man of 50, a stockbroker, with plump jowls and a bald head sparsely fringed with dark hair. His eyes were dark, rather protuberant, and looked oddly intense in the pink placidity of his face.

"You see, there's a lovely view from here," he said, waving at the window. "Nothing between you and the downs. You'll enjoy that, won't you? We thought of that when we asked you to come."

"How kind you both are, how very kind to me," Mrs. Gosse said, and just then would have been immensely pleased if she had been able to think of something more to say to make up to the Hassalls for the fact that in the past somehow she had never thought of them as particularly kind people. But no doubt there would be opportunities later to show her gratitude. She only added that she was feeling rather tired and would like to go to bed.

"And you're longing for a cup of tea too, aren't you?" Oliver said and hurried out so that Evelyn could help Mrs. Gosse undress and get into the bed in which the electric blanket had thoughtfully been turned on, waiting for her.

The next three weeks were very pleasant. It was true that Mrs. Gosse found them rather quiet. She missed the bustle of the nurses round her and the visits of her bridge-playing circle and of faithful Mrs. Jimson. Evelyn sat with her aunt when she could and Oliver generally paid her a visit when he got home from the City, but Evelyn lived a busy life, filled with voluntary work and committee meetings, and Oliver was usually tired in the evenings. And unfortunately the one thing the Hassalls' spare bedroom lacked was a telephone.

Mrs. Gosse loved chatting with her friends on the telephone and now that she was too far away for them to be able to drop in to see her, she would have liked to be able to ring them up and settle down for a nice long comfortable gossip. Always, of course, finding out from the operator how much the call had cost and paying the sum to Evelyn, for Mrs. Gosse would no more have thought of telephoning at the Hassalls' expense than of allowing them to pay for the stamps on the numerous letters she wrote to her friends and which Evelyn took away to mail for her.

It was the fact that none of these letters was answered that first began to worry Mrs. Gosse. She could not understand it. Her friends were not neglectful people. Always, when she or any of them had gone away on holiday, they had sent one another picture postcards. At Christmas, even when they were meeting every few days, they sent each other the season's greetings. And those who, because of infirmities or domestic problems, had not been able to visit her in the hospital had written to her.

But now there was silence. It seemed very odd. She began to get querulous about it and one day actually asked Evelyn if she was sure she had remembered to mail the letters.

Evelyn laughed and said, "Of course, darling. I don't forget things."

"But I haven't had any answers," Mrs. Gosse said. "I don't understand it."

"You're too impatient," Evelyn said. "Very few people answer letters by return mail. I know I never do."

"But you're quite, quite sure you did post my letters, aren't you?"

"Quite, quite sure."

Mrs. Gosse accepted it. Yet a nagging worry remained. She began to feel cut off from the world in a way that slightly scared her. But that, of course, was absurd. There was nothing for her to be afraid of. It was just that her relative helplessness and the long hours she sometimes had to spend quite alone were beginning to get on her nerves.

Then one day she and Oliver had a rather curious conversation.

It was Mrs. Gosse herself who thoughtlessly began it. Oliver had come into her room to bring her coffee after a particularly delicious dinner that Evelyn had cooked. She was an excellent cook and she understood how much it meant to an invalid to have a real meal served with shining silver and a pretty tray cloth. That evening there had even been a few snowdrops in a little glass jug on the tray. Mrs. Gosse was touched by the thoughtfulness.

"You're really so good to me, both of you," she said to Oliver. "You'll see, I won't forget it."

Rather to her surprise he answered with a self-conscious laugh. She had an odd feeling she had just said something for which he had been waiting. But he said, "Now, now, we don't want to talk about that sort of thing, do we?"

"But I mean it," she said. "You do so much for me and I couldn't bear it if you didn't understand how grateful I am."

"But there's no need to talk of things like that yet, is there?" he said. "Why, goodness me, I expect you'll outlive us all."

"Outlive—?"

Mrs. Gosse was startled. She realized he had thought, when she spoke of showing him and Evelyn that she would not forget their kindness, that she had been speaking of what she would leave them in her will. But in fact she had simply been thinking of making a present to Evelyn of a pearl and ruby brooch inherited by Mrs. Gosse from her grandmother, a very charming thing and probably quite valuable and which she was sure Evelyn would like. And Mrs. Gosse meant to think of something for Oliver, too. He was an incessant smoker and there was that gold cigarette case of Andrew's. Perhaps Oliver would like that.

But she did not want to embarrass Oliver by letting him know how he had misunderstood her.

"Oh, well," she said, "we all come to it sooner or later. There's no point in being afraid of thinking about it, is there?"

"Well, of course I've always hoped you'd remember Evelyn," he said, "but as the money was all Uncle Andrew's it wouldn't be surprising if you felt you had to leave your share of it to Judith."

As he spoke he was watching her with disconcerting intentness.

Mrs. Gosse sipped her coffee.

"No, perhaps it wouldn't," she said. "Of course, I made out my will thirty years ago and I've never thought of changing it. I remember when Andrew and I went along to the solicitor together and made our wills at the same time. Not that I had anything of my own to leave then. It was just to save trouble later if he should predecease me, as of course happened. We both agreed about the terms. They were very simple. Dearest Andrew, I should never think of doing anything I thought he wouldn't like."

"No, no, of course not, of course not," Oliver said and his eyes seemed to fill with a hungry kind of curiosity, as if he were trying to determine if the ambiguity of her reply was the result of deliberate evasiveness or merely of aged muddle-mindedness. Then suddenly he went hurriedly out of the room and let the door shut behind him with a loudness that was almost a slam.

Mrs. Gosse put her coffee cup down quickly on the bedside table because her hands had started to tremble violently and she was afraid of spilling coffee on the flower-patterned sheets. Clasping her hands together, she lay there rigid in the comfortable bed, trying to think clearly and not let confusion and a perhaps utterly irrational panic overwhelm her.

She told herself that Oliver had never had much tact and that it was just like him, if he was curious about her will, to blurt it out as crudely as he had. And what more natural for him than to be curious? Yet there was a callousness about it, an indifference to her feelings, which offended Mrs. Gosse deeply.

For the question of what would happen to her modest fortune when she died could be of no interest to Oliver and Evelyn unless they had already talked freely to one another about her death. And she was 82. Her mother had lived to 93 and her father to 97 and he had enjoyed a game of bowls on the very day of his death. And as longevity was said to run in families, wasn't it a little impatient, to say the least, of Oliver and Evelyn to be wondering about her will?

Unless—

Unless they had been told something in the hospital about her health that had been kept from her. Was her heart, for instance, not as strong as she believed? Was there anything the matter with her arteries? Had they some reason for expecting her to die soon? And was that why they were looking after her so assiduously, and while they were at it, keeping her virtually a prisoner, denying her all other human contact, perhaps never mailing the letters she had written, giving her no access to a telephone, and now beginning, when she was all too conscious of her complete dependence on them, to suggest to her that she should make a will in their favor?

No, that was all nonsense! She was letting her nerves get the best of her, allowing herself to be overcome by senile suspiciousness. Of course she was not a prisoner. She was being devotedly looked after. She ought to feel nothing but gratitude.

All the same she must think, she decided. She must think very clearly, without getting lost among hysterical thoughts and fancies. Lying still, except that her fingers plucked at the edge of the flowered sheet, she gazed at the ceiling and presently began to make what she thought was really a rather clever little plan. She meant it as something just to set her own mind at rest, and it would be so easy, so simple even for her to carry out that it seemed very sensible to try it. She would do it tomorrow.

Having decided on that, she dropped off almost at once into a pleasant doze, from which she did not awaken until Evelyn came into the room to settle her for the night and to give her her sleeping pills.

Mrs. Gosse put her plan into execution the next day, as soon as she heard Evelyn leave the house to do the shopping. Oliver, of course, had gone off to London some time before. So while Evelyn was out, Mrs. Gosse had the house to herself. Moving carefully and slowly, leaning on her crutches, she crossed her room to the door, opened it, went out into the hall, and hobbled along it to the door of Oliver's and Evelyn's bedroom. For there was a telephone in there. She had overheard both of the Hassalls speaking on it.

She had never suggested using it herself because this had never been offered and she regarded bedrooms as private places into which one did not intrude without an invitation. Yet really, with no one to see her, what was to stop her going in and ringing up, say, good Mr. Deane, her solicitor, and asking him to visit her?

She put a hand on the doorknob of the bedroom door. It did not open. It was locked. The Hassalls did not intend to let her reach that telephone extension to call Mr. Deane or anybody in the outer world. So her fears had not been crazy. She was, in fact, being held a prisoner.

With her heart beating in a way that frightened her, she made her way back to her room. At the head of the stairs she stood still and looked down. There was the front door. There was escape. If she gritted her teeth at the pain, could she somehow get down the stairs and reach the street?

But what would she do when she got there? Wave her crutches at passing cars? Hope some driver would not think she was mad and would give her a lift of 50 miles to her home?

Probably before a car stopped Evelyn would return and gently force her back into the house and her captivity. And anyone who saw it happen would be on Evelyn's side.

For the moment there was nothing for it but patience.

It was soon after this that a subtle change came over Evelyn's attitude to Mrs. Gosse. All at once she seemed to have become very tired of looking after the old lady. She hardly spoke to her, there were no pretty tray cloths, and the meals she brought in as often as not consisted of meat of some sort out of a can and a lump of mashed potato that had certainly come out of a box. And Evelyn's face seemed to have become all bony jaw and veiled, resentful eyes.

One day, just as Evelyn was leaving the room, Mrs. Gosse said on an impulse, "Evelyn dear, don't you think it's time I was going home?"

Evelyn paused in the doorway. "So you want to leave us," she said.

"It's just that I think I've imposed on you long enough," Mrs. Gosse answered.

"You can go home tomorrow if you want to," Evelyn said.

Mrs. Gosse tried hard not to look startled. "Just whenever it's convenient for you, dear."

"Only tell me one thing first." Evelyn's voice suddenly grated. "Let's stop pretending, both of us. Oliver and I want to know if you've left us anything in your will or does everything go to Judith?"

"I don't think that's a very nice thing to talk about," Mrs. Gosse replied. "I'd sooner not discuss it."

"But we want to know where we stand. It won't hurt you to tell us. We aren't as well off as we look. Oliver isn't as clever as he thinks about money."

Mrs. Gosse considered her answer carefully.

"Well, you know everything I have was left to me by Andrew," she said. "And Judith is his daughter. You're actually no relation of Andrew's at all. I wouldn't say you have any right to his money."

"Didn't he leave half of what he had to Judith and half to you, without any strings to it?" Evelyn said. "I remember his saying so once. You can do what you like with your share."

"And you think I ought to make a will leaving it to you?"

"I do. We're your only blood relations."

"And if I make this will, I can go home?"

"As soon as you like."

"And if not?" Mrs. Gosse asked quietly.

Evelyn hesitated, then seemed to make up her mind.

"After all, why should you ever go home?" she said with a tight little smile. "Your friends are already beginning to forget about you. When you first came here they were always ringing up to ask how you were, but it was quite easy to put them off and now they just think you've settled down with us and they've stopped worrying about you. You could stay on here in this nice room forever and ever and no one would ask any questions.

"And as I really find carrying trays up and down the stairs rather a tiring job, perhaps I might not bother with them quite as often as I do. And I might forget to change your library books. I don't mean, of course, that I'd ever do anything actually unkind, but you might find your life not quite as comfortable as it's been. And still no one would dream of interfering."

"But suppose I make a will of the kind you want," Mrs. Gosse said, "what's to stop me changing it when I get home?"

"If you promised you wouldn't change it, you wouldn't," Evelyn said. "That's what you're like."

"Are you sure?"

"Oh, yes, I'm sure. You'd never change it."

"No," Mrs. Gosse said thoughtfully, "perhaps not."

For, promise or not, once she had made that will she would be given no chance to change it. She would never get home. What she understood clearly as the result of this extremely upsetting conversation was that the Hassalls were going to see to it that she never left their house alive. Melodramatic as it sounded, that was the simple truth. It must be. No other explanation of their actions made sense. And she was in their hands, at their mercy.

After that day, as if it were already putting her threat into practice, Evelyn became more and more neglectful of Mrs. Gosse. Her food was often hardly edible. She had to struggle to make her own bed. The room was left to grow dusty and the sheets were not changed. And as she became better able to walk about she found, not much to her surprise, that she was locked into her room.

In a way she was glad to be left alone. She liked it better than those times when the Hassalls tried to make her discuss a new will. But sometimes she sat and cried from sheer loneliness and fear and hopelessness. The thought of giving in to them, trusting that at least the manner of her end would be merciful, began to seem almost attractive.

Then one afternoon, when she was in the bathroom, a noise in her bedroom startled her. It sounded as if the window had just been opened and closed. Then distinctly she heard footsteps and someone began to sing thickly and hoarsely.

" 'When they call the roll up yonder, when they call the roll up yonder, when they call the roll up yonder, I'll be there. . .' "

A burglar?

A burglar who came in daylight and sang hymns? Hardly likely. Yet burglars seemed to do the oddest things nowadays. One was always reading about it. And perhaps this one might turn out to be a friend. Limping into the bedroom as fast as she could, she saw a small, stout, red-faced man busily cleaning her window.

The window cleaner. The one intruder whom the Hassalls had forgotten to keep out. And luckily, just then, Evelyn was away from the house, doing the shopping.

"Oh, good day," Mrs. Gosse exclaimed excitedly. "What a beautiful day it is, isn't it?"

For almost every conversation with a stranger should begin with a remark about the weather, shouldn't it? It always eased things. Besides, for the first time in some weeks, she had just noticed how brightly the sun was shining.

He took no notice.

"Good day," Mrs. Gosse repeated, louder.

He went on cleaning and singing.

She went closer to him and tapped him on the shoulder with a crutch.

He whirled, his hands coming up as if to defend himself. Then, seeing her, he gave a loose-lipped smile and said, "Oh, good afternoon, missus. Didn't know anyone was in. Mrs. Hassall always says if I come when she's out to go ahead on my own and she'll pay me next time. Nice day, isn't it?"

Mrs. Gosse's heart sank. She could smell the beer on his breath. He was, she realized, both drunk and deaf.

She tested how deaf he was by raising her voice and repeating as loudly as she could, "It's a beautiful day."

He gave her a dubious stare, considered the situation, then said, as if he knew that it was a safe thing to say in almost any circumstances, "That's right." Then he returned to cleaning the window.

Mrs. Gosse stumbled hastily to the table where her writing paper and envelopes were. She lowered herself into the chair and began feverishly writing. Before she was half finished the window cleaner began to climb out of the window onto his ladder. She reached out with one of her crutches and jabbed him sharply. When he turned with a look of hurt protest she held up a finger, beckoning to him, and shouted, "Wait!"

He stayed where he was uncertainly.

Under the address she had scrawled at the top she wrote, "Dear Mr. Deane, I am being kept here against my will. I am in fear of my life. Please come and rescue me. This is urgent, very urgent. Yours sincerely, Margery Gosse."

She folded the sheet of paper, slid it into an envelope, and addressed it. She had an uneasy feeling that what she had written might sound merely insane. If she had more time to think she might have written more temperately. But the window cleaner was looking as if he might decide to descend his ladder at any moment. Then she realized she had no stamps. Taking 50 pence out of her handbag, she handed it to him with the letter, pointed at the corner where the stamp should be, and shouted, "Please! Please post it for me!"

At the sight of the 50 pence his face split into a grin.

"Thank you, missus," he said. "Very good of you. Thank you."

"But please post the letter!" In her own ears her pleading voice sounded hopelessly thin and ineffectual.

"That's right," he said cheerfully, then pocketing the money and holding the letter he disappeared.

Mrs. Gosse looked down after him. She saw him reach the bottom of the ladder, look at the letter in his hand in a puzzled way as if he wondered how he had come by it, then crumple it into a ball and drop it on a flowerbed.

Mrs. Gosse shouted down to him to be sure to post the letter, but the man moved on and was quickly out of sight.

She collapsed into a chair. For a few minutes she gave in to helpless sobbing. The bitter disappointment after the few minutes of exalted hope left her feeling far more desperate than she had before. She felt more exhausted than she ever had in her life. A cloud of blackness settled on her mind. Utter despair enveloped her.

Now, she knew, there was nothing left for her but the gamble she had been thinking about recently. A most fearful gamble. The thought of it terrified her. For it was only too likely to fail. But if it did, did she really care? Might that not be better than letting things go on as they were now? All the same, but for the agonizing disappointment of having seen her letter crumpled and dropped on the earth, she would probably never have had the courage to act.

As it was, she sat still, thinking, for what seemed a very long time. She had never been a gambler by nature. She enjoyed her bridge, but never for more than twopence a hundred, and once, when she and Andrew had been in Monte Carlo, she had become very agitated when he had risked a mere ten pounds at roulette. Yet here she was. thinking of risking all that she had. Literally all. Her life.

At last she got up. and staggering more than usual, from nervousness and a kind of confusion, she went into the bathroom, took her sleeping pills out of the medicine cabinet, and counted them. There were 47 in the bottle. And the lethal dose, she had once been told, was about 30. But when you were 82, perhaps it would not take so many to kill you. How could you tell? You must just guess and hope for the best.

Above all, you must not take too few. That would be useless. Counting out 30, she flushed them down the toilet. Then with shaking hands she filled a glass of water and set herself to swallowing the 17 remaining pills.

She was surprised at how calm she became while she was doing it. Walking back into her bedroom, she turned the cover of the bed down neatly, took off her shoes, and lay down. While she was waiting for the drug to begin to affect her she found the words of the hymn that the window cleaner had sung going round in her head. "When they call the roll up yonder..." Dimly the words comforted her.

She was far gone by the time Evelyn came in with her supper tray. Loud snoring noises came from the inert figure on the bed and the aged face on the pillow was paper-white. Evelyn stood still, staring, then shouted, "Oliver! Oliver, come at once!"

He pounded up the stairs.

"Look!" Evelyn cried.

"Oh, God, what's happened? What's she done?" he gasped.

Evelyn dumped the tray she had been clutching onto the table and shot into the bathroom. She came back with the empty bottle.

"It's her sleeping pills. She's taken the lot. What fools we've been, leaving them here! Why didn't we think she might do this?"

"How many were there?"

"Nearly fifty, I think."

"Then she hasn't a hope."

"What are we going to do? This is how we planned things. There'll be questions, a post-mortem. . .Oh, Lord, when I think of all the time I've spent on her—"

"Be quiet, let me think."

"We'd better get the doctor."

"Yes, yes, of course, that's unavoidable. But the question is, do we do it now—or when it's over?"

"It had better be now," Evelyn said. "If she's going to die anyway, it's going to look better if we do everything we can to save her. It might even give us some sort of claim on her estate."

"You can forget that now. That damned Judith will get it all. And suppose she comes round. Wouldn't it be better to wait? We can't have her talking."

"She'll never come round. Go and phone the doctor. We can tell him she was convinced she'd never walk properly again and that it has been depressing her. Go on."

"And you'd better do some cleaning up in here," Oliver said. "The place looks filthy. We've got to make it plain we've been doing everything we could for the woman. Hurry."

He went quickly to the telephone extension in the bedroom. Evelyn, giving the figure on the bed a look of the deepest malignancy, set about dusting and tidying.

Mrs. Gosse, in her deep coma, went on with her unconscious struggle for life, drawing one breath after another into her laboring lungs. The effort of each breath seemed to use up more of her vitality than she could possibly afford. She looked far too wasted and fragile to survive till rescuers came.

It was morning when she recovered consciousness in the hospital. Through a fog she became aware of people coming and going, of a bright young face under a starched cap bending over her, of voices nearby and of someone saying, "She'll do."

She could not think how it had come about. Her memory was a blank. But a sense of wonderful peace enveloped her. There was something beautiful about seeing human faces round her and the two rows of beds filled with other sick people in the long emergency ward. She smiled vaguely at a man who was standing by her bedside and murmured, "Are you from the police?"

"Of course not, I'm a doctor," he said. "And a lot of trouble you've given me. If you weren't as strong as a horse, we'd never have pulled you through. But we don't need the police just because you took a few too many of your pills, do we? That's all that happened, isn't it? You lost count. We don't need the police just because you were a little careless."

"The police," she said softly, as if the word charmed her, then she drifted off into a normal sleep from which she did not wake up for several hours.

When she awoke, Evelyn Hassall, holding a bunch of lilacs, was standing at the side of her bed.

Mrs. Gosse raised her head a little from the pillow and began to scream, "Nurse, nurse, nurse!"

Her mind was as clear as it had ever been.

"Shh, darling, don't, you'll disturb everyone," Evelyn said. She looked hollow-eyed, as if she had not slept during the past night, but she smiled sweetly.

"Nurse, nurse!" Mrs. Gosse shrieked.

The heads of the other patients in the ward turned toward her. A nurse came running.

"Now, now, what's this?" she said. "This is your niece, Mrs. Hassall. Don't you recognize her? She sat up all night while we worked on you and it was touch and go. She'll take you home again as soon as you're strong enough."

"Don't let her come near me!" Mrs. Gosse shouted so that everyone could hear. "She gave me that stuff to drink! She tried to kill me! I told her I was going to change my will because she and her husband were so unkind to me and she gave me all that poison in my tea before I could call my lawyer. My lawyer, Mr. Deane, I want to see him! Now! I want to see him at once because I mean to change my will immediately and leave everything I have to my stepdaughter Judith."

"*Change* your—?" Evelyn began.

"Yes, yes, I'd left everything to you, you knew that," Mrs. Gosse answered furiously. "When Andrew and I made our wills he said to me he was providing for Judith himself and that what he was leaving me was mine absolutely and that I should leave it, if I wanted to, to my own kith and kin. So I left it all to you and you would have had it if you hadn't been too impatient. Trying to poison me, that's further than I thought even you would go, and that's murder. Nurse, I want the police. I want to charge that wicked woman with trying to kill me."

"But I didn't know about your will. . .you didn't say. . .and I didn't give you anything, you took it yourself!"

Evelyn's eyes were wide and frightened in her pallid face. Her bony jaw trembled.

Suddenly she turned and went running out of the ward, dropping the lilacs as she ran.

Mrs. Gosse gave a deep sigh. Settling herself more comfortably in the high hard bed, she smiled up at the nurse.

"Of course, I knew there was something wrong with the tea as soon as I tasted it," she said. "But I thought perhaps the teapot hadn't been washed out properly. My niece is not as careful a housekeeper as she might be. But I didn't want to make a fuss. I never make a fuss if I can help it. And naturally I never thought of murder. But I'm afraid there's really no question of it. So now, dear, I'd really like to see someone from the police. After all, poisoners nearly always try again."

The nurse gazed at her with a look of shock on her face, then went hurrying away to consult her superior.

Perhaps because Mrs. Gosse was not wearing her false teeth, which were in a glass by her bedside, her gentle features looked more shrunken than usual, more hollow, so that her jawbone stood out, giving it almost as hard an outline as that of her niece Evelyn.

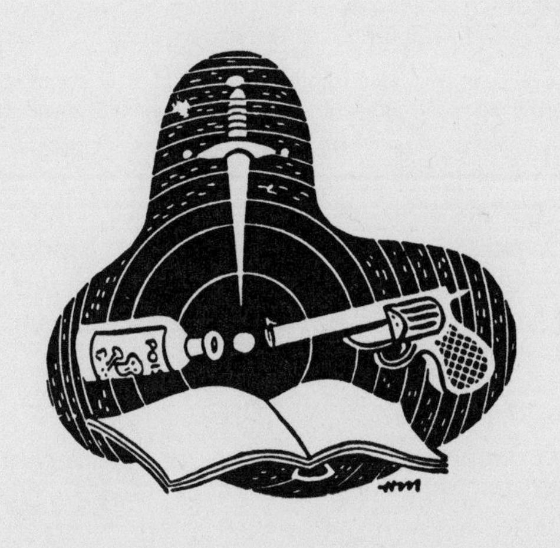

Gerald Tomlinson

Miss Ferguson Versus JM

An interesting duel of wits between Elsie Ferguson, a spinster librarian with a photographic memory for names and faces, and Joseph Moldavi, a handsome black-bearded borrower with a curious taste in reading matter . . .

P.S.: Can you deduce from internal evidence in this story the name of one of Gerald Tomlinson's favorite detective authors? But don't let this "Rossword Puzzle" distract you from the main business at hand—the battle of the experts. . .

Elsie Ferguson, a spinster with gold-rimmed granny glasses, had been a library clerk in Elm City for 43 years. She knew the Dewey Decimal System down to the fourth digit after the period. She knew the card catalogue from *A, A Novel* to *Zylstra, Henry.*

Despite her expertise neither library books nor catalogue numbers were her true forte. Names and faces were. She had a photographic memory for people.

Whenever a person brought books to the circulation desk at the Elm City Library, Miss Ferguson would close her eyes for a moment, match the face with a name in her files, smile over the top of the gray book-charging machine, and say, "It's nice to see you again, Mr.——, Mrs.——, or Miss——" and fill in the name.

But if the borrowers' names and faces were a challenge to Miss Ferguson, their reading habits bored her to blasphemy. The average reader carried away books that to Miss Ferguson seemed as dull as baseball and as mindless as bowling: mysteries, historical romances, Gothic novels, celebrity biographies, science fiction.

There was one exception. Miss Ferguson loved books on coin collecting. She had spent most of her life and most of her small income in building a collection of United States coins. It was a tiny collection compared with the great ones—the Smithsonian's or the American Numismatic Society's—but it was strong on early American Large Cents.

Miss Ferguson did not belong to the Tionega Valley Coin Club, and she avoided coin shows. She seldom exhibited her collection, but instead kept much of it stored in a vault of the First Tionega Canal Bank.

The quality of her collection was well known, however, and she had recently lent three of her rarest Large Cents, two 1793s and an 1804, to the Calvert Coin Museum in Baltimore.

Miss Ferguson was both a collector and a student of numismatics. On early American Large Cents she was one of the three or four living experts. She had written articles on the subject for *The Numismatist*, one of which had been published as a book and stood, to her satisfaction, in section 737.4 of the Elm City Library.

Once every couple of years she and her hobby were the subject of a feature column and a photograph or two in the local newspaper.

Coins fascinated her. So did books on coins. But she did not mix business with pleasure. At the library she watched people come and go, fed cards into the book-charging machine, and thought little about either coins or books.

Yet this people-watching was less a sociable exercise than an intellectual one, as Miss Ferguson knew. She said hello to more people in a day than most people did in a month, but still she was a loner, a dedicated loner. She had no close friends, no social life, and had never tried to have any. She cherished privacy. She had been followed by neither suitors nor trouble, and not for one moment in her 65 years had she thought seriously about marriage.

The names-and-faces ritual was simply a game she had made up to lighten the long leaden hours at the library. It was a form of escape. She did not consider it an especially praiseworthy pastime. She always tried to be honest with herself about her motives, not to lie to herself the way some people did.

The memory game had begun, she remembered, 40 years before when she learned that the then Postmaster General, James Farley, could pair off 50,000 names with 50,000 faces. She was impressed. She knew almost no borrowers by name in those early days. Now, four decades later, she figured her repertoire at 10,000 names and faces.

Although no one interested her very much personally, some people interested her more than others. There was one great hulk of a man in particular: Mr. Joseph Moldavi, a tall swarthy gentleman, black-bearded like Ivan the Terrible, a man whose choice of books caused Miss Ferguson to look twice at the borrower, and to wonder.

He was a strikingly handsome man, this Mr. Moldavi, a point that Miss Ferguson noted at first with more disdain than delight. Looks, like books, were suspect. Anyway, the small black mole on his left cheek marred his appearance; it looked to her like an ugly embedded insect. But it did give her a mnemonic hook on which to hang the name Moldavi: mole-Moldavi.

After a while, given her gift for observation, she could not help noticing how his reading habits matched—and matched alarmingly—what had been happening in Elm City.

Side by side with the usual street construction, school-budget defeats, and political corruption, Elm City was having a series of big-money burglaries. In the past two years there had been five spectacular thefts—an Elm City crime wave that coincided exactly, Miss Ferguson noted, with Mr. Moldavi's career as a borrower at the library.

First there had been three jewelry-store burglaries, clever nighttime heists with no clues and no suspects. The jewels were on the premises one day and gone the next. These events had followed hard on the heels of Mr. Moldavi's three-month concentration on books about gems and minerals.

Next there had been two art thefts. The Blauberg Art Gallery had lost two Ben Shahns in one night, the only two valuable paintings in the Blauberg collection. Less than six months later Langdon College found itself missing a Schneider Esch portrait of Mark Twain valued at $20,000. These two thefts had coincided with Mr. Moldavi's persistent enchantment with books on art.

Each of these five thefts had required expert knowledge, according to the Elm City Chief of Police, Thomas McEachern, a morose man with a gray crewcut and five nagging reasons to be morose. Only the best items in each place had been taken. And all the thefts had been executed, he said, by the same thoroughgoing professionals, men or women who knew jewels, art, locks, alarm systems, and enough else to stay out of suspicion and prison.

Miss Ferguson did not see herself as a detective. But there it was: Mr. Moldavi, the self-taught expert, the suave bookish thief. Black beard, black mole, black money. He had stopped borrowing books on art after the Esch robbery, and for the past two months he had been charging out armloads of books about wine.

This new interest puzzled Miss Ferguson. Jewels were understandable. So were paintings. But wine?

No one enjoyed a glass of white table wine more than Miss Ferguson. But her Sunday evening sauternes or riesling cost only $2 or $3 a bottle, not much more than the bottled spring water she drank on weekdays. She had never supposed that sauternes could be in a class with sapphires and Shahns.

Miss Ferguson, her suspicions aroused, decided to test her theory, to research the wine market on her lunch hour. The best place to investigate, she knew, was Parrish's Wine Cellar, a downtown landmark for three generations, a small shop on Charles Street with wide plank flooring and the smell of cheese. Even a teetotaler with a taste for TV dinners knew that Parrish's was the finest store in Elm City for wine, liquor, and cheese.

She drove to Parrish's in her rusted-out mauve Dodge, arriving a little after noon. She dropped a nickel in the meter out front, paused under the zebra-striped awning, and considered her strategy.

Inside the store Miss Ferguson addressed herself to a ruddy face behind a white goatee. "It's nice to see you again, Mr. Parrish," she said. She recognized him because he occasionally took out books on woodworking or some equally dreary subject. "I'd like to see your most expensive bottle of wine."

Alex Parrish smiled across the counter at her—a bit patronizingly, she thought. Probably he recognized her as a novice at wines. But he nodded and said, "Certainly. You realize, of course, that in order to see that particular bottle, we will have to go down into the cellar."

She looked at him steadily over her bifocals, not quite sure what he meant.

"Well," he explained, "I really can't afford to disturb a fine old Bordeaux unless you wish to purchase it." She looked innocent, questioning. "You usually buy a domestic riesling, don't you, Miss—?"

"Ferguson." She felt herself blushing. "Yes, I do." She was surprised that he remembered her. "But if it's not asking too much, Mr. Parrish, I would like to see your most expensive bottle today. A gift—"

"Of course, Miss Ferguson. Please step this way."

She was astonished at the extent of the Parrish wine cellar. A dozen ceiling-high racks stretched the length of a long room, and the racks were filled with thousands upon thousands of bottles.

Mr. Parrish led Miss Ferguson to the far side of the cellar where, under a hanging fluorescent fixture, he pointed toward a bottle with a slight covering of dust. "There it is." Then, observing her disappointed expression, he shrugged his narrow shoulders and slowly, carefully, drew out the bottle, using both hands, and tilted it ever so slightly to show her the label.

She could not read French and did not know the cryptography of wine labels, but she could see *Chateau Lafite-Rothschild* and *1945*.

He smiled at her. "Eight hundred dollars," he said simply, but in a reverent tone of voice.

Miss Ferguson gulped. She cleared her throat. "That's a bit more than I expected. Do you have any bottles for—well, maybe fifty dollars?"

The proprietor of the Wine Cellar chuckled as if he might have anticipated this sudden shattering of the dream. "Certainly, Miss Ferguson. Dozens, perhaps hundreds. In fact, many of them are Lafites such as this one. But not"—he paused and raised his eyes—"not the legendary '45."

"My goodness."

"Would you care to see a less expensive year from that Chateau? Or perhaps a Latour or a Margaux?"

"Thank you, Mr. Parrish, I do appreciate your courtesy. But perhaps I'd better think about it some more. May I come back another day?"

"By all means."

He returned the bottle to its resting place, and Miss Ferguson, in a state of mild shock, drove back to the Elm City Library.

That afternoon Mr. Moldavi returned five books on wine, pushing them firmly across the polished oak counter. Yes, indeed, he was a fine figure of a man. He strode down the dark tunnel into the stacks with that disturbing macho manner of his, a stride that both enchanted and annoyed her. He returned a few minutes later with four new books about wine.

Miss Ferguson met him at the book-charging machine, closed her eyes for an instant so as not to change her mnemonic routine—heavens, she knew *him* all right—then smiled nervously and said, "It's nice to see you again, Mr. Moldavi." She had been rehearsing a question to ask him about Chateau Lafite. Did she dare? "May I ask—?"

"Yes?" Mr. Moldavi smiled, displaying a costly set of capped teeth. "What can I do for you?" His voice was warm and ingratiating, an actor's or a prophet's voice. He made it sound as if he had been eagerly waiting for the moment he might be allowed to talk to her.

Miss Ferguson's heart jumped. This was a bit too heady. "Nothing." She bit her lip, steadied her shaking hand, and hurriedly punched the date cards. Mr. Moldavi watched her through colbalt-blue eyes.

As soon as he had left, she chided herself for her silly show of emotion. After a few minutes she crossed to a file of membership applications and took out Joseph Moldavi's card. According to the information on it he lived at 23 Strathmore Drive, West Elm City. His telephone number was 382-5968. His employer was Consolidated Prefabricated Homes, where he was a supervisor.

His reference—a line on the card required of all applicants but seldom checked—was Harvey Galton of 19 River Knolls, Northwood. Telephone 602-1948.

Miss Ferguson hastened to the telephone and dialed 602-1948. Mr. Galton. Her breath came in short puffs as she waited. Investigative work was stimulating, but it was not really in her line. A woman's voice answered. "Yeah?"

"Hello. Mrs. Galton?"

"Right on, dearie." The voice was fuzzy. "Except now I'm remarried. The name is Bowman."

"Oh, I see." Miss Ferguson frowned. "I'm calling from the Elm City Library, Mrs. Bowman. My name is Elsie Ferguson. We have received an application for a library card from a Mr. Joseph Moldavi. I would like to verify your husband's—that is, your ex-husband's—acquaintance with him."

"Hold on. Moldy-who? What are you talking about, hon?"

"Joseph Moldavi. Did your husband know him?"

There was a muffled curse on the other end of the line, aimed at either a pet or a child underfoot, followed by a noisy swallow. "Harvey Galton knew zip. Now he knows angleworms. He's dead."

"Oh, I'm sorry."

"I'm not. He was a loser from the word go. You know any losers?"

Miss Ferguson stared into the black holes of the mouthpiece. "I beg your pardon?"

"Don't beg, dearie. Never beg." A long pause; then Mrs. Bowman said, "Marvelous Harv, as I used to call him, was killed in a bank holdup in Albany two years ago."

"Oh, how terrible."

"Yeah, terrible. You said it, terrible. He had a satchel full of cash that never got past the State Street curb."

Miss Ferguson gasped. "He was holding up the bank?"

A high laugh rattled across the wire. "You're too much, hon! Where're you from anyway, the Little Sisters of Mercy, Seven Miles Outside the City of Jerusalem?"

"No. I mean—" Miss Ferguson stopped to think, trying to put her meager facts in order. Then she gambled for the second or possibly the third time in her life. "Mrs. Bowman, could you tell me if one of the other men in the bank holdup was a Mr. Moldavi? Joseph Moldavi?"

"Who's this guy Moldy you keep bringing up? I never heard of him. Wait a minute." Miss Ferguson heard the clink of ice against glass in the background. A moment later Mrs. Bowman's voice returned. "There was no Moldy in the gang, dearie. How about Larry Kincaid? Would he do? He got shot along with Harv. Died a couple of days later at Albany Hospital."

"I'm afraid not. Moldavi is the name."

"Well, call 'em like you see 'em, hon. I'll tell you what I know. There was one other guy on the bank job. Brad Eaton, who's now in Dannemora. Oh, yeah, there was also the lamebrain who planned it. Joe Masseno, the so-called genius of the operation. You get that? Joe the Genius." She snorted. "Some genius. But he backed out before they went to Albany—said the plan still needed work. It sure did. Huh, I guess maybe Masseno *did* have more brains than the rest of them."

"Joe Masseno? He was the one who planned it?"

"You deaf?"

"I'm sorry. And you say he backed out before they went to Albany?"

"Deaf as a fence post."

"Mrs. Bowman, could you tell me what Joe Masseno looked like?"

"Never saw him, hon. Never saw anybody except Harv. Only saw *him* about twice a month. Just heard him talk about the rest of the meatheads. Joe the Genius. *He* knew the score, Harv used to say. Yeah, he knew the score all right. The score was cops three, crooks nothing." She hiccupped.

"Thank you very much, Mrs. Bowman."

"Don't mention it, hon. A day's work for a day's pay, I always say. What do you always say?"

Miss Ferguson said nothing.

"Well, cheers then!"

"Yes."

"Roger and out!"

With a scowl Miss Ferguson lowered the receiver to its cradle. She immediately dialed 382-5968, the Moldavi number. She knew pretty much what to expect. When the answering voice droned, "The number you have dialed is not in service—" she smiled and hung up.

Joe Masseno. Initials: JM. She leafed idly through the M's in the Elm City phone book, not expecting a miracle. People with aliases were slippery and hard to find, she supposed, this being her first experience with aliases. There was no Joe Masseno listed in the directory.

But there was a Joseph Malloy, and suddenly Miss Ferguson's mnemonic system clicked into gear. JM. Somehow, for some reason, the name Joseph Malloy meant something. For the first time in 40 years her names-and-faces repertoire came up against a genuine, practical problem. She leaned back in her chair, excited by the sudden associations, and thought hard, concentrated, racked her memory, conjuring up mental images, grasping at mnemonic hooks.

Mallow, marshmallow, white skin, toasted marshmallow, brown, brown, not a name, brown marks, scars, the double *l*'s, parallel scars on one cheek. Malloy, Malloy, that was it. Joseph Malloy. She knew him. She squinted to clear up the haze of time. Thirty, thirty-five years ago, he had borrowed books at least a dozen times. The young Joseph Malloy, a high school kid, basketball injury to his face, bad teeth, tall—that was him.

Joseph Malloy was Joseph Moldavi as a young man. Thirty or more years ago. No question about it. Why hadn't she seen it before? And Joseph Malloy—she supposed that must be his real name—now lived at 278 Foster Avenue, Elm City. She whistled.

She ignored the phone number. The name and address were enough. They were like Large Cents from heaven, precious and hers alone. She had to see Joseph Malloy in person.

That evening after work Miss Ferguson began a new day-by-day routine. From the Elm City Library she swung her rusted-out Dodge north on Wycherly Boulevard for two miles, then east on Foster Avenue, a modest residential street. She drove slowly past 278, a white Cape Cod with dark blue shutters, a tidy and cheerful house. She peered and blinked, like a sparrow hawk hunting an insect.

For about a month she saw nothing. Just a quiet house and sometimes a nondescript car. Then, unexpectedly, on a dark muggy Thursday, with her Dodge clattering and the heat indicator touching red, she saw him—Joseph Malloy, Joseph Moldavi, one and the same—and Joseph Masseno, too, she assumed—mowing the lawn, sweating in a T-shirt, muscles bulging, tall body leaning into the curved handle of his power mower, glaring at her Dodge, unaware of the fate closing in on him like gray storm clouds over the Tionega River.

Miss Ferguson now knew all she needed to know. But what was she to do with it? Inform the police?

She considered the possibility. Mr. Moldavi-Malloy-Masseno would be arrested and convicted, she was sure of it. He would be sentenced to a long prison term.

And if Miss Ferguson gave the police an anonymous telephone tip, got him arrested that way, which seemed the safest course, there would be no chance of the trapped man blaming his arrest on her and perhaps later taking revenge.

But there were two problems. One: Miss Ferguson did not believe in prisons. She hated the idea of locking up human beings like cattle. She thought prisons were pestholes, breeding grounds for more crime, teeming swamps of brutality and nameless perversions.

The second problem was more personal. She had come to admire Joseph Moldavi and had finally come to realize it. Exactly why, she didn't know, but she admired him a great deal. He was a suave gentleman, handsome despite the mole, a wide reader, a man of action, a scholar of sorts, surely not a common thug.

The police—oh, dear, she knew the police by reputation. They would not treat their captive like a gentleman and a scholar. They would treat him like a criminal, like a found victim. Chief of Police McEachern obviously hated Mr. Moldavi already, without even knowing him, to judge by the Chief's comments to reporters.

No, Mr. Moldavi could not expect justice in Elm City. He would be demeaned, manhandled, confined, his talents scorned, and then he would be shunted off to prison, perhaps for the rest of his life. Miss Ferguson could meet him again, if at all, only behind bars, or at the morgue, or at the funeral.

No. It must not happen that way.

The next night, in the solitude of her small apartment, with the air conditioner whirring and the bright faces of a Norman Rockwell print beaming down on her, she sat at her Underwood portable and typed out a message on plain, untraceable 3x5 notepaper.

> Dear Mr. Malloy,
>
> Do not try to rob Parrish's Wine Cellar. The police have been informed of your plans. Mr. Parrish has been given your description and is armed. You are in grave danger in Elm City. You must move away. Please, for your own safety, leave town.
>
> An Admirer

She typed his name and address on the blank white envelope, pasted a stamp on it upside down, and made a special trip to the post office to mail it.

Three nights later, when she had worked up the nerve to drive past his house, she found it vacant, tidy but cheerless, a For Rent sign on the lawn.

Mr. Malloy-Moldavi-Masseno had left town, or gone underground. Parrish's Wine Cellar would not be burglarized. Miss Ferguson had succeeded where the Elm City police had failed.

She felt no sense of triumph. A tear trickled down her cheek. If she had been a more emotional woman, she would have drowned her sorrow in a pool of tears, then or later, for that was how she felt about her recent acts and their consequences.

An end to snooping, she vowed. For weeks afterward she concentrated on her coin collection, thankful more than ever for it. At the bank and in her apartment she studied the many faces of the ageless and aloof Miss Liberty, the unsleeping beauty of numismatics, whose copper profile glowed in low relief and whose eyes stared unblinking, unseeing, toward the edge of her tiny universe. Almost as penance she lent another of her precious possessions, a mint 1799 Large Cent, to the Calvert Coin Museum in Baltimore.

Mr. Moldavi was gone. Out of Elm City and out of her life. Forever, she supposed.

For three years.

It was late August when he reappeared, and at first Miss Ferguson did not recognize him. The mole was gone. The beard was gone. He had lost weight. His hair was longer and lighter in color. He wore a pencil-thin mustache, as if trying to impersonate the devil or Vincent Price.

He was carrying a black overnight bag.

As he entered the library, he glanced sharply around, alert but calm. He fixed his attention on the circulation desk and walked toward Miss Ferguson.

At the desk he leaned down, placed his black bag on the floor, and unzipped it with a flourish. He removed a green corked bottle, which he set on the oak counter in front of her.

Her heart jumped to her throat, and she stammered, "Hello. It's nice to see you again, Mr.—"

"Mohrmann," he said, flashing his ivory grin. "It's nice to see *you* again, Miss Ferguson. I brought you a little present—a bottle of wine from an excellent shop on Charles Street. Chateau Margaux '47. I hope you enjoy it."

"But—"

He leaned an elbow on the desk. Miss Ferguson backed away, a chill icing her spine. He continued to smile. "How did I learn your identity? Is that what you're wondering?" He ran a forefinger along his mustache. "It's elementary, my dear. I have a memory for cars—for makes and models and colors and years and dents and licenses. The same kind of memory you must have for names and faces. It's useful in my line of work."

Miss Ferguson had an intense urge to run away, to get to a phone, to call the police. Mr. Moldavi was no longer an object of her concern, he was an instant enemy. She wanted to move but couldn't. Her heart pierced by betrayal, she stood motionless.

"Now, you, Miss Ferguson, you drive an eleven-year-old Dodge Charger, unless you've gotten rid of it. It's reddish violet, rusted out, with a broken left taillight—which is probably fixed by now—and license number 398-KLV." He spread his arms wide, palms up, as if to make light of his talent. Joe the Genius.

She spoke haltingly, her thin voice trilling like a schoolgirl's in spite of her efforts to control it. "But why me, Mr.—? Why are you bothering with me?"

He pretended patience. "My dear lady, when a car goes creeping past my house night after night for two or three weeks, I pay attention to it. I find out who's driving it, and why. Your license number told me who—I have sources for that kind of information—and your charming note told me why."

She felt frightened and ridiculous at the same time. She summoned up her courage. She wanted him gone. "You were foolish to come back, Mr.— The police—"

Mr. Malloy-Moldavi-Masseno-Mohrmann smiled at her with no trace of humor. "I'm just passing through. I can work in whatever city I choose. I'm here for a goodbye look at my secret admirer, nothing more. The museum yesterday was my fourth and last target in Baltimore. I'm moving west."

Miss Ferguson said nothing. She felt a sinking sensation deep within her, touching her soul.

"Yes, I've come from there this morning," he said in an even voice, following her thoughts. His cobalt-blue eyes, the handsome eyes of doom, stared straight into hers. There was no liking in them, only mockery. "Since I won't be going back, Miss Ferguson, could you please mail these books to the Enoch Pratt Free Library in Baltimore for me? I wouldn't want them to be overdue."

He reached into his overnight bag again, and handed her, one by one, five books on coin collecting.

Janet Green

The Most Tattooed Man in the World

It is more than twenty years since we published Janet Green's "The Tallest Man in the World"—a haunting story that gave you an intimate glimpse behind the scenes of European theatrical life. Now we offer another of Janet Green's stories about, in this instance, English show biz . . . Certain backgrounds never seem to lose their fascination, their glitter and glamor. For example, the circus: there's something about it, something that is, as Janet Green's theatrical agent says, "magic all the way" . . .

The bell sounded urgent, insistent, the way only a telephone bell sounds at two o'clock in the morning. I lifted the receiver. Papa Gaudin was calling from Amsterdam. The Great Reinheimer's ulcer had finally killed him, and with a cat man there is never an understudy. Papa had lost his cat act.

I sat up, fully awake now. This was my business as well as his. It had taken me three years to persuade the old gentleman to bring his circus across the Channel. He had no regard for English audiences. He said that his kind of entertainment belonged on the Continent. But he knew, and I knew, that the truth was he spoke no English, and felt too old to learn.

It was clear to me that if I did not move quickly he would ask me to put in another circus. An aqua-show, an ice show, anything. I said I knew a cat man who was free, and when I cradled the receiver I knew I had to find one.

The problem stayed with me and would not let me sleep. I thought coffee might help. I make coffee carefully, slowly. Before the kettle boiled, I recalled a fellow I'd seen in Los Angeles two springs before, a young man with a lot of talent, panache, and no money to buy his own cats. He could step right into the Great Reinheimer's white kid boots and work the act as it stood.

At once I put in a person-to-person call. I chased it through the next two days, then ran him down across the Mexican border, tenting in Ensenata. I was in luck. The end of his engagement was in sight, he said, and he'd be glad to fly to Amsterdam.

After he'd hung up, I sat for a moment. His voice, throaty, vibrant, young, was playing on a memory. Then the picture slipped from the filing cabinet that I call my mind and I saw Jules. I saw how he looked, heard how he sounded. And remembered how I loved him.

I walked the park. Now that I had remembered, I wanted to forget. Quickly. Jules was the best cat man I ever saw, the bravest, the most beautiful, till a snow-leopard clawed his face in love and tore away his beauty. I was the first to see him after it and I went straight out.

Jules was proud. When they took the bandages off, and he saw the result of the Judas Kiss, he disappeared. Plastic surgery can't do much for the deep caress of a passionate leopard's paw.

It happens all the time in my business. They just drop away: the flyer who falls, the knife thrower whose arthritic knuckles betray his eye, the bareback rider who breaks her spine, the crocodile woman who looks on the fangs with fear and has to stop, the actor who can hold the words no longer. And the dwarf who dies. Dwarfs do not make old bones. Only clowns last. Look at Carko, 75 this year, and I have him with the Reislings at a top figure. My father was booking that shriveled old gentleman when I was small enough to run under the horses' bellies and shorter than the shortest dwarf.

I sighed. None of these thoughts ousted Jules. Then I told myself I would think of him as he had been and not as he became. Does he wear a mask? I wondered. Or does he wait for the night and then walk? It was no use. I could only remember the last I saw.

The American from Ensenata, tall and sandy, planed the Atlantic three days later. I met him at the airport and liked him. He was big, broad, ebullient. A good showman. But tense underneath, the way a cat man should be.

We flew to Amsterdam together and met the cats in the pewter-colored light of early morning. You'd have thought he was related, the way those sleepy majestic beasts took to him. He had the touch, the flair, like Jules. I pushed the thought away, saw Papa Gaudin embrace the boy, and knew the London season was safe. My heart lightened. I collect the ten percent, and it's never enough in my business. Expenses are so high.

The three of us left the empty tent together. Then I saw that there had been a fourth and he was leaving just ahead. A tall broad man who wore a heavy German topcoat. I've often thought that topcoats give a distinctive national stamp to a man. My English ulster gives me away everywhere I go. It's good tweed and I've had it years. This fellow walking in front of me was a German. I was sure of that.

Christmas came fast. For me it's always the busiest time of the year. I had artistes up and down the country, and most nights I slept in a train. But I made the Olympic for Papa Gaudin's opening.

That night he took the ring himself, splendid in a silk hat, white tie, red tails, and the tall traditional whip firm in his right hand. Speed. I never saw anything like it. Yet nothing overlapped. That's the secret of being a good ringmaster. Marry the acts without a second's wait, and back it all with a showy brass band that plays music, not just noise.

I sat and basked in the atmosphere. There's something about a circus audience. I suppose it's the kids. But it acts on me like a walk in front of the sea. And the circus itself. I love it all. The liberty horses, Indian flame eaters, Chinese tumblers, clowns, elephants at the end of the first half, the trapeze high up. And clowns again. And again. Magic all the way.

Now young Jacko was in the ring with his twelve entrancing ponies. What would the Education Authorities say if they knew he was only ten years old? I shrugged. They wouldn't believe it. Young Jacko's as good as his old man, Captain Jack. My father found him in Prague. He spoke no English, nothing but his native tongue, but when he died he knew twelve languages.

The atmosphere changed, tensed. The finale had come. Rapidly the riggers formed the big cage in the center ring. The cowboy with his lasso came to one side. The quiet man with the gun to the other. Then happened the sudden moment of darkness, the fine dull sounding call on the trumpets, and then the center arena full of lights to reveal the cat man dressed in the traditional costume of the Ruritanian Captain of Hussars, with gun in one hand and whip in the other. I stared. Sweated. Remembered. He was Jules, big, quiet, magnificent. My eyelids pricked. I shook my head. Jules was gone. This was the sandy American I had brought from Ensenata in old Mexico.

The atmosphere changed again. Heightened. The big thrill was here. The cats were coming, two black jaguars from the Equator, three black panthers from Sumatra, three spotted jaguars from Colombia, four North American pumas, three tigers, six lions and lionesses. And the snow-leopard.

To the syncopation of snapping jaws, throaty, snarling roarings, and flying claws, the American guided the varied felines to their pedestals, then turned his back and crossed the cage.

Now handing the whip through the bars he quickly followed with the gun, then unbuttoned his tunic, threw it from him, pulled off his white silk shirt, and stood. Glistening.

Jules again. Naked to the waist amid a collection of cats that hated each other, and one snow-leopard, whose love could change a man's face from beauty into beefsteak.

I watched the act coldly. The sandy boy was good. He worked well with the snow-leopard. But I knew he would not perform the Judas Kiss. Papa Gaudin cut it from the act after Jules went. There's no time, you see. No time at all. If anything goes wrong, what is it? A gasp. A sigh. And in the moment that it takes the first customer to scream, a career is out, a cat man is finished, and a freak begun.

I shivered. When did it happen? How long ago? Five years? No—six. And the place? Kôln on the Rhine. I got up suddenly. I could not watch the American. Jules was too strong in my memory.

I left the circus and strolled along the midway between the booths. As usual the concession was sublet and the lane was packed. It was grubby with discarded litter, raucous, and alive with human enjoyment. Bright unshielded lights illuminated red, yellow, and green painted posters specially designed to tickle the original sin in all of us. They brought even my jaded head around.

I watched the people, the customers, flooding to rubberneck the fat lady, the dwarf, the double-jointed man, to buy the pink clouds of candy floss, try for the packet of cigarettes at the rifle range, and risk their luck with the new number game. I stopped to see how this last one worked, twigged the gimmick at once, and laughed at their audacity. It was plain the two lads hadn't worked it for long, but they'd made a good start.

Next door the bearded lady had drawn her quota of gawpers. The last sniggering group was going in and just before the curtains closed, I saw her and wished I'd had a warning. By and large, freaks are conceited, arrogant, dirty, believing themselves entitled to special regard in man's esteem.

I'd seen this one completely. I'd marked the low-cut sequined gown showing thin white shoulders and the silky dark beard that fell to the tight canyon between her breasts. I shuddered. I felt the goose flesh on my arms. My father used to tell me I'd have to find some armor against these dislikes, but I never have. I've tried.

I've drawn ten percent before now on a fellow who swallowed live wriggling fish, I've even brought a dozen giraffe-necked women across two continents. Rancid, those. They smell of stale oil. But I've never touched a geek, although I do a certain amount of business in the States. Never could, never will. They bite the heads off chickens for a bottle a day. Blood. Feathers. Mustn't think about it.

I dropped the iron curtain and crossed abruptly to the opposite booth. Automatically my eyes registered the words: *Ulric, The Most Tattooed Man in the World*. I relaxed. This wouldn't bother me. Underneath the tattoo marks I knew he'd be normal, with the right amount of fingers and toes.

More with a sense of retreat than anticipation, I entered the booth. It was small, smelly, and stuffy. Standing among the tight press of people at the back, I watched Ulric, The Most Tattooed Man in the World, coming to the end of his act, his show, his performance, whatever he styled it. Really he did nothing.

He just stood there, tall and rainbow-hued, clad only in the briefest loincloth, flexing his muscles, while in pseudo, high-pressure Americanese his barker told the story of the legend pictured on the fine broad body. And the telling took him from the soles of Ulric's feet to the crown of his proud head.

I listened, following the tale on the body. When I reached the kaleidoscope of colors in his face and saw the eagle spread across the hidden features, something fell into place. This man had been tattooed in Japan.

You see, I read anything. Everything. Nearly always in trains, planes, hotel lounges. And I remember what I read. Now I remembered reading about a bargain, and the terms of it were these: in Japan, if a man agreed to be tattooed from top to toe and left his body on death to a certain university, then he earned himself $3,000. I knew this Ulric had made such a bargain and when he died his skin would join the other skins, stretched tight and taut at that university.

The booth seemed suddenly hotter. I thought I was going to fall, then inched myself to the exit, and outside breathed easier. Walking back to the circus, I tried not to recall the rest of what I had read. But my memory beat me and the air in the midway became as hot and stuffy as it had been in the booth.

This tattooing was a three-year job. It was done in small sections, because the subject could take only so many pricks at a time. No man's skin is less sensitive than another's, and the tattooist's needle is sharp.

I walked faster. I thought of the waterfalls in Japan, the coldest in the world, it is said. The stream that comes straight from the ice contains a curious fixing quality, so that between sessions the volunteer was required to stand beneath it for hours. So Ulric would have stood. He must have been in wild need of a career.

Glad to reach the normal atmosphere of Papa Gaudin's office, I embraced Madame Gaudin warmly, held her from me and praised the violet lace dress, and smiled to see her fat, comfortable, and heavy breasted. But at once the vision of a silky black beard leaped into my mind and would not budge. I asked for a straight Scotch. Quick.

The American brought the brimming glass. I saw that he was happy, the way only a performer whose ears still vibrate with the thunder of the customers' applause is happy. I liked the way he pulled the rug round Jacko's shoulders, where the ten-year-old lay fast asleep on Madame's couch. Jules had been gentle, too.

I looked at Madame and saw her eyes flicker away from mine, oddly and slyly. She knew I was thinking of Jules.

Now with the crack of his tongue, Papa had us all to business. This cat man was good, he told me, nodding sagely. Good enough to be exploited. Perhaps some articles, well-written, well-placed, to titillate the public's interest. Did I know a man?

I did. Harry Learoyd. A clever journalist, a man who could sense news before it was born, shape a story from almost nothing. I said I'd find him and bring him to see the cats and the sandy boy who worked them.

Learoyd wasn't difficult to trace. I only had to telephone six bars and four clubs. Our negotiation was as quick. He asked about a down payment and when I told him the notes were crackling in my hand, he was my man. I arranged to take him in front the following night.

We met in the foyer at the Olympic. I saw him first, a podgy man bulging out of his collar. He said he didn't want to see the whole of the circus, but only the cats, so I took him down the midway. I thought it was safer than a neighborhood bar, which is where he wanted to go.

He looked curiously at the booths that advertised the freaks and seemed disappointed that they weren't showing themselves. I explained that came later, when the midway was crowded. Then he asked where they lived, where they slept, and I pointed out the vans.

Just then a hand caught my arm and I turned. Of course, I knew the fellow at once. It was Harry Farr—Farr and Rix, a top-line patter act till Rix died. Harry tried to go on but one-half of an act is the same as one right-hand glove or one left-foot shoe.

I took quick stock of the jaunty check suit, the aging straw hat, and the dingy teeth in the spry old face. But when I automatically fingered my wallet, Harry stopped me, told me he was all right, minding the hoop-la with Maisie. I was glad they'd stuck together. There was a time when Rix said if Harry didn't throw Maisie out, he'd break up the act, but Harry stood by her and Rix had to give in.

We arranged to have a drink. But both of us knew it was a promise that belonged in the never-neverland. I've no time for drinks outside the ten percent. Harry understood that.

We shook hands warmly enough and then I looked for Learoyd. He'd disappeared. I found him peeking into a van, a van that more than likely housed a freak. I legged it hard toward him. They're touchy, these people. They don't mind being stared at in public, but they hate it in private.

When Learoyd saw me he put his finger to his lips, stepped aside, and indicated the chink between the curtains at the window. I shook my head. Then I saw that his eyes glittered, that his skin wore a sudden sheen, and I knew what it meant. Years of dealing with newspapermen has taught me to know them. Learoyd had a story.

I felt an odd chill and the hairs on the back of my neck beginning to tingle. Those hairs act like an alarm bell to me. Thinking I'd better assess the damage, I took Learoyd's place, looked between the curtains into the van, and then I gaped.

There she sat on the edge of the bed, the bearded freak, disdainful, indifferent, for all the world like a lady of fashion attended by a chic French maid. And as her beard was combed and brushed, carefully, tenderly, she turned her head and yawned.

I knew at once the cause of Learoyd's professional excitement. For the hand that held the brush was tattooed, and the face bent over hers was green, gray, blue. A whole eagle. The king of birds.

I shivered, straightened, came away from the van and looked at Learoyd. His eyes seemed larger and he was sweating.

"I suppose it's the imperfection in each that makes the bond," he said. His voice was husky, stimulated.

I told him sharply that the down payment had been given to publicize the American, the cat man, then I took him back to the circus.

Learoyd listened, watched, made his notes, asked me the correct questions, all with the right amount of considered attention; but I wasn't fooled. I knew he hadn't forgotten the bearded lady, and a fair-sized worry began to cloud my mind.

So I stayed at his heels, then drove him home, and we discussed Papa Gaudin, the circus, the American, and cats in general. But it's the last thing a man says that counts and when I dropped him in Chelsea I heard what he said quite clearly, although his voice was low and reflective.

"If they sleep together, they might have a child. Would it be born with a beard or an eagle's beak?"

I told Learoyd to concentrate on cats. I hoped I sounded like a man who was content with the night's work. Then I left him.

The articles appeared and they were good. Papa Gaudin was satisfied and I had nothing to worry about, till the old man told me that Learoyd was a friendly soul, who came to see them six days out of six. Then those alarm bells of mine began to work overtime.

In my business a hunch is as good as a black and white fact. Cutting a lunch date, I went down to the Olympic, telling myself I ought to pay the American some attention, the way he was paying me ten percent.

Papa Gaudin opinioned if he was anywhere, he'd be with the cats, so I went to find him. There was no sign of the sandy boy, but a big broad man in a German topcoat was standing in front of the cage that held the snow-leopard. I knew I'd seen him before. Then I remembered it. Amsterdam. I wasn't curious, I wasn't even interested. I just thought he might know where I could find the American. So I walked toward him.

He was talking to the white cat, his voice soft, fond, caressing, and I knew at once the coat had lied. He was not a German.

He heard me come behind him and turned sharply. I saw the eagle spread proudly where the features used to be. Then I looked into his eyes.

There was a little silence, while my thoughts shook into place. Now I said his name, his true name.

"Jules."

The tears started, and lay like drops of rain on the eagle's wings. I put up my hand to touch his face. I wanted him to know that I was reaching to the scars beneath and that I loved him.

He understood, and when he spoke it was to comfort me.

"I've made a life. Just sometimes I want to smell the cats."

There was another silence, then the sound of feline claws scraping jealously at the bars behind us.

Jules turned and with gentle Gallic words quietened the snow-leopard.

When next he spoke, his voice was rough.

"How long before the scribbler leaves her in peace?"

I knew that Learoyd's was a terrier's hold. He would not let go till he had his story. So I bought a little time. I made believe I hadn't understood and asked Jules to lunch with me, to sup, dine, or anything that suited him.

He raised his head, sharply and jerkily. "In my flat?" I added hurriedly.

Then Jules laughed and I saw the fine white teeth I remembered so well and experienced a generous moment that brought him back to me as he had been, healthy, strong, with a Frenchman's full appetite for wine, food, and women. Warm rounded women.

The mirage vanished and I saw only the beard.

Now anger took hold of me. I told Jules he was too young to hide himself behind a Japanese legend, too young to be alone.

He answered softly, "I am not alone. I live with the woman I love and who loves me."

I knew he meant the bearded lady.

"Why, Jules?" I asked helplessly.

"We are the same. Both imperfect. That is why we love each other."

I knew that theirs was a secret world and feared that if light fell on it they would be destroyed.

He took my arm and made me look at him. I regarded the part of the legend that I could see and remembered the other. Then he held out his fingers. Tiny Geisha girls danced from joint to joint, and on the palms of his hands I saw blossoms.

"Lovely blossoms in Japan," he murmured.

I marveled that there was no bitterness in his voice. Jules had triumphed.

"I'd like to meet her," I said suddenly. "Are you married?"

Jules's face darkened. I knew because his eyes changed color, and the wings of the eagle were momentarily dulled.

"No," he said.

The explanation came slowly.

"She is young. Just twenty-two. All young girls cherish dreams. She dreams of a knight on a white horse who will lift and carry her out of the circus."

His voice was compassionate. Jules had not always been a freak. He knew there would be no knight for the bearded lady.

"I'd like to meet her," I said again. "Now."

He took my arm and led me away from the snow-leopard.

"I saw you in Amsterdam," I told him. "I didn't recognize you." Then I added, "You must give up that German topcoat. Buy a new one in Paris."

"I never go to France," he said. "Never." And for the first time his voice held pain.

When we reached the van, I could hear her laughing. And I heard Learoyd's strong voice that provoked the laughter.

Jules pushed the door back and we went in. They sat together on the bed. A box of chocolates was open in front of her and she was a-tinkle with giggles. The small baby-pink bow in the silk of her beard was in keeping with her mood. The van was bright with electric light. I had thought it would be near-dark. Shadows are so much kinder to hair on a woman's face.

Mastering my repugnance, I bowed over her hand and saw the sharp pointed teeth before she turned her shoulder, looking at Learoyd, fluttering her eyelids and smiling secretly.

He stood up and stretched, a fat spaniel who had gnawed the bone clean. I knew that she had talked before he spoke Jules's name, his true name.

Then I looked at Jules, and I swear the feathers on the eagle's wings were ruffled as the face beneath contracted.

"You'll come again?" she asked Learoyd eagerly.

"Sure."

"Soon."

"I'll be around."

I knew that he was lying. Learoyd had his story. There was only stale meat here.

When I looked at Jules, I saw that he knew also. He turned to take up the brush and the comb and there was pity in his eyes. As he moved to her I knew it was time for me to go, so I followed Learoyd.

Outside the booth, he lit a cigarette and drew on it as if he'd been without for several weeks.

"Revolting, isn't she?" he said. And shuddered. . .

It was over breakfast in Liverpool where I had a Christmas show that I read his story. It was brilliantly graphic, the tale of the cat man who became a tattooed freak and loved a bearded lady. I guessed Learoyd had made a packet. The Sunday papers pay well.

But suddenly for some reason I wanted to see Jules again, so I skipped Leeds and caught the midday express back to London.

I found him with his love. Today the little bow was white and there was candy in front of her, there was perfume, there were long silk gloves, and there was even a flotsam of black nylon lace.

"You're spoiled," I told her. And the sight sickened me.

She put her head down on the table and sobbed. I said that Learoyd's story would be wrapping fish in a week, then I saw how Jules looked at her down-bent head and spread his varicolored fingers helplessly.

"She misses him," he stated simply.

I guessed that the ugly printed words had passed him by. He was lost in the greater tragedy of her craving for the man who wrote them.

"Learoyd's a busy man," I announced quite loudly. "He hasn't forgotten you. It's work that keeps him away."

She raised her head. Sharply. Fiercely. The hair was all about her face, thick round her brows as well as on her chin.

"It isn't work," she spat. "It's this. This beast."

And she tore at the beard as if it were alive, apart from her, a separate thing.

Jules moved quickly, taking away her hands. "No, no, no!" he cried, as if the black silky strands she tugged trailed from his own chin.

Suddenly she quieted and I saw the pointed teeth holding her lower lip, before she pulled away from Jules's rainbow hand and screamed at both of us, "Leave me, leave me!"

Taking his arm, I drew him toward the exit. But I looked back and marked the small ugly hands with their brightly painted nails clench and unclench, then fold tightly into fists. Above the beard her brown-bead eyes steadied suddenly. I wished I knew what she was thinking.

Jules and I went to see the cats and there in front of the snow-leopard we talked. I swear I was more afraid than Jules, certain that he had lost her. Again it was he who comforted me. The beard was the screen, he said. Behind it they had their world. Just him and her. She would forget Learoyd.

I marveled at his patience, his pity, his love, then left him wooing the snow-leopard. The French words sounded soft and caressing and I could hear the beast responding, clawing and chafing at the bars.

The days went quickly after that. Sam Ellerman called me from Los Angeles. We're old enemies, but sometimes when it suits us we take in each other's washing. He had a beefsteak character making a movie in Rome. There was script trouble. Big trouble. I guessed the character couldn't speak lines. So I went over to tell the director that most movies are better without the dialogue anyway.

It was pleasant in Rome, and I let the argument linger. Sam was footing the bill and I remembered those dollars of mine he'd spent when Maxie opened in Chicago and the dwarfs took exception to the chimp man's billing and let those man-like monkeys loose on the city roofs.

When I returned to England the crocuses were out and the circus was ending. I spoke to Papa Gaudin on the telephone. He told me they were sold out right to the end. Then the old man boasted. He could speak English now, order a drink, pay for it, and tell the waitress she looked a honey. He demanded I go down on Saturday morning to bid the company farewell. I promised and went.

Of course, I looked for Jules first and found him with the American. Since Learoyd's story they had become big friends and in off times shared the key to the snow-leopard's cage. I guessed that Jules had emptied his memory bin for the younger man, and I hoped that in the giving he had been blessed.

He waited for me to inquire after the bearded lady, and when I did he smiled, said she was content again, enjoying life, had made several expeditions to the West End to shop. Today she'd gone to buy gloves.

My face, I knew, mirrored the shock I felt; then Jules explained she wore a veil fixed cleverly over her chin and tied behind her neck. She'd need to, I thought, or they'd be calling 'Beaver' after her. Then I chided myself. But I swear it wasn't only the beard I'd hated. Those little hands, the sharp white teeth, the mouth that I could just see, wetly red, the brown-bead eyes—those were the things that acted on me like a spider crawling down my back.

With a sensitive smile the American left us, and we found our way to the vans. There was a light in the third one and Jules exclaimed, "She's back!" His voice was gay.

As we neared the van, the light flickered and seemed to beckon. He took my arm and we hurried. Jules went in first. I followed.

She had her back to us and was taking off her gloves. The hair was thick at the nape of her neck. And the hair at the nape of mine began to tingle.

I knew before she turned. Her face was smooth. The beard was gone.

Defiantly she moved full into the light. I saw the weak rabbit chin, the small, moist, spiteful mouth, all the mean features that added up to that ugly, white, peaked face. And the tiny dark pin-pricks where the hair had been.

She was more horrible without the beard than with it, and when she smiled I looked away.

Jules went to her, uncertain, dazed. And the beardless lady turned on him such a look of loathing that I felt as if she had stripped and shown me an ugly scar on her body.

When she spoke, her voice was harsh and thin and made plain that she hated him. "Get away—*freak!* All the electric treatment in the world wouldn't cleanse your skin!"

Running her hand round her hideously bare chin, she looked at me and smiled again. "You can tell your friend to come back. I've made myself pretty for him."

I saw Jules's face, saw how the wings of the eagle fluttered, saw how his eyes filled and flooded over. Then I took his arm and drew him from the van.

Inside she was laughing as she pulled the curtains sharply, shutting herself away with her beardless chin.

I tried to reach Jules, tried to hold him. I would have taken him into the smartest, brightest, most crowded restaurant, called him my brother, anything to keep him with me.

But he put aside my hand and said, "I loved the imperfection. It healed me."

Then he went away. I knew I could not call him back. He would not hear. And if he did he would not turn.

I found Learoyd, not because I wanted to hit him or scourge him with my tongue, but because I wanted to share my filthy knowledge.

We shared it and several bottles.

The newspapers were already on the mat when Learoyd saw me to my flat. Then he stooped to lift the paper.

Jules had bound and gagged the beardless lady and put her in with the snow-leopard.

There was nothing left where the beard once grew.

Donald Olson

The Intricate Pattern

The touching and revealing story of two people—the owner of a bookstore and a dirty homeless dropout of a boy . . . and of "the only real mystery of life, which is the mystery of why and how things happen as they do. And this thought was like the delicate quivering of the web that first alerts the innocent ego to the artful designs of the spider-wiled subconscious" . . .

Myrna greeted him with one of those peck-like salutations which only vaguely resemble kisses. "You're late," she said.

"Last minute customer." It was his only reference to the boy.

"Have a good day?"

He could have pinpointed the second when she would ask this, and thereupon he would give her the sales figure for the day and would relate bits of gossip. "Mrs. Antonucci came in, terribly excited. She's had another message from Outer Space. There's going to be a momentous Cosmic Discovery that's going to change all our concepts about the universe. But we mustn't be afraid, she said. It's going to change our lives drastically, but it'll be to our benefit."

And he would dry the dishes for her and they would watch Walter Cronkite and the news and would settle down, he on the sofa, she in the swivel rocker, and they would read advance copies of the new books and presently, yawning, he would get up and move toward the door and she would ask him where he was going and he would answer, "Just outside to check on the weather."

It was the way they communicated—ritual phrases, with smiling glances that didn't quite meet.

Outside he would look at the stars and wish for impossible things.

It wasn't that he disliked the bookstore. After 20 years in the insurance company office it was in many ways a perpetual vacation. He liked books, and by and large the customers were agreeable enough, and yet it was far from the ideal life of which he'd always vaguely but persistently dreamed; it was not the freedom he'd always wanted, though what he meant by freedom he couldn't have said, aside from knowing it was not mere comfort.

At times he thought freedom might be adventure; at other times, peace of mind. Had it been some concrete ambition he would likely have attained it by now, at 38, but it was more a thing of the spirit—one of those hankerings which do not age with the body but rather intensify with the shrinkage of time, as the mind begins to realize there is no longer a limitless future in which to discover the heart's desires.

Often of late he thought that what he truly wanted was his *own* life, not somebody else's, for at times he actually felt he was living a life designed and intended for someone else, and this evoked obscure feelings of guilt, secret yearnings to be punished in some way for the things he had. His life, however, seemed as charmed as it was false. For years he'd saved his money and invested it indifferently, scarcely caring if these investments were sound or foolish, as if it were an enemy's property he was disposing of, or a stranger's. Still, in spite of this, he was left with more gains than losses.

The bookstore turned out to be as confining as the insurance company office. It did not represent freedom, only independence, and the cry still sounded in his heart.

The boy had come in one day just as Edward was closing up. He was slim and blond and had a pug-nosed, blue-eyed Huckleberry Finn face. He wore a ragged blue sweat shirt and shorts made from a pair of jeans. His feet were huge and bare and remarkably dirty, and silver-colored chains around his right ankle had left a greenish brown ring on his skin.

Edward was about to tell him the store was closing when the boy lunged toward one of the racks of paperbacks. "Hey, you've got it! *Born Free!*"

Clumsy brown fingers fished into pockets so frantically the cloth ripped, but came out of each pocket with nothing. He looked sheepishly at Edward. "I guess I forgot my money. Okay if I pay you tomorrow?"

Edward looked into the boy's strange blue eyes. Saying it perhaps because he was tired or because he felt a flash of envy for the boy's youth and spirit, and hating himself for saying it, he said, "It'll still be here tomorrow."

"I'll come earlier tomorrow," the boy said, unoffended. He looked around. "I never even knew this place was here."

On the way home Edward drove out into the country along a road from which you could see far off into a deep purple-misted valley glade. The air was dry and cool and smelled of pine. More urgently than ever before, he was touched by that poignant and mysterious sense of something drifting irretrievably out of his reach.

The boy came back the next day, but again he had no money and this time he stood by the rack with his nose in *Born Free.*

"If you want to read it but not own it I'm sure the library must have a copy," Edward felt impelled to remark.

"That's okay," said the boy, one of those teenage put-off replies which Edward found unanswerable.

He must have been an exceedingly slow reader, Edward decided, because he came back every day at three o'clock and stood there deeply absorbed in the same book. By then, however, Edward was curiously intrigued by the boy—he wasn't as annoyed as he ordinarily would have been by an habitual nonbuying browser; and he actually began to look forward to seeing him every day. He learned that his name was Tom Rodack and that he went to the high school, or said he did, although none of the other high-school students who stopped at the store ever spoke to him or appeared to recognize him.

Edward assumed that once the boy had finished *Born Free* he would not return, but by then he had discovered *Living Free* and *Forever Free*—thanks to Edward's pointing them out.

Occasionally, as the weeks went by, Edward gave him simple duties to perform, such as dusting the books and washing the windows. But there was a reckless clumsiness about the boy; his attention span was limited, and his enthusiasm, though quickly sparked, was of short duration.

Nevertheless, the hours when Rodack was not there began to seem empty to Edward, and when the boy did show up, a certain oppressiveness lifted from Edward's heart and the lines of his mouth became less rigid.

Like most complex people Edward was seldom bored by candor and simplicity, when they were genuine, as Rodack's were. That may have been why he tolerated Rodack's presence, or it may have been that he was grieved to think of that wild blue light being extinguished from Rodack's eyes, of the tiresome obligations of life crippling the pride of that stalwart body. The boy was all instinct, all feeling, with a lopsided nature that would make life a never-ending struggle.

One morning Edward got the shock of his life when he arrived at the store at his usual time, 8:45, unlocked the door, switched on the lights, and walked into the back room, where he found Rodack asleep in the wicker lounge chair.

Edward knew he should have been angry; in fact, he was angry at first, but still he didn't choose to awaken the boy, finding something touching about the vulnerability of his sleeping face. And by the time Rodack awoke, Edward's anger had changed to perplexity.

"Easy," grinned Rodack, when Edward asked him how he'd got in. "I sticky-fingered your key one day and had a duplicate made."

"But, Tom, you had no right to do that."

"But, gee, you might get sick someday or something and want me to open up for you."

"What time did you get here this morning?"

"Came in last night."

"You've been here all night?"

"Sure."

"But your folks must be worried about you."

"They're dead."

Edward had studiously avoided ever asking Rodack any personal questions. Knowledge seemed always to confer a kind of obligation, which Edward wished to avoid.

"Then whom do you live with?"

"I kind of move around."

Rodack was in and out of the store all day; he seemed unusually eager to please Edward, to do odd jobs and run errands, and that afternoon when it came time to close he said he would lock the door when he left.

"Well, it's closing time right now," Edward said, turning off the lights.

"Can't I hang around for a while?"

Edward looked at him. "What for?"

"You know that creep who came in and tried to sell you his watch? I didn't like the way he kept looking at the cash register."

"You know I don't leave money in the register overnight."

"Yeah, but he might not know it. I better stay here and keep watch. You know, just in case."

Edward surprised himself by not objecting. He knew it was wrong, knew that Rodack simply wanted to stay the night, yet he hadn't the heart to refuse.

The following morning Rodack was gone when Edward got to the store, but in the back room he found an army blanket and two empty boxes of animal crackers.

All this time he had said nothing to Myrna about Rodack, although it would be on the tip of his tongue to relate some especially amusing bit of nonsense the boy had come out with; but then he would stop, for some reason unwilling to have Myrna know anything about the boy. It was inevitable, of course, that sooner or later Myrna and the boy would meet, considering how much time Rodack spent at the store.

As it happened, an epidemic of Asian flu spread through the town. Edward caught it, and one morning he was too sick to go to work. That night Myrna came home, fixed his supper on a tray, and brought it up to him with the evening paper.

"Darling," she said, tucking the napkin under his chin without looking into his eyes, "the horridest boy came into the store today. I had the dickens of a time getting rid of him. He *said* he was a friend of yours."

"Tom Rodack," said Edward laconically, sipping his tomato juice.

"He reeked of perspiration. I could still smell him after he'd gone. Doesn't he have a mother?"

"I suppose so," he lied.

"Well, she ought to make him get a haircut and get some decent clothes. He talked as if you two were great pals. Does he come in often?"

"Rather, yes."

"You shouldn't let people like that hang around. Mrs. Wilcox and her daughter came in. You should have seen the looks they gave him. I finally had to tell him to leave if he wasn't going to buy anything."

Edward looked at her coldly. "You shouldn't have done that."

She laid a hand on his hot forehead. "Before you know it he'll be bringing all his friends. Kids are always looking for a new hangout."

"He hasn't any friends."

"Well, if he thinks you're his friend couldn't you tactfully suggest he take a bath more often?"

Edward smiled to himself. Rodack was scornful of such concessions to civilization, and Edward secretly admired him for it. Life was, after all, a record of such concessions, and with each one of the individual sacrifices some essential part of himself; for each concession exacts a price until one is bereft of all the wild free impulses of his nature and becomes a plodding creature of motive, his body shaved and scented and clothed according to the dictates of fashion, his mind furnished with the proper attitudes of the day.

Suddenly, lying there in bed, he knew what he meant by freedom, that elusive abstraction that sounded on the lips like the soaring flight of some great white bird; freedom was the courage not to make concessions.

One evening shortly after, Edward lay watching a movie on television; he seldom read any more. Myrna sat with a book by the window. About eight o'clock she stood up and looked out into the street.

"Edward, come here."

"What is it?"

"He's standing out there on the corner, under the streetlight."

"Who is?"

"That boy!"

Edward felt a strange excitement. He didn't look away from the screen. "What boy?"

"Your *friend*. The kid who came in that day you were sick."

"Can't be."

"Come here and look."

"He doesn't even know where we live."

"Well, come here and look, can't you?"

Edward got up slowly and stood beside her, looking out.

"Well, it's him, isn't it?"

"Yes."

"He doesn't even have a jacket on. Just that ragged filthy sweat shirt. He must be insane. He'll catch pneumonia."

"I'd better tell him to come in."

She clutched his sleeve. "No. Don't."

"Why not?"

"I don't know. I'd just rather you didn't."

For a moment he really hated her. "You'd rather he stood out there and caught pneumonia?"

"He ought to have his head examined."

"I'm going to have him come in and I'll give him one of my jackets."

"Can't you just take it out to him?"

But Edward didn't go out. How could he have explained to Rodack why he couldn't invite him into the house?

Rodack said nothing to Edward the following day about his standing outside the house; Edward said nothing to the boy. But something did happen that day, a revelation that added an element of deep pathos to Edward's feelings about Rodack. It was inventory time and Edward put the boy to work reading off titles to him from the shelves. Rodack said he didn't want to do it.

"It's silly," he objected.

"Silly or not, it has to be done."

"But, heck, you can see what books are here. You know where every single book in this place is. So why do you want to write them down?"

"That isn't the point." And he tried to explain the purpose of the inventory.

"I'll wash the windows instead. Or let me dust the shelves."

This puzzled Edward, for he knew how much Rodack really disliked those chores. "The windows are okay, and the shelves don't need dusting."

"Then I guess I can't help you."

Neither insolence nor defiance characterized this remark, but a curious sort of resignation touched with sadness, and it alerted Edward to something happening behind the boy's placid inscrutable face.

"If you're going to hang around here, Tom, you've got to help out when I need you."

Rodack looked gravely down at his toes. "I wouldn't be much help with the inventory. I can't read."

At first Edward thought he was being funny, and then he realized he was in dead earnest. The grin faded from Edward's face. "What about *Born Free*—and *Living Free*—and *Forever Free?*"

"I saw the movie of *Born Free*. You told me what the others were. I wouldn't have known."

All those hours, standing there with his nose in those books, staring at them, pretending to read them. Why? *Why?* The prodigious injustice of it all struck Edward like a dizzying blow. Had no one cared enough to teach him?

"They tried," Rodack admitted. "Something was wrong. I just couldn't hack it."

"But they have special kinds of instruction these days."

"Not where I come from."

"Tom, where *did* you come from? You've never told me."

Rodack looked sly, mysterious. "Heck of a long ways from here. Don't ask me 'cause I ain't ever goin' back."

Edward kept thinking of all those hours when Rodack had wandered among the rows and racks of books, touching them, staring at them, thumbing slowly through them, and always, he now realized, with a look of baffled wonder that Edward had mistaken for enchantment. While all the time the real enchantment was denied to him. And Edward had thought Rodack was free!

For the first time in his life Edward felt the stirring of a cause within his soul, the first inkling of a positive ambition.

"Would you like to know how to read, Tom?" Edward asked quietly.

"What's the use? I can't."

"Oh, yes you can. I'm sure you can."

Nothing else was important, not really, after that. Only the lessons. Edward was the soul of patience, the ideal instructor, for he was truly inspired. And now he would deal curtly and perfunctorily with anyone who came into the store. If someone asked for a certain book he would often say no, they didn't have it, rather than take the time to check or find it; and sometimes, if the interruptions were so numerous they still didn't have time to complete the daily lesson, he would pull down the shade and turn out the front lights as much as an hour or two early.

Meanwhile his own paperwork suffered. It had always been his practice to type up special orders the same day they were received, so that his customers could be assured of two- or three-week delivery. Now he was letting these orders pile up, and the larger the stack grew the less inclined he felt to tackle the chore of typing them up. Complaints began to mount, orders were canceled, and business began noticeably to fall off.

"It beats me," said Myrna, balancing up at the end of the month. "Business isn't half of what it was last year. What do you think is wrong?"

Edward shrugged. "Don't forget, they warned us the retail book business was an interesting way to make very little money."

"I can't say you're even showing much interest lately."

Edward said nothing. She persisted. "Is it beginning to bore you, darling? Is that it?"

This he denied, but without conviction. She said nothing more until later, over dessert. "Edward, I've been thinking. I know we had an agreement. You would run the store, I would run the house and keep the accounts. But I'm left with so much time on my hands. Why not let me take care of the store for two or three days a week, or in the afternoons? You wouldn't feel so confined."

"Have I complained?"

"Not exactly."

He felt she was being dishonest. "Are *you* complaining?"

She regarded him with mild impatience. "I'm not complaining about a thing. But I'm smart enough to know that something's wrong. Let's face it, figures don't lie. The business is in trouble. Serious trouble."

"And you think it's my fault."

"I'm suggesting it may be mine. I'm quite willing to shoulder more of the burden."

In fact, she developed the unnerving habit after that of dropping into the store on frequent and unexpected occasions, quite like some sort of inspector, and Edward's resentment was magnified because of her uncanny ability to pop in at the most inopportune moments.

"But you never *told* me, Edward," she scolded. "You're obviously encouraging that kid to hang around."

"My God, Myrna, haven't you heard a word I've said? This boy is eighteen years old and can't *read*."

"But, darling, that's not your fault. We're running a bookstore, not a remedial reading clinic."

He didn't quite know how to explain to Myrna that for the first time in his life he felt that he was doing *his* thing, not somebody else's. Perhaps freedom, in its purest sense, meant service, a heretofore untraveled road by which he might resume his long-stalled journey toward fulfillment.

The experience of helping someone who so desperately needed help proved a heady and self-nourishing sensation, especially when his efforts met with far greater success than he had dared hope. Where professionals had failed, he was succeeding, and once he had overcome Rodack's conditioned-by-failure apathy the boy forged ahead with remarkable speed.

Myrna was the only obstacle, and it soon became clear to Edward that she was jealous of Rodack, intensely jealous, and when he would summon all the patience he could muster to prove to her how foolish this was she would merely get angry and rave all the more violently.

"I guess it was a bad idea after all," she finally declared. "The bookstore, I mean. It's losing money—*my* money, I don't have to remind you—and you're running it deeper into the ground every day. I think it's time we bailed out."

He looked at her, astonished. "You mean—sell?"

"Yes, sell. Only an idiot throws good money after bad."

Rodack was aware of all this tension—Myrna left *him* in no doubt at all of how she felt about his presence in the store; but he couldn't believe, any more than Edward could, that she was serious about selling out. He had begun now to sample all the riches of the written word and the experience wrought a swift and amazing change in the boy's personality: it opened him up and healed the budding neurosis that had made him so jumpy and cantankerous, and he even began to take more pride in his appearance.

Edward told him there was no reason now why he couldn't get himself a good job. "And you'll be able to find yourself a room." Now that he could read, Rodack had seemed to find the bookstore the perfect place to live.

"Can't I just bunk in here like I've been doing—till you sell the place, I mean?"

Edward agreed that he could, and Rodack looked absurdly grateful.

"I'm going to repay you, you know. For all you've done for me. No one's ever been this good to me."

"You don't owe me a thing, Tom."

"Oh, yes I do. And I'm going to pay you back. Some way."

Meanwhile Edward had been giving a great deal of thought to what had happened, and it occurred to him that there must be hundreds of people in the same fix as Rodack—people with serious reading difficulties who might respond to the same sort of unconventional therapy. Perhaps the bookstore could even be converted into a remedial reading clinic. The idea excited him.

"But that would take money," he confided to Tom. "Even if Myrna would agree. Which she won't."

Myrna, in fact, thought of nothing but selling the store, the sooner the better, and Edward was disconcerted by the swiftness with which she came up with a prospective buyer—a couple of retired schoolteachers with some money saved and a desire for a respectable small business of their own. Edward could see they were serious about wanting the store, and when it was proposed that the two ladies spend an entire day or two there to get an idea of the clientele and amount of business transacted on an average day, Edward had no choice but to comply.

"And listen to me, Edward," Myrna made it clear. "I want that *boy* out of there. I don't want him sticking his nose in the door while the ladies are there. I don't want him within a *mile* of the place. Otherwise I'm calling the police and having him arrested for trespassing."

Edward tried as tactfully as possible to explain this to Rodack, who wasn't the least abashed.

"That's okay, Ed. There's something I've got to do anyway."

"Don't be silly. I said you didn't owe me a thing."

"Yes, I do. It's funny, you know. It seems to me now that I was meant to come in here that first day. I mean, gosh, think of all the places I could have gone that day! And yet I came in here. I mean, *why?* Unless I was meant to. I think you were the one person in the world who could help me."

For some mysterious reason this little speech of Rodack's filled Edward with a secret and extraordinary satisfaction, as if he'd been given a glimpse of the intricate pattern of his life and how innumerable unrelated events had been interwoven to form this pattern; and he thought with wonder and awe about the only real mystery of life, which is the mystery of why and how things happen as they do. And this thought was like the delicate quivering of the web that first alerts the innocent ego to the artful designs of the spider-wiled subconscious.

Still, this did not keep him from hoping that business would be so bad on the day the prospective buyers were present that they would immediately lose interest.

Unfortunately, this was not the case. It seemed, on the contrary, that every customer the store ever had had suddenly and perversely taken it into his head to buy a book or stationery or a greeting card or *something*. Edward could tell from the delight on the ladies' faces that their minds were now firmly made up: they would buy the business.

He went home later than usual that night, having stopped off at a bar for a couple of drinks, which was something he had never done before. Never.

When he did get home and found the house dark, the degree of his surprise was affected by the slight intoxication of his senses, and it must be assumed that this was why he felt neither alarm nor apprehension. He let himself in. No aroma of cooking food, no clatter of dishes and silverware from the kitchen. Only a pervasive silence. He went from room to room looking for Myrna and never paused to wonder why he did not even once call out her name.

He found her in the bathroom, but she was not taking a bath. Her head was totally submerged in the tub.

Apparently she had slipped while getting out of the bathtub and fallen back, striking her head on the end of the tub, becoming unconscious, and sliding under the water. The police asked a number of routine questions and took the trouble of confirming with the two ladies that he had been in the store all day. The doors of the house had been locked; there was no reason to believe that Myrna's death was anything but an accident.

Still, Rodack's candor the following day was oddly disconcerting, for the boy was as blunt-spoken as ever and his smile was unevasive and congratulatory.

"Now you're free to do whatever you want to do," he told Edward. "You can open that reading clinic if you want to and help other people just like you helped me."

"And what will you do?"

"Shove off, I guess. I've had enough of this burg."

"What did you do all day yesterday?" Edward's voice was carefully toneless.

Rodack still smiled. "Looked for the present I wanted to buy you."

He handed Edward a small package. "Don't open it till I'm gone."

Edward kept it, in fact, for several days before opening it; he was busy with funeral arrangements, and Rodack had left town by the time Edward got around to seeing what was in the package.

At first it seemed like a rather tasteless joke. It was a book—a noted journalist's factual account of a notorious crime. Rodack had probably taken the book from the shop without bothering to pay for it.

There was an inscription in the boy's bold scrawl, along with a house key taped to the title page. Edward recognized the key, a duplicate of one he always carried and which he'd often left on his desk in the back room of the store.

Edward skimmed through the book that evening. It recounted the case of a prominent society woman who had been murdered by being struck over the head and submerged in a bathtub full of water. The woman's lover and alleged assailant had been arrested and tried, but the jury had acquitted him—there had been insufficient evidence that her death was not an accident. A misplaced key had been one of the prosecution's minor exhibits.

Before closing the book, Edward turned back and reread the boy's inscription: *Dear Ed—Without your help I would never have been able to read this book. With lasting gratitude, your friend, Tom Rodack.*

Ellen Arthur

The Scene of the Crime

Ellen Arthur's first story, "Cal Always Said," appeared in the November 1971 issue of EQMM. Her second story, "The Scene of the Crime," reminds us of what we wrote about Lika Van Ness's second story, "Something Like Growing Pains," in our November 1972 issue: it "shows a considerable advance, both in technique and telling; but even more important is the deeper substance of what the author has to say." Yes, our new writers advance impressively—they are the lifeblood of our field for the future...

"Could you let me have Number Twelve if it isn't occupied?" I knew it wasn't—I wouldn't have been standing there asking for it if it was. I told him that twelve was my lucky number, that I had a sale to close in the morning, and the motel clerk looked up, a decency he'd neglected till then. He was a little man with fuzz on his ears and glasses that bit into a sharp nose, a nose that appeared locked in mid-sniff.

I could see that he didn't care for me, as some short men do not care for tall men, and I could also see that he was wondering if I knew about Number 12. But he gave me the key, and I was able to turn my back and drop the visiting-fireman act.

I took the Volkswagen around, parked it in front of the cluster marked *Rooms 10–20,* and carried my suitcase down the covered cement walk. I paused to look down a tunnel-like opening between Room 15 and Room 16; there was a door with a bug light above it and a sign under the light: *LAUNDRY*, and, beneath that, *ICE*. As I passed windows, some lighted, others dark, all with drawn curtains, I thought of my sister, Cara, taking this walk two weeks earlier, walking with a young sailor beside her. What on earth had gone wrong? How could she have angered him? What could she have refused that young man—Cara, who never refused anyone anything?

The Lord knows I had tried to find out, tried my best to see the sailor, but his lawyer was inflexible. A man with no handles. Just a few hours ago he'd thrown me out of his office again, actually threatening me with a Peace Bond.

I unlocked the door of Number 12 and thought how much of a child Cara had been. Even at 34 she had been a child. She'd gone into this room like a little girl crawling into an abandoned refrigerator, full of anticipation, thinking of spooky secret fun, and finding death instead. She must have been terrified. Peering into the dark room I was suddenly ashamed. I called myself a voyeur, a morbid and foolish man. There was nothing rational in my coming here, and I like to think I'm rational.

Yet I reached inside for the light switch and entered the room—because Cara's death had unsettled me so, and because I couldn't shake the notion that here, alone in the place where she had died, away from family and friends, I might be able to understand what had happened.

I closed the door and looked around at once for the ice bucket, deliberately putting off a study of the room until I could make a drink. A few minutes later, filling the bucket, standing in the gloomy light that haloed the ice machine, I felt like the murderer himself. He had been here and had bought a soft drink from that machine over in the corner—he had admitted that much.

There was some validity in identifying with him. I *was*, in one sense, Cara's killer. Because I loved her best. If anyone could have deflected Cara, I was the one. I loved her best. It was wrong of me to care for her more than my good sister Rachel, more than my decent parents; but it had always been so. Perhaps if I'd tried harder. . .

Sometimes I could reach her. I had stopped her drinking. That was years ago, and not until she'd wrecked her car and put our father in the hospital, but I did it. I stayed with her day and night. By the time she came to trial, Cara was finished with drinking for good—though the Lord knows she must have needed it now and then.

I went back to Room 12, fixed my drink, and examined the room. I tried hard to see something meaningful, but of course I couldn't. What an idiot I was! The room was like every other motel room—reproduced by cloning, marching to infinity, living up to the promise of all its twins: it would tell nothing, not a whisper.

Everything in the room confirmed it: soap in a sealed wrapper, glass in a transparent paper bag, writing paper in an envelope in the center drawer. Who has been on the road in America and could not find his way stone-blind around such a room? What had I hoped to learn?

I sat with my Scotch, going slow because I knew I would make another as soon as the glass was empty. How else could I sit where the murderer must have sat before he put his hands around my sister's throat? Why had he done it? My one brief look at him had left me baffled. He seemed incredibly young, didn't look strong enough or cruel enough. But he'd done it, and then, stricken by what he'd done, had fled barefoot in the night, leaving Cara for the maid to find.

He had, of course, denied it when they caught him. He claimed to have gone out for a soft drink and returned to hear voices in the room: "What's the matter with you? This is me, Carolyn!" And an angry male voice: "I know who you are." The young sailor said he ran, assuming that Cara had a husband who had tracked them to the motel. He had not known she was dead, he said, until they arrested him two days later.

A single word in his story, the name Carolyn, caused me to doubt his guilt momentarily. I thought George Kiley might have killed her—Cara had been married to him, and I must admit she gave him reasons to murder her. But that was a long time ago, and I realized at once that George wouldn't have bothered with Cara; he would never have slipped so clumsily between the rungs of the ladder he was climbing. George was a big man now, and he meant to be bigger.

No, the sailor did it. Cara must have mentioned her given name in some context or other, and he cleverly decided it would give his story the sound of truth. Well, he would pay now for whatever joy Cara might have brought him. People always did.

I sat listening to the anonymous sounds: traffic on the highway, crickets, a television playing, indistinct voices in the room next door, an occasional thud. Cara had died among such sounds.

I had seen her two nights before her death. She was appearing at the Court Lounge, and I went to see her. No one else in the family kept any contact with her, but occasionally I drove reasonable distances to hear her sing, to sit and talk with her. She had a moderately good voice and a strikingly intimate way of using it—a sort of piano-lounge voice. I enjoyed it. No—more than that—I was grateful for it, because, to be truthful, all of us, even I, had been relieved when Cara found this way to make a living. It kept her out of New England a good part of the time, and we'd been wondering how to do that. She became Cara, billing herself by the one name, and not troubling our lives.

I remember that she sang well that last time I saw her, seemed more beautiful than ever, and I was proud of her. Her soft smoky songs suited her; they were all of a piece with her tilted eyes and her full unsubtle mouth. She did surprise me with her final number. *Those Were the Days.* It wasn't a tempo she would ordinarily choose, but she handled it well, and I think of it now particularly because it was the last enjoyable part of that evening.

We had coffee together after closing and I bullied her. I was angry that she hadn't told me she was coming to the Court, that I'd picked up the information by hearing her voice on a local radio talk show—a promotion for her current appearance. I was also more than a little annoyed at the things she'd told the talkmaster. They were views I knew she held, but I never expected to hear her speak of them on the radio. "Suppose Mother had heard you?" I asked. "Or Rachel?"

She looked at me strangely, as if trying to place these people I'd mentioned. "Did they?"

"I don't know. I don't think so."

She shrugged. "Well then? Anyway, the man wanted a good interview—I couldn't let him down. But I'm sorry you heard it," she said, and I knew she meant it.

I argued and made her sad. I accused her—a stab I knew was false—of aping the new generation. I tried to make her consider the family. I spoiled that meeting, and even though I didn't know it was our last, I went away angry with myself as well as Cara.

Taking these thoughts with me to the window of the motel room, I parted the curtains and stared out at the highway, at the occasional car moving in the night like someone breathing in and out. I told myself that I couldn't have changed her, that she was never very different, not even when she was small and we had called her Carolyn. Hadn't she always given what was asked—anything—toys, candy, clothes, her company, her complicity? Once she pulled a fire alarm and would only say that she was asked to do it. Lord. how she tormented our parents, such dutiful people, so religious. . .

I closed the curtains abruptly. The thought of my parents, the image of my mother at Cara's graveside—Rachel, too—their patient animal eyes. . .It was impossible to sit quietly, so I prowled the motel room, opening drawers, slamming them shut. I saw the extra blankets in the deep drawer, thick maroon blankets, probably never unfolded. Who needed them in a motel room? Such a warm place, full of the warmth of flesh. And, ah, yes, there was the writing paper—even more useless. People found other things to do, and the paper stayed pure in its pure packet.

I decided to tear it up, make a change, dent the complacency of the room. The maid would be astonished at having to replenish the silly envelope. I was standing with the paper in my hand, ready to rip, when I noticed something on the back of the envelope that I'd tossed onto the dresser. I can remember seeing myself in the mirror, seeing my astounded face looking back at me.

It was a foolish thing that I saw marked on the envelope—or would have been if I hadn't known what it was. A scribble. Two small crosses inked thoughtlessly there; each with three tiny circles, two in the upper angles of the crossbeam, and the third enclosing the intersection of the cross. The doodle had religious significance, the three circles representing the members of the Holy Family. I knew because I had often drawn it myself—in imitation of my father. He had learned it sometime in childhood, perhaps putting it at the top of his papers in parochial school. My father. An usher in church, taking time between his duties to kneel in a rear pew, praying for Cara, praying with suffocating monotony.

I didn't have to ask myself why my father had done it; only why *now*, when Cara's life touched his so seldom? There had been times when I wouldn't have blamed him, times when Cara must have ground his soul too fine. Why, for example, hadn't he killed her that dawn when he found her, after a long night of searching, asleep on a littered beach, curled up on the sand, some man's shirt clutched in her upflung fist, and a smile on her still face? That was a time for murder.

Shortly before Cara died, I was reminded of that awful scene. I was walking along a pond beach, feeling disturbed by the carelessness of people—the discarded cans, the empty cigarette packs, the profusion of flip-top tabs, looking like female symbols, cheap aluminum statements of sin. Suddenly I was seized with the fear that if I kept walking I would see Cara stretched out amid the trash, perhaps just beyond the next bend. . .Three days later she was dead. Perhaps it was a premonition meant to prepare me for her death. But nothing, nothing could have prepared me for that motel room or lessened the impact of that damning scribble I held in my hand.

The envelope with the scribble had to be burned. With shaking fingers I began to tear it and stack it in the little ashtray. I struck a match and watched the flame catch up the crosses, curling and twisting them. Tiny stickmen dancing in fire. How had my father come to make them, I wondered. Had he stayed in the room with Cara's body? I couldn't imagine it.

Then I thought of the young sailor. My father had, appallingly, been waiting for him to return! Good God! The sailor had done right to flee—*"Let him who is in the field not turn back to take his cloak."* He had certainly saved himself.

But *had* he? I understood then for the first time the difficulty facing me, and I wished to God I had never come to this room. I did not want to know that the sailor was innocent and that he was not at all safe. He and my father could not both be safe. It lay before me like a physical law: two bodies cannot occupy the same safety at the same time.

I lifted the telephone, replaced it, and drank. Then I lifted it again, replaced it, and drank again. Cara, I thought bitterly, would have no problem about this. She would save the sailor because he was the immediate one; later she would give all her comfort to our father. But I was not Cara. And my father was very beloved to me.

I was still struggling with this enormity when I heard footsteps coming along the walk. They stopped at my door, and someone knocked sharply. Who? No one knew where I was. No one. Puzzled, I opened the door and saw two men. One was a detective—I knew him, Sergeant Mooney; the other one I'd never seen. Mooney spoke. "Hello, Mr. Kane. This is Detective Pierce. Can we talk for a few minutes?"

I nodded dumbly. They had discovered something. Why else would they come? Oh, my poor father. "Of course, Sergeant. Come in. How did you know I was here?"

Mooney and I took the chairs and Pierce sat on the bed. I offered them a drink and they turned it down. Mooney's serious face made me increasingly certain that they knew about my father's guilt. At least I hadn't been the one to tell them.

"How did you know where to find me?" I asked.

"The clerk," Mooney said. "He remembered seeing you at the

inquest and he thought it was strange—you coming here and asking for this room."

"Of course," I said. "I should have realized. But then I was so upset that day. I suppose he would have been there, wouldn't he?" I tried to speak calmly, aware now that they *didn't* know about my father. They had come simply because the nosey little man at the desk had called them.

"Why *are* you here?" Mooney asked. He was a big man, ponderous, kind. I'd known him for years. We met at Cara's trial. After the car crash. He was with the Accident Investigation Unit then. He tented his fingers now and peered at me. It was a gesture I'd seen him make before. Pierce sat silent on the bed.

"I thought I could understand something about Cara's death if I came here alone." It sounded lame now, even to me. Policemen are very realistic. It's difficult to speak to them about fancies.

"You know, Mr. Kane," Sergeant Mooney said, "when we got this call I kind of thought it might be you. The clerk didn't remember who you were—just that he'd seen you in court. It was the second call I got about you. The other one was from the sailor's lawyer. You were there again."

The other detective got up suddenly and moved toward the dresser. He motioned to Mooney and we all stared at the ashtray. "Were you burning something, Mr. Kane?"

I tried to distract them by speaking of my need to see the sailor, to question him. But it was useless. The one called Pierce put the charred curls into a small plastic bag, and Mooney turned to me. "We have several unidentified prints from this room," he told me, "prints that don't belong to your sister or the sailor or the help. We assumed that previous occupants had left them. Do you think some of them are going to turn out to be yours, Mr. Kane?"

I sat down and covered my face. I could see where my bungling was leading. "No, Sergeant, they won't be mine. I may as well tell you. I can see you're going to find out. It was my father. He needs help." I told him the story then, hating myself for telling it. I finished by asking him if the burned envelope could be reconstructed.

Mooney didn't answer. His eyes were curiously opaque; there was something in them I couldn't read. "Are you feeling okay?" he asked. "Who's your family doctor, Mr. Kane? And your lawyer?" Then he launched into a torrent of words, and I knew, incredibly, that he was reading me my rights. It made me wild.

"What's wrong with you? Haven't you been listening? My father killed her—he needs help!"

Sergeant Mooney took me by the arm, gently. "Do you remember when we first met?" he asked. It seemed an odd question under the circumstances. "Do you remember that your sister went to prison for manslaughter? In connection with the death of your father?"

My head began to pain as I tried to figure out what he was up to. Was this lie supposed to shock some additional information out of me? Did he think I was holding back? We went outside, the three of us, and I saw the little man, the clerk standing on the walk. What on earth could be happening? I decided to ask him.

"Pardon me, sir. I wonder if you know anything about the laws of this state concerning vehicular homicide?" My question appeared to unnerve him. His eyes loomed large behind his glasses, his face paled. I shall never forget how he looked standing there as we drove away, hopping, agitated, just like a disabled bird.

I think of him now as I stare sourly at the doctors. I am so ghastly weary of doctors. That little man is the one who needs a doctor. These doctors need doctors. They crouch around me like crocodiles, their mouths yawning, their mouths full of insinuations and lying questions. This is the most godawful place I've ever stayed in—worse than a motel.

These people are inordinately interested in personal matters. They would give anything to know, for instance, why I've never married. A gross invasion of my privacy. They also question me closely about the crosses and circles that I pen idly while they talk. They suspect some deep inner meaning—no matter that I tell them it's a common doodle, that my father frequently scribbles it quite unconsciously. One of them tried to tell me that my father never recovered from the accident, that he died years ago. He's in collusion with Sergeant Mooney, I see that now clearly.

But they are all liars in one way or another. Their mouths are filled with soft cottony lies. I watch the wisps move gently at the back of their throats as they breathe in and out. I'd like to put out my hands and stop them, squeeze off the air. They won't leave me alone, and I need time to sort out my sister's death.

I will never rest until I discover why that sailor killed Cara. She wouldn't have refused him anything. I know that. I'm certain that if I could get out of here, if I could go to the place where she died, sit in that motel room, that I could find the answer.

Michael Innes

A Matter of Disturbing Incidents

As a relief from his high-pressure duties at Scotland Yard, Sir John Appleby tackles what appears to be a lighthearted little case involving Aunt Jessica's poltergeist . . . and the happy result is a fine example of suave and sophisticated English crime-writing . . .

Detective: SIR JOHN APPLEBY

"Aunt Jessica had a poltergeist," Judith Appleby said, as she watched her husband pour drinks. Sir John had got home from Scotland Yard after a hard day. High-powered criminals were very much abroad in the land, and he had conferred at length with half a dozen of his senior officers about one large-scale villainy or another. He deserved to be entertained with a little relaxing family gossip.

"In that case your aunt had better keep a sharp eye on the new kitchen maid." Appleby handed Judith her sherry. "Better ring her up and tell her so."

"There isn't a new kitchen maid. In fact, kitchen maids are no longer heard of."

"In the kind of household your Aunt Jessica runs I'll bet they are, although there may be a new name for them. In any event, what the old lady must look out for is an adolescent girl, preferably of worse than indifferent education and necessarily of hysterical temperament. If poltergeists exist, it's almost invariably when some such young person is around that they get busy toppling the furniture and chucking the china about the house. If they don't exist, one has to conclude that dotty girls can develop surprising skill in putting on such turns themselves. The subject is a perplexing one. Parapsychologists are by no means in agreement about it."

"Isn't that because there's often such a mixup of straight fraud and genuinely inexplicable happenings?" Judith felt she was at least getting John's mind off bank robberies and muggings. "For instance, a man finds he can make billiard balls roll about the table simply by glaring at them. Then he is investigated by professors and people who turn out to be an unsympathetic crowd. His powers begin to desert him in these new conditions, and soon he is doing it with magnets or something hidden up his shirt sleeves."

"I've never heard of the billiard-balls man."

"No more have I. I've made him up. But that sort of thing."

"I agree there have been plenty of such cases. The ladies known as physical mediums are the best documented of them. But it's more interesting when the thing operates the other way round. The professional stage illusionist makes a few passes, mutters some abracadabra, and the pretty girl in the box vanishes. It's done too often and the girl *really* vanishes, never to be seen or heard of again."

"I've never heard of *that,* John."

"Of course not. I've made it up. And now tell me more about your poor aunt's predicament. I hope the manifestations are confined to the kitchen."

"They're not. The poltergeist has managed to smash a white porcelain dish of the Liao dynasty. And that, you know, means a hundred years before the Norman Conquest."

"Good God!" Appleby was genuinely shocked. "Anything else of that order?"

"An eight-faceted vase of *mei-p'ing* shape. Underglaze blue with dragons in waves."

"That would be Yüan—and I think I remember it. This must be stopped. Has the old lady called in the police?"

"She called in the vicar, and the vicar produced an ecclesiastical exorcist, specially licensed for the job by the Archbishop of Canterbury. There's been bell-book-and-candle stuff all over Anderton Place. But the poltergeist hasn't been incommoded so far."

"Then the good Lady Parmiter must be persuaded to try the local constabulary after all—and just as a last resort." Appleby, far from amused, frowned at his untouched sherry. "It's monstrous, Judith. A vast great country house absolutely crammed with treasures waiting to be smashed to bits by some unfortunate child of disordered mind! And nothing done about it, you say, except in terms of clerical mumbo-jumbo? The old dear ought to be locked up."

"Don't be so cockily rationalistic, John. Of course you're right about the treasures. Acres and acres of the things. But acres and acres of utter junk as well. Aunt Jessica's late husband was enormously wealthy. As a collector he was also as guileless and tasteless as they come. The result is that Anderton Place must be unique among the dwellings of men."

"But does your aunt *know?* What's genuine and what's fake, and so on?"

"It's impossible to tell, but she certainly likes living with the old higgledy-piggledy effect perpetrated by my uncle. Loyalty to the deceased, perhaps. Her trustees must have accurate inventories based on adequate expertises made by museum people and so forth. The insurance position would be chaotic without that. But Anderton Place itself *is* chaotic, as you've seen for yourself."

"Not so chaotic as it will be when this precious poltergeist is finished with it."

"That's how it looks, I must say." Judith Appleby glanced at her husband with caution, and confirmed her view that he had been working far too hard. There were even dark rings under his eyes. "Yes," she said. "It *ought* to be stopped. Why don't you stop it?"

"What's that?"

"Aunt Jessica has a high regard for you—"

"Judith, are you suggesting that I take time off to run this blessed poltergeist to earth? The idea's absurd."

"You said yourself she ought to call in the police. And since there's a policeman in the family—"

"More sherry? It's almost dinner time."

"John, dear, don't be evasive. And think of all that stuff. Sung and T'ang and heaven knows what. And only poor old Aunt—"

"Poor old fiddlesticks! Your precious aunt is as formidable a dowager as any of her kind in England."

"Don't you feel you could handle her?"

"Of course I could handle her." As he uttered this boast Appleby caught his wife's eye and grinned. "Oh, very well," he said. And he reached for the telephone beside him. "I'll cancel things," he said. "Just for tomorrow, mind you. I can't play truant for longer than that."

"The poltergeist may not last even that long with *you* on the job, darling."

And with this very proper expression of confidence uttered, Judith Appleby went to see about the dinner.

It is well known that poltergeists, in common with other agents of the supernatural, frequently sulk when attracting the interest of persons skeptically inclined. Aunt Jessica's poltergeist may have regarded the Applebys not as skeptical but merely as open-minded; certainly it lost no time in showing that it remained in business.

Appleby hadn't finished his polite inquiries about Lady Parmiter's health—indeed the butler who had announced the visitors hadn't yet left the drawing room—when the unmistakable sound of breaking china announced the poltergeist's presence. From a high unglazed shelf crowded with stuff a medium-sized jar had tumbled to the parquet floor and exploded like a fragmentation bomb.

Appleby strode over to the resulting small disaster and picked up a couple of the larger pieces. Although scarcely an expert on Oriental ceramics, he had no difficulty in identifying what had been destroyed. The Parmiter Collection—so enormous and so eccentrically miscellaneous—was the poorer by one of those nicely manufactured pots in which one buys preserved ginger at rather superior shops.

"Sometimes T'ang and sometimes Fortnum and Mason," he said rather grimly to Aunt Jessica. "Your visitant must certainly be described as having catholic tastes."

"As my dear husband himself had." Aunt Jessica produced this odd rejoinder with dignity. She certainly wasn't at all an easy old lady.

"Yes, of course." Appleby spoke absently. Taking the freedom of a fairly close relative, he had scrambled on a chair and was investigating the shelf from which the jar had fallen. It stood close to a high window of which the upper sash was open. Nobody had been looking that way when the thing happened. Beyond this, there was nothing to be seen.

He got down, collected a brush and shovel from the fireplace, composedly swept up the bits and pieces, and deposited them in a wastepaper basket. Performing this more or less menial action appeared to put something further in his head. "How many indoor servants have you got at present?" he asked.

"Fewer, certainly, than some years ago." For a moment Lady

Parmiter seemed to feel that this was as precise a computation as she could fairly be expected to arrive at. But then she tried harder. "Seven," she said. "Or eight? No more than that."

"I suppose you can just manage," Judith said without irony. Unlike her husband, she had been accustomed to large establishments in youth. "I take it they are all reliable and have been with you for a good many years?"

"I fear not. The minds of domestic servants, Judith, are undeniably unsettled. I sometimes judge, too, that a nomadic habit is establishing itself among them. Their faces are frequently unfamiliar to me, so I think they must come and go. My housekeeper, Mrs. Thimble, would tell you about that. I don't, of course, include Mrs. Thimble in the eight. She is almost a companion to me in her humble way. Unfortunately she is absent for a few days, owing to some bereavement in her family."

Appleby had betrayed some impatience during these unhelpful remarks, and had received a warning glance from Judith. Now he tried again.

"I know," he said, "that you don't much care for the police. But you might—"

He broke off, having been interrupted by a series of bumps and shudders, followed by a splintering crash, apparently from just outside the drawing room. He ran to the door and threw it open. Anderton Place rejoiced in a very grand marble-sheathed hall and a correspondingly imposing marble staircase.

The hall was now littered with the debris of an enormous wardrobe. Minor bits and pieces—the first to detach themselves from the tumbling monster—lay here and there on the stairs. The bizarre effect was enhanced by the fact that the wardrobe had apparently contained a large collection of Victorian and Edwardian clothing. This, too, now lay all over the place.

"I was about to remark," Appleby said calmly when the startled ladies had joined him, "that two courses are possible. You might, Aunt Jessica, call in one of the big security firms. They would send you a few skilled people, in the guise of accountants or solicitors' clerks or indignant clergy deserving a country holiday—"

"Quite out of the question." Lady Parmiter made no bones about this. "I should regard anything of the sort as most objectionable."

"Alternatively, there are highly reputable bodies devoted to the pursuit of psychical research. Archbishops and Prime Ministers have been among their active members from time to time. Their attitude is totally objective and disinterested, just as is that of any other learned society. They possess great experience alike in assessing the significance of genuine paranormal phenomena and in detecting imposture. If you cared—"

"I will have nothing to do with anything of the sort, John. Dear Adolphus would not have approved of it. Judith, is that not so?"

"Yes, Aunt Jessica, I suppose it is. But then Uncle Adolphus was never up against a peculiarly destructive poltergeist."

"There is the luncheon bell, my dear. Your uncle always liked an old-fashioned bell. I have had to instruct this new butler—whose name escapes me—to refrain from entering and announcing meals. And that reminds me. We shall not discuss these disturbing incidents before the servants. I hope the man has remembered the Andron-Blanquet. I recall it, John, as your favorite claret. Malign spirits may be at work, but at least they have made no attack on the wine cellar."

And Lady Parmiter, a spirited woman, led the way to her dining room.

The meal was uneventful. Spoons and forks didn't tie themselves into knots or take to the air and vanish. The only mishap was a minor one, when a young parlormaid contrived to spill an uncomfortably hot potato into Judith's lap. Appleby found himself giving an eye to this girl. If she was a professional, it didn't seem to be at waiting at table.

And to his trained sense her relationship to the anonymous butler was detectably odd. This might be taken to count against the view that she was the standard hysterical female of canonical poltergeist literature. Appleby rose from table with a dim theory stirring in his mind.

Then—again claiming family status—he took a prowl through Anderton Place alone. Even more than he remembered, it was a mad museum from cellars to attics. In the cellars there was plenty of that sound and modest claret; there was even more claret that was very rare indeed; there was also a bewildering amount of wine for which the late Lord Parmiter must have scoured every fifth-rate wine shop in the country.

The attics were full of rubbish—some of it honest-to-goodness rubbish, and some of it fake furniture of the most pretentious sort. But every now and then one came on something which would have satisfied the most exacting taste in the age of Louis Quatorze. The effect was a kind of security nightmare. It cried out for skilled pillage.

And so with the rest of the house. As the crazy Lord Parmiter had originally disposed everything, so was everything disposed now. It would take the entire staff of the British Museum a month's labor, one felt, to separate the wheat from the chaff.

There were several further "disturbing incidents" (as Aunt Jessica had termed them) while Appleby prowled. At one point a worthless but lethal bracket clock hurtled past Appleby's ear and smashed into a cabinet containing some decidedly precious Dresden china. The whole affair was clearly mounting to a crisis.

Back in the drawing room Appleby found that Judith had been trying to persuade her aunt to take drastic emergency action. She ought to send her entire staff away on board-wages, shut up the house, and leave merely a thoroughly reliable caretaker in charge. Appleby didn't think much of this plan. Nor—more conclusively—did Lady Parmiter. If the poltergeist really was a poltergeist (and on this she, too, professed an open mind) the result might merely be major disaster. More poltergeists might simply move in, and the last state of Anderton be worse than its first.

Appleby agreed, or professed to agree. He had an alternative suggestion. The most experienced packers in London should be hastily brought in. Working under Lady Parmiter's direction, they could crate up everything of the first value for immediate removal to impregnable strongrooms in the metropolis. Poltergeists were invariably confined to one stamping ground. They wouldn't be able to follow.

Lady Parmiter turned this down too—but with a shift of ground. Such a proceeding would be abhorrent to the shade of dear Adolphus and was therefore not to be entertained for a moment. It seemed an impasse. Appleby produced what seemed to be a final throw.

"But doesn't Anderton run to something like a strongroom of its own?" he asked. "I seem to remember Judith's uncle speaking of something of the kind, and being rather proud of it."

"We simply call it the safe, John, but it is in fact a large room and entirely burglarproof. I always lock my dear mother's Queen Anne silver away in it when I have occasion to leave Anderton."

"That's very prudent of you." Appleby was wondering if he

could possibly bring this perverse old person to see reason. At least he mustn't give up without a further attempt. "May I see it?" he asked. "Your husband was extremely wise to have such a room constructed. No great house should be without one."

The request, thus framed, was well received. The Anderton strongroom looked tremendously impressive—and had looked that way for at least 50 years. Indeed, it might have been some triumph of metallurgical skill triumphantly displayed at the Great Exhibition at Crystal Palace in 1851. If Appleby was amused at this outmoded affair he managed not to betray the fact.

"Look," he said, "couldn't we simply put everything that is really valuable in here? I'm sure Lord Parmiter would have approved. We have on our hands just the sort of situation he must have been envisaging when he ordered so spacious an affair. If what we're up against is simple human vandalism or madness, then we defeat it in this simple way. If it's something supernatural, we're at least no worse off than we are at present.

"Of course you're the only person who knows what's what, who can quickly pick out the really precious things from those which are to be classed as primarily of sentimental value. I honestly feel you should do this, Aunt Jessica. It's your duty as the guardian of all the marvelous things Lord Parmiter gathered together. And it can all be done this afternoon. You show us what, and the whole household can help with the stowing."

Perhaps surprisingly, Lady Parmiter agreed to this plan at once. The undisturbed disposition of things at Anderton was very dear to her as one of the pieties of widowhood. She was a good Victorian, after all, and the impulse was the same as that which had prompted a more famous Widow to preserve intact the arrangements on her deceased Prince Consort's writing table.

On the other hand, she had a shrewd sense of what things were worth, and no reason to believe that dear Adolphus would have smiled on the indiscriminate massacre of his wildly heterogeneous treasures.

The task was accomplished by a late dinnertime, the bewildered servants having been directed (in the absence of the bereaved Mrs. Thimble) by the butler without a name. Anderton didn't look that denuded when the job was finished. All the same, objects worth many hundreds of thousands of pounds had been segregated and placed under lock and key. The poltergeist was thwarted—or so it was to be hoped.

The Applebys drove back to London in the dark, but not before Appleby himself had contrived a short private conversation with Lady Parmiter.

"Lucky your aunt turned out to know the stuff fairly well," he said to Judith on the way home.

"Yes."

"I doubt whether much that's really first-rate now remains outside that strongroom."

"I suppose not."

"You'd agree, Judith, that Aunt Jessica has been persuaded to do the rational thing?"

"Clearly she has—unless it really is a supernatural agency that's at work."

"You'd also agree that what she has done is the *obvious* thing in the circumstances?"

"Well, yes. But I don't see—"

"The *predictable* thing?" It was almost with anxiety that Appleby appeared to wait for his wife's acquiescence this time.

"Absolutely."

"Then I think all's well. Yes, I'm pretty sure of it. By the way, just give a glance at the spare bedroom tomorrow. Your aunt's coming to stay with us."

"To stay with us!"

"Oh, not for long. Just for two or three days. She's telling that butler tonight that she's coming to us in the morning."

"How very odd! But at least we can get a good night's sleep first."

"Very true. Just one telephone call, and I'll be ready for it."

"A telephone call?"

"To the Thames Valley Constabulary, my dear. Anderton is in their territory, so I must liaise with them, as people now say." And Appleby laughed softly as he swung the steering wheel. "You see, I set the trap. But they spring it."

"All caught," Appleby announced a couple of mornings later. "Butler, phony parlormaid—"

"I recall remarking," Lady Parmiter said, "that servants tend to be rather unreliable nowadays."

"Quite so—in fact, two more were in the pay of the gang. All small fry, of course, the butler included. Fortunately, their bosses decided to be in at the kill. Our Thames Valley friends nicked the lot while they were happily treating your strongroom, Aunt Jessica, like a hunk of old cheese."

"We had really done quite a lot of their work for them?" Judith asked.

"Just that. Exactly the point. They count as top-ranking villains, but happen not to be all that clued in on the fine-art front. By themselves they could only have made a purely random haul. Hence the poltergeist, who made us work like mad doing all the sifting for them—separating the wheat from the chaff."

"But, John, what about the tumbling jar? That *did* look like the real thing."

"Not to me. A little bladder at the end of a long tube passing through the window. Squeeze a bulb at the other end, and the trick's accomplished. You just pull the tube out through the window again, and there you are. Literally a trick. Every kid's conjuring set includes a miniature version of the same thing."

"I must go upstairs and pack at once." Aunt Jessica announced this firmly. "It would be the wish of dear Adolphus that the *status quo ante* at Anderton be restored forthwith. And Mrs. Thimble must find me a new butler. His first task, my dear John, will be to pack up every bottle of Andron-Blanquet I still possess. And I needn't tell you where it will be dispatched to."

Joe Gores

Kirinyaga

Something different from Joe Gores, and "clear and convincing" proof of his writing versatility . . . an adventure-crime story about mountain climbing in East Africa, with as authentic and chilling a background as you have ever read . . . You won't forget Kendrick's heroics for a long time . . .

The climber looked like a fly at this distance, Kendrick thought. Because of the anorak he wore, like a bright red fly. Clinging to a rock face of vertical slabs and deep horizontal sections which together formed a massive staircase with hundred-foot risers.

The fly had reached the top of a trough-like diedre in one of the risers. Broken rock there. Brought up closer, the fly began working toward a niche in the edge of the step above. Not a bad show for a man recovering from his annual bout of malaria, Kendrick thought.

Closer yet. He could see the three-color zigzag design of the knitted balaclava helmet. Hesitating at the foot of a bulging rock face split by a shallow groove. Get on with it, Kendrick thought. Right up through the bloody overhang to the stance above. You know you have to do it.

Good show. Tight on the head and torso now. Fingers groping above for purchase. It was coming now. Head turning so that sunlight struck off smoked goggles. Unshaven, teeth clenched, sweat rivuleting the cheek and line of jaw even in the subfreezing temperatures of 17,000 feet. Now. Just here.

The climber slipped, swung free of the rock, only the fingers of the right hand still holding their grip. A gasp went up. Kendrick grinned. Yes. A good bit, that. Unexpected.

The image disappeared and the lights of the stuffy crowded viewing room came up to the clearing of throats and muttered comments. Kendrick paused in the hallway, sweat starting to dry on his lean muscular body, made leaner by recent illness. A couple of inches under six feet, with straight, prematurely white hair and a deeply tanned mid-thirties face.

Morna tucked a proprietary arm through his as the production people and distributors' reps and studio flacks flowed around them.

"Don't you think it's wonderful footage?" Her clear, very blue eyes smiled up into his. Morna was his ex-wife. "Aren't you glad I got you on as guide and Kenya technical adviser?"

"I can use the money," Kendrick agreed. He said, "You look wonderful yourself, luv. London must agree with you."

He still had her note from two years before, when she had packed it in. *This bloody damn country* . . . He had found it when he'd returned from a fortnight on staff at the Outward Bound Wilderness School on Kilimanjaro. Hadn't been strong enough to hold her.

"You look awful," she said. "Thin and—"

"The annual bout of malaria. It's finished now."

She tugged at his arm, skin like satin and untouched by the sun, auburn hair worn long and straight and parted in the middle like an Asian's. "Let me buy you a drink. I'm meeting Burke at The Thorn Tree."

Let her buy, Kendrick thought. She'd have plenty of pence now, living with the great Burke Hamlin. He felt a stab of jealousy.

They went out into bright Kenya sunshine, then under the colorful umbrellas shading The Thorn Tree's sidewalk tables. Hamlin was already there, surrounded by the usual sycophants, newspaper and media people; three tables had been pulled together to accommodate them. Perkins, the young reporter on the *East African Standard*, was asking a question. Kendrick knew Perkins from the Kenya Mountain Club.

"How *did* you get that superb climbing footage? I've been on scrambles up Kenya myself, and that camera angle—"

"Two cameras, both set up on the edge of that glacier on Point Lenana." Art Kaye, the hulking bespectacled chief cameraman, had taken it as a technical question on the difficulties of location shooting over three miles above sea level where cameras would want to freeze up. "What you saw was put together out of both magazines. Aeroflex 35mm's, one with a 120mm zoom for the loose stuff, the other with a Questar for in tight."

A woman reporter put the focus back on Hamlin. Morna had sat down next to the actor and had an unconsciously familiar hand on his thigh with Kendrick's drink forgotten.

"Mr. Hamlin, when you slipped and were hanging by only one hand—was that deliberate? Or—"

Burke Hamlin leaned back in his chair and sipped thoughtfully at his drink, a faraway look in his pale blue eyes. A grin split his craggy features. He had a rolling masculine voice that went well with the six-three physique and fifty-inch chest.

"Let's just say it makes damned good theater."

Kendrick used that as an exit line, sliding backward out of the crowd as Morna's lips formed the words: *Call me*. Behind him, Hamlin's voice, beautifully projected, was explaining that Kenya was a corruption of a much older Kikuyu word, Kirinyaga—which meant, literally, mountain of whiteness. The house of god, home of Ngai, the creator.

Kendrick had told him that himself a few days before.

Over their first drink Morna said, "A few days in Nairobi and I remember why I left East Africa."

"Thanks for them few kind words, ma'am."

Kendrick had felt a suppressed masculine excitement ever since picking her up at the hotel. They'd been good together, and he'd found single-life sex unexpectedly conventional and bland, like British cooking. Morna laughed and laid a warm hand on his.

"Present company excepted. You don't much care for Burke, do you?"

"Should I?"

"Beyond the machismo bit, I mean. After all, isn't he the sort you've always professed to admire? A real man who can come out here to your world and excel—"

It slipped out drily before he realized it. "You mean like he did in that climbing footage?"

"Exactly." She pushed aside the ruins of her steak. God, she was beautiful, face alight, eyes sparkling, perfect lips curved. Small wonder he'd not been man enough to hold her. She said, "Catch-up time."

Not much to tell. White hunting, what was left of it, had become a black man's game by government fiat, so he'd drifted into the Kenya Game Department as a park warden. And spent his spare time climbing, of course—Kili, Kenya, the Aberdares, the Ruwenzoris.

"The Mountains of the Moon!" he exclaimed. "Took us three

weeks to get in and up to the top of Rarasibi, and it rained every bloody day. Except near the top, where it snowed."

"I'll take Carnaby Street."

She had literally, in fact, returning to the mannequin's job from which Kendrick's whirlwind courtship during a long leave in England had snatched her. It was in Carnaby Street that Burke Hamlin also had found her, modeling a wardrobe for his latest dolly who'd quickly become ex-dolly.

"It's permanent with you and Burke?"

"I leave decisions to him, he's superb at them." The hotel elevator bore them upward. "I enjoy the sex-object role."

Sex-object for Hamlin, thought Kendrick a bit bitterly over the brandies in her room. If he'd been a stronger man, more self-confident like bloody Hamlin, she'd still be his. Then she surprised him with that special look he'd never been able to forget, was kicking off her shoes and unzipping her dress with one flow of sensuous movement. Her eyes were enormous and dark and unfocused in the dim room.

"Just between us, darling," she said. "Old times."

It was better than old times. It was better than anything else would ever be, Kendrick thought as he dressed by the soft glow from the open bathroom door. She was lying on the bed, watching him with solemn, sated eyes.

"I'd forgot," she said, "just how—" She stopped. "Burke will be busy again on Thursday night."

To his own surprise Kendrick said, "I'll be back up on Kenya by then." It came out rougher than he wanted. But if he remained in Nairobi he wouldn't be able to stay away from her, and he didn't want that. She was another man's woman now.

"You just came down off that bloody mountain," she said curtly.

There wasn't any answer to that. He kissed her and let himself out. He was glad he hadn't told her the truth about that climbing footage of Hamlin. Hamlin was right for Morna, the strong, aggressive individual she'd always wanted and hadn't found in Kendrick.

By the time he reached the summit of Point Lenana, only an hour up the ridge from Top Hut, it was snowing again and the two major peaks, Nelion and Batian, had been blotted out. It was just a scramble, nothing more strenuous than kicking steps in each day's new snow. He'd been up to Lenana each morning for the past three days, waiting for a window of decent climbing weather to try the twin central peaks.

Going down, the snow-blanketed breadth of the Lewis Glacier lay to his right, the clouds now pouring up over it and across the ridge like smoke off dry ice. It was snowing in earnest when he swung open the door of Top Hut, itself at 15,730 feet, and stomped his feet clean. Only then did he realize two more climbers had arrived.

"We wondered where you'd got to, with all your climbing gear still here," said Perkins. The reporter from the *Standard* was a slightly built youth, pale-skinned and pale-haired and, right now, looking white and drawn around the mouth. The other climber was Burke Hamlin.

"A scramble up Lenana." Kendrick stripped off outer clothing. "Touch of mountain sickness?"

Burke Hamlin made a grandly dismissive gesture. He looked immense in his climbing clothes. "Not me. Young Perkins."

"You want some aspirin or Panadol for the head?"

"Some of the Panadol, if I may," said Perkins.

Kendrick watched him down the pills with water and fought a rising anger. What the hell were these two doing up here? Perkins, easy of course: hero-worship of Hamlin, and a possible feature in one of the big London dailies. But why Hamlin? A talkative bellhop at the hotel?

"Want to check the peaks," grunted Kendrick.

He left the hut without looking back, knowing the actor would follow. Bloody fools. Hamlin, even Perkins, had never seen Kirinyaga frown. Now, with the wet season pushing the snow line down, that frown could be deadly to climbers. He turned when he heard Hamlin's boots crunching behind him.

"Neither of you is a good enough climber for any real rockwork."

Hamlin gave him that wide and famous grin that celluloid villains saw just before the choreographed mayhem began. "Maybe I want to revise that estimate for you. Or maybe I want to say I don't mind your sleeping with my woman, but why did you tell her the truth about that climbing footage?"

Morna herself must have told Hamlin of their coupling. Why?

"I didn't know there was any bloody great secret about that footage, Hamlin. But for what it's worth, I didn't tell her."

"She says you did."

He shrugged. "Maybe Kaye mentioned it. I didn't have to."

In a surprisingly mild voice Hamlin said, "You're rather a louse, aren't you?"

"Listen, Hamlin, any fears you might have that I'll get Morna away from you are purely make-believe. Just for the effect. But this mountain is real. Take the boy back down tomorrow. His sickness gives you a good excuse."

"While you stay up here? Mighty mountaineer turning back the lowly actor because the mountain is too dangerous for him? No, thank you."

"For Pete's sake," said Kendrick in a pained voice.

He went back inside. Perkins was lying on one of the bunks with a forearm over his eyes. Kendrick knew the symptoms of oxygen starvation vividly himself—headache, loss of appetite, nausea, vomiting. But he also knew Perkins, hero-worshipping all the way, would struggle up the peaks if Hamlin did—unless he could deflect the youngster himself. Hamlin couldn't very well try it alone.

"That film you saw of Hamlin climbing," he told Perkins. "That was me. Hamlin's no better climber than you are, doesn't know a damned thing about any really tricky rock or ice-work. Standard III, maybe. You'll be facing Standard V pitches up there, and ice and snow."

Perkins sat up, swung his feet to the floor. He said, hesitantly, "You're saying we'd be fools to go on?"

"Bloody fools. Rest here the night and head down in the morning. Will you do that?"

Perkins finally nodded. He looked very ill. Kendrick stood up.

"I'll spend the night at Two-Tarn Hut," he said. "Neither Hamlin nor I would be comfortable if I dossed here."

He settled into the shabby wooden hut that crouched near the bleak shore of Hut Tarn well before dark. He found himself fighting a vague uneasiness. He finally isolated it: Hamlin wouldn't be fool enough to try for the peaks alone, would he?

Golden sunlight slanted through the window to wake him. It was late, nearly 6:00 A.M. Kendrick yawned, sat up, began pulling on layers of clothing. The hut was icy. When he opened the door, the dazzling white and black peaks towered starkly above, surely close enough to touch across the miles of snow and icefields flanking the glaciers.

Kendrick hurriedly lighted the primus and set water heating in the sufuria. Amazing to get a window of weather this far into the season, he ought to make the most of it. He poured boiling water over the tea leaves, sugar and dried milk in his cup, and to the remainder in the sufuria added white corn meal, dried milk, and salt to make *ugali*. Porter's rations, that, not European fare; but he could subsist on ten pounds of food a week up here.

He ate at the window. As he had thought. Already wisps of cloud were forming in the cleavage between Nelion and Batian, where the Diamond glacier sparkled. The cloud falling on the ice made it gray and cold-looking. Kirinyaga's usual rainy season tricks. Sunshine, then—

Kendrick's spare hard body tensed. He never would have seen them if the window hadn't framed them, given them scale.

Bloody stupid idiots! He glassed the distant figures with his binoculars. Hamlin in the lead, Perkins behind, trying the southwest ridge of Batian. He should have known Perkins' acquiescence had been the mountain sickness working. When that had lessened, and with Hamlin whispering in his bloody ear—

"The blind leading the blind," Kendrick said in a vicious voice.

The southwest ridge. A tough ascent even during the climbing season. On the south side a snowfield, where they'd have to cut steps across. At the head of that, a rock bulge that would be treacherously verglassed this time of the year.

He jerked on sweaters, anorak, knitted mitts with split palms, stuffed balaclava and waterproof gauntlets into pockets, jammed a soft floppy-brimmed army fatigue hat on his head.

To the snout of the Darwin glacier he moved at a slow trot, then angled up the true right bank of the ice floe, reversed himself, went left up snow-sheathed rocks to the southwest ridge notch. He followed their tracks across the snowfield, his cheeks burning with cold. The sun had gone, the wind was moaning at him from the east. He paused to don the balaclava, saving the gauntlets for the real cold ahead. He had always hated heroics, and now he was involved in those of a posturing ape.

They had somehow made it up and over the rock bulge, verglassed as it was with frozen rain. He felt a spurt of adrenalin-like hope; that had taken nerve and strength. But ahead, between him and the main ridge, lay a hundred yards of steep black broken rock. And beyond that—

A sudden shrill scream cut through the wind's low moan. He

needed no clatter of falling rock to confirm it; he'd heard men fall before. He went up the hundred yards of tumbled rock in a single ferocious sustained rush that left him on the narrow ridge panting and nauseated. The screams had cut off. Dead? In shock? One or both?

He hallooed. No answer. He was aware of intense cold stinging his nostrils and lungs. Of thin air pushing his pulse to 160. And of fatigue. Bone-chilling fatigue. The annual fever bout was not as far behind as he had thought.

Kendrick hallooed again. This time a weak voice answered.

They'd come to grief at the crux of the climb, a two-hundred-foot buttress of exposed rock dismally bare of good handholds. His eyes searched the swirling, snow-laden clouds above. There! A dark shape clinging to the sheer wall.

One dark shape.

"Are you all right?" he called.

"Help! For God's sake, help!"

The rock bulged out toward Batian's west face, so his weight was carried by his arms and the strain of thighs and knees against the rock. Up, and up. The face mercifully eased to merely vertical. Thirty feet. Forty. Burke Hamlin was clinging spreadeagled to good holds, face white and strained, eyes absolutely wild.

"Get me down from here," he said hoarsely.

Kendrick was well to the side. Terrified climbers were like terrified swimmers, they'd take anything within reach down with them.

"Are you hurt?"

"I—don't know. For God's sake, man—"

Kendrick's fingers were numbing with cold; he regretted the gauntlets. Snow swirled around them. The actor's safety rope had parted a couple of feet below his belt. Kendrick had to find Perkins, but before he could he had to get Hamlin down the ledge formed by the ridgetop and the base of this exposed buttress.

"Move when I tell you, where I tell you," he said in the voice of someone calming a spooked horse. "Don't look down. Okay, left hand down six inches . . . good! Now, left foot . . . "

It was a bad twenty minutes. Hamlin collapsed on the four-foot width of the ridgeline. Kendrick followed the ledge, found the safety line with Perkins still attached to it. He'd been probably twenty feet below Hamlin when he'd fallen and the rope had parted, had struck the ridge, and had kept going over and down the sheer face.

Kendrick crouched on the ledge. Visibility was so bad he could barely see the blond youngster's limp body hooked around a knob of rock fifteen feet below. Three feet to either side, Kendrick thought, and he'd still be bouncing.

He belayed around an out-cropping, then roped down to assess the damage. One leg was shattered just below the hip, so the jagged white end of femur was thrust out through a rip in the flannel trousers. The red meat exposed by the tear was already freezing. Internal, Kendrick could only guess. A pulse, yes, but—

The eyes suddenly opened in the deathly pale face a yard away.

"It's numb now."

"Anything broken inside that you know about?"

"My chest stabs when I breathe. I think it's ribs. I did two of them at rugger once and it feels the same." He closed his eyes, opened them. "I've had it, haven't I?"

Kendrick laid a momentary palm on his shoulder. "I'll get you up to the ledge."

He went up his rope hand over hand. On the ridge Hamlin was hunched in the lee of the buttress. He was shivering. There was a blue line around his mouth and the rim of his nostrils.

"He's fifteen feet below the ridgeline," said Kendrick. "I'm not sure I'm strong enough to get him up alone."

The wind moaned. Hamlin raised shock-dulled eyes. "He's still alive?"

"He won't be if we keep fooling around. We'll have to—"

He stopped there. Hamlin's mouth was set.

"I can't." His teeth had begun chattering. He was stripped of pretense. "Can't—face it. Can't—pull him up to the ledge, can't make it down—can't . . . arm broken."

Kendrick had seen men do remarkable things hampered by a broken arm. But he had also seen men like Hamlin before—stunned by the sudden terrible mortality that Kirinyaga could thrust upon you. Men who, faced with that realization, shriveled up inside. It was in search of that insight that others climbed.

He left Hamlin there and returned to Perkins. He braced, took a turn around his left hand, and began hauling. He was aware of Hamlin, watching him like a ferret; the actor's naked ego had begun peering once again from the rocks into which it had scuttled. The lift was the hardest thing Kendrick had ever done.

When it was finished, he walked downwind from the crumpled youth and threw up.

"Lie down next to him, Hamlin. I've dragged him back under the face of the buttress where there's some shelter from the wind."

"Where are you going? You can't leave me here! You can't—"

"Grow up," said Kendrick.

The descent to Two-Tarn Hut wasn't too bad; the whining press of wind cut visibility with swirling snow, but gave him a fixed direction on which to depend. He gathered up his bedroll and blankets and started back up. He didn't like to contemplate the next hours. He was wearing down already; and besides the wind which in exposed places threatened to flick him off, his fatigue itself was dangerous. It made him treat tricky bits of rock-work with a numb, casual contempt.

The light was muddy as he dragged himself up the final yards to the narrow ridge. Anger stirred him.

"Dammit, Hamlin, I told you to lie down next to him."

"I—couldn't move."

"Move now or I'll kick your arm!"

Hamlin moved, crabwise, his back against the rock, his right arm hanging limply at his side. They got two of the blankets around Perkins and rolled him into the sleeping bag. A pulse of sorts, still breathing, but no outcry when they handled him. Just as well, Kendrick thought. At the very best he was going to lose his leg.

Hamlin snatched at the two remaining blankets.

"I'll need more than this, Kendrick! I'll freeze."

"You'll be all right. Keep moving around, work your fingers and toes. And make sure Perkins stays covered."

Kendrick entered a curious limbo of exhaustion where he moved solely by his superb mountaineer's sense. He had a flashlight, but here on the peaks it merely reflected back from swirling snow. During the rock-work he kept his mind awake with speculations of times and distances. Twenty-five miles to his VW down at the 9000-foot level, say. Easier going downhill, of course, but in the dark, in the snow and, below that, rain . . .

He fell the first time going down the steep scree north of Shipton's Peak, twisting instinctively and landing on a shoulder rather than on his face in the loose, sliding volcanic debris. By the time he reached the stream at the head of Teleki Valley he had fallen twice more. It was utterly black, pouring icy rain; he'd left his poncho at Two-Tarn Hut. At old ruined Klarwill's Hut he jettisoned ice axe, crampons, piton hammer, and ropes. He went on down the long hollow of moorland dotted with giant lobelia and euphorbia.

Below this was the vertical bog, several miles of coarse matted tussocks with water between. He lost track of his falls there. Only the vague starlight following the rain kept him floundering, splashing, cursing his way down.

Ahead, the dark mass of the treeline. He fell on it as on a banquet. Stunted, gnarled nidorellas bearded with moss. The Naru Moru forest track plunged down into the rainforest's impenetrable darkness. Sodden branches slapped at his face, clawed at his eyes. He used his flashlight here, made plenty of noise so he wouldn't surprise an elephant or leopard on the trail. Once the light limned great streaming piles of fresh buffalo dung.

At the Meteorological Clearing at 10,000 feet, he found Hamlin had left the keys in the Land Rover. That would cut 45 minutes and three miles afoot from his descent. He rested his forehead against the steering wheel as the four-wheel vehicle grumbled itself awake.

Midnight. Another day beginning. Good Lord, he'd never been so tired. And he still had to get back up again.

He sent the Land Rover careening down the narrow red murram track, almost sideswiped his VW, and as soon as he cleared the forest area swung off the route toward a distant farmhouse owned by a middle-aged Scots family originally from the Republic. His horn brought them awake so he could shamble through the welcome triangle of yellow lamplight, hollow-eyed and gaunt and caked with mud.

"Accident up on Batian."

"Full mountain rescue drill?" The farmer was already at the phone; his wife was heating tea water and cutting bread.

Kendrick nodded and drank scalding tea. All the farmers on Kirinyaga's approaches knew about accidents on the mountain. The call would go through the Nairobi police, who would relay by shortwave. He set aside the mug regretfully. The farmer was full of objections.

"Man, you'll be in no condition to make it back up."

"And they'll be in no condition to wait up there alone."

He remembered little of the climb after he had smashed and bulled the Land Rover two miles uphill beyond the Meteorological Clearing before bogging down entirely. Watery dawn slashed through renewed rain to greet him at the treeline. The bog should have finished him; then, fording the rapid rain-swollen Naru Moru by Teleki Hut, he knew he was all through.

He kept on.

At Klarwill's he collapsed on what was left of the floor. He cried. He collected his climbing gear and went on.

The sun appeared to taunt him while he was on a lateral moraine from the track to the stream below the Lewis Glacier. He made the stiff scramble to Two-Tarn Hut and passed it without pausing. The rest of the climb was made by instinct and will power only. His body merely continued to respond in familiar physical ways to familiar stimuli. Moving was as involuntary as breathing.

He got there too late. Waiting for the rescue party, he knew he'd driven his body beyond the normal limits of endurance because he had feared from the beginning that he would be too late.

The press conference was held two afternoons later in the lounge of Nyeri's Outspan Hotel. Burke Hamlin had refused hospitalization beyond having his arm set and being treated for exposure. He lounged on one of the superbly comfortable old couches, hemmed in by reporters, tourists, onlookers, flacks, studio people. Cameras and mikes. His cast already scrawled with bawdy sentiments, a large whiskey at his elbow. As he'd said in an earlier context, damned good theater.

"Does the broken arm hamper you much, Mr. Hamlin?"

"I tend to spill more drinks."

"The mountain sequences were finished. What were you looking for up on Kirinyaga?"

"Read *The Snows of Kilimanjaro.*"

"That isn't really an answer, is it, Mr. Hamlin?"

"It is for me."

"What can you tell us of the tragic death of Mr. Perkins?"

Stern sorrow molded the craggy features. The drink was set aside unspilled. Kendrick, in a doorway well back from the crowd, thought it was an excellent performance.

"What can one say when his best is not good enough? He died of cold and exposure and shock before the rescuers arrived."

It broke up. Kendrick wandered tree-shaded paths, his nostrils full of the rich scents of tropical blooms. Warm air caressed his skin. He had slept the clock around. The Outspan was an old Colonial hotel, airy, spacious, quiet, civilized.

Cold and exposure and shock.

He looked between the branches of a scarlet-flowered Nandi flame tree toward Kirinyaga, 40 miles away, with her head buried in clouds of her own making. Here, deep blue sky filled with stately gray-hulled clipper ships which would close ranks and fire salvos of rain at four o'clock.

Cold and exposure and shock. Neat and cosmetic, antiseptic as a hospital bed.

Reality was a bit more gross. Perkins was frozen solid. Lips pulled back from the canines in a perpetual trapped hyena snarl. Fingers clawed into blunted parodies of a leopard's talons. Eyeballs staring through their contact lenses of ice.

And Kendrick couldn't really condemn Hamlin for it. Blind panic. How many cracked in battle under similar stress, and while surrounded by companions and trained to it besides? Alone, on a mountain ridge with Kirinyaga slavering above you—

Couldn't condemn, but couldn't let it happen again so someone else would die. He knocked on the actor's door just before four o'clock, under a clouded sky with pre-rain wind dancing dust devils in the parking lot.

"It's open."

Hamlin was alone, sitting in a chair with his bare feet crossed on the foot of the bed. He had a drink in his left hand.

"Pulling out at first light," said Kendrick.

"And you came to say goodbye? How touching." The magnificent leonine head followed Kendrick across the room as if to camera cues. He set his bare feet on the rug. "Did I forget to thank you for saving my life?"

"And for not saving Perkins'?"

"Meaning what, precisely?" asked Hamlin carefully.

Kendrick relaxed against the wall. The assurance he'd sought was in the raw edges of Hamlin's voice, in the whiteness of his fingers around the glass. Kendrick shook his head chidingly.

"It won't do, Hamlin. The ends of the safety rope. The broken arm. The zipped-up sleeping bag."

Hamlin stood up. He swayed slightly, not from drink. His face was pale, something akin to terror was in his eyes.

"I'm not going to listen to this, Kendrick. My arm—"

"—was broken by yourself, deliberately, when you saw me coming up the mountain the next morning. You were clinging to that rock face with both hands the first time I saw you. *Both hands.* I'll grant it takes courage of a sort to jam your forearm between a couple of rocks—" He made a snapping motion with his hands. "It's the image that's all important, isn't it? The image is everything."

"Don't think I'll admit—"

"And the safety rope. Brand-new Perlon, a thirty percent stretch factor to absorb shock—you could have bounced Perkins up and down on it like a yoyo and it wouldn't have broken."

"It broke." Sweat stood on Hamlin's face; his eyes were like knobs of bone in spoiled meat. They found the closed bathroom door, returned to Kendrick. "Broke. Broke. You weren't there, you couldn't know. It broke, I tell you."

"Two feet off your belt where it would have no chance to be rubbed through? It was cut. Perkins started sliding, screaming, you panicked and cut him loose."

"Who—who would believe—"

Kendrick laughed. It wasn't a pleasant laugh. Poor bloody Perkins. Poor bloody Hamlin, for all that.

"Nobody has to. I just wanted you aware that *I* know. So if you ever get your nerve back and are ever tempted again—"

Hamlin sat down heavily. He stared straight ahead.

"The cold," he said in a strangled voice. "The altitude." He shuddered abruptly. "Do you think I ever again—"

"Good." Kendrick's face hardened. "That leaves Perkins. Frozen solid in his sleeping bag and his blankets."

"You—you found him yourself."

"Only if he'd been *out* of the sleeping bag. *Out* of the blankets. Even in delirium he couldn't have unzipped that bag. But you could. You still had both arms then, you could take away the blankets and bag for yourself, put them back when you saw me on my way. You were afraid of freezing."

"He was finished. Done for." Hamlin was panting, sweating, hunched in his chair like a man who'd been fed arsenic. "Just a vegetable. Oh, it's easy for you! You're never tired. Never frightened. I was afraid to die. Afraid. Can you understand that? Can you?"

The bathroom door opened and Morna came out. Must have

gone in there when Kendrick had knocked and stayed there quietly, listening. No wonder Hamlin had tried to keep him from talking about it. Morna, who wanted a strong man, a self-sufficient man; Morna, who had dumped Kendrick because he hadn't measured up. Now Hamlin had been stripped, exposed to her scorn.

"No, he can't understand that, Burke," she said in a low deadly voice. "He's never needed anyone or anything in his life." She met Kendrick's gaze, a strange look on her lovely face. "Is it true? The things you've accused him of?"

Kendrick shrugged. "I wasn't accusing. Just telling him what I know. It doesn't go any further."

"All right, you've told him. Now get out and leave us alone."

She was on her knees beside the sobbing actor, her arms around his massive shoulders, cooing soft words to him. She looked at Kendrick past the magnificent shaggy head, her eyes ablaze.

"*He* needs me!" she cried triumphantly.

Kendrick felt as if he had narrowly missed being struck by a train. He also felt nauseated. He said, "Yes. He needs you. God help him."

He left the room. The first broad drops of rain were making dime-sized splotches on the tarmac, making it smell of wet tar. Kendrick looked instinctively to the east. Just gray cloud massed there now, all the way to the horizon. But somewhere behind it—

He shuddered. Morna had been wrong, of course, when she'd said he had never needed anybody or anything. He stared at the clouds, as if able to see through them to Kirinyaga, waiting there with her fangs bared and gleaming.

Waiting. For Kendrick.

"Q"

William Brittain

Mr. Strang and the Cat Lady

Mr. Leonard Strang, the gnomelike old science teacher at Aldershot High School, is a trained observer. He sees everything—not only what is there but what is not there. And when the clue in this murder case proved to be something missing, Mr. Strang saw it as clearly as if the clue were not missing at all . . .

Detective: LEONARD STRANG

It was a Wednesday in late fall. The fifth period was almost over, and Mr. Strang stood at the window of his classroom. The crumbs of the sandwich that had been his lunch lay unnoticed on his jacket lapels and rumpled necktie. He was speculating on how many more days it would be before the maple trees in front of Aldershot High School would be completely bare of leaves when he felt a tugging at the far reaches of his consciousness. Something odd had happened. Or rather, something had *not* happened, and that was equally odd. But it was several minutes before he realized what it was.

Miss Pinderek had not passed the school on her daily walk to the grocery store.

Until 17 years before, Agnes Pinderek had been a history teacher at Aldershot High. Then, at the age of 72, she had retired, with a minimum of fuss and fanfare, to her little cottage just around the corner. Few of the present staff even knew Miss Pinderek existed. But Mr. Strang knew, remembering the advice and encouragement she had showered on him long ago when he was only a young teacher just out of normal school. Mr. Strang ran gnarled fingers through his sparse crop of gray hair, realizing that by now Agnes Pinderek must be almost 90.

And yet every day at 12:15, in spite of her age, Agnes Pinderek walked by the school on her way to the grocery store three blocks away. And every day at one o'clock she returned, head erect and spine ramrod-straight, clutching a small paper bag as if daring someone to try and take it from her. Rain, snow, sleet, and hail did not deter her. Through them all she marched at her appointed times. In retirement she was the same as she had been in the classroom—proud, punctual, self-sufficient.

But on this day Miss Pinderek had not appeared.

Mr. Strang decided to pay her a visit as soon as school was over. He knew this would not please her. While she sometimes returned to school to see old friends, she was adamant about refusing to allow visitors to her home. "I'm an old lady, Leonard," she had told Mr. Strang on one occasion when he'd requested the privilege of making a call. "I've worked hard for my privacy, and now I intend to have it. Besides, I've spent so long in school that you might not recognize me away from it. I'd love to chat with you in your classroom after school, but my home is not open to visitors."

And that had been that.

Still, Miss Pinderek might be ill. Perhaps too ill to summon help. And he might not need to even enter the house. If he shouted through the door at her and received an answer, that would be enough to reassure him.

For the rest of the day Mr. Strang's classes came and went. Chemistry, general science, biology. And through them all the old teacher couldn't get Miss Pinderek out of his mind. Finally the school day ended. Mr. Strang placed a sign on his door canceling the meeting of the Science Club, took his keyring to the main office, and left the building just as the last of the buses was pulling out of the driveway.

Miss Pinderek's tiny front yard was overrun with ivy which not only choked out the weeds but climbed the clapboard sides of the house, partially obscuring the fact that the structure was badly in need of paint.

Mr. Strang pressed the doorbell. He heard no chime or buzz from inside the house. Finally he rapped loudly on the front door, his knuckles avoiding the panes of glass, three of which were cracked, while the fourth was missing, the opening blocked by a piece of cardboard.

No answer. He knocked again. Then he rattled the doorknob. The door creaked open a scant twelve inches and then struck against something.

The teacher pushed his way through the opening. He found

himself standing between two towering piles of boxes, one of which had kept the door from opening fully. Beyond the boxes piles of ancient magazines and newspapers filled the entryway, leaving only a narrow passage along which the teacher walked.

"Agnes! Agnes Pinderek!" he called. The piles of debris muffled the sound of his voice. There was no answer except for a faint rustling which told of mice scampering for safety. Finally he reached the living room.

It was there he found the body of Agnes Pinderek.

Even as he absorbed the shock of finding the dead woman, Mr. Strang's brain was considering what must have happened. She had died painfully, horribly. The threadbare rug was pulled and twisted where her body had thrashed about on the floor, and an old brass lamp had been toppled, breaking its white glass bowl. Several of the piles of books about the room had been dragged down, and a copy of Charles Dickens' *Bleak House* was lying beneath the body. The old lady's long fingernails had pierced the palms of her hands, silent testimony to the agony she had suffered.

Someone had to be notified. Mr. Strang looked around for a telephone and found none. He walked toward the rear of the house, shivering uncontrollably. What kind of illness or injury could have caused such suffering?

He found the box of rat poison on the shelf in the kitchen. It was almost empty. In the sink were two white china cups and a teaspoon, all washed clean.

Pale and queasy, Mr. Strang left the house and hurried to the telephone booth on the corner in front of the school. From there he called the Aldershot police and asked to speak to Detective Sergeant Paul Roberts.

As if by magic a crowd collected in front of Miss Pinderek's house shortly after the arrival of the first police car. A pair of uniformed patrolmen, beefy and poker-faced, was stationed at the front door, and others were keeping the onlookers behind hastily erected barricades. Official-looking men carrying brief cases, cameras, and bags of investigative equipment moved back and forth between the house and the line of cars parked at the curb. Miss Pinderek's body, covered with a sheet, was brought out on a stretcher to be taken to the morgue for examination.

Paul Roberts came out of the house and beckoned to the teacher. Mr. Strang followed the bulky detective through the crowd until they reached a car at the curb. As Mr. Strang opened the door and got in on the passenger's side, he couldn't help thinking how much Agnes Pinderek would have disapproved of all this fuss being made over her. Proudly independent for nearly 90 years, she was receiving in death the attention she had spurned while alive.

Roberts sprawled onto the seat beside him and braced a clip-board against the steering wheel. "Do you have any idea who did it?" asked the teacher.

"I dunno. She didn't seem to have any enemies, according to the neighbors. She lived a pretty lonely existence, as far as we can make out."

Mr. Strang removed his black-rimmed glasses and rubbed at his eyes. "Paul," he said, "are you sure it's murder? After all, Agnes—Miss Pinderek—was an old lady. Couldn't she have just died of natural causes?"

Roberts shook his head. "The police surgeon said it was poison. Arsenic—all the classic symptoms. Apparently she died sometime yesterday afternoon."

"The rat poison?"

Roberts shifted the holstered pistol at his hip to a more comfortable position. "That's how we figure it," he said. "A couple of spoonfuls of that stuff would contain enough arsenic to kill a horse. We tried to lift prints from the box, but the cardboard was so wrinkled and greasy we couldn't get anything worthwhile. The cups and the spoon in the sink were clean too."

"Two cups," said Mr. Strang. "So there probably was a visitor. But up to now Agnes has never allowed a visitor in her house. Not even her best friends."

"Yeah," said Roberts musingly. "Well, she had one yesterday, all right."

"Any idea who it could have been?"

"We've got a pretty good—" Suddenly Roberts clamped his mouth shut and looked at the teacher, shaking his head. "Always want to play detective, don't you—?" he grinned. "Suppose I ask the questions and you give the answers."

"All right, Paul. Fire away."

"Okay. Since Miss Pinderek didn't allow visitors, how come you picked today to come calling?"

The teacher told Roberts about Miss Pinderek's daily trips to the grocery store.

"But today she didn't go, eh?"

Mr. Strang nodded. "For the first time I know of in years. I came over thinking something might be wrong. But I never suspected—"

"Yeah." Roberts slapped the clipboard onto the seat next to him. He turned the key in the ignition, and the starter whirred. "Let's take a ride. It's not much of a lead, but I'd better follow it up."

"Follow what up, Paul?"

"The grocery store. That would be the supermarket on Ripley Street. It's the only one in walking distance from here. I'd like to know what Miss Pinderek usually bought there every day."

In the parking lot Mr. Strang waited in the car while Roberts entered the supermarket. He was gone less than fifteen minutes. Returning, he opened the door, sat down, and shrugged dejectedly. "Cat food." He frowned into the rearview mirror. "Damn!"

"What's the matter?"

"The clerks remember her, all right," Roberts replied. "One or two of the older ones used to have her for a teacher. Every day she'd come into the store at about twelve-thirty. She'd pick up a few vegetables, maybe, or a loaf of old bread on sale. But there's one thing she bought every day. A can of Tabby-Yum catfood—tuna flavor."

"Well, that's innocent enough," said the teacher. "I doubt anyone would murder Miss Pinderek just because she kept a cat."

"Okay. But tell me this. What happened to the cat?"

"I beg your pardon?"

"About thirty men have gone through Miss Pinderek's house with a fine-tooth comb. There was no sign of any cat."

"Perhaps it ran away."

Roberts shook his head. "No way, Mr. Strang. I know cats. We've got two of 'em at home. They tend to hang around wherever they've been used to getting chow."

"Maybe it's at a neighbor's house."

Roberts rubbed his chin thoughtfully. "Could be. But you'd think we'd have found a food dish or a litter box—something to show a cat lived there."

"Paul, are you saying the murderer took the cat?"

"That would explain why it's missing, at least. If the killer was after the cat and if Miss Pinderek caught him—"

"What then?" Mr. Strang shook his head. "I doubt she'd have offered him a cup of coffee or tea."

"Yeah, that's true. But how's this? Miss Pinderek's visitor is let in. She offers him something—tea, probably. The visitor spikes Miss Pinderek's tea with the rat poison. She drinks it. She dies. Then the killer takes away the cat and all its equipment. How does that grab you?"

"Frankly, Paul," said Mr. Strang, "it leaves me with a good many questions unanswered. Why, for example, did Agnes allow this one person in when she'd kept all visitors out for years? And why did the killer choose a slow-acting poison like arsenic? And why was the cat taken away at all?"

"This is a weird one, all right," said Roberts with a shake of his head. "The whole thing's crazy. No motive. The killer steals a cat. If we're dealing with a maniac, he's going to be devilishly hard to locate."

"But you do have another lead, don't you, Paul?" Mr. Strang regarded the detective with an owlish stare.

"Like I said, that's police business," said Roberts, starting the car. "You stick to school-teaching. C'mon, I'll take you home."

It was two days later, on Friday evening, that Roberts called on Mr. Strang at the teacher's room in Mrs. Mackey's boardinghouse. Mr. Strang offered the detective a chair, which was accepted, and a brandy, which was refused.

"I gotta have your help on the Pinderek case," said the detective reluctantly.

"Why, I wouldn't think of meddling in police business," said Mr. Strang, a smile playing across his lips. "I'm a schoolteacher, remember?"

"Okay, so I shot my mouth off," said Roberts. "But you've got to help me on this one. Seems like everybody in Aldershot knew of Miss Pinderek. They've been demanding action on her murder. The chief's been catching all kinds of flak, and he's dropped the whole thing in my lap. I've got twenty-four hours to come up with an answer."

"But how can I help?" Mr. Strang asked.

"Do you know a kid in the high school named Gary Eklund?"

Mr. Strang stared intently at Roberts. "What's Gary got to do with this?"

"I just want to talk to him, that's all. But if I drop around at his house by myself, the whole family's going to start getting excited—a detective questioning their son and all that. But I understand Gary's in one of your classes."

Mr. Strang nodded.

"Well, that's the answer then," said Roberts. "You come with me. You're his teacher. He'll be more open with you."

Mr. Strang shook his head. "Gary lives with his mother, Paul. The father's been dead less than a year. I'm not about to use my position as Gary's teacher to make him say things he wouldn't talk to a detective about. You'll have to do your own dirty work."

"Okay." Roberts stood up and jammed his hat onto his head. "I thought it would be easier this way, that's all. I guess I'll just have to pull the kid in for questioning."

He was almost to the door when Mr. Strang stopped him. "Paul, wait. You must have some evidence against Gary. Tell me what it is. If what you've got is legitimate—if you're not just going on a fishing expedition—I'll help you. I'm afraid of how Gary's mother would react to his being arrested."

Roberts moved back into the room and sat down again. "Evidence," he said. "Yeah, we got evidence. Apparently Gary Eklund was the visitor Miss Pinderek had on the day she died."

From a coat pocket he took out a notebook. Opening it, he removed a small piece of paper. "This," he said, "is a receipt form for the school edition of the *Morning Record* newspaper. According to what we've found out, young Eklund handles the delivery of those papers in Aldershot High School. Is that right?"

"Yes. I take it myself. Seven cents a day, thirty-five cents per week. A special school rate. Gary earns a few dollars by distributing the papers to the classroom."

"But he's not supposed to deliver anywhere except in school," said Roberts. "Correct?"

"Yes, but—"

"Then how come this receipt was found in Miss Pinderek's house? It was under the rug next to the body. It's dated the day of the murder—last Tuesday. It's got Miss Pinderek's name on it, Mr. Strang. It's made out for thirty-five cents. And the words *Cancel Subscription* are written across the front of it. Last but not least, Gary Eklund's signature is at the bottom."

"Then Gary was in that house the day Agnes was murdered," said the teacher.

"That's right. And there's another thing. Have you taken a look at Gary's left hand in the last couple of days?"

"No, I—"

"According to his friends, Mr. Strang, there are scratches across the back of it. Scratches that look like they were made by a cat."

The teacher sat down limply. "But Gary's only a boy."

"I know that, Mr. Strang. That's why I want you to be the one to ask him about the receipt and the scratches. Hell, maybe it was an accident. I dunno. I'm not out to frame the kid. I just want to find out what really happened in Miss Pinderek's house last Tuesday."

"When do you want to see Gary, Paul?"

"Right away."

"I'll get my coat."

It was nearly eight o'clock when Roberts and Mr. Strang arrived at the Eklund house, a small shingled bungalow at the far end of town. Mr. Strang rapped at the door, while Roberts hung back in the shadows.

The door was opened by a frail woman with graying hair, wearing a faded housedress. "Why, Mr. Strang," she smiled, swinging the door wide. "What a pleasure to see you. Won't you come in?"

Mr. Strang entered the house, followed by Roberts. "We'd like to talk to Gary for a few minutes, if you don't mind, Mrs. Eklund. This man is a detective with the Aldershot—"

There was a sudden scurrying at the rear of the house and the sound of a door opening and closing. Immediately Roberts reopened the front door and raced out into the darkness.

For a moment there was only the slap of footsteps circling the house. Then a scuffling sound, followed by a shrill yell. Finally Roberts' loud voice echoed through the evening stillness.

"Get up, Gary, and come inside. I don't want to hurt you."

Roberts entered, almost carrying a youth wearing blue jeans, a flannel shirt, and once-white sneakers.

"Gary! Mr. Strang!" gasped Mrs. Eklund, her eyes wide and the palms of her hands pressed against her face. "What's happening? I don't understand."

"Sit down, Mrs. Eklund," said the teacher softly. "There really isn't any easy way to say this. You see, Detective Roberts believes Gary knows something about Agnes Pinderek's death last Tuesday."

"But—but that's impossible, Mr. Strang. Gary wouldn't—"

"Tell me something, Gary," said Roberts, staring down at the boy. "Did you visit Miss Pinderek at any time last Tuesday?"

"I don't have to talk to you." Gary turned uncertainly to the teacher. "Do I, Mr. Strang?"

After a glance at Roberts, Mr. Strang shook his head. He knelt beside the boy's chair.

"Gary," he said softly, "I'm on your side. I don't think you did anything wrong."

Slowly Gary raised his eyes toward his mother's worried face. "But I did," he whimpered. "I did do something wrong."

There was a gasp from Mrs. Eklund. But Mr. Strang went on as if he hadn't heard. "What was it, Gary? What did you do that was wrong?"

"It was on Tuesday. I sneaked out of school during my study hall the last period. You see, Miss Pinderek asked me to come to her house. And old Mrs. Lewis never takes attendance in study hall anyway. So I thought nobody would know."

"Why did Miss Pinderek want to see you?" asked Mr. Strang. Behind him, Gary's mother had gripped Roberts' sleeve, and her thin body was trembling.

"She takes the paper, Mr. Strang. Oh, I know I'm only supposed to deliver to people in school. But one day last year I saw her in the hall and she said she'd like to take the paper if it was at all possible. She seemed real nice, and it was no trouble at all to go over there before homeroom, so I did it. I guess when they find out about this, they'll take my job away."

"So you've been delivering the paper to Miss Pinderek every day, is that it? That's the 'something wrong' you were talking about? And she asked you to stop by on Tuesday so she could pay you?"

"Yes, sir. She owed me for the week. It was then she said she wanted to cancel the subscription. I made out a receipt just so I'd have a carbon copy for the circulation manager."

"Did you go *into* the house, Gary?"

The boy nodded. "It was the first time she ever let me inside. It was kind of spooky in there, but she made me a cup of tea. I don't like tea, but she was so nice I drank it so I wouldn't hurt her feelings."

"Did you see a box of rat poison?" asked the teacher.

Gary stared at him blankly. "I don't know anything about rat poison, Mr. Strang. After we'd had our tea, Miss Pinderek paid me, and I left."

"Is that all, Gary?"

"That's all. Honest. The next day I was leaving school when I saw all the police cars by Miss Pinderek's house. When I got home

I heard on the radio that she'd been—been—"

Roberts tapped Mr. Strang on the shoulder. "That story's all fine and dandy," he said. "But he still hasn't said anything about how the cat put those scratches on the back of his hand."

Gary considered his left hand as if seeing the scratches for the first time. "What's he talking about?" he asked Mr. Strang.

"The cat," Roberts said. "What did you do with the cat?"

"Cat? What cat, Mr. Strang?"

"Gary," said the teacher, rising stiffly to his feet, "Mr. Roberts wants to know how you got those scratches on your hand. Was it Miss Pinderek's cat that did it?"

"It wasn't any cat," said Gary. "It was a girl. We were down at the Malt Shop after school on Wednesday. In a booth. I was kind of—you know. Playing around a little. She got mad. So she dug her fingernails into my hand. I pulled it away, and that's how I got scratched."

"Holy Moses on a bicycle!" Paul Roberts shook his head in disgust. "Where did you dream up that fairy tale? If a girl did that, what's her name?"

Tight-lipped, Gary stared at the floor, shaking his head.

"I dunno," said Roberts. "There's no way to get a straight answer out of the kid. And we haven't gotten a single bit of information about the cat. Or the rat poison. Or—"

The teacher sank into a chair, staring at the opposite wall. "Rat poison," he murmured. "Rat poison. That's got to be it."

"Got to be what, Mr. Strang?" asked the detective.

The teacher rose and faced the little group before him. From a jacket pocket he took his glasses and began polishing them on his necktie. "Paul," he said, "it's pretty obvious that you think Gary is lying."

"Sure he's lying. How do you explain his taking off as soon as he found out I was a detective? And what about that business of the girl? He won't give her name. Why? Because there wasn't any girl. It was a cat, I tell you. Look, I'll grant I haven't figured out his motive yet. But of all the crazy yarns—"

"Paul, I want you to do something for me. It won't be easy for you, but try your best."

"Sure, Mr. Strang. Anything to get to the bottom of this. What is it?"

"I want you to assume for a short while that Gary is telling the absolute truth, that he has left out nothing of importance."

Roberts stared at the teacher in amazement. "Oh, come on!" he barked in an outraged tone.

"Now if Gary told the truth," Mr. Strang went on calmly, "then he paid Miss Pinderek a visit but left her alive and well. A day later, however, he finds out she's been murdered. As perhaps the only visitor Miss Pinderek has had in years, he realizes he'll be the Number One suspect. And then this evening a detective comes to his home. Wouldn't that explain his sudden flight out the back door? Gary tried to escape not because he was guilty but because he was afraid you thought he was."

"Well, yeah, maybe. But what about that business of the girl scratching him? That's a lot of—"

Mr. Strang held up a warning finger. "We're assuming Gary's telling the truth, remember? Paul, when you were young, did you ever get fresh with a girl?"

The answer came grudgingly. "Yeah. Couple of times. One of 'em took a good sock at me."

"Would you have been willing to discuss those times with adults if they'd asked you?"

"Not on your life. I mean—"

"So much for Gary's silence concerning the girl," the teacher went on. "Yes, Gary's afraid. He's afraid he'll lose his paper route because he was doing an old lady a favor by making a delivery outside of school. He's afraid he'll be disciplined for cutting school during a study hall. He's afraid you suspect him of a murder he never committed. But still, I'm convinced he's telling the truth. He went to see Miss Pinderek on Tuesday afternoon. He collected what was owed, gave her a receipt, then left. That's all."

"And what about the cat?" Roberts asked.

"Ah, yes, the elusive cat. I'm glad you brought that up, Paul, because that's what convinced me Gary was *not* lying."

"Where is it, then?" the detective demanded.

"The cat, which you thought made the scratches on Gary's hand, and which the killer supposedly did away with, can't be found for the simple reason that it never existed. The fleeing feline is a figment of the imagination, Paul. A phantom."

"But there had to be a cat!" Roberts exclaimed.

"Why, Paul? Why?" Mr. Strang continued relentlessly. "There was no sign of one. No bedding, no food dish—nothing. And once we eliminate the non-existent cat from our thinking, Agnes Pinderek's death is much easier to explain."

"Now, hang on, Mr. Strang." Roberts held up a hand like a student during a class discussion, then furiously jerked it down again. "We know Agnes Pinderek bought a can of Tabby-Yum every day. So how can you say she never owned a cat?"

"Because of the rat poison. Paul, why would a woman who kept a cat—a cat big and healthy enough to consume a can of cat food every day—need rat poison? And yet the box of poison was old and stained, and nearly empty. Now, not even the most determined poisoner would need an entire box of rat poison. Clearly the poison was there because Miss Pinderek was plagued with rats. But whoever heard of rat poison being necessary in a home where there's a healthy cat? Therefore, Miss Pinderek did not own a cat."

There was a long silence. "Why, I—I—" Roberts stammered.

But Mr. Strang pressed on. "Furthermore, when I first entered Miss Pinderek's house I distinctly heard mice playing among those boxes. Surely mice wouldn't run about so freely if there was a cat in the house."

"No cat," said Roberts slowly. "Okay, Gary seems to have been telling the truth. But if Miss Pinderek was all right when he left the house, what did happen? As far as we know, she had no other visitors. Who could have killed her?"

"The only person possible. Agnes herself."

"Suicide?" Roberts whispered the word. "But why?"

"Paul, I knew Miss Pinderek for several years before her retirement. She was a fiercely independent woman. She told me many times of her dread of one day being forced to accept charity."

Mr. Strang removed a handkerchief from his pocket and blew his nose loudly. "Seventeen years ago Agnes Pinderek retired. She'd made a few investments and felt that with the income from those plus what she got from the retirement fund, she'd be able to get along.

"Now, whether the investments were bad or rising prices were more than her fixed income could take, I don't know. But look at her house. It's rundown in a way she'd never have allowed if she'd had the money for its upkeep. I'd also imagine you'll find it's mortgaged to the hilt. She took to saving everything and anything that might one day be turned into cash. She bought stale bread, and even got the newspaper at school rates to save a few cents a week.

"Paul, the woman was a pauper. But still she wished to maintain her independence. Therefore she allowed herself no visitors who might see how badly off she was and take pity on her. Pity was the one emotion she couldn't tolerate when it was directed at her.

"And then one day she realized she could go on no longer. It became impossible for her to support herself. Accept charity? Never—not Agnes Pinderek. But there was another way. A solution that a proud woman of ninety might have found quite acceptable. Certainly from her point of view much more honorable than the indignity she would have suffered from accepting public assistance.

"But first her affairs had to be put in order. And that involved paying all her debts—including what she owed Gary. She invited him inside. We can only speculate on why she did this after having kept visitors away for so many years. But he was, after all, the last human she'd ever see. And she remembered to cancel the newspaper. At her death she would leave no loose ends behind.

"Once Gary had left the house, Agnes made a second cup of tea in the same cup she'd first used and mixed in the arsenic. Being tasteless, it was easily swallowed. Then she washed the cups and spoon, not to conceal evidence, but simply from force of habit. The cramps and stomach pains didn't come until later."

Mr. Strang rubbed one hand across his eyes, which were glistening wetly.

"You've drawn a helluva lot of conclusions from a box of rat poison and a missing cat," said Roberts. "How can you be so sure that—"

A tear ran down Mr. Strang's cheek.

"It really had to happen the way you said, didn't it?" Roberts murmured softly. "I'll run a check on Miss Pinderek's finances to make sure, but—well, how else could it have been?"

With one hand he rubbed at the back of his neck. "But I still don't understand about the cat food."

"Tabby-Yum costs about one-third the price of a can of tunafish," said Mr. Strang. "For the past few years it was about the only thing keeping Miss Pinderek alive."

"Q"

Michael Gilbert

Return of the Hero

"The mother of Sisera looked out of her window and cried, 'Why is his chariot so long in coming? Why tarry the wheels of his chariot?' "

As Detective Inspector Patrick Petrella of Q Division said, "It was pure Old Testament" . . .

Detective: INSPECTOR PATRICK PETRELLA

That morning, because his wife and small son were away at the seaside, Detective Inspector Patrick Petrella cooked his own breakfast. He should have been with them, but his stand-in had broken his wrist in an argument with an Irish truck driver and his second-in-command had mumps.

As he walked through the sun-baked streets, from his flat in Passmore Gardens to the Divisional Substation on Patton Street, there was an ache at the back of his neck and a buzzing in his ears, and his tongue felt a size too large for his mouth. Any competent doctor would have diagnosed strain from overwork and packed him straight off on holiday.

The morning was taken up with a new outbreak of shoplifting. In the middle of the afternoon the telex message was brought into his room.

"Important. Repeated to all stations in Q Division and for information to other Divisions. Arthur Lamson's conviction was quashed by the Court of Criminal Appeal at 3 o'clock this afternoon."

Petrella was still trying to work through all the unpleasant possibilities of this message when Superintendent Watterson arrived.

He said, "I see you've had the news, Patrick. It was that ass Downing who did it."

He referred, in this disrespectful manner, to Lord Justice Downing, one of the more unpredictable of Her Majesty's Judges.

"I was afraid it might happen," said Petrella.

He spoke so flatly that Watterson looked at him and said, "You ought to be on leave. Are you feeling all right?"

"It's the heat. A decent thunderstorm would clear the air."

"What we want," said Watterson, "isn't a decent thunderstorm. It's a decent bench of judges. Not a crowd of nit-picking old women. I wonder if they've got the remotest idea of how much damage a man like Lamson can do."

"There'll be no holding him now," said Petrella.

Arthur Lamson was once described by the newspapers as the unofficial mayor of Grendel Street. He ran a gymnasium and sporting club there, was a big donor to all local charities, and had a cheerful word and a pat on the head for any child, or a pinch on the bottom for any pretty girl. He was also a criminal, who specialized in protection rackets, employing the youths who hung around his gymnasium to break up the premises—and occasionally the persons—of anyone who refused him payment.

Since he took no part in these acts of violence himself he had been a difficult man to peg. Indeed, he might have continued untouched by the law for a very long time if he had not fallen out with Bruno.

Bruno was a fair-haired boy, with a deceptively open face and a smile that showed every one of the thirty-two teeth in his mouth. He was a great favorite with the girls, and it was over a girl that the original trouble arose. There were other differences as well. Bruno had an unexpected streak of obstinacy. When he was not paid as much as he had been promised for a job he had done for Art Lamson, he spoke his mind, and spoke it loudly and publicly.

Lamson had decided he must be disciplined. The disciplining took place in a quiet back street behind the Goods Depot.

While Bruno was in the hospital, having half of his right ear sewn back on, he came to certain conclusions. He told no one what he proposed to do, not even Jackie, the girl he was secretly engaged to. He went one evening to a quiet public house in the Tooley Street area, and in a back room overlooking the river he met two men who looked like sailors. To them he talked, and they wrote down all that he said, and gave him certain instructions.

A month later Bruno said to Jackie, "I don't think any of the boys know you're my girl, so you ought to be all right, but you'd better lie low for a bit. I'm going to have to clear out of London."

Jackie said, "What are you talking about, Bruno? What's going to happen? What have you done?"

"What I've done," said Bruno, "is I've shopped Art Lamson. The Regional boys are picking him up tonight. With what I've been able to tell them, they reckon they've got him sewn up."

Jackie put both arms round Bruno's neck, her blue eyes full of tears, and said, "Look after yourself, boy. If anything happened to you I don't know what I should do."

Very early on the following morning two cars, with four men in each of them, slid to a stop opposite Lamson's house. Two men went round to the back, two men watched the front, and four men let themselves into the house, using a key to unlock the front door. Petrella was one of them. Grendel Street was in his manor and it was his job to make the actual arrest, and to charge Lamson with the crime of conspiring with others to demand money with menaces and to commit actual bodily harm.

The nature of the information received became evident at the preliminary hearing in the Magistrate's Court. It was Bruno. And it was noticed that never once, while he gave his evidence, did he look at Lamson or Lamson at him.

This was in March.

The trial started at the Old Bailey in the first week of June. Bruno was brought to the court, from a safe hideaway in Essex, in a police van which had steel bars on its windows and bulletproof glass.

On the second afternoon he gave his evidence to the Judge. Under the skillful questioning of his own counsel he repeated, even more clearly and comprehensively, the facts he had already stated to the Magistrate. At four o'clock he had finished, and the Judge said, "It will be convenient if we break now. We can begin the cross-examination of this witness tomorrow morning."

Counsel bowed to the Judge, the Judge bowed back, the Court emptied, and Bruno was taken down a flight of steps to the basement where the van awaited him.

As he stepped out of the door, a marksman on the roof of a neighboring building, using an Armalite rifle with a telescopic sight, shot him through the head.

"And that," said Watterson, "was that. The Jury had heard Bruno's evidence, and they convicted Lamson. Of course, there was an appeal. The defense pointed out that although plenty of people had given evidence of being intimidated, the only witness who actually identified Lamson as the head of the organization was Bruno."

And Bruno had not been cross-examined.

"How can you accept his evidence," said Mr. Marston, Q.C., in his eloquent address to the Court of Criminal Appeal, "when it has not been tested, in the traditional way, by cross-examination? Bear in mind, too, that the witness was himself a criminal. That he had, by his own admission, taken part in more than one of the offenses with which the accused is charged. The law is slow to accept the evidence of an accomplice, even when it has stood the test of cross-examination—"

And so, at three o'clock on that hot afternoon in August, Arthur Lamson descended the stairs which lead from the dock in the Court of Criminal Appeal and emerged, a free man.

A considerable reception awaited him. The committee of welcome consisted of a number of reporters, mainly from the sporting papers, but a scattering from the national press as well; one or two minor celebrities who didn't care where they went as long as they got into the photograph; members of the Grendel Street Sporting Club; and friends and hangers-on of both sexes.

The party started immediately in the bar of the Law Courts, but this was too small to contain everyone who wanted to get in on the act. A move was made to a small club behind Fleet Street which was broad-minded about membership and seemed to observe its own licensing hours.

By six o'clock the party was larger than when it had started, and much louder. Lamson had a six months' thirst to quench, and he stood, at the center of the noisiest group, a schooner of whiskey in his large right hand, the sweat running in rivulets down his red face, a monarch who had been unjustly deposed and was now returning in triumph to his kingdom.

"I got a great respect for the Laws of England," he announced. "They don't put an innocent man in prison. Not like some countries I could name."

"That's right, Art," said the chorus.

"I'm not saying anything against the police. They've got their job to do, like I've got mine. If they're prepared to let bygones be bygones, I'm prepared to do the same."

This offer of a treaty of friendship to the police force was felt to be in the best of taste, and a fresh round of drinks was ordered.

Back in Grendel Street extensive preparations had been made for the return of the hero. Streamers had been placed in position, from top-story windows, spanning the street, and banners had been hung out with WELCOME HOME, ART embroidered on them in letters of red cotton-wool. The two public houses—The Wheelwrights Arms at one end of the street and The Duke of Albany at the other end—were both doing a roaring trade, and the band of the Railway Recreational Club was starting on its favorite piece, which was the William Tell Overture.

The organizer of these festivities was seated at her bedroom window, in a chair, looking down on the street. This was old Mrs. Lamson, Art's mother, the matriarch of Grendel Street. Ma Lamson was a character in her own right. She had married, outdrunk, outtalked, and outlived three husbands, the third of whom was Art's father. A stroke had paralyzed her legs, but not her tongue. Confined to a wheel chair, and rendered even more impatient by her confinement, her shrill voice still dominated the street.

"Fix the end of that streamer, you big git," she screeched. "It's flapping like a lot of bloody washing on a line. That's better. My God, if I wasn't here to keep an eye on things, you'd have the whole bloody lot down in the bloody street. And Albert"—this was to a middle-aged man, one of her sons by her first marriage, himself a grandfather—"clear those bloody fools back onto the pavement."

She indicated the drinkers outside The Wheelwrights Arms who were sketching an informal eightsome reel to the strains of William Tell. "We want Art to drive straight down the street when he comes home, don't we? He can't do it if they've turned it into a pally-de-dance, can he?"

By eight o'clock the original party had moved from the Fleet Street club and re-established itself in the backroom of a public house near Blackfriars Station. Its constituents had gradually changed. The journalists had slid away, to write up their impressions of the event for next morning's papers. The minor celebrities had gone in search of the next happening to which they could attach themselves. What remained was a hard core of serious drinkers, a few friends of Art's, but mostly friends of friends, or those complete strangers who seem to have a knack of attaching themselves to any party which has reached a stage of euphoria.

One of the few men there who knew Art personally said, toward nine o'clock, "You ought to be getting back sometime soon. Your old lady'll be expecting you."

"That's right," said Art, "she will." He made no attempt to move.

"She's got a sort of reception organized, I understand."

"She's a lovely person," said Art. "I'm lucky to have a mother like that. Have you got a mother?"

The friend said that he had a mother, a lovely person, too.

Toward ten o'clock the black clouds which had been piling up from the west had blotted out moon and stars and the air was electric with the coming storm.

The party was showing signs of disintegrating. There were no formal farewells. People drifted out and did not reappear. For some time now Art had been conscious of the girl. To start with, there had been quite a few girls in the party. This one had sat quietly in the background drinking whatever was put into her hand and minding her own business. Nobody knew exactly who had brought her, but nobody minded because she was a good-looking chick, with blue eyes, black hair, and lots up top. Not obtrusive, but enough to catch the eye.

Art found his thoughts centering on the girl. Drink was not the only thing he had been deprived of for the past six months. When she looked up at him and smiled, what had been vague stirrings became clear desire.

How it happened he was not clear. At one moment he was putting down an empty glass on the counter, at the next he was in the back of a taxi with the girl.

He slid one arm around her waist. She said, "Don't start anything here, love. The taxi driver'll sling us out. Wait till we get there."

"Where are we going?"

The girl sounded surprised. "Back to my place, of course."

Art was happy to wait. He was three out of four parts drunk. One thing was puzzling him. If this chick really had been knocking back all the drinks that had been offered to her, she should have been blind drunk, but she sounded sober. A bit tensed up, he thought, but cool. Perhaps she had a very hard head. She certainly had a beautiful little body.

Her place was a surprise too. It was certainly not a tart's pad. It was on the third floor of an old-fashioned house and had the look of a working-girl's flat, small but neat. She sat him down on the sofa, and said, "What about a bite of food, eh?"

This seemed to Art to be an excellent suggestion. He needed something solid to absorb the alcohol he had poured into himself. The girl gave him a drink from a bottle on the sideboard. She said, "I won't be a minute," and disappeared into the small room which was evidently the kitchen.

Art sipped his drink and lay back on the sofa. He had had so much luck lately that this little extra bit seemed a natural bonus. The only trouble was that he was feeling bloody sleepy. It really would be a bad joke if, with this gorgeous chick offering herself to him, he couldn't stay awake to do anything about it.

He laughed and the laugh turned into a strangled snore.

Five minutes later the girl reappeared. She picked up the glass, which had rolled onto the floor, and stared down at Art, full length on the sofa, his face red and sweating, his mouth wide-open. There was no expression in her blue eyes at all.

First she moved over and shot the bolt on the door. Then she went to a closet in the corner of the room. It seemed to have household stuff in it. She selected what she needed, and came back.

When the storm broke, Petrella was sitting in the charge room at Patton Street talking to Superintendent Watterson.

"This should cool their heads," said the Superintendent. "They've been jazzing it up since opening time."

"Has the great man put in an appearance yet?"

He was answered by the telephone. It was Ma Lamson. Her voice had in it anger, vexation, and an edge of fear. Petrella found it difficult to make out what she was saying.

He said, "Hold on a minute," and to Watterson, "She says Art hasn't turned up, and she's worried something may have happened to him. I can't really make out what she wants. I'd better go down and have a word with her."

"Watch it, Patrick. They all know it was you who pulled him in. They'll still be hot about it."

"No one could stay hot in this weather," said Petrella. The rain was now coming down solidly. He drove down to Grendel Street in a police car, stopped it at the end, turned up the collar of his raincoat, and went forward on foot.

The street was empty, its gutters running with water. Overhead the banners of welcome flapped, damp and forlorn. The band had cased its instruments and hurried home.

Only Ma Lamson kept vigil at her upstairs window. The rain, blowing in, had soaked her white hair which hung, in dank ropes, on both sides of her pink face.

"Where is he?" she screeched. "Where's my boy? Art wouldn't let us down. Something's happened to him, I know. 'E'd got enemies, Inspector. They'll have been laying for him. You've got to do something!"

Petrella stood in the pelting rain and looked up at the old woman. The release of the storm had cleared his head. It had done more. It had made him almost light-headed. He felt an almost hysterical urge to laugh.

Restraining it, he promised that a general alert should be sent out, and made his way back to Patton Street.

He said dreamily to Watterson, "It was pure Old Testament."

"What are you talking about?"

The Superintendent knew that Petrella had a reputation for eccentricity. He had once quoted poetry at a meeting of the top brass at Scotland Yard, and had got away with it because it was Robbie Burns, who happened to be the Assistant Commissioner's favorite poet.

"The mother of Sisera looked out of her window and cried, 'Why is his chariot so long in coming? Why tarry the wheels of his chariot?' "

"Who the hell was Sisera?"

"He was a king in Canaan. When he was on his way back to a triumphant welcome, organized by his mother, he was lured into the tent of a young lady called Jael."

"And what did she do?"

"He asked for water, and she gave him milk. She brought forth butter, in a lordly dish."

"I see," said Watterson doubtfully. "And what happened then?"

"Then she took a mallet in one hand and a tent peg in the other, and she smote him. At her feet he bowed, he fell. Where he fell, there he lay down, dead."

"What you need is a holiday," said Watterson firmly. "You're going on leave first thing tomorrow, if I have to stand in for you myself."

Five days later, when the police, alerted by worried neighbors, broke into the third-floor flat of Bruno's girl, Jackie, they found Art Lamson.

Jackie had driven a six-inch nail clean through the middle of his forehead, and had then cut her own throat. But Petrella knew nothing of this. He was helping his small son to construct a sand fort and adorn its battlements with shells from the sea.

Edward D. Hoch

Captain Leopold and the Ghost-Killer

"It started as a simple case"—a murder with five credible witnesses, all making positive identification of the killer. It turned into an impossible case—one of the toughest cases Captain Leopold ever tackled. . .And we should warn you: keep your mind sharp and your wits alert—or you too may believe in ghosts! . . .

Detective: CAPTAIN LEOPOLD

It started as a simple case, without a hint of ghosts or impossibilities—Lieutenant Fletcher's case, really, with Captain Leopold along only because he'd been working late that night and Grant Tower was on his way home. The time was 9:25 and downtown was deserted except for the usual street people. Some of them were standing around outside the 20-story building—which qualified as a Tower in Leopold's city—when their car pulled up, and for a wild moment Leopold feared the one closest to him might ask for his autograph.

The trouble was on the 15th floor and a uniformed cop was waiting when they came off the elevator. "Cleaning woman here in the building, Captain. Martha Aspeth. Her husband shot her."

Fletcher was already bending over the body of a middle-aged woman, sprawled in the doorway of an insurance office. There was blood beneath and around her, soiling the freshly polished floor. "Any witnesses?" Leopold asked.

"Five women who work with her," the officer said. "They all saw it happen. I've got an APB out on the husband."

More technicians were arriving, to photograph the scene and dust for prints. Fletcher straightened up from the body and said, "At least three wounds, Captain. Maybe four."

Leopold nodded. "Let's talk to some of these women."

A stout white-haired woman with rolled stockings and a dumpy-looking print dress stepped forward. "I was right next to her! I saw the whole thing!"

Two white-coated morgue attendants had arrived with a stretcher, but they stood aside while the medical examiner checked the body. "I was on my way home," the M.E. told Leopold. "Doc Hayes takes over at nine. Hell of a thing, grabbing a man on his way home. Going to take that telephone out of my car."

"I was on my way home, too," Leopold said. "Cheer up." Then he led the woman to a sofa in the open office. "What's your name?"

"Hilda Youst. Martha and I started together over at the bank building. She was like a sister to me."

"What about her husband?"

"They didn't live together. He wanted younger ones. Can you imagine that? Martha was only forty-two and he wanted younger ones!"

"Had they quarreled before?"

"All the time!"

"Up here?"

"Sure! He came up regularly, usually on paydays. Wanted money for drink and women."

"Was tonight a payday?"

"No."

"Exactly what happened?"

"It was"—she glanced at the wall clock—"about twenty-five minutes ago, just after nine o'clock. He got off the elevator and asked one of the girls where Martha was. She was in here with me and she heard his voice. She said, 'God, not him again,' and she went to the door to see what he wanted. He just pulled out his gun and started shooting."

"He didn't say anything first?"

"I think he called her a filthy name."

"How many shots did you hear?"

"Four, I think."

"Then what happened?"

"He ran out the fire door and down the stairs. I phoned the police. The other girls were in terrible shape. They never saw anything like this before."

"Did you?"

"Did I what?"

"See anything like this before?"

"No, of course not! But I'm older. I been around more."

"Would you recognize the killer if you saw him again?"

"Kurt Aspeth? Of course I'd recognize him!"

Leopold found Lieutenant Fletcher talking to the other four witnesses. Three of them were Puerto Rican girls, barely out of their teens. One was close to hysteria, her body shaking with sobs. Leopold noticed that the photographer and the medical examiner had finished their jobs. The body was covered now and the white-coated men were lifting it onto their stretcher.

"They all tell the same story, Captain," Fletcher reported. "He got off the elevator, asked Miss Sanchez here where Martha Aspeth was, then pulled out the gun and fired the moment he saw her."

"It seems clear enough," Leopold decided. "I guess we can leave the details to the rest of the men. We'll want statements from all five witnesses, of course, and from relatives. Find out where Kurt Aspeth lives and put someone on the address, in case he goes back there."

"I'll take care of it, Captain," Fletcher assured him. "You go on home now."

Leopold grinned. "I keep forgetting it's your case. See you in the morning."

The morning was in May, with golden sunshine and a spring warmth that robbed him of energy. Leopold simply sat in his office, wondering as he gazed out the window if this bout of spring fever was a sign of increasing age or merely a return to youth. He was still thinking about it when Fletcher came in a few minutes after nine.

"You know that killing last night, Captain?" Fletcher asked, settling into his favorite chair. "I've got some good news and some bad news."

Leopold grunted. "What's the good news?"

"We found Kurt Aspeth. His car hit a bridge abutment on the Expressway, about a mile from the Grant Tower building. He was killed instantly."

"What's the bad news?"

"The accident happened at 8:27—a good half hour or more before Kurt Aspeth is supposed to have killed his wife. . ."

The city morgue was located across the street from police headquarters, in a faded brick building soon to be demolished for urban renewal. Doc Hayes was still there, on duty from the night before, following some rotating schedule which had always baffled Leopold. He'd known Doc for some years, through numerous homicides on which Hayes had functioned as acting medical examiner. He was a grim, efficient little man somewhere past 40, who sometimes looked as if he'd be more at home teaching at a medical college.

"What is it?" Hayes asked when he saw Leopold and Fletcher coming in. "That Aspeth thing?"

"Right. We're trying to establish a time sequence. The police officer's report lists the time of the accident as 8:27. We're wondering if that could be a mistake."

Doc Hayes shook his head. "That's the time, all right. He was killed instantly, so the officer didn't bother with an ambulance. As I understand it, a doctor pronounced him dead and they called for the morgue wagon. His body was already here when I came to work at nine." He consulted the book in front of him. "Checked in at exactly nine. Made the notation myself. Damn busy night—Aspeth and a hit-and-run and then Aspeth's wife. Damn busy."

"There's no possibility of error?"

"Error? The man is certainly dead, if that's what you mean."

"But what about the time? Could it have been an hour later?"

Doc Hayes snorted. "Daylight-saving time started three weeks ago. Our clocks are all correct. Besides, the officer's records couldn't be wrong, too."

"All right," Leopold said, moving to another possibility. "Are you sure it's really Kurt Aspeth?"

"*I'm* not sure," Hayes said. "I never met the man. But he was driving Kurt Aspeth's car, carrying Kurt Aspeth's driver's license, and Kurt Aspeth's brother identified the body early this morning."

"Brother?"

Doc Hayes nodded. "Felix Aspeth."

Leopold had a wild thought.

"*Twin* brother?"

"Hardly. Felix is ten years older."

"Still, they might resemble each other. What's his address?"

Hayes looked it up in his records and gave it to him. "Now, get outa here, will you? I have to take my car into the garage and then get home for some sleep. This is supposed to be my day off!"

"Thanks, Doc." Outside, Leopold said to Fletcher, "I'm going to check on this brother. You get Hilda Youst and the rest of the cleaning crew down here to identify the body before it's moved."

"You think they will?"

"Who knows? Maybe the brother is pulling some sort of trick."

Felix Aspeth's address was an apartment building in a rundown section of the city. The neighborhood was racially mixed, sprawling through six blocks of what had once been a downtown college campus. The college, sensing change, had moved to the suburbs, from the city streets. The old buildings had become apartment houses.

Felix Aspeth answered the door with a suddenness that startled Leopold, as if he'd been waiting on the other side. "What is it?"

"Captain Leopold of the Violent Crimes Squad. It's about your brother."

Felix Aspeth grunted and motioned him inside. He was a tall man with stringy black hair and a black mustache flecked with gray. There was something a little seedy about him that matched the sparsely furnished apartment in which he lived. "I'm making funeral arrangements now," he said. "I can only spare a few minutes."

Leopold sat down gingerly on a straight-backed chair. "You know, of course, that your brother's estranged wife was shot to death last night, at just about the time of the fatal accident."

"Yes."

"Witnesses say Kurt was the one who shot her."

"I have no doubt of it. He was always a bit crazy on the subject of Martha. He was crazy to have married her anyway."

"I understand he was your younger brother?"

Felix Aspeth nodded. "Ten years younger. He was just thirty-one. They got married about ten years ago, when he was just out of the army. He picked her up in a bar one night. I told him that wasn't the sort of girl you married, but he wouldn't listen."

"How long had they been separated?"

"The whole ten years, off and on. One of them would walk out and then after a while they'd get back together again. There were no children, and he was never much of a worker. Martha was on welfare for a year before she got that job cleaning up at Grant Tower."

"You said he was thirty-one. She seemed older than that."

"She was. Over forty, I'd say. That's one of the reasons I was against the marriage in the first place. But you just couldn't talk to Kurt."

"There seems to be a time discrepancy of about an hour in our records. Though Kurt was positively identified as the murderer by five witnesses who knew him, the records of the accident bureau show the smashup occurred about thirty minutes earlier."

"I see," Felix Aspeth said.

"You see? Well, I *don't.*" Leopold was growing irritated with the man. "Suppose you explain to me how that could be possible."

"Kurt couldn't leave this earth without settling the score with Martha. Call it love or hate or whatever you will, he had to take her with him. Martha was murdered by my brother's ghost."

When Leopold returned to headquarters he found Fletcher in his office with policewoman Connie Trent. "You look tired, Captain," Connie said. "Want some coffee?"

"I could use something. How about it, Fletcher? Did those women view the body?"

"It was quite a struggle, Captain. A couple of them just didn't want to look at him. But they all made positive identification. His face wasn't damaged in the accident, and they say there's no doubt about it. That's Kurt Aspeth, all right—the same man who killed Martha Aspeth last night."

Connie returned with coffee. "Fletcher said you had a hunch it was Aspeth's brother. Did you see him?"

"I saw him," Leopold said sadly. "He thinks his brother's spirit killed Martha, after the accident."

"Spirit? You mean, a ghost?" Fletcher snorted. "I don't buy that, Captain. Ghosts don't run down stairs."

"And they don't fire pistols, either," Leopold agreed. "Whoever shot her, it wasn't Kurt Aspeth's ghost."

"How about the brother? Do they look alike?"

Leopold thought about that. "Not really, though Felix without the mustache might pass for an older version of Kurt. It's hard to say, never having seen Kurt alive. They look like brothers, I guess. No more than that."

"But in the excitement of the shooting, couldn't the witnesses have been mistaken?" Connie asked.

"Five of them? Not likely. Especially the older one, Hilda Youst. Nothing would shake her."

"Then the thing is impossible," Fletcher said.

"It happened," Leopold reminded him. "Which officer was first on the accident scene?"

Fletcher consulted his file. "Pete Franklin, a motorcycle cop. Good man."

Leopold glanced at his watch. It was just after three o'clock. "Connie, hop down to the police garage and see if you can catch Franklin. He must be on the four-to-midnight shift, and he should be coming in soon. Find out everything he knows about the accident."

"I'll even ask him if he saw any ectoplasm leave the body and head downtown," she said.

Officer Pete Franklin was tall and handsome, and Connie Trent did not in the least mind interviewing him. She found him in the garage adjusting his leather puttees and awaiting the arrival of the duty sergeant with the orders of the day. When she'd introduced herself, Franklin said, "I've seen you around headquarters. The prettiest policewoman in the department."

She ignored the compliment. "Captain Leopold's a swell man to work for. He took me on last year after I blew my cover on the Narcotics Squad."

Pete Franklin nodded. "I see Lieutenant Fletcher occasionally."

"Do you like riding a motorcycle?"

"It's great in the summer. Come winter I'm back in a patrol car."

"Captain Leopold was wondering about that fatal accident last night—Kurt Aspeth, the man who hit the bridge abutment?"

"I know. The car was a mess. I was only a few blocks away when I heard the crash."

"You were first on the scene?"

"The first officer. The only one, really. Some motorists stopped, and a doctor. He was dead, so I called for the morgue wagon on my radio."

"What do you think caused the crash?"

"Somebody told me today he'd killed his wife. I suppose he smashed the car deliberately. A lot of one-car accidents are really suicides."

"There were no bad road conditions?"

"No, except that it was dark, and that section of the Expressway isn't too well lighted."

"What time was it?"

"Around 8:30. That's in my report."

"You know Aspeth's wife wasn't shot till after nine?"

He frowned and scratched his head. "I heard there was some confusion about the times. It doesn't make sense. The witnesses must have been wrong."

The duty sergeant had arrived and Connie could see her time was running out. "One more thing. Which way was the car going on the Expressway—toward downtown or away from it?"

"Away from it. The guy'd just shot his wife, hadn't he? I figure he was trying to escape and just decided, the hell with it, and smashed up the car."

"Maybe," Connie conceded. "If we can just account for that time difference we'll be all set."

"I gotta go now," he said. He started to turn away, then had another thought. "How about dinner some night? I'm off tomorrow."

She was about to decline automatically, then said instead, "Sure, I'm free tomorrow night."

"Give me your address and I'll pick you up at seven."

Hilda Youst opened the door and stared at Leopold without recognition. "What do you want?" she asked.

"We met last night at Grant Tower, Mrs. Youst. I'm investigating the killing of Martha Aspeth."

"Oh, yes—Captain Leopold. I remember you now. Come in."

Like Felix Aspeth's, her apartment was in a poorer section of the city. But there the resemblance ceased. Where his had been sparsely furnished, hers was jammed with trinkets and trophies. One small corner table was covered with religious statues of all sizes and shapes, while a table in the opposite corner held a single large trophy with a golden figure on the top representing a woman in a long gown. She saw Leopold looking at it and explained, "I won a weight-watching contest two years ago. I lost the most weight of any member in the whole state."

"That's fine," Leopold said.

"I got a crown and a dozen roses. Then I came home and put the weight all back on."

"That's life, I guess. I wanted to ask you more about last night."

"What about last night?" She didn't ask him to sit down, so he stood.

"You see, all five of you positively identified Kurt Aspeth as the murderer of his wife. And you identified the body at the morgue as being his."

"That's right."

"But he died around 8:30, and you didn't report the shooting till about 9:05."

"That's when it happened," she insisted.

Leopold sighed. "The thing's an impossibility, Mrs. Youst. Two things seem certain—Aspeth was dead at 8:30, and Aspeth shot his wife a half hour later. One element *must* be wrong. The killing must have taken place a full hour earlier than you said. Why did you wait an hour before summoning the police, Mrs. Youst?"

"But I *didn't!*"

He couldn't doubt her words. The idea of five cleaning women dancing around the body in some obscene rite for an hour before calling the police was just too preposterous. And yet, if he accepted her story, he was left with no one but Aspeth's ghost as the murderer.

"Maybe the shock was so great you lost all sense of time. An hour might have gone by without your realizing it."

"Impossible! For one thing, we have our schedule. I never reach the fifteenth floor till nine o'clock. That's where I was, so it had to be after nine."

"All right," he said. There was no attacking her logic. But as he started to leave, a new thought struck him. "If you just reached the fifteenth floor at nine, how was it that the floor was already freshly polished?"

She sighed, as if at his stupidity. "I said *I* got there at nine. The girls who do the floors work about twenty minutes ahead of me."

He left her standing in the doorway and went home to meditate on the ghost of Kurt Aspeth.

In the morning Fletcher had more bad news. "We checked out the fingerprints, Captain. The dead man really is Kurt Aspeth. He's got a minor record for drunkenness and assault."

"Is the body still at the morgue?"

"The brother claimed it. There's a funeral service this morning."

Leopold stared out the window, wondering what had happened to the bright May sunshine of the previous day. It was a good day for a funeral, but not much else. "We've hit a blank wall so far,

Fletcher. Let's see what happened around 9:27 that night, at the time the accident *should* have occurred. Communications keeps a tape on incoming accident and trouble calls. Get it over here and let's play it. There has to be something we're missing, and I want to find it before the press gets onto this story."

But the tape that Fletcher produced an hour later seemed merely a jumble of radio calls and phone conversations. It took them some time to sort out the accidents from the crime reports, and this was what they heard, in part:

". . .8:05—truck-bicycle collision at Maple and York. Car 124 responding. . .8:27—car accident near the Wilson Avenue exit on the Expressway. Cycle 404 radioed in from scene. . ."

"That must be Pete Franklin," Fletcher said.

"Let's hear what happened later."

". . .8:54—two-car collision at West and Saratoga. Injuries. Car 212 responding with ambulance. . .9:02—Cycle 404 investigating possible hit-and-run fatality on Small Street. . .9:06—Police? A woman's been shot! She's been murdered! I'm on the 15th floor of Grant Tower! Come quick!. . ."

"That was Hilda Youst," Leopold said.

Fletcher nodded. "The patrolman got there first and verified it was a murder. That's when I was called along with the medical examiner, the technicians, and the morgue wagon."

"Let's see what else there is."

But there was no other accident recorded until *". . .9:59–two-car collision on Park Place. Car 23 responded. Drivers will see own doctors. . ."*

"Nothing around the right time," Leopold grumbled. "What was that hit-and-run?"

"The boys are working on it. Terrible thing—a high school girl on her way home from the store, cutting across a narrow alley behind some apartment houses. Nobody even saw it happen. Some damn fool swung out of the parking area too fast, I suppose."

Leopold puzzled over the tape, rewinding it to play it again. Finally he gave it up. It was nearly time to start believing in ghosts. . .

Connie Trent was ready when Officer Pete Franklin rang her bell at seven. He looked different out of uniform—less handsome, somehow—and she felt a bit cheated.

"All set?" he asked. "Where do you want to eat?"

"Your choice." She knew his salary as a motorcycle cop would exclude the sort of places she really liked.

"I know a great place down on the Sound, if you like fish."

"Love it! Let's go."

Over an expensive dinner of lobster and white wine she began to change her opinion of Pete Franklin. His easy-going manner with women was something of an act, and he used money to compensate for some lack he felt in himself. "That cost you a lot," she said as they left.

"I'm celebrating. I may be coming into some money soon. Besides, it's a long time since I've been out with a girl as pretty as you."

As he pulled out of the parking lot, Connie asked, "Where to?"

"It's a great night for a drive. Look, the moon's even come out from behind the clouds. Let's ride around a bit, then go back to my place and listen to records. How's that grab you?"

"Fine." She was already plotting excuses for an early escape, but it was only nine o'clock, just barely dark, and she could hardly ask to be taken home that early.

His apartment was on the north side of the city and they reached it a half hour later. He drove around back and pulled into an assigned space in the parking area. "This place must cost you something," she commented.

"It's not cheap."

He helped her out of the car and they headed across the dark asphalt toward the lighted rear entrance. Connie saw the figure in the shadows first and she tugged at Franklin's sleeve. "Pete, someone's there!"

"Who is it?" Franklin called out.

The answer was a blinding blast from a shotgun that toppled Pete Franklin backward like a giant fist. Connie felt the edge of the shot pattern rip into her left arm and side even as she tried to pull her own gun free from her purse. Then she went down too, seeing nothing, hearing only the running footsteps that gradually faded into silence.

Lieutenant Fletcher had phoned Leopold at home as soon as the word reached headquarters. They caught up with Connie Trent in the emergency room at General Hospital, where a doctor was bandaging her wounds with professional ease.

"She's all right," he told them. "I removed eleven shotgun pellets, but none of them were deep."

Connie was trying to sit up. "Fletcher! Captain! What about Pete Franklin? They won't tell me a thing around here!"

"Pete caught the full blast in his chest," Leopold said quietly. "They couldn't save him."

"Oh, God. . ."

"Did you see who did it?"

"Nothing but someone standing in the shadows, waiting for him. I tried to use my gun—"

"Don't blame yourself, Connie."

She lay back and closed her eyes for a moment. Then she opened them. "He told me he might come into some money."

"What else did he say?"

"Nothing. But I think it was tied into the Aspeth killing."

Leopold frowned. "Why do you say that?"

"He said something odd when I talked to him yesterday. That's why I went out with him tonight—to find out more about it."

"What did he say that was odd?"

"That it was dark at the time Kurt Aspeth smashed up his car. But it doesn't get dark these nights till a little before nine. At 8:27, when the accident was supposed to have happened, there'd still be daylight."

"Thanks, Connie," Leopold said. "I think you've solved the case for us."

"But not soon enough to save Pete Franklin's life."

When they left the hospital, Leopold and Fletcher drove over to Small Street, a narrow alley that ran behind some old apartment buildings near the Expressway.

"A hell of a place to end your life," Fletcher said.

"Any place is," Leopold said. "What was her name?"

"Rose Sullivan. She was only seventeen."

"Pete Franklin again?"

"Yeah," Fletcher said. "We should have caught that on the tape. Cycle 404 responded to both accidents, even before a call came in."

"We had no reason to catch it. When he radioed in that he was investigating a 'car accident near the Wilson Avenue exit on the Expressway,' it naturally sounded as if the accident was *on the Expressway*. Actually it was here on Small Street, a half block from the Wilson Avenue exit. He must have been coming off the exit ramp on his cycle when he saw it happen. And see that fence down the end of the alley? I'll bet that overlooks the Expressway. He was still here on Small Street when Aspeth cracked up nearly an hour later on the Expressway."

"What do we do now, Captain?"

Leopold shrugged. "I guess we go back to the morgue."

Doc Hayes was on duty again, because it was after nine. He let them in himself and led the way to his office in the rear. "Quiet night," he said, "except for poor Pete Franklin, of course."

"What time did they bring him in?"

"Around ten. I was late getting here myself. Had a flat tire."

"Damn lot of car trouble lately, Doc. You were taking it into the garage yesterday, weren't you?"

"Yeah. These things happen."

"Doc. . ."

"What is it?"

"Killing the girl was only manslaughter at worst. With Pete Franklin it's first-degree murder."

There was a sudden flash of wildness in Hayes's eyes and he started to move, but Fletcher was on him, handcuffing his wrists.

Connie Trent was released from the hospital the following morning and was in Leopold's office an hour later. "What's all this about arresting Doc Hayes? I can't believe it!"

"He killed two people, Connie," Leopold said.

"He shot Pete? And Martha Aspeth?"

"Pete, yes—but not Mrs. Aspeth. She was killed by her husband, just as the witnesses said. We spent our time investigating that case when we should have been investigating the hit-and-run killing of a high school girl named Rose Sullivan. You see, the answer to the problem of Aspeth's ghost was a very simple one—the times of the two accidents were *switched*."

"But how was that possible? And why?"

"Doc Hayes made a full statement last night, after his arrest. You see, he goes on duty at the morgue at nine o'clock each night. He'd been visiting the apartment of a lady friend earlier in the evening and was pulling into Small Street in a hurry to get downtown when his car hit and killed the Sullivan girl. On that back street, at dusk, no one saw the accident. But Pete Franklin, cruising the area on his motorcycle, came along just after."

"What time was this?"

"Probably very close to 8:27, the time that was later ascribed to

Aspeth's fatal accident. Franklin's first reaction was to radio in a report that he was investigating an accident. Once that report was on the record, as of 8:27, Doc Hayes's troubles began. He knew Pete, of course, and maybe he even knew that Pete wasn't above taking a little graft to keep up a nice apartment. Doc was in big trouble at this point. He'd killed a girl with his car, and if he admitted it he'd also have to explain what he was doing there. I guess he saw his marriage and his career both threatened in that moment, and he made a fatal mistake. He offered Pete Franklin money to let him go."

"And Franklin took the money."

Leopold nodded. "It was dark by this time, and the street is little more than an alley anyway. No one came along. Doc Hayes drove away and Franklin must have spent the next several minutes tidying up the scene—picking up bits of chrome or headlight glass that might have served as clues. Then he was ready to call headquarters on the radio and report a hit-and-run, which he finally did at 9:02. The only trouble was, there was still his 8:27 report on the record. He'd called in an accident, nothing more, identifying it simply as being by the Expressway—which Small Street is. The detectives who came to examine the scene didn't know about the earlier call, or about the missing thirty-five minutes, but it was still on the record. That was when fate brought Kurt Aspeth onto the scene."

"He'd already killed his wife and was escaping on the Expressway. And he probably did hit that abutment deliberately."

"Could be," Leopold said. "Small Street dead-ends at the Expressway. Franklin could have seen—or at least heard—the crash from where he was. He got there on his motorcycle almost at once, saw that Aspeth was dead, and called for the morgue wagon. Only this accident he *didn't* report. This accident became the 8:27 accident he'd already radioed in to headquarters."

"But. . ." Connie still wasn't convinced. "What about the detectives investigating the hit-and-run? They must have heard Aspeth's crash, too. What about the other motorists who stopped? What about the morgue records?"

"The detectives already had their hands full. The motorists would never see the time on Franklin's report. The morgue records were easily changed by Doc Hayes. It was a one-car accident, remember, so there wasn't likely to be any court case where witnesses would be testifying. Franklin saw a lucky chance to switch the order of the two accidents and thereby explain his earlier radio report. Fortunately for him, he hadn't mentioned Small Street in the earlier report, only the Expressway. And luckily no other patrol car happened along while he was at Aspeth's wreck. Luck was all on his side till he asked Hayes for more money."

"But how did you know all this?" Connie wondered. "How did you know enough to arrest Doc Hayes in the first place?"

"When you repeated Franklin's remark about it being dark at the time Aspeth smashed up, we knew he hadn't died in the 8:27 accident. That had to be something else Cycle 404 investigated. But Franklin had only two accidents in the crucial period—Aspeth and the hit-and-run on Small Street. If it wasn't Aspeth at 8:27, it had to be the hit-and-run. Fletcher and I went over to Small Street last night and saw how close it was to the Wilson Avenue exit. So Franklin lied about the hit-and-run. Why? Only one answer went with his expectation of money—he was blackmailing the driver."

"All right—but why Doc?"

"Three things pointed to him. First, he lied when he said Aspeth's body came into the morgue before nine. Second, he told us he had to take his car into the garage, implying some necessary repair work. And third, at the time of the hit-and-run he would have been in his car, driving to the morgue. Circumstantial, sure, but it was circumstantial too when he said he had a flat tire that made him late for work while Franklin was being killed."

"You took a gamble accusing him on that evidence."

"I take gambles every day in this job, Connie. Just the way Pete Franklin did. After he thought of switching the accident times he had to phone Doc at the morgue and tell him to switch his records, too. The records were the important thing. The morgue drivers would never be asked, any more than those passing motorists. The time of Kurt Aspeth's death would be an unimportant fact buried forever in police files. It would have happened that way too, except for one crazy thing—Kurt Aspeth had just come from murdering his wife. When that fact became known, Franklin asked Doc for more money to keep quiet. And Doc got out a shotgun to pay him off."

"It kept building up, didn't it?" Connie said. "From an auto accident to bribery to murder. But at least it wasn't Aspeth's ghost on the prowl. I was almost beginning to believe that."

"So was I," Leopold said.

Ellery Queen

The Adventure of Abraham Lincoln's Clue

We cannot resist quoting Anthony Boucher's editorial introduction to "The Adventure of Abraham Lincoln's Clue" in BEST DETECTIVE STORIES OF THE YEAR: *21st Annual Collection. Mr. Boucher wrote: "Ellery Queen has written very nearly as many different types of detective stories as he has edited; but my favorites are largely those that might almost be called fantasies: tales of a looking-glass world in which people create the most improbable mystifications for the most unlikely reasons, yet always leaving some trail of mad logic for Ellery (and the reader) to follow—problems that are as unbelievable as they are acutely solvable. 'The Adventure of Abraham Lincoln's Clue' is especially appealing because it involves two of the deepest passions of both Queen-the-character and Queen-the-author: the lives of Abraham Lincoln and Edgar Allan Poe.*

"Ellery Queen appeared in BEST *#18 with a long novelet, and in #19 and #20 with short-shorts. Now we have him in a regulation-length short story—and one of the most characteristic Queenly stories in his long and rich career."*

Detective: ELLERY QUEEN

Fourscore and eighteen years ago, Abraham Lincoln brought forth (in this account) a new notion, conceived in secrecy and dedicated to the proposition that even an Honest Abe may borrow a leaf from Edgar A. Poe.

It is altogether fitting and proper that Mr. Lincoln's venture into the detective story should come to its final resting place in the files of a man named Queen. For all his life Ellery has consecrated Father Abraham as the noblest projection of the American dream; and, insofar as it has been within his poor power to add or detract, he has given full measure of devotion, testing whether that notion, or any notion so conceived and so dedicated, deserves to endure.

Ellery's service in running the Lincoln clue to earth is one the world has little noted nor, perhaps, will long remember. That he shall not have served in vain, this account:

The case began on the outskirts of an upstate-New York city with the dreadful name of Eulalia, behind the flaking shutters of a fat and curlicued house with architectural dandruff, recalling for all the world some blowsy ex-Bloomer Girl from the Gay Nineties of its origin.

The owner, a formerly wealthy man named DiCampo, possessed a grandeur not shared by his property, although it was no less fallen into ruin. His falcon's face, more Florentine than Victorian, was—like the house—ravaged by time and the inclemencies of fortune; but haughtily so, and indeed DiCampo wore his scruffy purple velvet house jacket like the prince he was entitled to call himself, but did not. He was proud, and stubborn, and useless; and he had a lovely daughter named Bianca, who taught at a Eulalia grade school and, through marvels of economy, supported them both.

How Lorenzo San Marco Borghese-Ruffo DiCampo came to this decayed estate is no concern of ours. The presence there this day of a man named Harbidger and a man named Tungston, however, is to the point: they had come, Harbidger from Chicago, Tungston from Philadelphia, to buy something each wanted very much, and DiCampo had summoned them in order to sell it. The two visitors were collectors, Harbidger's passion being Lincoln, Tungston's Poe.

The Lincoln collector, an elderly man who looked like a migrant fruit picker, had plucked his fruits well: Harbidger was worth about $40,000,000, every dollar of which was at the beck of his mania for Lincolniana. Tungston, who was almost as rich, had the aging body of a poet and the eyes of a starving panther, armament that had served him well in the wars of Poeana.

"I must say, Mr. DiCampo," remarked Harbidger, "that your letter surprised me." He paused to savor the wine his host had poured from an ancient and honorable bottle (DiCampo had filled it with California claret before their arrival). "May I ask what has finally induced you to offer the book and document for sale?"

"To quote Lincoln in another context, Mr. Harbidger," said Di-

Campo with a shrug of his wasted shoulders, " 'the dogmas of the quiet past are inadequate to the stormy present.' In short, a hungry man sells his blood."

"Only if it's of the right type," said old Tungston, unmoved. "You've made that book and document less accessible to collectors and historians, DiCampo, than the gold in Fort Knox. Have you got them here? I'd like to examine them."

"No other hand will ever touch them except by right of ownership," Lorenzo DiCampo replied bitterly. He had taken a miser's glee in his lucky finds, vowing never to part with them; now forced by his need to sell them, he was like a suspicion-caked old prospector who, stumbling at last on pay dirt, draws cryptic maps to keep the world from stealing the secret of its location. "As I informed you gentlemen, I represent the book as bearing the signatures of Poe and Lincoln, and the document as being in Lincoln's hand; I am offering them with customary proviso that they are returnable if they should prove to be not as represented; and if this does not satisfy you," and the old prince actually rose, "let us terminate our business here and now."

"Sit down, sit down, Mr. DiCampo," Harbidger said.

"No one is questioning your integrity," snapped old Tungston. "It's just that I'm not used to buying sight unseen. If there's a money-back guarantee, we'll do it your way."

Lorenzo DiCampo reseated himself stiffly. "Very well, gentlemen. Then I take it you are both prepared to buy?"

"Oh, yes!" said Harbidger. "What is your price?"

"Oh, no," said DiCampo. "What is your bid?"

The Lincoln collector cleared his throat, which was full of slaver. "If the book and document are as represented, Mr. DiCampo, you might hope to get from a dealer or realize at auction—oh—$50,000. I offer you $55,000."

"$56,000," said Tungston.

"$57,000," said Harbidger.

Tungston showed his fangs.

"$60,000," he said.

Harbidger fell silent, and DiCampo waited. He did not expect miracles. To these men, five times $60,000 was of less moment than the undistinguished wine they were smacking their lips over; but they were veterans of many a hard auction-room campaign, and a collector's victory tasted very nearly as sweet for the price as for the prize.

So the impoverished prince was not surprised when the Lincoln collector suddenly said, "Would you be good enough to allow Mr. Tungston and me to talk privately for a moment?"

DiCampo rose and strolled out of the room, to gaze somberly through a cracked window at the jungle growth that had once been his Italian formal gardens.

It was the Poe collector who summoned him back. "Harbidger has convinced me that for the two of us to try to outbid each other would simply run the price up out of all reason. We're going to make you a sporting proposition."

"I've proposed to Mr. Tungston, and he has agreed," nodded Harbidger, "that our bid for the book and document be $65,000. Each of us is prepared to pay that sum, and not a single penny more."

"So that is how the screws are turned," said DiCampo, smiling. "But I do not understand. If each of you makes the identical bid, which of you gets the book and document?"

"Ah," grinned the Poe man, "that's where the sporting proposition comes in."

"You see, Mr. DiCampo," said the Lincoln man, "we are going to leave that decision to you."

Even the old prince, who had seen more than his share of the astonishing, was astonished. He looked at the two rich men really for the first time. "I must confess," he murmured, "that your compact is an amusement. Permit me?" He sank into thought while the two collectors sat expectantly. When the old man looked up he was smiling like a fox. "The very thing, gentlemen! From the typewritten copies of the document I sent you, you both know that Lincoln himself left a clue to a theoretical hiding place for the book which he never explained. Some time ago I arrived at a possible solution to the President's little mystery. I propose to hide the book and document in accordance with it."

"You mean whichever of us figures out your interpretation of the Lincoln clue and finds the book and document where you will hide them, Mr. DiCampo, gets both for the agreed price?"

"That is it exactly."

The Lincoln collector looked dubious. "I don't know . . ."

"Oh, come, Harbidger," said Tungston, eyes glittering. "A deal is a deal. We accept, DiCampo! Now what?"

"You gentlemen will of course have to give me a little time. Shall we say three days?"

Ellery let himself into the Queen apartment, tossed his suitcase aside, and set about opening windows. He had been out of town for a week on a case, and Inspector Queen was in Atlantic City attending a police convention.

Breathable air having been restored, Ellery sat down to the week's accumulation of mail. One envelope made him pause. It had come by airmail special delivery, it was postmarked four days earlier, and in the lower left corner, in red, flamed the word *URGENT*. The printed return address on the flap said: *L.S.M.B-R DiCampo, Post Office Box 69, Southern District, Eulalia, N.Y.* The initials of the name had been crossed out and "Bianca" written above them.

The enclosure, in a large agitated female hand on inexpensive notepaper, said:

Dear Mr. Queen,

The most important detective book in the world has disappeared. Will you please find it for me?

Phone me on arrival at the Eulalia RR station or airport and I will pick you up.

Bianca DiCampo

A yellow envelope then caught his eye. It was a telegram, dated the previous day:

WHY HAVE I NOT HEARD FROM YOU STOP AM IN DESPERATE NEED OF YOUR SERVICES

BIANCA DICAMPO

He had no sooner finished reading the telegram than the telephone on his desk trilled. It was a long-distance call.

"Mr. Queen?" throbbed a contralto voice. "Thank heaven I've finally got through to you! I've been calling all day—"

"I've been away," said Ellery, "and you would be Miss Bianca DiCampo of Eulalia. In two words, Miss DiCampo: Why me?"

"In two words, Mr. Queen: Abraham Lincoln."

Ellery was startled. "You plead a persuasive case," he chuckled. "It's true, I'm an incurable Lincoln addict. How did you find out? Well, never mind. Your letter refers to a book, Miss DiCampo. Which book?"

The husky voice told him, and certain other provocative things as well. "So will you come, Mr. Queen?"

"Tonight if I could! Suppose I drive up first thing in the morning. I ought to make Eulalia by noon. Harbidger and Tungston are still around, I take it?"

"Oh, yes. They're staying at a motel downtown."

"Would you ask them to be there?"

The moment he hung up Ellery leaped to his bookshelves. He snatched out his volume of *Murder for Pleasure,* the historical work on detective stories by his good friend Howard Haycraft, and found what he was looking for on page 26:

> And . . . young William Dean Howells thought it significant praise to assert of a nominee for President of the United States:
>
> > The bent of his mind is mathematical and metaphysical, and he is therefore pleased with the absolute and logical method of Poe's tales and sketches, in which the problem of mystery is given, and wrought out into everyday facts by processes of cunning analysis. It is said that he suffers no year to pass without a perusal of this author.
>
> Abraham Lincoln subsequently confirmed this statement, which appeared in his little known "campaign biography" by Howells in 1860 . . . The instance is chiefly notable, of course, for its revelation of a little suspected affinity between two great Americans . . .

Very early the next morning Ellery gathered some papers from his files, stuffed them into his briefcase, scribbled a note for his father, and ran for his car, Eulalia-bound . . .

He was enchanted by the DiCampo house, which looked like something out of Poe by Charles Addams; and, for other reasons, by Bianca, who turned out to be a genetic product supreme of northern Italy, with titian hair and Mediterranean blue eyes and a figure that needed only some solid steaks to qualify her for Miss Universe competition. Also, she was in deep mourning; so her conquest of the Queen heart was immediate and complete.

"He died of a cerebral hemorrhage, Mr. Queen," Bianca said, dabbing at her absurd little nose. "In the middle of the second night after his session with Mr. Harbidger and Mr. Tungston."

So Lorenzo San Marco Borghese-Ruffo DiCampo was unexpectedly dead, bequeathing the lovely Bianca near-destitution and a mystery.

"The only things of value father really left me are that book and the Lincoln document. The $65,000 they now represent would pay off father's debts and give me a fresh start. But I can't find them, Mr. Queen, and neither can Mr. Harbidger and Mr. Tungston—who'll be here soon, by the way. Father hid the two things, as he told them he would; but where? We've ransacked the place."

"Tell me more about the book, Miss DiCampo."

"As I said over the phone, it's called *The Gift: 1845*. The Christmas annual that contained the earliest appearance of Edgar Allan Poe's *The Purloined Letter*."

"Published in Philadelphia by Carey & Hart? Bound in red?" At Bianca's nod Ellery said, "You understand that an ordinary copy of *The Gift: 1845* isn't worth more than about $50. What makes your father's copy unique is that double autograph you mentioned."

"That's what he said, Mr. Queen. I wish I had the book here to show you—that beautifully handwritten *Edgar Allan Poe* on the flyleaf, and under Poe's signature the signature *Abraham Lincoln*."

"Poe's own copy, once owned, signed, and read by Lincoln," Ellery said slowly. "Yes, that would be a collector's item for the ages. By the way, Miss DiCampo, what's the story behind the other piece—the Lincoln document?"

Bianca told him what her father had told her.

One morning in the spring of 1865, Abraham Lincoln opened the rosewood door of his bedroom in the southwest corner of the second floor of the White House and stepped out into the red-carpeted hall at the unusually late hour—for him—of 7:00 A.M.; he was more accustomed to beginning his work day at six.

But (as Lorenzo DiCampo had reconstructed events) Mr. Lincoln that morning had lingered in his bedchamber. He had awakened at his usual hour but, instead of leaving for his office immediately on dressing, he had pulled one of the cane chairs over to the round table, with its gas-fed reading lamp, and sat down to reread Poe's *The Purloined Letter* in his copy of the 1845 annual; it was a dreary morning, and the natural light was poor. The President was alone; the folding doors to Mrs. Lincoln's bedroom remained closed.

Impressed as always with Poe's tale, Mr. Lincoln on this occasion was struck by a whimsical thought; and, apparently finding no paper handy, he took an envelope from his pocket, discarded its enclosure, slit the two short edges so that the envelope opened out into a single sheet, and began to write in a careful hand on the blank side.

"Describe it to me, please."

"It's a long envelope, one that must have contained a bulky letter. It is addressed to the White House, but there is no return address, and father was never able to identify the sender from the handwriting. We do know that the letter came through the regular mails, because there are two Lincoln stamps on it, lightly but unmistakably cancelled."

"May I see your father's transcript of what Lincoln wrote out that morning on the inside of the envelope?"

Bianco handed him a typewritten copy and, in spite of himself, Ellery felt goose-flesh rise as he read:

> Apr. 14, 1865
>
> Mr. Poe's The Purloined Letter is a work of singular originality. Its simplicity is a master-stroke of cunning, which never fails to arouse my wonder.
>
> Reading the tale over this morning has given me a "notion." Suppose I wished to hide a book, this very book, perhaps? Where best to do so? Well, as Mr. Poe in his tale hid a letter *among letters*, might not a book be hidden *among books?* Why, if this very copy of the tale were to be deposited in a library and on purpose not recorded—would not the Library of Congress make a prime depository!—well might it repose there, undiscovered, for a generation.
>
> On the other hand, let us regard Mr. Poe's "notion" turnabout: suppose the book were to be placed, not amongst other books, but *where no book would reasonably be expected?* (I may follow the example of Mr. Poe, and, myself, compose a tale of "ratiocination"!)
>
> The "notion" beguiles me, it is nearly seven o'clock. Later to-day, if the vultures and my appointments leave me a few moments of leisure, I may write further of my imagined hiding-place.
>
> In self-reminder: the hiding-place of the book is in 30d, which

Ellery looked up. "The document ends there?"

"Father said that Mr. Lincoln must have glanced again at his watch, and shamefacedly jumped up to go to his office, leaving the sentence unfinished. Evidently he never found the time to get back to it."

Ellery brooded. Evidently indeed. From the moment when Abraham Lincoln stepped out of his bedroom that Good Friday morning, fingering his thick gold watch on its vest chain, to bid the still-unrelieved night guard his customary courteous "Good morning" and make for his office at the other end of the hall, his day was spoken for. The usual patient push through the clutching crowd of favor-seekers, many of whom had bedded down all night on the hall carpet; sanctuary in his sprawling office, where he read official correspondence; by 8:00 A.M. having breakfast with his family—Mrs. Lincoln chattering away about plans for the evening, 12-year-old Tad of the cleft palate lisping a complaint that "nobody asked me to go," and young Robert Lincoln, just returned from duty, bubbling with stories about his hero Ulysses Grant and the last days of the war; then back to the presidential office to look over the morning newspapers (which Lincoln had once remarked he "never" read, but these were happy days, with good news everywhere), sign two documents, and signal the soldier at the door to admit the morning's first caller, Speaker of the House Schuyler Colfax (who was angling for a Cabinet post and had to be tactfully handled); and so on throughout the day—the historic Cabinet meeting at 11:00 A.M., attended by General Grant himself, that stretched well into the afternoon; a hurried lunch at almost half-past two with Mrs. Lincoln (had this 45-pounds-underweight man eaten his usual midday meal of a biscuit, a glass of milk, and an apple?); more visitors to see in his office (including the unscheduled Mrs. Nancy Bushrod, escaped slave and wife of an escaped slave and mother of three small children, weeping that Tom, a soldier in the Army of the Potomac, was no longer getting his pay: "You are entitled to your husband's pay. Come this time tomorrow," and the tall President escorted her to the door, bowing her out "like I was a natural-born lady"); the late afternoon drive in the barouche to the Navy Yard and back with Mrs. Lincoln; more work, more visitors, into the evening . . . until finally, at five minutes past 8:00 P.M., Abraham Lincoln stepped into the White House formal coach after his wife, waved, and sank back to be driven off to see a play he did not much want to see, *Our American Cousin,* at Ford's Theatre . . .

Ellery mused over that black day in silence. And, like a relative hanging on the specialist's yet undelivered diagnosis, Bianca DiCampo sat watching him with anxiety.

Harbidger and Tungston arrived in a taxi to greet Ellery with the fervor of two castaways waving at a smudge of smoke on the horizon.

"As I understand it, gentlemen," Ellery said when he had calmed them down, "neither of you has been able to solve Mr. DiCampo's interpretation of the Lincoln clue. If I succeed in finding the book and paper where DiCampo hid them, which of you gets them?"

"We intend to split the $65,000 payment to Miss DiCampo," said Harbidger, "and take joint ownership of the two pieces."

"An arrangement," growled old Tungston, "I'm against on principle, in practice, and by plain horse sense."

"So am I," sighed the Lincoln collector, "but what else can we do?"

"Well," and the Poe man regarded Bianca DiCampo with the icy intimacy of the cat that long ago marked the bird as its prey, "Miss DiCampo, who now owns the two pieces, is quite free to renegotiate a sale on her own terms."

"Miss DiCampo," said Miss DiCampo, giving Tungston stare for stare, "considers herself bound by her father's wishes. His terms stand."

"In all likelihood, then," said the other millionaire, "one of us will retain the book, the other the document, and we'll exchange them every year, or some such thing." Harbidger sounded unhappy.

"Only practical arrangement under the circumstances," grunted Tungston, and *he* sounded unhappy. "But all this is academic, Queen, unless and until the book and document are found."

Ellery nodded. "The problem, then, is to fathom DiCampo's interpretation of that *30d* in the document. 30d . . . I notice, Miss DiCampo—or, may I? Bianca?—that your father's typewritten copy of the Lincoln holograph text runs the *3* and *0* and *d* together—no spacing in between. Is that the way it occurs in the longhand?"

"Yes."

"Hmm. Still . . 30d . . . Could *d* stand for *days* . . . or the British *pence* . . . or *died*, as used in obituaries? Does any of these make sense to you, Bianca?"

"No."

"Did your father have any special interest in, say, pharmacology? chemistry? physics? algebra? electricity? Small *d* is an abbreviation used in all those." But Bianca shook her splendid head. "Banking? Small *d* for *dollars, dividends*?"

"Hardly," the girl said with a sad smile.

"How about theatricals? Was your father ever involved in a play production? Small *d* stands for *door* in stage directions."

"Mr. Queen, I've gone through every darned abbreviation my dictionary lists, and I haven't found one that has a point of contact with any interest of my father's."

Ellery scowled. "At that—I assume the typewritten copy is accurate—the manuscript shows no period after the *d*, making an abbreviation unlikely. 30d . . . let's concentrate on the number. Does the number 30 have any significance for you?"

"Yes, indeed," said Bianca, making all three men sit up. But then they sank back. "In a few years it will represent my age, and that has enormous significance. But only for me, I'm afraid."

"You'll be drawing wolf whistles at twice thirty," quoth Ellery warmly. "However! Could the number have cross-referred to anything in your father's life or habits?"

"None that I can think of, Mr. Queen. And," Bianca said, having grown roses in her cheeks, "thank you."

"I think," said old Tungston testily, "we had better stick to the subject."

"Just the same, Bianca, let me run over some 'thirty' associations as they come to mind. Stop me if one of them hits a nerve. The Thirty Tyrants—was your father interested in classical Athens? Thirty Years War—in Seventeenth Century European history? Thirty all—did he play or follow tennis? Or . . . did he ever live at an address that included the number 30?"

Ellery went on and on, but to each suggestion Bianca DiCampo could only shake her head.

"The lack of spacing, come to think of it, doesn't necessarily mean that Mr. DiCampo chose to view the clue that way," said Ellery thoughtfully. "He might have interpreted it arbitrarily as *3*-space-*0*-*d*."

"Three od?" echoed old Tungston. "What the devil could that mean?"

"Od? Od is the hypothetical force or power claimed by Baron von Reichenbach—in 1850, wasn't it?—to pervade the whole of nature. Manifests itself in magnets, crystals, and such, which according to the excited Baron explained animal magnetism and mesmerism. Was your father by any chance interested in hypnosis, Bianca? Or the occult?"

"Not in the slightest."

"Mr. Queen," exclaimed Harbidger, "are you serious about all this—this semantic sludge?"

"Why, I don't know," said Ellery. "I never know till I stumble over something. Od . . . the word was used with prefixes, too—*biod,* the force of animal life; *elod,* the force of electricity; and so forth. *Three* od . . . or *triod,* the triune force—it's all right, Mr. Harbidger, it's not ignorance on your part, I just coined the word. But it does rather suggest the Trinity, doesn't it? Bianca, did your father tie up to the Church in a personal, scholarly, or any other way? No? That's too bad, really, because Od—capitalized—has been a minced form of the word God since the Sixteenth Century. Or . . . you wouldn't happen to have three Bibles on the premises, would you? Because—"

Ellery stopped with the smashing abruptness of an ordinary force meeting an absolutely immovable object. The girl and the two collectors gawped. Bianca had idly picked up the typewritten copy of the Lincoln document. She was not reading it, she was simply holding it on her knees; but Ellery, sitting opposite her, had shot forward in a crouch, rather like a pointer, and he was regarding the paper in her lap with a glare of pure discovery.

"That's it!" he cried.

"What's it, Mr. Queen?" the girl asked, bewildered.

"Please—the transcript!" He plucked the paper from her. "Of course. Hear this: 'On the other hand, let us regard Mr. Poe's "notion" turn-about.' *Turn-about.* Look at the 30d 'turn-about'—as I just saw it!"

He turned the Lincoln message upside down for their inspection. In that position the 30d became:

POE

"*Poe!*" exploded Tungston.

"Yes. crude but recognizable," Ellery said swiftly. "So now we read the Lincoln clue as: 'The hiding-place of the book is in *Poe*'!"

There was a silence.

"In Poe," said Harbidger blankly.

"In Poe?" muttered Tungston. "There are only a couple of trade editions of Poe in DiCampo's library, Harbidger, and we went through those. We looked in every book here."

"He might have meant among the Poe books in the *public* library. Miss DiCampo—"

"Wait." Bianca sped away. But when she came back she was drooping. "It isn't. We have two public libraries in Eulalia, and I know the head librarian in both. I just called them. Father didn't visit either library."

Ellery gnawed a fingernail. "Is there a bust of Poe in the house, Bianca? Or any other Poe-associated object, aside from books?"

"I'm afraid not."

"Queer," he mumbled. "Yet I'm positive your father interpreted 'the hiding-place of the book' as being 'in Poe.' So he'd have hidden it 'in Poe' . . ."

Ellery's mumbling dribbled away into a tormented sort of silence: his eyebrows worked up and down, Groucho Marx-fashion; he pinched the tip of his nose until it was scarlet; he yanked at his unoffending ears; he munched on his lip . . . until, all at once, his face cleared; and he sprang to his feet. "Bianca, may I use your phone?"

The girl could only nod, and Ellery dashed. They heard him telephoning in the entrance hall, although they could not make out the words. He was back in two minutes.

"One thing more," he said briskly, "and we're out of the woods. I suppose your father had a key ring or a key case, Bianca? May I have it, please?"

She fetched a key case. To the two millionaires it seemed the sorriest of objects, a scuffed and dirty tan leatherette case. But Ellery received it from the girl as if it were an artifact of historic importance from a newly discovered IV Dynasty tomb. He unsnapped it with concentrated love; he fingered its contents like a scientist. Finally he decided on a certain key.

"Wait here!" Thus Mr. Queen; and exit, running.

"I can't decide," old Tungston said after a while, "whether that fellow is a genius or an escaped lunatic."

Neither Harbidger nor Bianca replied. Apparently they could not decide, either.

They waited through twenty elongated minutes; at the twenty-first they heard his car, champing. All three were in the front doorway as Ellery strode up the walk.

He was carrying a book with a red cover, and smiling. It was a compassionate smile, but none of them noticed.

"You—" said Bianca. "—found—" said Tungston. "—the book!" shouted Harbidger. "Is the Lincoln holograph in it?"

"It is," said Ellery. "Shall we all go into the house, where we may mourn in decent privacy?"

"Because," Ellery said to Bianca and the two quivering collectors as they sat across a refectory table from him, "I have foul news. Mr. Tungston, I believe you have never actually seen Mr. DiCampo's book. Will you now look at the Poe signature on the flyleaf?"

The panther claws leaped. There, toward the top of the flyleaf, in faded inkscript, was the signature *Edgar Allan Poe*.

The claws curled, and old Tungston looked up sharply. "DiCampo never mentioned that it's a full autograph—he kept referring to it as 'the Poe signature.' Edgar *Allan* Poe . . . Why, I don't know of a single instance after his West Point days when Poe wrote out his middle name in an autograph! And the earliest he could have signed this 1845 edition is obviously when it was published, which was around the fall of 1844. In 1844 he'd surely have abbreviated the 'Allan,' signing 'Edgar *A.* Poe,' the way he signed everything! This is a forgery."

"My God," murmured Bianca, clearly intending no impiety; she was as pale as Poe's Lenore. "Is that true, Mr. Queen?"

"I'm afraid it is," Ellery said sadly. "I was suspicious the moment you told me the Poe signature on the flyleaf contained the 'Allan.' And if the Poe signature is a forgery, the book itself can hardly be considered Poe's own copy."

Harbidger was moaning. "And the Lincoln signature underneath the Poe, Mr. Queen! DiCampo never told me it reads *Abraham* Lincoln—the full Christian name. Except on official documents, Lincoln practically always signed his name '*A.* Lincoln.' Don't tell me this Lincoln autograph is a forgery, too?"

Ellery forbore to look at poor Bianca. "I was struck by the 'Abraham' as well, Mr. Harbidger, when Miss DiCampo mentioned it to me, and I came equipped to test it. I have here—" and Ellery tapped the pile of documents he had taken from his briefcase "—facsimiles of Lincoln signatures from the most frequently reproduced of the historic documents he signed. Now I'm going to make a precise tracing of the Lincoln signature on the flyleaf of the book—" he proceeded to do so "—and I shall superimpose the tracing on the various signatures of the authentic Lincoln documents. So."

He worked rapidly. On his third superimposition Ellery looked up. "Yes. See here. The tracing of the purported Lincoln signature from the flyleaf fits in minutest detail over the authentic Lincoln signature on this facsimile of the Emancipation Proclamation. It's a fact of life that's tripped many a forger that *nobody ever writes his name exactly the same way twice.* There are always variations. If two signatures are identical, then, one must be a tracing of the other. So the 'Abraham Lincoln' signed on this flyleaf can be dismissed without further consideration as a forgery also. It's a tracing of the Emancipation Proclamation signature.

"Not only was this book not Poe's own copy; it was never signed—and therefore probably never owned—by Lincoln. However your father came into possession of the book, Bianca, he was swindled."

It was the measure of Bianca DiCampo's quality that she said quietly, "Poor, poor father," nothing more.

Harbidger was poring over the worn old envelope on whose inside appeared the dearly beloved handscript of the Martyr President. "At least," he muttered, "we have *this*."

"Do we?" asked Ellery gently. "Turn it over, Mr. Harbidger."

Harbidger looked up, scowling. "No! You're not going to deprive me of this, too!"

"Turn it over," Ellery repeated in the same gentle way. The Lincoln collector obeyed reluctantly. "What do you see?"

"An authentic envelope of the period! With two authentic Lincoln stamps!"

"Exactly. And the United States has never issued postage stamps depicting living Americans; you have to be dead to qualify. The earliest U.S. stamp showing a portrait of Lincoln went on sale April 15, 1866—a year to the day after his death. Then a living Lincoln could scarcely have used this envelope, with these stamps on it, as writing paper. The document is spurious, too. I am so very sorry, Bianca."

Incredibly, Lorenzo DiCampo's daughter managed a smile with her "*Non importa, signor.*" He could have wept for her. As for the two collectors, Harbidger was in shock; but old Tungston managed to croak, "Where the devil did DiCampo hide the book, Queen? And how did you know?"

"Oh, that," said Ellery, wishing the two old men would go away so that he might comfort this admirable creature. "I was convinced that DiCampo interpreted what we now know was the forger's, not Lincoln's, clue, as 30d read upside down; or, crudely, ·POƐ. But 'the hiding-place of the book is in Poe' led nowhere.

"So I reconsidered. P, o, e. If those three letters of the alphabet didn't mean Poe, what could they mean? Then I remembered something about the letter you wrote me, Bianca. You'd used one of your father's envelopes, on the flap of which appeared his address: *Post Office Box 69, Southern District, Eulalia, N. Y.* If there was a Southern District in Eulalia, it seemed reasonable to conclude that there were post offices for other points of the compass, too. As, for instance, an Eastern District. Post Office Eastern, P.O. East. P.O.E."

"Poe!" cried Bianca.

"To answer your question, Mr. Tungston: I phoned the main post office, confirmed the existence of a Post Office East, got directions as to how to get there, looked for a postal box key in Mr. DiCampo's key case, found the right one, located the box DiCampo had rented especially for the occasion, unlocked it—and there was the book." He added, hopefully, "And that is that."

"And that *is* that," Bianca said when she returned from seeing the two collectors off. "I'm not going to cry over an empty milk bottle, Mr. Queen. I'll straighten out father's affairs somehow. Right now all I can think of is how glad I am he didn't live to see the signatures and documents declared forgeries publicly, as they would surely have been when they were expertized."

"I think you'll find there's still some milk in the bottle, Bianca."

"I beg your pardon?" said Bianca.

Ellery tapped the pseudo-Lincolnian envelope. "You know, you didn't do a very good job describing this envelope to me. All you said was that there were two cancelled Lincoln stamps on it."

"Well, there are."

"I can see you misspent your childhood. No, little girls don't collect things, do they? Why, if you'll examine these 'two cancelled Lincoln stamps,' you'll see that they're a great deal more than that. In the first place, they're not separate stamps. They're a vertical pair—that is, one stamp is joined to the other at the horizontal edges. Now look at this upper stamp of the pair."

The Mediterranean eyes widened. "It's upside down, isn't it?"

"Yes, it's upside down," said Ellery, "and what's more, while the pair have perforations all around, there are no perforations between them, where they're joined.

"What you have here, young lady—and what our unknown forger didn't realize when he fished around for an authentic White House cover of the period on which to perpetrate the Lincoln forgery—is what stamp collectors might call a double printing error: a pair of 1866 black 15-cent Lincolns imperforate horizontally, with one of the pair printed upside down. No such error of the Lincoln issue has ever been reported. You're the owner, Bianca, of what may well be the rarest item in U.S. philately, and the most valuable."

The world will little note, nor long remember.

But don't try to prove it by Bianca DiCampo.